THE NAPOLEON AFFAIR

A SEAN WYATT ADVENTURE

ERNEST DEMPSEY

138 PUBLISHING

JOIN THE ADVENTURE

Visit ernestdempsey.net to get a free copy of the not-sold-in-stores short story, RED GOLD.

You'll also get access to exclusive content not available anywhere else.

PROLOGUE

VALLETTA, MALTA 1798

"You cannot go in there!" the old priest commanded. "This is a holy place, not a place of war and death."

"Get him out of here," the General said. He marched through the hall, taking long strides with every step, though *long* was subjective for the diminutive leader.

Two of his soldiers grabbed the priest under the arms and dragged him backward. The man yelped and shouted. He'd been speaking French before, but the curses and warnings emitted now were in Latin. As he was pulled farther from the general, the priest's angry protests faded to muted whimpers.

The Co-Cathedral of Saint John the Baptist was crawling with soldiers rushing between cells, rooms, and offices, carelessly tossing furniture, papers, and other ordinary day-to-day items onto the floor. They moved like locusts swarming through a harvest and consuming everything in their path; never satisfied, their hunger never filled.

The general stopped at an intersection in the corridor and looked back at his men. This was hardly the way he desired to search the house of God; then again, he wasn't a very religious person. He'd been baptized as a child into the Catholic faith, but the church's dogmatic views and guidelines had never truly taken root with him. He did, however, appreciate the measure of control religion could hold over people. In that regard, he almost admired the church, occasionally wishing that he, too, could exercise such sway over not only the nation of France but the entire world.

He respected most religions and believed that all belief systems should be honored. The general was not only a tolerant man, but wise beyond the understanding of many of his contemporaries. He believed that people should be permitted to worship as they chose; to embrace the cultures they'd established long ago. And he also understood the strategic advantage of honoring those who dwelled in the lands he conquered. It was no ruse, no falsehood that he told his soldiers to respect Christians, Muslims, Jews, and any others of different beliefs. He truly embraced that approach. He also embraced the benefits that came with such teachings, such as the ability to control the masses. And Napoléon was all about control.

Alas, he was only a man, alone in the world as a beacon of light and hope shining toward a brighter future for all—an ideal he believed to his very core. Wars, disease, pestilence, and death had all ravaged Europe, and little mercy had been meted out to his beloved France. All the while, those at the top of society had suffered little, sending out their soldiers to do their dirty work, fight their wars, claim them new lands and titles, all of which would be taxed to the breaking point—of course.

To the populace, Napoléon had represented change, something new for the people of France. He'd offered them hope in the unusual form of a squat general with a knack for military strategy and tactics.

Leading the people through a series of fantastic victories, he'd set his sights on foreign territories to further expand his...interests. Napoléon had the ambition of a lion—his thirst for power unrivaled —and only a few of his trusted advisers, his only real friends in this world, knew of his ultimate goal.

To achieve it, though, he would need something of note, a catalyst that would enable him to lay a legitimate claim to new realms, an artifact of unprecedented power and esteem. It would also have to be a holy relic, something that gave him authority—both of earth and of heaven.

He'd known about the island nation of Malta for a long time, but it was only recently that he'd learned of the treasure housed in this very place, this temple to the Almighty.

Napoléon often questioned loyalty to a master that seemed so uncaring, so ambivalent toward his own creations. He certainly believed that there was a higher power at work in the universe; he just didn't believe that higher power cared about him as an individual, or about his nation.

Turning from his men he continued walking straight ahead and then turned right into the church's atrium. It was a glamorous lobby, but nothing he'd seen so far compared to the opulence of the grand sanctuary. Most of the halls—including the one in which he now stood—featured grandiose archways coated in gold filigree and separated by masterfully painted scenes from the Bible. The sanctuary was a larger version of the other corridors: much taller, wider, and grander in every conceivable way.

For the briefest of moments, the battle-hardened general was taken aback by the splendor of the cathedral. Designed by the baroque master Mattia Preti, the interior was every bit as spectacular as the exterior was rudimentary and functional. Not that the Maltese limestone, out of which the building had been constructed, wasn't beautiful. It was, however, designed to look as much like a fortress as a place of worship. That, perhaps, was due to those who had engineered it.

The Knights Hospitaller, also known as the Order of Malta, had been responsible for that holy task. They took it upon themselves to design and even fund the structure, with much of the money coming from their own coffers as well as from personal contributions from within their own ranks.

While they'd made the outside look almost imposing, the interior was more exquisite than many palaces Napoléon had seen. The high,

gilded archways above separated scenes depicting the life of Saint
John the Baptist.

There were nine chapels that branched out from the main sanctuary, each dedicated to various languages, peoples, and sects, but all
equally as magnificent as the rest of the building, simply smaller.

Napoléon marched through the center of the sanctuary, his boots
irreverently clicking on the marble tiles underfoot as he made his
way toward the front of the church where the presbytery was located.

Two of his guards stood either side of a priest who was kneeling
before the altar. Napoléon focused his attention on the man, doing
his best to avoid the myriad distractions of glitter and shine all
around him, however he did catch something of note as he stalked
toward the front. One of the columns was emblazoned with the
letters *RC*. Another featured the letters *NC* in long, diagonal rows.
Between the grouped letters was the easily recognized cross of the
Order of the Knights of Malta, the Knights Hospitaller. They'd also
been known by a few other names, the more apt of them being the
Knights of Saint John or the Order of Saint John.

The Siege of Valletta and subsequent takeover had seen resistance from the Maltese people, especially from the knights. They'd
fought valiantly, honorably, and died in the same way. Napoléon
knew that some had escaped, but eradicating an ancient sect of a
fading chivalric order was not his primary goal here. Neither was
taking over the island for any length of time. He would leave a small
contingent, probably around three thousand soldiers, in the garrison
on the island. That represented roughly 10 percent of his forces,
enough to make it look like he was trying to establish a stronghold in
the Mediterranean but not so many that it would hurt his advances in
Egypt.

His plan was to leave as soon as possible, making for Alexandria
the moment he had the relic in his possession. The priest was the key
to finding said relic.

Napoléon walked the last fifty feet with his eyes focused directly
on the man in the priestly vestments. He paid no attention to the

marble tiles beneath his feet that marked the graves of 375 knights, all entombed within the confines of the church to be forever under the protection of God and of his servant Saint John the Baptist.

Napoléon stopped with a click of the heels, standing at attention behind the priest kneeling between the two soldiers. One of the men in uniform was an officer, a lieutenant in Napoléon's personal guard. He was loyal to a fault, never questioning his general's orders but always willing to pose alternative outcomes for situations the general had, perhaps, not foreseen.

"He won't move, sir," the lieutenant said. He was a tall man, easily two inches over six feet, and towered over his general.

Napoléon didn't let that bother him. He'd learned to deal with it over the years. Most people, especially men in the army, were taller than him. It was one reason he'd had to work so hard to quickly climb the ranks.

The lieutenant went on. "He just keeps praying, General. Saying the same prayer over and over again."

"Leave us, Lieutenant," Napoléon said with a curt nod.

His second didn't take the order as rude. It was how the general spoke to everyone, and all in his ranks knew not to take it personally or become afflicted by emotions over his often short and direct approach to conversation or issuing orders.

"Yes, sir." The man nodded to the other soldier, and the two stepped away from the general, walking twenty feet before they spun around and faced the two men at the altar, just in case this priest was up to something nefarious, however unlikely that might have been.

Napoléon stepped up to the right side of the kneeling man and lowered himself to the prayer step at the base of the altar. He was surprised at how firm the pad was—considering it had been created to ease the discomfort of kneeling when praying to the Most High.

He folded his hands and bowed his head. His two men probably wondered what he was doing, wondered if he'd had a change of heart and suddenly become a devout, religious man.

He said nothing, instead letting the priest finish his prayers.

"You must leave this place," the priest said. "There is nothing for you here. God will punish you for such blasphemies."

"Blasphemies?" Napoléon questioned. "I know not of what you speak, good Father. I am simply here to collect something, an item of some importance." He spoke heavily accented English to the priest, though he suspected the older man spoke fluent French. Most of the Maltese population was trilingual, able to speak French, English, and Maltese, though there were still others who knew Spanish and Portuguese, as well.

"I know what you are here for. You're nothing more than a brigand, a common thief. You have no right to it. It is a holy relic. It belongs in the house of God."

Napoléon looked around for a moment as if trying to find something. It was a mocking gesture, though the priest didn't really see it unless it was through his periphery. His eyes were still focused forward, on the floor just ahead of where he was kneeling.

"This house?" Napoléon asked, pointing at the tiles at his feet. "Why not some other house of God? There are so many."

"It was brought here by our founders, the knights ordained by God through His holy church. It belongs here, on Malta. Go on your way, General. Leave the ring here, I beg you, or it will lead to great disaster for you."

"Very well," the General said. He grabbed the priest by the collar and hoisted him up off the floor.

The priest was surprised at how strong this small man was. While his stature may have been unimpressive, there was a hidden strength beneath his military uniform.

"Take me to the reliquary, or I will start killing. Your monks, your other priests, your servants, and if you don't take me to it after all of that, I will start killing citizens from the city."

That got the priest's attention. The old man turned to the general with shock in his eyes. "You can't do that. This is a house of worship."

"And I will not kill in this...holy place," Napoléon sneered, his comment layered in cynicism.

He'd often wondered about the splendor of the temples and

churches of religion, why people felt it important to ordain their places of worship with such riches when the deity they worshipped offered no gratitude and certainly didn't need the money. He nearly chuckled to himself at that thought but refrained since doing so would have eradicated any sincerity of his threat. It wasn't that he didn't believe God should be honored; but with so much splendor and expense?

Footsteps clicked on the tiles behind the two men, and the priest couldn't stop himself from turning around to see who was approaching, perhaps hoping it was his savior, come to remove this outlaw general. The priest knew what was going on. He knew that the general had illegally invaded Malta—a neutral country.

The priest's eyes widened as his heart filled with hope. One of the knights approached, though he didn't seem to be in a hurry to save the older man. His sword was still at his side, a musket strapped over his shoulder. The priest knew there were any number of other weapons hidden on the man. The knights were well armed but never displayed their full personal arsenal until it was necessary.

Why was this guardian of Malta not rushing to the priest's aid? Instead, he was stalking toward the two men with patient intensity.

"Ah," the General said, seeing the man approach. "I'm glad you're here. Our friend, the priest, doesn't seem to want to tell me where the artifact is."

"Of course he doesn't," the knight said. He spoke fluent French, the accent hinting at an ancestry stemming from Toulon, the very place where this entire campaign began. "He's sworn to protect it."

"Oh, I see. So, death it is then, Father?" Napoléon had no intention of killing a priest. Even with his lackluster fervor for religion and his casual ideologies regarding it and other customs, he didn't want to tempt fate. Just in case.

"If you must," the priest said. "I will gladly die to keep it out of your hands."

"So dramatic," the knight said. His name was Jean-Antoine Courture. A Frenchman to his core, he was one of the many knights in the battle for Malta who had defected to the French side, the side of their homeland. "Come, General. I will show you to the reliquary."

Napoléon's eyebrows lifted, and he smirked at the priest. "So, it would appear we do not need you to give us the ring. Still, I would like you to accompany us."

The knight grabbed the priest by the shoulder and motioned toward a door off to the right.

The priest shook his head. "But the reliquary, my son, it's that way." He pointed in a different direction.

"No," the knight insisted. "Not the one for the parishioners and the patrons of your church. Did you think I was not aware of the true location of the hand of Saint John?"

The priest swallowed hard, afraid his mistake might have cost him everything. Then he nodded. "No, I supposed not."

The knight led the way to the door and opened it, motioning the priest through first. He followed behind, allowing the general to take up the rear.

The three men walked through a short corridor lined with iron sconces. Candles burned in their nests, dripping wax onto the black iron cups. The small flames flickered dimly, casting an eerie yellow glow through the passage. They proceeded down the hall until they reached another door. This one was heavy, made from oak and set in place with tough iron hinges and a matching looped latch. It was very different, stark almost, when compared to the ornately gilded door from the sanctuary.

"Open it," the knight said.

The priest briefly considered lying, telling him that he didn't have the key. Not only would the knight not believe him, telling a falsehood was against the priest's creed, the very fiber of his being. What was he if not honest?

He reached in a pocket of his vestment and retrieved a small key ring. There were only four keys on it.

Napoléon imagined that one was for some of the main doors to the building; another for his private cell; the third would likely be for other rooms—offices, perhaps. The fourth, he knew, belonged to this door.

The old man inserted the prescribed key into the hole and twisted it. The lock clicked, and the door inched open. A damp, musty smell wafted out and the scent became stronger as the gap widened. Beyond, a darkened staircase spiraled down into the bowels of the cathedral, the general uncertain as to what awaited them. At this point, he was beyond what he'd learned about this place and was in the full trust of Jean-Antoine.

The knight reached over to the wall and took a candle from a sconce. With the wax stick still fixed to its housing, he passed it to the general and then took his own from across the hall.

"You may proceed," the knight said to the priest. His tone was kind, reverent, and it bore no ill intent.

Perhaps the knight's demeanor set the priest's mind at ease because he gave a long nod and stepped onto the dark staircase.

The three ventured downward for a few minutes, carefully navigating the damp steps, aware that one wrong step could result in broken bones, gashed skin, or potentially a far worse injury.

It didn't take long for the three men to reach the bottom. They stopped at the base of the spiral staircase and found themselves in a crypt and surrounded by stone tombs, each marked with the names and titles of those buried within, their likenesses carved onto the lids, emulating the way the deceased might have looked when they were alive or newly dead.

In the back of the crypt, the three men glimpsed something flashing as the candlelight flickered.

"There it is," the General said, staring into the darkness. He raised his candle to the level of his right shoulder and the dim illumination widened, carrying all the way to the other side of the room.

He took the lead, walking across the length of the crypt before stopping short of the shrine. The table was made of pure marble, surrounded by an altar made of gold and silver with intricate carvings and reliefs adorning every inch of it. On the table was the prize

Napoléon had been set on the moment he announced his plan to invade Alexandria.

The ancient Egyptian city was certainly the target. It would weaken his British enemies in that region and would also give him claim to a vast new land, passing titles and acreage to his men.

Alexandria, however, was only part of Napoléon's grand scheme, merely a piece of the puzzle. What lay hidden in this golden shroud would give him the ability and the power to bring all the other pieces together.

He set the candle reverently on the marble surface. His eyes fixed on the item next to the candelabra. It was a golden glove with a matching metallic sleeve extending all the way up to the elbow. One finger was bent awkwardly toward the palm, the others remained straight and extended outward. A flap built into the backhand of the glove displayed a fragment of bone within.

Napoléon discarded his temporary reverence and picked up the object.

The priest gasped and instinctively stepped backward, afraid he might be struck down by the Almighty for such sacrilege.

"What are you doing?" the old man asked with a quiver in his voice.

Napoléon didn't look back at him. "You know exactly what I am doing."

"That is the hand of Saint John the Baptist!" the priest exclaimed. "You are not permitted to touch such a holy relic. Only those ordained by God may do so." The man crossed himself multiple times, probably whispering a prayer for forgiveness at the same time.

"I know who it is." The general slid the forearm out of the golden glove. The hand followed, grinding along the inside of the relic's housing until the fingers came free. There, on the ring finger of the skeletal hand, was what he'd come for. He reached out his left hand and with thumb and forefinger plucked a golden ring from the bone. Napoléon admired the jewelry for a moment, taking in its shimmer in the candlelight. There were no precious gems set into the metal, only words carved in Aramaic. He couldn't read them and didn't care to learn. He was here for the ring not a language lesson. He removed his leather gloves and slipped the ring onto his own finger.

It was a perfect fit.

"My God, forgive us!" The priest prayed out loud this time, crossing himself again. "Put that back or be forever cursed."

The warning slid off the general's shoulders.

"You keep the hand of the Baptist," Napoléon groused. "The ring belongs to me now."

1

INLET BEACH, FLORIDA - PRESENT DAY

S ean Wyatt wished he had one of those little plastic grocery baskets. No matter how many times he went shopping, he still made the same mental miscalculation from time to time. He'd pass by the grocery carts and the stack of baskets thinking all he needed was his two paws since his list of items was relatively short.

Almost every time, he ended up in this exact situation.

Well, not *this* exact situation.

Usually he was in a grocery store, this time it was a convenience store. He'd come in to get some drinks before he and his wife, Adriana, walked down to the beach.

And it wasn't just the store that was different, it was also the fact that there was a gunman standing at the register and holding a pistol in the face of the cashier.

The terrified young woman was unable to move or even process what was happening. Her red hair wasn't natural, but colored the shade of faded cherries and cut just below the chin at an angle so it grew shorter toward the back. There was a streak of white in it that dangled in front of her left ear. She was pale, almost as if she'd never been in the sun before, which would make her a unique citizen in this part of the world. Most people who lived along the Emerald Coast worshiped the sun, hitting the sand of the Gulf of Mexico as often as they could.

She couldn't have been more than twenty-one or twenty-two years old. She had a nose ring in her right nostril and several other pieces of metal dangling from her ears. There was also a butterfly tattoo on her neck. Now she was being threatened by a thief.

Sean stayed quiet and instinctively bent his knees to crouch down a little, partially blocking his view of the criminal.

"I said open the safe and the register!" The masked man was yelling again. It was his initial command to the cashier that had caught Sean's attention.

Sean had just grabbed four Cokes from the refrigerator at the back of the store to take to the beach and was heading toward the register when the shouting began.

The gun wagged back and forth in front of the girl's face. Sean wished he had his pistol with him. That was his second regret. He almost never left home without his Springfield .40-caliber XD, but he was on vacation—at the beach no less. Surely he could take a little time off without having to go all cowboy on someone.

Yet here he was, standing in a gas station with a clutch of Cokes in his hands and no weapon. If he'd had a basket, he could have easily set down the drinks and moved around to a better vantage point to get the thief's attention–or something like that. As long as the thief pointed the gun away from the cashier, that was all that mattered. He knew there would be a panic button behind the counter. Probably a gun, too.

Most convenience stores operated on similar systems, where they would take the money out of the register and deposit it in a safe. Less frequently, a manager—or in some instances, an armed guard—would come and collect the money to take to the bank or to a deposit drop-off. The thief was obviously aware of this, and of the safe wedged into the wall behind the counter.

"I...I don't have access to the safe," the cashier stammered. It was the first time Sean had heard her speak since the robbery began.

The man swore at her, calling her some unsavory names in the process. "I know you're lying. I've seen you open it before."

There was one little clue. This guy was a regular customer. He'd been here before and watched her as she went about her tasks, probably during down times when there weren't many customers. Right now was one of those times, and Sean found himself to be the lone consumer in the store. Sure, some cars drove by outside, but none of the drivers stopped for gas or snacks. It wasn't exactly a prime location for travelers, though it was perfect for him since it was within walking distance of the IAA beach house.

Sean could tell by the sound of the man's voice that he was nearing the end of his proverbial rope. When that happened, bad things would follow. There was a desperation in the man's voice that Sean easily recognized. His training in psychology and with the federal government had taught him not only to read body language but to interpret vocal intonation as a means of predicting a target's true aims.

There was no question in Sean's mind: if he didn't act soon, the girl behind the counter was going to die.

He quietly maneuvered backward, careful to mind that he didn't brush up against a rack of crackers and potato chips; effectively giving away his position. He was fine with that since taking the thief's eyes off the cashier was going to be his number one priority. Doing so before he was ready, however, would not be acceptable.

Once he was at the end of the row, he stepped to the side and crouched down carefully. As he'd grown older, Sean noticed that his knees cracked more often when he bent them. Thankfully, this time they didn't make a sound.

He set two of the Cokes down on the floor and kept two in his hand. The cold cans were frosty against his skin, but now they were no longer refreshments for a day at the beach. In his hands, they were deadly projectiles that could save a young woman's life.

Sean stepped back into full view.

The young woman saw him and her eyes grew wide.

Sean knew that she would express some form of surprise. That was fine. In fact, he'd planned on that. He would much rather the robber turn around as a result of something he knew she was seeing than from hearing a sudden sound from behind. That tended to startle most people, criminals especially.

This one seemed especially jumpy, and if Sean were to say anything or make the slightest sound, the guy's itchy trigger finger was apt to twitch and put a bullet through the poor girl's skull.

Sean's awareness of the situation and his prediction of the robber's reaction were spot on.

The second he saw the young woman's eyebrows rise slightly, he spun around with the gun leveled, ready to take out whatever threat was there.

Except there was no threat. No one was there. Behind him, something slammed shut. The gunman spun around again, only to realize that the cashier had disappeared. She wouldn't be hidden long since there was only one place she could be hiding at that point. He started for the counter, probably to vault over it to pursue the girl, but a voice halted him in midstride.

"I wouldn't do that," Sean said. He spoke loudly and clearly enough that there would be no mistaking his commands, or that someone else was in the building.

He assumed, which he rarely did, that this thief hadn't considered there might be someone else in the store. Thieves, while often intelligent in regard to their work, tended to be careless about other things, such as social awareness. A smart person would have assumed that there could be someone else in the store who'd walked over from the nearby beach community of Rosemary.

This thief, however, hadn't considered that. Now he found himself alone in the convenience store facing a ghost.

Just like before, when he turned around to find where the voice was coming from, he was presented with two empty rows. He couldn't see down the length of the other three rows, which presented a problem. Clearly, there was someone else in the building, and they were meddling with his plans.

"Where are you?" he snarled. "Come out or I shoot the girl."

The man was playing on society's chivalrous instincts. Despite how little of that seemed to be present in the modern day, it was still ingrained in many people, and criminals often sought to exploit that weakness. Some called it a savior complex. Others decried it as a Good Samaritan complex. Either way, criminals knew that when faced with harm to others, people would run, either to help or to get to safety.

This robber was clearly okay with either.

If Sean were to run, which wasn't even remotely in his bank of options, he would expose his position to the thief and make for an easy target. At the moment, Sean knew that he still had the element of surprise and the element of evasion.

The thief was too focused on where he believed the sound had come from to notice the reflections on the glass doors of the refrigerators. Sean had shifted to his left and quickly made his way down the last row until he could get a clear view of the gunman's reflection in the last door. The guy was still pointing his gun toward the end of the row where Sean had been only a moment before.

"I'm going to give you to the count of three to show your face, or I start shooting."

For a moment, Sean wondered what the girl was doing behind the counter. Surely there was a gun back there, though he doubted she knew how to use it. Maybe if she had been a few years older she might have had some kind of training, even if it was as simple as a basic firearm safety course. He didn't blame her, though. This was a difficult situation, terrifying for someone who'd probably never had a gun pointed in their direction before, much less in such a threatening manner and at such close range.

Sean plucked a stick of beef jerky from a rack in front of him and waited for a second.

"One!" The gunman shouted with a grunt. His accent was local, probably from one of the farms or small towns a little north of there between the Florida and Alabama border, perhaps a few miles across said border.

Where he was from didn't matter to Sean. All that mattered was taking him down.

He flicked the jerky through the air and watched it sail over three rows before it disappeared from view just a moment before striking what he assumed was a bag of chips.

The crinkling sound may as well have been a grenade going off in the otherwise suddenly quiet convenience store. The man twisted slightly to his right and fired the weapon twice. Bags of tortilla chips exploded, sending corn fragments into the air and spilling into the next row.

The sound was deafening in the confined space, but Sean remained calm. He'd been in more gunfights than he could count and figured himself fortunate not to have a bad case of hearing loss at this point in his life. Those two reports probably wouldn't help with that, but there was nothing he could do about it. The situation was what it was, and he'd have to make the best of it.

He picked out another stick of jerky and waited, watching the man's reflection in the refrigerator as the criminal stepped toward the second row. Sean flung the second stick through the air, this time letting it sail higher and farther than before, but his trajectory was different. Noticing the gunman was near the end of the row, Sean had thrown this one toward the counter. It struck a rack of chewing gum in front of the register and rattled to the floor. Again, the gunman turned, though this time he didn't fire any shots.

Sean was thankful for that. There would be no sleep for the rest of his life if the young girl behind the counter was somehow accidentally shot.

By the time the man had spun around to see where the second noise came from, Sean had already taken a third stick of jerky. He threw it hard toward the front-right corner of the store and listened as it struck something plastic, probably the stack of bottled water in that section of the store.

The man fired the gun again, this time charging back to his left and nearer to the exit where the first row came to an end.

That was Sean's chance. He rose as the guy reached the end of the row and, clutching one of the Coke cans in his right hand, reared back. He'd never had a great arm in baseball. He'd pitched some, but only because he could throw strikes. It had little to do with his ability to generate velocity. In this instance, accuracy was also paramount. If he missed, he had one projectile left, and there would be little time to take a second try.

He took a step as if throwing a baseball from third base to first, and whipped his arm forward. The can was out of his grip by the time the gunman saw movement out of the corner of his eye. The Coke flew through the air, streaking straight for the guy's head. He fired his weapon, probably out of fear, and the bullet bounced harmlessly off the ground and struck a quart of oil on the nearest row. The thick golden liquid immediately began leaking, but the thief never saw it.

Sean's aim had been true, and the base of the can struck the guy square in the right eye.

The gunman had been both lucky and unfortunate. Getting hit in the eye by an aluminum cylinder full of cola was excruciating. As the base of the can hit his face, the hardened rim crunched the bone, fracturing it and causing the eye to droop within a second. That was the unlucky part.

The fortunate part was that he could have been hit in the temple and died right there. Then again, that might have been preferable.

The man howled in agony, dropping his weapon to the ground as he grasped at the wounded eye.

Sean didn't wait for an invitation. He leaped from his hiding place and sprinted across the room, plowing his shoulder into the man's ribs even as the guy was still moaning from the wound to his eye.

A loud "oof" escaped his lips as Sean tackled the gunman and drove him into a metal frame between the huge windows that made up the store's façade. The left side of the guy's face hit the metal column with an audible crunch, no doubt shattering more bones on that side.

Sean felt the body go limp in his arms and he slowly lowered the thief to the ground. Blood was oozing down the side of the guy's face where the Coke can had struck his flesh, cutting a deep gash into the cheek.

Sean instinctively turned to where he'd heard the weapon fall from the guy's hand a moment before and scooped it up. He rapidly pulled the slide several times until no more shells came out of the weapon's ejection port. Then he released the magazine, tossed it on the floor, and rapidly removed the slide from the gun, dumping some of its parts on the tile next to the unconscious man.

"He's out," Sean said in a casual tone, hoping the girl wouldn't pop up with a shotgun thinking he was the robber. "My hands are up," he added, stuck on that last potential issue.

The girl hesitated, but she realized quickly that the man speaking didn't match the voice from before. "Okay," she said. "I'm coming up."

Two pale hands appeared behind the countertop, and she gradually rose from her hiding place on the floor. Her face was flushed red, and there were tears filling her eyes.

"It's okay," Sean said.

The girl's green eyes flashed toward the body on the floor. A new look of fear washed over her. "Is he..."

"Dead?" Sean finished the sentence for her. "No. I don't think so. He's gonna be in a lot of pain when he wakes up, though. Speaking of that, you should probably go ahead and call the cops."

She nodded rapidly and reached for her cell phone that was sitting next to the register.

"Do you mind if I..." Sean motioned to the back of the store, as if he still had some shopping to do.

The girl looked baffled for a moment then nodded as someone answered the call on the other end.

She began telling them what was happening, that someone had tried to rob the store but that the thief was unconscious on the floor.

Meanwhile, Sean grabbed four more drinks and then made his way to the front of the store. The girl shook him off as he reached for his wallet.

He shook his head and pulled out a ten. He set the bill on the counter and then mouthed, "Keep the change."

"Wait," she said, ignoring what the person on the phone was saying. "Where are you going?"

"Vacation."

2

ROSEMARY BEACH, FLORIDA

Sean's vacation had to wait for nearly forty minutes.

No sooner had he stepped outside than Sean heard the familiar whine of sirens heading his way. He was surprised at the response time—considering there was a pretty broad area to cover along this part of the Florida Panhandle and he knew of very few police stations along that stretch of road.

Most of the cops would be centralized in Panama City to the east, or about an hour to the west in Pensacola. Of course, there were several other small precincts in between. There were so many little beach communities, though, that most of the area was patrolled by county and state officers.

These first responders, Sean thought, must have already been in the area.

He answered all their questions, gave them his information, explained what happened, and then left when it was clear the police were done with him for the time being. He knew what that meant. They could and often would come around to ask more questions. Since he wasn't local and had technically committed no crime, they had no reason to keep him and no cause to press charges.

The reporters had started trickling in at the news of some hero who'd interrupted a robbery. They locked on to Sean when they saw him speaking to the police. Evading the reporters had been tricky, but he knew a back way through the cluster of trees and bushes behind the convenience store. It cut out onto a side road just off US 98, where he could return to the main road and walk back down the sidewalk to the beach house.

Once he was back on a walkway, he fished the phone out of his pocket. There were a dozen text messages. Some were from Tommy, some from Adriana.

Tommy had purchased the beach house to use as a company getaway for the International Archaeological Agency, the organization he built to help with the recovery and safe delivery of priceless artifacts. He and Sean had been best friends for most of their lives, so it had been a natural fit for Sean when he left Axis, an ultra secret government operation based in Atlanta.

Sean didn't put up an argument when Tommy mentioned purchasing the beach house. Sean had always loved this area, known as the Emerald Coast. He'd even lived up the road in Destin for a short time several years prior, but it hadn't worked out. Sean came to realize that this part of the world was only a small portion of his life —a periodic refuge. There were other places he was needed and where *he* needed to be.

He sighed and picked up the pace to a jog until he hung a left on East Water Street.

Sean made his way through the winding maze of little streets and walkways that cut between the gulfside homes of Rosemary Beach. He didn't bother texting his companions back because he didn't see the point. He'd be there in a minute anyway.

When he opened the door to the home and stepped inside, Tommy, Adriana, and June were all standing in the kitchen with worried looks on their faces. The moment they saw him, relief replaced the concern, visibly washing over their faces.

"Where have you been?" Adriana asked in the tone only a wife could use properly. It was the sound of love and anger all mixed into one spicy margarita.

Sean shrugged. "Went out to get the Cokes for the beach."

"We heard sirens," Tommy said.

"Yeah, I heard those, too," Sean admitted slyly and walked over to the counter with the cans. He set them down and then made his way over to the freezer. He scooped some ice out with his hands and placed it in a cooler to the left. Then he turned around and saw the other three were staring at him, arms crossed, and eyes narrowed with suspicion.

"What?" Sean asked.

"What did you do?" Adriana asked, arching one eyebrow. Her hands lowered and planted on her hips. She cocked her head to the side, her brunette ponytail hooking to the right shoulder.

"Hey, easy there, Spanish Inquisition." Sean put both hands up to surrender.

Tommy chuckled at the nickname. Adriana Villa came from the countryside just outside the Spanish capital of Madrid. The three had met under desperate and dangerous circumstances, which was how Tommy met his wife, too. June Holiday, a striking blonde, who turned out to be a secret agent, had met Tommy in an equally harrowing situation.

It was only natural all three of them suspected something crazy had happened in the hour Sean was away.

Sean sighed and dropped his hands. "Okay, fine. Fine. You win. There was a kitten in a tree. I...I fought through my fears and...thankfully, I was able to rescue the kitty and return it to its owners, a four-year-old girl and her parents." Sean said dryly, laying on the cynicism thicker by the syllable.

"You're being irritating," Adriana said, taking a step toward him. She was in a pair of running shorts and a tank top with her bikini on underneath. Her muscular arms pulsed; her leg muscles tweaked with each step. "And I don't like being irritated."

He licked his top lip, suddenly nervous, then took a step back and put his hand up to stop her. It was too late.

Adriana leaped through the air and crashed into him. He stumbled and then fell backward onto the floor with her straddling his torso. Sean laughed as she grabbed his wrists and pinned him down.

"Schultzie, would you mind leaving us alone for a few minutes. Family...um, matter."

Tommy shook his head and stalked toward the two on the floor, June at his side.

"Just tell us what happened, Sean, and I won't have my friend here hurt you." He motioned to Adriana and did his best version of an evil mastermind.

Sean let out an exasperated sigh. "Fine. There was a robbery— attempted robbery—at the convenience store."

"Oh, okay. You took out the bad guy. Didn't you?"

"Yes," Sean admitted. "I didn't have a choice."

June shook her head. "I don't get it," she said. "You three get into more trouble than anyone I've ever met."

"And you don't?" Sean asked.

"Girl's gotta make a living," June quipped.

"Touché."

"So, what happened?" Adriana stood up as she asked the question. She extended a hand to her husband, which he took graciously.

He grunted to his feet and dusted off his behind, even though there was certainly no dirt on it. "Just some idiot," Sean said. "He was trying to knock off the register and the safe. Sounded like he'd been watching the store for a while to get the timing of money transfers just so."

"That doesn't sound stupid, other than robbing someone."

"Yeah, I guess idiot isn't fair, although he didn't account for someone being in the back of the store. I was lucky."

"Here we go again," Tommy rolled his eyes and clapped his hands on his hips. "Always with the modesty thing."

Sean gave a laugh. "Anyway, the cops showed up and had a bunch of questions for me. So, I'm sorry it took so long."

Everyone else joined in a tentative laugh. Adriana put her arms around him and kissed him hard. When their lips parted, she leaned her head back and gazed into his grayish-blue eyes. Her right hand reached up and she tousled his scruffy blond hair.

"What?" he asked, wondering what she was thinking.

"You certainly do have a knack for finding trouble, *mi esposo*."

"*Quizas*," he answered with the Spanish word for "perhaps."

"You guys still want to go to the beach, or is that not the plan anymore?" June asked. She picked up one of the cans on the counter and tilted it to the others. "Because I think I'm still going. I haven't hit warm sand in way too long."

"I'm with her," Tommy said, suddenly taken away from the previous discussion by his wife's cute grin. Tommy picked up a can and turned toward the door, but froze in place the second he was facing the exit.

June was standing just short of the doorway. She stood perfectly still, staring up at a tall figure with broad shoulders. The man's face was tanned and clean shaven. His hair was brown and cut short in a military style. His jaw was strong and broad, coming to a fine point at the chin. From the looks of him, he spent a lot of time working out. His shoulders and pecs bulged in the tightly tailored suit.

Sean slid his left foot a few inches to the side. He'd stored a gun in the top drawer next to the dishwasher. It wasn't his usual .40-caliber, but it would do the job.

"There's no need to go for the weapon in the drawer, Mr. Wyatt. I'm not here to hurt anyone." The man raised his hands slowly in a show of peace. He spoke with a strange accent that the others couldn't immediately place.

"You know I have a gun in here," Sean said, "which makes me think you're kind of dangerous. And if you're that level of dangerous, I'd say it's a good bet you've got some backup outside somewhere. If I didn't know better, I'd say someone's got their sights on me at this very second."

"Very astute," the man said. "Of course, I would expect nothing less. It would seem, at first glance, your reputation is well deserved. There are no guns pointed at you, though I do have men outside in our cars. I thought it best if I came in alone since bringing four armed men in suits might send the wrong message."

Sean chuckled at the joke. "I like you." He motioned to the drinks on the counter.

"No, thank you. I don't drink sodas."

"So," Adriana crossed her arms and stepped back as if standing within striking distance of a snake, "who are you? How did you find us? What do you want?"

"Those are a lot of reasonable questions, and I will answer all of them since I anticipated you might ask those and more. My name is Gabriel Bodmer."

A pin flashed on the collar of his suit. Sean's breath caught as he realized immediately what it was.

"I am the current commander of the Swiss Guard."

Three sets of eyes darted from one to the other.

Sean's didn't. His remained fixed on the commander. Now Sean recognized the accent. Bodmer was a Swiss name, and the way in which he spoke revealed an upbringing where multiple influences blended into one culture. That made many of the accents initially hard to pin down, even for some trained linguists. Now that he knew, Sean could easily make out the combination of French and German. His English, however, was perfect, which was to be expected from someone in his position.

The Swiss Guard was tasked with protecting the Vatican and, most importantly, the pope himself. He crossed one leg over the other as he eased back into a seat at the dining table.

"As to your questions," Bodmer continued, "I hope I don't have to explain how I found you. Let's just say we have resources. To your last question, and to the point as to why I am here, we need your help."

3
_____

ROSEMARY BEACH

"You need our help?" Tommy asked.

"The Vatican?" June added in disbelief.

"Yes," Bodmer confirmed. "May I?" He pointed to the left breast of his blazer. The hosts nodded in unison and he stuck his hand into his jacket for a moment then pulled out a letter. He set it down on the table and nudged it forward. "This will certify who I am and why I am here—in case you need to see an official state order."

Everyone was curious as to what that might look like from the Vatican, but no one reached for the envelope.

"We had a murder in the Vatican," he said plainly. The statement was harsh and unexpected. Everyone's mouths hung agape at the news. "Right now, no one outside the Vatican walls knows of this except for you four. I trust that won't be a problem."

It wasn't a question, it was a statement—one that left little doubt as to its meaning.

"We can keep a secret," Sean said. He took a wary step forward. "But the question is, why would it be a secret? That would only be the case if there was someone with a high profile potentially involved."

"You're not saying the pope..." June cut herself off.

"Not His Holiness," Bodmer clarified. "One of the cardinals."

"That's still a big deal," Sean said. "You obviously don't want that kind of attention at the Vatican, and you certainly don't want the source of that attention to be a murder committed by one of the cardinals."

"Not just one of the cardinals. He is considered to be the next in line to be elected pope."

"Is the current pope sick?" Tommy blurted.

"Not that I am aware of, but he is older now. We know that day will come sooner or later. Cardinal Alfred Klopp is the favorite at this time. He's been an excellent leader. I would not be surprised if he were to win, if not for this...incident."

"See, you keep calling it an incident like it isn't a homicide."

"Make no mistake, Mr. Wyatt—"

"Sean," he corrected.

"Very well. Make no mistake: We are treating it as a homicide, but this is no ordinary homicide. It must be handled delicately."

"Just like every other government in the world." Sean nearly spat the words.

"Sean, I appreciate your cynicism, but the fact remains that we have a killer on the loose, and we need your help."

Bodmer motioned at Tommy, too. "We have to track him down before it's too late."

"Track him down?" Tommy asked. "He's on the loose? But you said you know who did it. Cardinal Cup or something?"

"Klopp," the man said. "Yes, he is under house arrest in the Vatican. The Italian authorities have been contacted and are aware of the situation."

"You don't think he did it," Sean realized. He leaned against the nearest doorframe, which led into a hall. He looked at the man sitting at the dining table. The table's surface was a pale, exposed timber, giving it a farmhouse feel. The building's designer had done much the same look with most of the interior décor. "That's why you're here, because you don't believe Klopp is guilty, which means you have no leads."

"No. We do not believe the cardinal did it. We believe he was framed."

"Framed?" Adriana asked after a moment's thought.

"The man who was killed was also a cardinal." There was regret in Bodmer's voice. The victim must've been someone he knew, someone he saw on a regular basis. In the confines of Vatican, it was likely that you saw some of the same people semi-frequently. In the case of the Swiss Guard, a high-profile cardinal would be someone he knew personally. It would be his job to make sure that man was safe, along with all the other men of God. "He was a good man, but he and Klopp differed on several key ideas."

"Sounds like he had motive," Sean said.

"Indeed. However, Cardinal Klopp wasn't home that night. Someone snuck into the apartments and murdered Cardinal Jarllson in his sleep." It was the first time he'd mentioned the name of the victim, and it renewed the sadness in his voice.

"So, Klopp hired someone to do it, conveniently stayed out of the building that night. Get the competition out of the way, and he's on his way to the top."

"I can understand your thinking on this matter, Sean. But it is incorrect. Klopp is not behind this. He is a victim in this case. Not to mention he is also a man of God."

"Sounds like you're at an impasse, Commander," June said. "Why bother coming here?"

"Yeah," Tommy agreed. "Don't the Italian police or Interpol take over from here?"

The visitor responded by reaching into his right breast pocket. He withdrew another envelope. This one was nothing like the first. It was dirty and weathered. It looked like it had possibly gotten wet at some point, though at second glance Sean realized it was simply very old.

"How many pockets you got in that jacket?" Sean asked jokingly.

The commander ignored him. "We were given this letter by Klopp. It was he who requested your help." He slid the envelope across the table. "The cardinal wasn't at his apartment that night because he was with me. He told me that he was concerned that someone he didn't know had approached him about this letter."

"What's the letter about?" Tommy asked. "Who approached him?"

"That's what we were hoping you could help us with." He eyed the two men with determination. "The police are already involved and have examined the crime scene, but it's still cordoned off for now. The body of Cardinal Jarllson has been moved. I'm certain that the investigators are working around the clock, but they won't find anything."

"Why's that?" Adriana asked.

"Because it was clean."

"Clean?" Tommy asked. He thought he knew what the man meant by that, but he wanted to be sure.

"The killer left no trace, no clues, nothing. He was professional. Whoever killed Jarllson knew what they were doing. They knew the ins and outs of all the Vatican's security protocols, the timing of every guard change and patrol, the locations of every camera he'd need to avoid to get to his target."

"Or her target," June added with a tilt of the head.

For a second, the commander didn't catch what she was saying. "Yes, or her."

"Murder weapon?" Sean asked.

"Some kind of blade—inserted into the base of the skull and pushed through to the brain. Death was instantaneous. The dagger was no wider than four centimeters, and there was a limited amount of blood. This person knew exactly how to kill someone without making a mess."

"Why worry with keeping it clean?" Sean asked. "Or that clean, anyway. I understand the need to hide one's tracks," he clarified, "but why worry about the blood?"

"Perhaps that has something to do with the killer's training."

"Training?" June asked, taking a step forward.

"The killer left a calling card at the crime scene." He slid his phone across the table next to the letter. There was a picture on it of the crime scene with the dead man lying facedown on the floor in his priestly sleeping attire.

Commander Bodmer had been right. There was almost no blood,

only a thin sliver on the back of the dead man's neck that indicated where the blade had slid into his skull. That wasn't what Bodmer had wanted Sean to see. The rest of the crew leaned in close, huddling around to get a better view.

On the man's back was a piece of cloth. It looked worn, like an old kitchen rag. On it was a white shield that featured a black cross.

"What is it?" Sean asked. "You thinking this was an inside job or something?"

Bodmer shook his head. "You don't know what that is?"

Sean shook his head.

Tommy remained eerily silent. "I believe I know what that is, but —" He stopped, cutting off the words that were sitting on the cusp of his lips, ready to leap out.

"But what?" Bodmer asked.

"That couldn't be. They're...they're a charity organization now. Last I checked, they're not a military group anymore."

Bodmer leaned back in his seat, clearly pleased at Tommy's recognition of the mark.

"So you know it."

Tommy rolled his shoulders, still uncertain if he should say it.

"Know what?" Sean pressed.

"That emblem," Tommy said, pointing to the shield that was emblazoned on the cloth atop the dead man's back. "It's one of the crests used by a group that is no longer around, at least not in the way they used to be. If I'm not mistaken, that's the military crest of the Order of Teutonic Knights."

"Very good. I had my doubts about coming here, but I see Klopp wasn't entirely incorrect. He told me you were the best at this sort of thing. Quite the exploits you two have had over the years. Even a trip or two to the Vatican." He arched one eyebrow.

"Yeah," Sean said. "The library is impressive."

"Indeed." There was a hint of disdain.

"So, I don't understand," June said. "If you know who left that rag there, why don't you just track them down yourself and arrest them?"

"We only know the symbol of the order—one of the symbols,

actually. There are a few. As your...husband here said before, the Order of the Teutonic Knights was disbanded long ago."

Tommy nodded his agreement. "Yeah, I can't remember the exact dates, but they were dismantled in the early 1800s. Maybe 1803?"

"It was 1805."

"Oh, I was close," Tommy said excitedly.

"They were reinstated in 1834 as a charitable organization. As far as we know, they have not been involved in any military or clandestine training or operations for the last couple of hundred years. Following World War I, they were officially recognized as a spiritual organization within the Catholic Church, which did little except give them more authority in their charitable operations."

"It would seem that assumption wasn't entirely correct."

"Indeed. The letter"—Bodmer pointed at the envelope—"was thought to be nothing more than the ramblings of a dying man. They were his final words, and he was in an immense amount of pain. He was struggling to keep his mind right in his last days. Several of his friends thought he'd gone mad. That letter was kept in our archives for nearly two hundred years. Then, a few weeks ago, Cardinal Jarllson discovered it. We have the records of his visit to the vaults, making a copy of the original letter, and whom he shared it with."

"Who did he share it with?" Adriana pressed.

"Only Klopp. Jarllson sent him an email about it, knowing that Klopp also had a deep interest in history. He thought Klopp would like to see the letter, perhaps in hopes that Klopp could make sense of it all. Unfortunately, Jarllson was murdered the day after he sent the email. Klopp had this copy of the letter and requested that it be sent to you. He said he couldn't decipher it but knew of someone in the United States who could."

"I wonder how this Klopp heard of us," Sean quipped, casting a sidelong glance at Tommy.

They could tell their guest was intent on them opening the letter. He stared at it, begging silently for someone to open and read it.

"I guess the beach isn't happening," Tommy said, reaching over to pick up the letter. "This isn't an original, is it? Because it should really get better care than...well, this." He wagged the envelope.

"That old envelope is a ruse. Nothing more. As I said before, the real letter is safe. It's in the Vatican archives, deep within the vault. It is as secure there as it could be anywhere in the world. That envelope isn't more than a few years old; though it's certainly seen better days."

Tommy accepted the explanation and removed the letter, spreading it out on the table. He wanted to smack himself in the forehead for already forgetting what the commander had said about the vault.

It was written in French. The letters were swooping, dramatic cursive. The ink had faded, not just from being copied, but the original ink was clearly very old.

"My French is...a little rusty," Tommy said.

He passed the letter to Sean, who waved a hand. "I know enough to get by, but reading that..."

"Give it to me," Adriana said. Before Tommy could even nod or start to say yes, she snatched the paper and started scanning over it. She stopped in the middle of the page and looked up, meeting the eyes of Commander Bodmer. "This is a deathbed confession."

"Yes, that is correct," he said as if it were obvious. Maybe it should have been since he was talking about that before.

She continued reading, and when she reached the bottom of the page, her eyes shot wide in disbelief.

"This isn't real," Adriana said flatly. "It has to be a fake."

Bodmer shook his head ominously, as if he was keeping a great and foreboding secret from the rest of the group. "I assure you, it's real. Of course, your friends here can analyze it if they choose. I'm certain Thomas, or Tommy as you call him, has the equipment and the means to determine its legitimacy. We've already run those tests, of course, in the labs at the Vatican. But be my guest." He waved one hand dismissively as if he didn't care what they did with the thing.

"What?" Sean asked, looking at her intently. "What is it?"

"It's a letter," she said plainly, then paused for dramatic effect, "from Napoléon Bonaparte."

4

MALBORK, POLAND

Lucien Berger picked up the phone and pressed the green button on the screen. "Details."

It wasn't a question, it was an order, and the man on the other end of the call didn't flinch. Berger was direct and efficient. He didn't have time for pleasantries, and there was, in his opinion, no call for them.

His accent was native French. He'd been born in Toulon, a coastal town in the South of France. It was a city with a rich maritime and military history.

He'd moved to Germany long ago, though, and hadn't looked back. This was where he belonged—despite the location of his birthplace.

The other voice came quickly through the phone's earpiece. "Bodmer is meeting with them right now, sir." This new voice was decidedly German, hinting from somewhere in the north of the country.

Berger nodded. He knew that was going to happen. Things had been put into play now, and there was no going back. Not that he intended to stop.

"And?" Berger asked.

"It sounds like they're going to the Vatican with the Guard's commander."

Berger thumbed at his mustache and picked the goatee on his chin with the side of his index finger. "Good. This is exactly what I hoped you'd tell me."

"Sir?"

The man didn't have to clarify what he meant. It was evident in his voice that he thought Wyatt and the others coming to Europe would be problematic. He was right—if the proper precautions were ignored. Sean Wyatt and his sidekick had a bad habit of getting into trouble no matter where they went. Their exploits were well known across the globe. Most of the time, they were working on historical projects, helping other archaeologists transport their finds to secure locations and, occasionally, working on dig sites themselves.

These two, however, were more than what they seemed on the outside. While Berger didn't think Schultz had any formal training in weapons or hand-to-hand combat, he knew that the man possessed a certain amount of skill when it came to a fight. If he hadn't, he would have been dead by now.

Wyatt, on the other hand, was trouble, plain and simple. He was highly skilled in the art of combat, was extremely proficient with firearms and other kinds of weapons, spoke a few languages, and had gone through rigorous paramilitary training before moving into service with Axis, which had led him to even more clandestine operations.

Once he was with Axis, most of his file seemed to evaporate. That agency had very few leaks, and little was known about it, other than its director answered only to the president of the United States. None of their exploits, none of their missions, and none of their agents, apart from Wyatt, were known to anyone.

Berger didn't need to penetrate their headquarters, though, since Wyatt no longer worked for them.

IAA, on the other hand, had been easier to hack. The databases, while well protected, were relatively easy to get into, though they contained nothing helpful, just some information about certain budgetary spending and inventory of their vault.

There was very little in the way of anything useful.

None of that mattered, though, when Berger executed the priest in the Vatican. He'd ended Jarllson's life with ease, inserting the dagger in the man's neck and driving the tip into his brain. It was a clean kill, and the cardinal didn't suffer—even though Berger had wanted him to.

He wanted all of them to suffer, and they would, but he would have to bide his time and be patient, waiting for the final moment.

"Do not worry," Berger said to his man on the phone, "all is going according to plan."

"They're talking about visiting the Vatican, the crime scene specifically."

"Good. If Cardinal Klopp won't hand over the true letter, then perhaps these Americans can lead us to it."

There was an uncomfortable pause on the other end of the line, as if the other man wasn't sure he should say what he was thinking.

"What is it, Michael?" Berger asked. "You have something you want to say but aren't saying it."

How did he know? The other man on the phone was actively wondering that very thing. He was relatively new to the order and didn't yet understand that the organization's grand master had the keen ability to not only read body language, but to detect inconsistencies in conversations, sometimes even when they were extremely subtle.

"Yes, sir. I do. The Americans...they have a copy of the letter."

"Interesting." Berger didn't sound concerned, even though he probably should have been. If they had the letter, that meant they had a head start.

He'd killed Jarllson for it, only to later learn that the dead man had given it to Klopp. He'd tried a different tact and was cordial, borderline friendly with Klopp, and made an exceedingly generous offer. The cardinal, however, had turned him down. Apparently, he was one of the powerful men in the church who had morals. Berger detested those types, particularly because he knew so much of the truth behind the history of the Catholic Church and what they had done, whom they had wronged, and the atrocities they were responsible for.

He did his best not to get angry, but the little flame flickered in his gut, sparked from old embers that had been smoldering for most of his life—ever since he'd learned the truth.

"Stay close to them, Michael. We don't want to lose them."

"Sir, I won't be able to follow them. They're going to get on the Vatican's private jet and head back to Rome."

Obviously, Michael couldn't get on the plane with Wyatt and company. He flew in on his own, on a commercial jet. Now, he would have to find a way to get back quickly.

"I'll have a charter waiting for you at the airport. Did they say when they're leaving Atlanta?"

"Sounds like tonight, sir."

That made sense. The group would fly through the night, sleep on the plane, or at least try to, and then start fresh the next morning with their search of the Vatican.

"You're a tourist," the grand master said. "Get a tour of the Vatican, and follow closely behind them."

"Begging your pardon, sir, but I won't be able to gain entry into restricted areas if I'm disguised as a tourist."

That was true. Berger had to commend his apprentice for bringing up that issue. What to do, then?

The answer was elegantly simple. "You're a priest, then. See our man Rafael in Rome. He will take care of your clothes and everything you need to look and feel the part. Once you're inside, you know what to do."

Michael did know. It was the same thing as always when it came to following someone and getting information. Stay close but not so close that the targets became suspicious. He'd done that dozens of times before, had gone through painful training to learn how, and was now an expert of stealth reconnaissance. Berger trusted his trainee's talents, so the reminder was superfluous.

"Yes, sir. I do."

"I'll send you your itinerary and where to go in the airport." He didn't have to tell the younger man not to be late. That was a given.

"Thank you, sir. I'll be in touch when I land in Rome."

"Good. We will speak then."

Berger ended the call and laid the phone on his desk. The fire crackled in the stone hearth ten feet away. He looked around the room at the papers strewn across the desk, the pictures, books, maps, and notes that were scattered haphazardly on the floor, on the chairs, and on the sofa.

The room was old, built several hundred years ago to serve as an underground tavern. It had become his headquarters when he was brought into the order by the previous grand master. Now Lucien Berger was in charge, and he swore to his leader on the man's deathbed that he would see to it that all of the man's plans came to fruition.

It was the least Berger could do.

Watching his mentor die was a difficult thing despite being trained to be immune to such emotions. There were still little flecks of Berger's prior life, his prior humanity, that, to this day, would still haunt him from time to time.

Whenever it did, he had to actively push it away.

Emotions caused rash decisions, mistakes, erratic behavior that almost always led to disaster. He'd been taught that during his training and had almost eliminated emotional responses from his psyche, but now and then there was a moment, however fleeting, that caused feelings to surge up from his chest and fill his mind.

In this instance, it was thinking of his master on his deathbed and the promise that Berger had made.

The old man had brought Berger in as a young boy, little more than a toddler. He was an orphan, out on the streets, trying to beg for enough money to buy one meal a day and maybe a bottle of clean water now and then. Back then, Berger was scrawny, feeble. He was the definition of pitiful.

His parents had died when he was very young and had left him nothing. Their house was repossessed, and he was sent to a boys' home since his mother and father had no other relatives in the area. Both sets of grandparents had passed, and as far as he knew, there were no aunts or uncles who could swoop in and provide for the young man.

Berger quickly learned that he didn't want to be at the boys' home. There were sick things that happened there, things that revolted him even to this day, though he forced himself to reframe those events as necessary to make him who he was. He would never have arrived at the order without going through those hardships, and he certainly wouldn't have ever gained ambition enough to climb to the top of the food chain.

Now, here he was, the grand master of the order, and Lucien Berger had every intention of living up to the promise he'd made the dying man. He would restore them to their former glory and renew their place in the world as the true holy military power.

There were just a few things standing in his way. They would be handled soon. Everything was coming together according to plan.

5

ROSEMARY BEACH

"**N**apoléon Bonaparte?" Tommy asked. "As in the general?"

"You know of another Napoléon Bonaparte?" Adriana fired back, lifting an eyebrow as she did so.

"Gah, I always walk right into those."

"You really do," Sean agreed. "So, what does the letter say, honey?"

She grinned at the way he used the term of endearment. She liked it. That tenderness was in stark contrast to the side that was accustomed to killing, the side that even enjoyed the killing at times.

They'd been relatively lucky the last few months. Not much had happened since their big encounter out in the Pacific Northwest, giving their merry band some time to take a few trips to dig sites in Europe and Asia.

It was the first time in her life that Adriana got into a dig site with all the necessary tools to actually do archaeological work. She was given trowels, brushes, a tool belt, and several other things to do the painstaking job of removing hundreds of years of debris and dirt in hopes of finding a clue as to how an ancient civilization might have lived.

Doing manual labor was soothing. It was relaxing in a strange sort of way. It was a concrete task. You knew exactly what you had to do and how long to do it. The parameters were clear, and even though she didn't find anything on the first day, she felt a sense of accomplishment simply from the fact she'd moved a section of earth out of the way in search of a piece of history.

Adriana realized that doing that kind of work took her mind back to Spain where she used to work on her parents' plantation. They grew wine in the rolling hills outside of Madrid, and as a child, Adriana often found herself helping the hired workers with their tasks.

Now, it seemed the vacation was over. Not just their literal one, but the period of time where nothing insane popped into their lives had, apparently, gone out the door the second Commander Bodmer walked through it.

"It's...confusing," Adriana said. "Is this real?"

"I assure you," Bodmer said, "it is legitimate. The problem is that we don't understand what it means. It would seem that he didn't fully trust those around him when he died. The question is, what was he trying to keep from them and, if he was trying to hide a secret, why the letter?"

"Heavy lies the crown," Sean chirped.

"Yes, except he had no crown when he died. He was in exile. And toward his end, he began saying things that were nonsensical. He descended rapidly into madness, and once that happened there were only bits and pieces that his friends and family could interpret."

"But he wasn't going crazy," Adriana said. "Was he?"

"No, I don't believe so. Although the unbearable pain from the cancer eating away at his gut likely did create new mental issues for him. It's a natural progression of the mind to take one's thoughts to another place, another plane where the pain goes away."

"So, what's with the flower at the bottom of the page?" Adriana asked, looking over her shoulder and pointing to a faded rose.

"Funerary," Sean said, glancing at Bodmer for confirmation.

"That's what we assumed as well," the commander agreed. "Since it is customary to give flowers when someone dies, we think that might be what this flower is doing on the letter."

"A single rose," Sean whispered, contemplating the meaning. "He was so egotistical that he gave himself a rose before dying."

"Read the letter to us," Tommy said to Adriana.

She didn't hesitate. "It says that he feared that the Battle of Waterloo was not going to go as planned. He claims to have had a premonition, a vision of the outcome in which he and his men were defeated."

"That would explain the desperate tactics he used in the battle," Tommy said.

"Indeed," Bodmer agreed.

"It goes on to say that without the relic the odds were too great against him. He also says that with his greatest strength missing, there was no chance they could be victorious."

"What relic?" June asked. "Does it say which one he's talking about?"

"No," Adriana answered, looking back over the letter. "No mention of a specific item by name. He just calls it the relic. I wonder what relic could have made a man as skeptical as Napoléon believe in its power."

"And you have no idea what he could be talking about?" Sean sounded like he wasn't sure if he should buy what the commander was selling.

"I do not. If I did, I assure you, I would tell you. The sooner this entire mess can be solved, the better. It is my desire and that of the Vatican for this to be resolved quickly and discreetly. It seems, however, that there is some sort of riddle here, one that none of our top experts could solve."

"And that's where we come in," Tommy said.

"This letter seems incomplete," Adriana said, still looking at the page.

"Again, this is why we need your assistance," Bodmer reiterated.

Sean looked over his wife's shoulder at the letter, and then it hit him. "It's incomplete because this is, get ready for it, the first in a series of clues!" He used his best game show announcer voice, elevating his volume and tone toward the end of the sentence.

Bodmer stared blankly at him, clearly not understanding the joke.

Tommy figured it was appropriate to explain. "We get this kind of thing a lot, Commander. A clue that leads to another clue and so on."

"Yes, well, if Napoléon hid a powerful relic somewhere and this is the beginning of the trail, then you surely must see the inherent danger involved with a search of this kind."

"You mean the danger that led one of your cardinals to be murdered within the confines of the Vatican?" Sean asked. "Or that led to more threats?"

"Yes." Bodmer said the word plainly and without hesitation.

Sean decided to cut to the chase. They'd wasted enough time already if the commander truly did want them to be part of the investigation. "What do you want us to do, Commander Bodmer? You flew all the way here to show us this letter and those pictures of the crime scene. I guess that means you would like us to come back to the Vatican with you?"

"If you think that is the best place to start."

"Vatican?" Tommy groused.

"What's the problem?" June asked.

"I mean, it's our last day of vacation." He turned to his wife and looked at her longingly. He looped his hand around her waist and pulled her close. "I was hoping to hit the beach one more time and just relax, maybe check out the stars over the gulf tonight, sit by a fire in the sand and listen to the waves lapping against the shore."

"Honey, we've literally done that every night we've been here. It's okay."

Tommy sighed. "I know. I just...I'm enjoying it, and I know that you're going on an assignment for Emily in two days."

"Which means I can't come with you. Aww, honey, that's very sweet of you. You're going to miss me, huh?" She put her arm around his neck and kissed him.

Bodmer looked away, casting a stare out the window toward the water as he was immediately uncomfortable with this situation.

"Hey, guys. There are still some of us here in the room with you," Sean said. "You want us to leave, or you gonna go up to your room?"

"Can you shut up, ever?" Tommy said. It came out as a muted, squished sentence with his lips pressed against his wife's.

"Anyway, Commander," Sean turned back to Bodmer, "yes, I think we need to visit the Vatican. Would it be possible for us to investigate the crime scene? I know you said it has been cleared, but it might be helpful if this weekend we take a look around."

"Certainly. I'll make all the necessary arrangements. I know you have your own plane with your organization," he said to Tommy, who was just now letting go of his wife, "but I would be honored if you would accompany me on the Swiss Guard's private jet. We will get through customs faster, and you will be able to bring anything you need, including weapons."

Sean raised an eyebrow at this last statement.

"I see you've done your research on us," Sean said with a smirk. "We find it best not to leave home without some protection."

"Protection..." There was doubt in the word.

"Well, we don't start fights," Tommy said.

"But we certainly finish them," Adriana completed the thought.

"We will find your killer," Sean said. "And we will figure out what relic Napoléon was talking about in this letter. Usually, it works in the reverse order, though."

"How do you mean?"

"I mean, what typically happens when we take a job like this is that we'll start looking for whatever lost artifact needs finding, then we get chased by the bad guys, in this case it seems like that would be Teutonic Knights or someone impersonating them."

"The knights have been gone a long time," Bodmer corrected. "At least in their military form."

"You don't think it's possible they laid low for the last couple hundred years, waiting, biding their time until the right moment?" Tommy asked.

"No. I don't. The symbol left on the body of Cardinal Jarllson was a distraction. Nothing else."

"You didn't happen to keep that piece of cloth, did you?"

"Of course. It's evidence. We never discard evidence. We operate exactly like a police department would when it comes to solving crimes. If you would like to see this cloth, though I have no idea why you would, I can present it to you when we arrive in Rome."

Sean seemed satisfied. He turned to his friend with the question in his eyes that the two of them always shared just before they began a new project.

"What do you think, Schultzie?" Sean asked.

Tommy Schultz ran a hand through his thick brown hair, his fingers combing chunks of strands as he pushed them to the back of his skull.

"Sounds too interesting to pass up," Tommy said. "Besides, no one has tried to kill us in the last couple of months, so I'd say we're due for some bullets and death threats to come our way."

"There you have it, Commander," Sean said. "Count us in."

He glanced over at Adriana, who crossed her arms and flung an irritated glare at him.

"What?" he asked, putting his hands out wide like a child who claimed to have done nothing wrong, all the while standing around a broken cookie jar.

"You forgetting someone?" She put her hands on her hips and kicked her left hip out. It was both cute and terrifying. That stance meant she wasn't happy, and he was going to catch grief for it.

"Honey, of course I figured you'd want to go. You love this kind of stuff."

"Oh, so you're speaking for both of us now?"

He felt his skin blushing bright red. Heat swelled in his cheeks and on his forehead. "No, I'm...I'm sorry. I just thought you would enjoy it. You're the one that always says we don't go to Italy enough."

She cracked a smile, revealing the truth. "I know. I'm just messing with you."

Tommy shook his head. "He's so easy, right?"

"He really is," Adriana said.

"You guys are hilarious." Sean turned to the commander. "I'm coming alone."

"Are you sure?" Bodmer asked, taking Sean's comment literally. "I thought they said they were coming, too."

Sean rolled his eyes. "Okay, we're going to need to work on your sense of humor if we're going to be spending a lot of time together."

6

THE VATICAN

Sean listened to the echoes of shoes clicking on the marble-tiled floor as he and the others stalked purposefully through the Vatican. No one paid them any mind save for a few tourists who thought, curiously, that perhaps Sean and his entourage were famous or of some importance.

The group followed Commander Bodmer through the immense corridors, under frescoes depicting scenes from the Bible, set between high-vaulted Gothic domed arches. The splendor rivaled the beauty of any palace or temple that was ever built, no doubt an effort by the architects to provide the Most High with a suitable home on Earth.

They had entered through one of the side doors, both to avoid attention and because they weren't there to see the grandeur of the Sistine Chapel. They were there to find the reason a cardinal had been murdered in cold blood and to see what, if anything, the killer may have left behind.

Bodmer led the way through the corridors of the Apostolic Palace and up to the floor that housed the guest apartments. Some of the priestly quarters were used by cardinals and other men of the cloth on a more permanent basis, while many were reserved for those who were only visiting temporarily. The most notable of the latter happened upon the unfortunate death of a pope, when cardinals would assemble for the conclave to vote on who would become the next head of the church.

Sometimes, papal conclaves would last for weeks, requiring much deliberation, debate, and prayer over who should be the next to lead the papacy. That required accommodation for the many cardinals to sleep, not to mention all of the other preparations that were needed. They would need to be fed, given clean linens, have their vestments and other clothing laundered, and provided with bathrooms, all things that most people took for granted.

These men did not support themselves. For most of their lives, they had lived to serve the church, and so the church took care of them in exchange for their service.

The hallways were beautiful, and more than once Sean caught Adriana admiring their opulent décor.

Bodmer stopped in front of a door on the left and fished out a key from his pocket to open the door. He stepped inside, giving no concern for contaminating the area simply by being there, not to mention smearing his fingerprints all over the door latch.

It was this action that caused Sean to raise an eyebrow, though he didn't say anything. Once they were inside, he understood the lack of caution on the commander's part. The room had been cleaned, thoroughly. The body was long gone, and any sign of a struggle or forced entry were likewise unnoticeable. The apartment was tidy, just as it would have been on the day the late cardinal arrived.

"Looks like you did a little cleaning," Sean said.

"Yes. And we took down the crime scene markings on the door. We don't want to distress the rest of our tenants. The police tape only served to remind other priests of what happened here and what could happen to them. That's not good for anyone. Besides, all of the evidence has been collected and is being analyzed, although I doubt we will find anything useful."

"Why's that?" Tommy blurted.

Bodmer turned to him. "Because whoever did this didn't leave a trace of evidence that could identify them. The room was scoured for clues as to the mysterious killer's identity. We looked everywhere but could find nothing, nothing of course except for the emblem we found on the body."

"The Teutonic Cross," Sean said.

"Correct. That was the lone item the killer left behind. Other than that, there was nothing."

Sean looked around in wondrous disbelief. The room was the complete opposite of the grand hallways just beyond the door. While the corridors that interconnected the immense structure were richly decorated to look more like a king's palace, this apartment was ordinary by comparison. The walls were white; the furniture a dark brown, almost black; and the windowsills dark brown to match the furniture.

Sean liked the interior decorating. He was pleasantly surprised at the elegant simplicity that was used to put the apartment together. He had half expected to find portraits of dead saints and popes in gilded frames, furniture overlaid with gold, enormous beds that could sleep a soccer team, and vast closets full of fine clothing.

There was none of that.

The room defined minimalism the same way most palaces defined grotesque overabundance.

"As you can see," Bodmer went on, "there isn't much to find in here."

"So why did you want to bring us here?" Adriana asked. She had an idea but wasn't sure.

"I wanted you to see this place first because I thought you could use some context."

"Context?"

"The killer entered through the window."

"How do you know that?" Tommy asked.

"Because if they had gone through any of the corridors leading to these apartments, we would have seen them." His face turned deathly serious. "We watch everything very closely. As you can imagine, protecting His Holiness is no easy feat."

"I guess not."

Adriana still looked befuddled. "You don't have cameras outside?"

"We do," Bodmer confirmed. His response was curt but not rude. "Unfortunately, we experienced several thunderstorms during the night in question. Our external camera system had a few technical issues."

He could see the three guests were about to ask what that meant. "Over the course of the night, we noticed three significant times when our camera systems failed."

"Failed?"

"The monitors went dark. We corrected the situation each time, and after the third, there were no more issues. We believed it was lightning strikes close by."

"But now you're not so sure," Sean offered.

"Precisely." Bodmer turned away from the group and stepped around the bed. "The cameras were only down for a few seconds on two of those occasions. They blinked off and then came back almost immediately. The other time, however, the system was down for nearly a full minute."

"Doesn't sound like a lot of time," Tommy said. "Especially if the killer had to scale the wall outside, break in through the window, do the deed, and then get out."

"Indeed. We are dealing with a professional of the highest order, an assassin of immense skill."

Sean and Tommy glanced at each other at the mention of an *assassin*. They'd had a run-in with that sort before, and things had gotten messy. The two would have much preferred to never deal with their kind again. The thought caused them both to cringe.

Sean had faced his share of challenges as a special agent, and many times after leaving that line of work. Few were as tough as the bout he'd had with the Assassins, an ancient order bent on waging war with the Templars.

He shrugged off the concern and forced his mind to stay focused on the facts at hand, not the past. Besides, as far as he knew, those assassins were gone, extinct. Bodmer wasn't necessarily insinuating it was an actual member of their secret organization, simply a stealthy killer. That didn't change the fact that the word sent a chill up his spine.

"So, you're telling us that whoever got in here went up the wall and through that window in less than a minute?" Tommy asked as he drew nearer to the window and looked down. It wasn't the highest room, but it would have taken incredible skill and agility to make that climb and get through the window without detection.

"Impressive," Sean added. "They would have had to know the layout."

"Agreed," Bodmer managed.

Sean stepped closer to the window as well and looked down into the alleyway below. It was narrow, too narrow for a car, and barely wide enough for a large motorcycle. It took him less than five seconds to realize how the killer got up the wall and into the apartment. While he didn't know how the murderer might have opened the window from the outside, a short inspection of the locking mechanisms told him that even the most inexperienced of thieves could have gained entry, more so for someone who was an expert. And that was exactly what they were dealing with.

"Whoever killed your cardinal used both walls," Sean stated. There wasn't an ounce of doubt in his voice or in his mind.

"What?" Everyone turned to face him, but it was Bodmer who spoke.

Sean pointed out the window at the narrow gap between the two buildings. The wall across from them was only four or five feet away.

"It's too far for someone to push their back against one wall and their feet against the other. And they certainly didn't do the splits and shimmy up. That would have taken too long, and we'd be looking for someone nearing seven feet tall. I doubt there are that many people out there that tall, and also with the agility to accomplish that particular task."

"So, how did they do it?" Tommy asked.

"Parkour," Sean said. "I've seen guys on videos climbing two or three stories that way before jumping through an open window. Someone with the right training could have done this. Heck, high school and college kids do it just from practicing all the time. Take someone who's an expert in that sort of thing and a killer to boot? Wouldn't be all that daunting."

"That's a long drop," Bodmer countered. "Not to mention he'd have to somehow land perfectly on the narrow ledge outside the window without falling, then pry the window open."

Sean shook his head and pointed at the windowsill. "No sign of forced entry." He instantly realized he sounded like a cop when he uttered the words. "There are no scratches, no evidence that the window was broken or tampered with. Just like the commander said."

Bodmer agreed with a nod of his own. "Exactly. We found no evidence of that. And the window was locked when we arrived."

"That's interesting," Sean agreed. He didn't voice his curiosity further, but he found it odd that the window was locked when investigators arrived on the scene.

"What is that supposed to mean?" Bodmer sounded irritated, almost as if he understood Sean's insinuation, but the question indicated he didn't.

Adriana crossed her arms and listened as her husband explained. Tommy, too, paid close attention to his friend.

"There are no signs of forced entry because there was no forced entry. The killer was invited into the cardinal's apartment."

Bodmer scoffed with an audible "Pfft." He looked incredulous. "What? You're saying the cardinal invited his own killer into the apartment?"

"It's the only thing that makes sense...unless you have a better theory."

Bodmer pinched his lips together.

Sean continued in order to answer the next question he knew was coming. "The victim invited the killer here, but not so the visitor would kill him. I'm not suggesting the cardinal was suicidal. He had another reason for his guest to visit that night, but something went wrong." Sean slowly pivoted and looked around the room; his eyes scanned the walls, the corners, the ceiling, the floor, and every inch in between within seconds. It was an old habit, one that he'd developed during his first year in training with the government. Now he did it all the time, even when he was going out to eat at a nice restaurant. Always assess every situation. That's what he was trained to do. It was the best way to ensure the safety of himself and others. In this case, it was his way of making sure he hadn't missed a tiny detail.

Bodmer appeared irritated, bordering on angry. "Are you suggesting that the deceased cardinal, a man ordained by God to lead his church and oversee one of the largest parishes in the world, was involved in some kind of criminal activity?"

Sean rolled his shoulders. "If the shoe fits."

"This is an outrage!" Bodmer roared. "You can't just walk into the Vatican, the seat of the Holy See, and make wild accusations like that!"

"First of all," Sean said, keeping his tone firm but calm, "*you* brought *us* here. We were doing just fine back in the old US of A when you came knocking. You wanted to know what we thought, what I thought. Well, there it is. That's what I think happened. I understand," he cut off Bodmer as he was about to speak again, "how you all feel about these priests and cardinals and whatnot. I get it. They're holy men to you, people who are infallible. What I'm suggesting is that, perhaps, he didn't realize what his visitor was up to until it was too late. Maybe it was someone who he thought could help him attain the papacy, take over for the pope when the time came."

"The pope will not die anytime soon."

"Good. That's wonderful." Sean tried to sound like he cared, but he was focused on his task, and right now his brain was running faster than he could keep up. "I'm just saying that the only way in here without detection was the window. You said the cameras went out for a short amount of time, but enough time for someone skilled enough to climb between the two walls and get through into this room. The window wasn't pried open, so that means it was either wide open for some fresh air to get in, unlikely, or the cardinal left it open for his visitor. What we need to know is why he had that visitor and what that visitor wanted."

"It is also highly unorthodox for a killer or any criminal to leave a calling card," Adriana chimed in, "unless of course they wanted to be caught. Seeing that the murderer has not yet been found, I would say that isn't the case."

"But they did want us to know something about them," Tommy added.

"Indeed."

Bodmer's head was spinning. He was doing his best to keep up, but there was so much information coming so fast that it made the job difficult. He felt like he was watching a tennis match between superhumans, his eyes and head twisting back and forth as the information passed between them.

"We need to see Cardinal Klopp," Sean said abruptly.

The others turned to face him.

"No, that can't happen," Bodmer said.

"We need to know what he has, what he knows. Where is the cross you found on the body of Cardinal Jarllson?"

"The cardinal, he is safe, here on the grounds of the Vatican in a secure location."

"Well, we need to see him, and I want to have a look at that cross you were talking about. Or we can just let you guys continue your investigation without us, but I think there is something going on here that you don't know about. I'm sure Klopp won't mind that you just sent the three of us back to the States without solving anything."

He let the words hang in the air for a couple of seconds. He knew that he'd struck a nerve.

Bodmer couldn't afford to let these three go without getting a few answers, something he could share with the cardinal and the rest of the higher-ups. They wanted information, and the three people in the room with him were the best chance of getting it.

Bodmer sighed reluctantly. He'd brought them there with the intent of taking them to Jarllson's quarters to see if they could find anything, but that was starting to feel like it wouldn't bear fruit. Besides, Bodmer and his men had already gone through the apartment with great diligence and still dug up nothing. Perhaps taking these three to see the cardinal would yield something useful.

"Fine," he relented. "Come with me."

7

THE VATICAN

The group stepped off the elevator and into the bowels of the Vatican's Swiss Guard headquarters. They'd made their way through the palace, the immense halls, and the maze of empty corridors, before finally arriving at the main office of the Vatican's elite security forces. At first, Tommy thought that was their destination, but he'd been wrong, unaware that there was a more secure, underground facility that housed an extensive armory, computer terminals, living quarters, and yes, even a jail.

The jail wasn't like those known to the rest of the world. It consisted of old monastic cells that had been converted to a detention area, and was larger and more comfortable than prison cells.

Bodmer led the way through the short hallway until they reached a closed door at the end. It was wooden, made from lumber that had been cut down centuries ago, and was well oiled and cared for to maintain its luster as well as its strength. There was a hole cut into the top half, with iron bars forming a sort of cross that resembled a tic-tac-toe board. Through that opening, the visitors could see inside the little apartment beyond.

Sean took a moment to absorb his surroundings. The corridor was sparse, made from stone blocks that had been quarried long ago.

There were Gothic archways holding up the ceiling, much like he'd seen in other buildings of the Vatican. However, the rest of the facility's underbelly didn't feature the frescoes, the paintings, the sculptures, or the gilded molding and trim that occupied the aboveground areas. It was stark, minimalist, and without seeing inside the cells, you would think you were in the basement of an old castle.

The commander reached out and opened the door. To everyone else's surprise, it wasn't locked.

"Tight security," Tommy quipped.

Bodmer shot him a questioning glance, missing the sarcasm.

"Never mind."

The door swung open without a creak, the iron hinges apparently well cared for and well oiled by the caretakers of the holding area.

Candles flickered in the cell, casting a wavering yellow glow throughout the room, barely dispelling the darkness.

"Father," Bodmer said reverently, "you have some visitors." He spoke in English, which told the others their interaction with the priest would be for their benefit. Most of the higher-ranking men of the cloth were fluent in many languages. It was no surprise that someone such as the cardinal would as well, especially considering that he was most likely going to be the one who took over from the pontiff someday. Popes were required to travel extensively and interact with millions of people all around the world. That meant adhering to cultural and linguistic norms.

"Visitors?" Klopp asked. He only spoke a single word, but his German accent was obvious.

"Yes, Father. The men you sent me to find in America. Along with"—Bodmer looked at Adriana with questions in his eyes—"a woman."

"A woman?" The cardinal stood from his place at a humble wooden desk and turned to face the group.

"I didn't mean to cross a line, sir," Bodmer explained, sounding almost pleading.

As Klopp raised his eyes, the man's features came into full view. His face was smooth, belying the years he'd lived. It was tanned but not dark. His hair was gray under his priestly cap and came down just above his ears, brushing them slightly. He was around five feet, nine inches tall and probably 175 pounds, with much of that weight settling in around his midsection, though it was difficult to get an accurate picture because of the flowing robes around his body.

"Ah," Klopp said. "Yes, Mr. Wyatt, Mr. Schultz." The cardinal nodded and took a step forward.

"Yes, sir," Sean said and motioned to Adriana. "This is my wife, Adriana."

She bowed her head low in a show of respect. "At your service, Father."

She wasn't Catholic, but she respected the religion and those who were a part of it. She chose to ignore the scandals and hearsay that seemed to ever-revolve around the church and its clergy, instead preferring to believe that these people, men and women, had given their lives to service and worship.

"Ah, your wife," Klopp said. His tone was the mildest, most calming sound Sean thought he'd ever heard come out of a human being's mouth. Even he felt a strange sense of peace wash over him at the man's words. "Welcome, my child. All of you, actually." He looked around as if assessing his quarters with regret, the way a person would upon receiving an unexpected guest, wishing they'd tidied up first. "I'm sorry our meeting isn't under more...formal circumstances."

"No need to apologize, sir," Tommy said.

"We are keeping the cardinal here for his safety," Bodmer explained.

Sean had already figured that out. The two guards at the top of the elevator and the one by the door were there for the man's protection, although Sean had his doubts about those three. There were other measures in place, he knew, such as cameras, sensors, and other technology to keep a close watch on Klopp to ensure his safety, but if the man who killed Jarllson was anywhere close to as skilled as Sean figured him to be, none of that stuff would be good enough to stop him. The man was an elite, even more so than the Swiss Guard occupying the fortress of the Vatican. He wasn't about to say that, though, since doing so could be perceived as offensive. Sean certainly wouldn't want anyone telling him that his security detail was inadequate against such a threat.

"Yes, well, I don't quite see why that is necessary. God will protect me." The cardinal was insistent, but that theory hadn't worked out so well for Jarllson. That was another thought Sean and Tommy both decided to keep to themselves.

"They are here to ask you some questions," the commander said.

"Ah, about the letter," Klopp acknowledged.

"Yes, Father," Sean said. He took a step closer and stopped near the door. He noted the rest of the cell's interior. It was a deep space, going back at least twenty feet or more and was about that wide. A large bed with white linens and a dark oak frame occupied the right side. The bed was made and appeared to have been freshly cleaned. The floors were spotless, made from smooth stone tiles. There were a few chairs situated opposite the bed where the cardinal could receive a guest or two. In the back corner was the desk where the man had been sitting, and opposite it in the other corner was a small kitchenette. There was a door fixed into the far wall that Sean assumed was the bathroom, again another feature that wouldn't be found in any other prison in the world, not that he'd seen.

"Please, then, come in. Commander Bodmer?" The cardinal turned to the leader of the Swiss Guard. The man's head tilted up. "Could you bring in another chair for our guests?"

"Certainly, Father." Bodmer turned and said something in Italian to the guard by the door. The man nodded and hurried into one of the empty apartments and returned a moment later holding a wooden chair just like those in Klopp's room.

"Thank you, Marco," Klopp said with genuine gratitude.

"Of course, Father." Marco hurried past the group and placed the chair next to the others and then retired to his post by the door without saying anything else.

"Please," Klopp motioned into the room as if inviting guests into his house. "Come, sit. I will help you as much as I can."

The three visitors stepped into the room and took a seat.

Klopp waited until they were all seated and then made his way to the empty one across from them. Bodmer stayed at the door, clearly having no designs on sitting down on the job.

Once he was in his chair, Klopp leaned back and sighed as if taking the weight of the world off his shoulders. He steepled his fingers and rested his elbows on the armrests. "I assume Commander Bodmer filled you in on what happened."

"He did, sir," Sean confirmed.

"I also took them to the...to Cardinal Jarllson's apartment," Bodmer added.

"Ah." The cardinal's head tilted back in an affirming nod. "So, what do you think?" He stared straight into Sean's eyes.

Sean didn't have to work hard to assess the man. There was no lie in his eyes, no deceit, no cover-up of some heinous act. His innocence was easy to read. This man had done nothing wrong, committed no crime. Bodmer was right about that—if that was indeed the position he was taking with the matter.

"About the..." He paused for a second. Sean wasn't sure how delicate he should be with the subject of the murder. He didn't want to be insensitive, but things couldn't be changed now. The fact of the matter was, Cardinal Jarllson was dead, and walking on proverbial eggshells wasn't going to bring him back.

"The murder?" Klopp said, easing Sean's mind.

"Yes."

"It's unfortunate, my son, but there is no point in prancing around the subject. We must find the one responsible for this. Jarllson and I had our differing viewpoints on certain subjects, but he was a brother in Christ and a good man. He would have made a fine pope had he been elected."

Sean nodded at the comment and then dove right into his hypothesis. "I believe the killer went in through the window. They would have had to scale the wall using the opposite wall for leverage, maybe even as jumping points."

"They call it parkour," Tommy interjected.

The cardinal's eyes flitted to Tommy for a moment. The priest was clearly confused by the term, but nodded absently, absorbing the new information as if to store for later use.

"Yes, parkour," Sean said. "It's a sort of...game that people play. They make use of ordinary objects, buildings, railings, park benches, that sort of thing to do exercises."

"Exercises?"

Sean sighed, frustrated. "I don't feel like I'm doing a good job describing it. All you need to know is that people who are highly athletic can do some pretty amazing things with everyday, stationary objects. I believe this person was able to climb the wall with remarkable speed due to those skills."

"And then they broke into the window? Bodmer tells me there was no sign of forced entry."

"That is correct, sir. I came to the same conclusion. There was no sign that the window had been tampered with. The door, either. That, to me, can only mean one thing."

"What's that?"

"I think the killer was invited into Jarllson's apartment that night. The window must have been left open. The commander said there were several instances that night when the security cameras went out. The disruptions didn't last long, but they were long enough for an expert to ascend the exterior wall of the apartment building."

"Even at the top, a master thief couldn't have balanced there on the narrow windowsill to pry open the window. I would know." Adriana arched one eyebrow.

The cardinal acknowledged her comment with an open mouth that formed an O.

"She is highly skilled in those kinds of things," Sean explained, hoping to avoid more questions about Adriana and her past. "The point is, sir, I usually go with the simplest answer, the one that makes the most sense."

"Occam's razor," Klopp muttered.

"Yes, sir. Cardinal Jarllson knew the killer was coming, though he likely didn't know what the person's true intentions were. The best I can figure, the intruder wanted something, something that Jarllson wouldn't give him. When he refused, it would have been simple enough for a trained assassin to execute the man. Which brings me to the method by which he was killed."

Sean stopped for a moment to assess the priest's demeanor again. Sometimes talking about such things could make a person queasy, unnerving them to the point of nausea. The first sign was typically a loss of skin color as the blood drained, producing a pale, ashen look on a person's face. There was no sign of any such reaction from Klopp, so Sean went on.

"The knife that was used was small, easily concealed. It would be lightweight, also a necessity for someone who intended on climbing walls and doing a significant amount of jumping, even possibly some acrobatics if necessary. The weapon was used expertly, sir," Sean said with an even tone. "It was inserted at the base of the skull and pushed into Jarllson's brain. The man died instantly, I assume."

Sean glanced at Bodmer for confirmation. The commander gave a single nod.

"That kind of attack produces almost no blood. It's quiet, too. There would have been no struggle. That tells me the killer was in the room, talking with Jarllson. If the priest had resisted, even a little, there would be some kind of evidence to that effect. According to what Commander Bodmer tells us, the crime scene was lacking in that regard, as well."

Sean watched as the old priest considered his words. He raised one hand and cradled his chin with his index finger, rubbing the side of his jaw with his thumb as he contemplated everything he'd heard.

"That *is* interesting," Klopp said after a long minute of thought. "All of it makes sense, except for one thing."

"Why did Jarllson invite that person into his apartment under the cover of dark?" Tommy asked.

"Yes."

"If I had to guess," Sean said, "Cardinal Jarllson was coerced. Or perhaps you didn't know him as well as you thought you did."

Sean gauged the cardinal's response with interest, hoping he hadn't jabbed the man in the wrong place with his comment.

Klopp's reaction was stoic, his expression unchanged. "Do we ever really know anyone?" He nodded. "Of course, it's possible that the late cardinal was up to something, but I doubt it."

"Why is that?" Adriana asked. She leaned forward and planted her elbows on her knees.

"Because he warned me about the killer."

8

MALBORK

L ucien Berger sat at his desk, watching the birds eat seeds from the platform feeder just outside the massive window to his right. There were several different varieties, each beautiful in their own way.

He'd taken an interest in birds when he was younger. It was one of the few childish luxuries he'd been afforded as a young member of the order. Childhoods for the Teutonic Knights went by quickly, and there was very little time for play. Since early childhood, he'd been raised to be a warrior, a killer. He didn't regret that. There were no emotions buried deep within him that yearned for playtime with other kids, or for the toys he'd never received under the Christmas tree. Those sentiments were for the weak, for those who were bred to be society's puppets. Not him, not his kind.

Beyond the shrubs and ornamental trees outside his window, he could see the roof of the castle in the distance. It had been the home of his order for centuries. Now it was a museum, a UNESCO World Heritage Site.

The notion angered him. World Heritage Site? The world had done nothing for them except steal what they'd rightfully gained so long ago.

Berger pushed aside the foolish pity he'd momentarily allowed to creep into his mind. He wasn't that weak. He didn't want anyone's pity. The only thing he desired was justice, justice for a wrong that had been committed long ago.

He stared at the red-tiled roof of the castle and the brick walls leading up to it. The towers and parapets looked much as they might have seven hundred years before when the castle was expanded. Berger never had the privilege of staying there, issuing orders from there, or sitting by the fire in a great hall with his fellow knights while they sipped wine and discussed their conquests.

No, they were resigned to the shadows, hidden from the rest of the world as they conducted their operations in secret. That had been fine, for a while. But his predecessors had grown prideful and complacent. With the immense wealth they'd amassed over the centuries, the grand masters of the order had grown sloppy. Drunk on wine, power, and money, they had lost sight of the principles that had guided their kind for so long, principles that had kept them safe and out of the crosshairs of the papacy, along with most of the world's governments.

The fatter the leaders grew, the more susceptible they became to infiltration, both from within and without.

Berger understood why it happened, why the leaders of one of the greatest military states in history had become weak. Such was the nature of victory and peace. They'd become one of the most powerful organizations in the world at the time. They were feared, even by empires and kingdoms.

Heavy lies the crown, he thought.

With so much, the order became targets of jealousy. Kings and popes alike were not happy with the power the order wielded and the brazen way they went about their business. The knights believed themselves untouchable, not only because of their military prowess, but also because they believed themselves holy, above others, and in some cases, nearly equal to the pope himself.

The result, in hindsight, was obvious. Berger wondered if he would have seen it coming were he the grand master in those days.

He believed that he wouldn't have fallen prey to such snares, but it was impossible to say. He was also wise enough to know that no one was immune to such temptations. He'd made mistakes along the way, but he'd learned from them. That was the key to success.

Throughout history, empires had risen and fallen. Kings had clawed their way to power through blood and sweat on the battlefield or through political subterfuge. The Knights of the Teutonic Order were no different than any other kingdom or government. They were composed of men, fallible human beings who made mistakes, who were prone to rust if left on the shelf too long.

That, Berger knew, was exactly what had happened to his order, but like any other, he also believed that there would come a time when they would rise from the ashes, soaring into the stratosphere once more to bathe in the sun and assert their rightful place in the world.

He'd watched with disdain as the pope, along with the church, had wilted under the pressure of politics and the growing infection that was spreading throughout the world like a virus. That virus was immorality, tolerance, acceptance of things that Berger knew to be unholy.

Recently, the pope had gone too far. The pontiff had said on a live broadcast that a peace between Jews, Christians, and Muslims needed to be reached so that there could be a greater peace on Earth.

When Berger received the news, he was angered, but there was nothing he could do about it. In the old days, centuries before, the grand master would have made it his personal responsibility to take care of the situation. The pope would have come down with an illness, one that would have been incurable and fast acting. Upon his death, the knights would appoint a new pope of their choosing from a selection of cardinals they approved.

Things didn't work like that anymore. Their resources were thin. While their armory boasted enough weapons and ammunition to take over a small town, the order was a far cry from the wealth and power they'd enjoyed so long ago. Now, their number was down to almost nothing.

They had their pawns, the members of the order who knew nothing of their real mission. Those men operated the charitable arm of the organization. It had always been a part of their way. The order, after all, was based on Christian values of assisting the needy. There was no need for that arm to know what the other was up to. That arm was the one that held the sword, and it hadn't had a blade to heft in many years.

Berger had been resigned to watching and waiting, just as his predecessors had done. They operated according to business as usual, running their various charities, while in the shadows he and his operatives watched and listened.

It was sheer luck that Jarllson had discovered that piece of parchment in the Vatican vaults. Why the man had been snooping around there in the first place remained a mystery to Berger, but he took it as a divine sign that their time to return to the light was close at hand.

He believed he could turn Jarllson. The cardinal was one of the favorites to succeed the pope when the man died, though there was no telling when that would happen. The pontiff seemed to be in good health and could live another decade or more. Even with his considerable skills, Berger knew the pope was nearly untouchable. A cardinal, however, not so much.

He'd insinuated to Jarllson that if he were to give him that letter, Berger would make sure the man was rewarded. He didn't have to say what the reward would be. It was implied. Being a man of the cloth, Jarllson didn't seek reward by nature, though there was one position he clearly desired. He believed he should be the one to guide the church into the next phase of its existence, but there was a roadblock in his way. Klopp had the support of the current pontiff and most of the conclave. It would be nearly impossible for Jarllson to achieve the office—unless he had outside help.

The cardinal, it seemed, was above those sorts of tactics. He'd turned down Berger's offer and taken the precaution of giving the Napoléon letter to Cardinal Klopp for safekeeping.

Now Klopp was being kept in the Vatican prison, if it could be called that. While the place was hardly maximum security, getting in there was next to impossible. This meant that if Berger wanted to get his hands on that letter and the information it contained, he would have to take another route.

As luck would have it, his actions opened the door of opportunity. The death of Jarllson caused Klopp to reach out to a group of American archaeology experts. The IAA was renowned, apparently, for their exploits in recovering and safely delivering rare artifacts. Until Klopp's contact with the group, Berger had never heard of them or of the two men who were in charge.

Tommy Schultz, it seemed, was savvy with money he'd inherited long ago. He'd built his agency into a powerful entity in the historical world and had gained tremendous respect for his work in salvaging important artifacts. The man didn't appear to be a threat, save for the fact he was now possibly in possession of the letter. That detail was still unclear.

Sean Wyatt, on the other hand, had the potential to be trouble. Finding his records had been difficult. That was a huge red flag. All Berger could discover was a few things about the man's collegiate career. After that, it was as if he'd dropped off the map. The only current information about Wyatt was from news articles revolving around the IAA and their various missions.

When Berger dug deeper, he learned information that was considerably more valuable, and disconcerting.

When he combined information about Wyatt's exploits in taking out would-be killers or thieves with the lack of information about his past, it wasn't a difficult conclusion to jump to. The man was clearly former special operations of some kind. Which branch of the government was unclear, meaning it was probably one of the more secretive ones.

Most people knew about the FBI, the CIA, the NSA, and a couple other agencies that ran the spy game for the United States government. Very few people knew about the shadow organizations, the ones that didn't make the headlines or that weren't paraded around in movies. Berger knew there were others, those that did the jobs the mainstream agencies didn't want to handle, or simply couldn't. Those suicidal jobs fell to the most hardened agents; those who had been trained in a fire unlike anything but a rare, hearty few could endure.

That's what Berger believed he was dealing with now. This Wyatt character was like him, an elite warrior and one that could prove problematic. Berger was certain he could deal with Schultz. Wyatt would require care. As would the woman.

She was something of a mystery. Now the wife of Sean Wyatt, she'd become more visible with the IAA over the last few years, but beyond the sparse collection of articles Berger could muster that featured her likeness, there was almost nothing about her anywhere in the world. She was a ghost, and Berger wasn't a man given to superstition. This woman, however, spooked him. There was nothing about her. Getting her name, Adriana Villa, was one thing, but there were no records of that person, at least not matching her physical description, anywhere in the world.

Berger hadn't had a challenge like this in a while. He relished it in a way, excited to have a secret to unlock, a mystery to solve. Yet there was no key. At every turn, he was greeted with an abundance of wrong answers. Part of him wondered if she was an orphan who had changed names in the middle of her life. That could account for the lack of information, but based on the company she was keeping, Berger doubted that was the answer.

His deeper suspicions about the woman were unsettling, even for a hardened warrior such as himself.

There were whispers in the shadows, in the darkness of the criminal underworld, in the bowels of haunts only the foolhardy or the powerful would dare visit. Going to such places had become a necessity for survival: a fact Berger knew well. A holy man in an unholy place might have been frowned upon centuries before, but now it provided him and the order with vital information from time to time. Walking with sinners, after all, was the Christian thing to do.

He bowed his head and scratched at the back of it for a moment as he considered the woman named Adriana. He shook off the notion for the hundredth time. She was no Assassin, no Templar, no member of some ultra secret organization of warriors. Those were just ghost stories, designed to keep people awake at night. She might be a former agent of some kind, perhaps MI6 or the KGB, though her Spanish origins refuted that possibility for the most part.

Whoever she was and whatever she was, Adriana Villa would have to be handled with care.

Berger stood from his desk and took a step to the window. Most of the birds took off in a fluttering fury of flapping wings and feathers.

He continued to gaze out the window, peering at the red roof of the castle. That fortress was his by all rights. His order had designed and built it long ago. Now they were resigned to this place. He glanced around the room as he'd done hundreds of times before, with disdain and agitation.

It wasn't that bad. Truth be told, most people would be grateful to have such a manor. The house was two hundred years old and had been renovated dozens of times. The building was two stories tall and occupied nearly six thousand square feet of space. By many standards, some would consider it a small palace.

The home had been built on a small patch of farmland just outside the city of Malbork, right on the outskirts in the north of Poland. Its original purpose had been to serve as both a security outpost on that side of the city, as well as a steady source of agricultural goods for the Teutonic Order. The knights were highly progressive in that regard, depending more on their own abilities and hard work than on serfs or peasants. While kings and emperors relied on taxes on the poor to build their kingdoms, the Knights of the Teutonic Order earned nearly everything using business savvy, trade, and almost every form of commerce to establish themselves as the financial powerhouse in the region. They were truly a self-made government, built by common men with an uncommon purpose.

This house was all that remained of that powerful regime and was a reminder of better days, days when the knights were feared and unquestioned rulers.

The way it was meant to be.

He planted his hands on the windowsill and watched the leaves flitting in the trees just beyond the double-paned glass.

Their allies, however, had turned on them and stripped them of everything they'd worked so hard for. The grand master—one of the strongest, most brilliant military minds the order had ever known—had been unable to hold back the tides that surged through the gates.

The combined forces of Rome, regional lords, and powerful monarchs had been too great. This home was all that remained in their possession, and only because it had been well disguised, positioned as a sort of safe house for those who opposed the Teutonic Order.

People, it seemed, never changed. They believed what they were told to believe. The citizenry, the encroaching armies all visited the manor but found no signs of the knights, only a few nobles who swore their allegiance to the pope and to the kings of this land.

The sheep had no idea the very nobles they were talking to were the grand master and his associates.

The move had been a savvy one, and the only way that the order had survived in its military capacity.

Under the grand master's leadership, they immediately adapted to their environment, as they'd always done since their founding at the doomed city of Acre. They became mercenaries, assassins-for-hire. It hadn't been their preferred way of operating, but necessity trumped all. They kept their identities secret, their allegiances in shadows. No one knew the knights still existed, at least not at the time. They were believed to have been vanquished, but all the while the Teutonic Knights continued to reinvent themselves, rebuild their lives, and work toward reestablishing their order as a dominant force in the world. They'd evolved, becoming spies as well as hitmen. The information they sold was extremely valuable, often incriminating. Other times, it was of a military nature.

One of the order's best customers was the fledgling nation across the Atlantic. The United States had built a rudimentary spy network during its revolution, but from the start the Americans' efforts had been stymied by both the British themselves and allies of the crown, those who resented the early success of the upstart nation. The Teutonic Knights, being the astute observers they were, noted this weakness with the young country and were more than happy to offer their services—for a price.

Most of the clandestine and intelligence operations systems and strategies that the United States used were derived from those early days of working with the knights. Of course, there was no history book that would shine a light on that fact. No one knew, and no one could, that the knights had become consultants, evolving again into something different and elusive, impossible to track or find, not that anyone was looking anymore. They'd successfully achieved something that was all but impossible for most organizations as prominent as theirs had been: they'd become invisible, both in the present and in the annals of history.

The world was constantly changing. It had always been like that. Only the strong and those willing to adapt could survive.

Over the centuries, the knights managed to accumulate a small measure of wealth that now sponsored a greater scope of activities. They were still nowhere near as powerful as they'd been at the height of their kingdom, but they were able to afford high-tech surveillance and intelligence equipment. Their land holdings were vast, purchased under names and titles that were designed as shelters that would never link back to the order, not that anyone would think such a link existed. The order, as far as most of the world was concerned, was dead.

As he gazed out at the land around them, the land that his kind had dominated so long ago, he knew that the time had come for a resurrection. Once they had the relic, there would be no stopping them.

Berger mused over the notion, allowing an ever-so-slight grin slip to one corner of his lips. The world had been misled. It had fallen into disrepair, much the same as happened in ancient Israel. He glanced over his shoulder, his eyes falling on the open Bible on his desk. It was open to a chapter he'd read many times, in a book he'd pored over for years.

The book of 1 Kings had become his guiding light. Within the pages of that section of the Bible were the tales of a kingdom of God's chosen people who continually rebelled against the Lord and his teachings. After a time of punishment and pain, the people would repent and come back to God.

Berger believed—no, he knew—that this was a similar time in history, when the people of Earth had turned away from the holy path. They'd rejected God, the Word, all of it, just as the kings of ancient Israel had done.

During every one of those moments in the history of Israel, God had sent a prophet to warn the leaders, to correct them in their ways. Often, this meant harsh punishment to teach the people a lesson, one that they wouldn't forget for a generation or more.

Berger didn't consider himself a prophet. He would never allow himself to think such a thing. To do so would be blasphemy. He'd never had a vision, never performed a miracle. He was an instrument, a tool for the Almighty.

He might not be a prophet, but he could certainly be a shepherd. Now, all he needed was the staff, and when he had that, he could return the flock to their home.

9

THE VATICAN

"He warned you?" Tommy blurted. The words were lathered in disbelief. "What do you mean, he warned you?"

Klopp sat up a little straighter and then eased back into his seat once more. The chairs weren't comfortable; then again, they were in a holding cell, so the fact that they had chairs at all was a luxury.

"Jarllson approached me the day he was murdered. He told me that there was a man—he didn't give me a name—who was looking for something that had been stolen from him long ago."

"The letter," Sean realized.

"Yes," Klopp said. "The letter. Cardinal Jarllson had a fondness for history. I share that same interest. Knowing that, he sent me a message about it, though I'm not entirely certain why he didn't just tell me in person. We saw each other that day at lunch, but there was something off about him."

"Off?"

Klopp nodded. "He looked afraid—worried about something. Now, it seems, his concerns were valid."

Adriana pressed the conversation. "Did he mention anything about who was coming to see him?"

"No," the old cardinal said with a shake of the head. "He said nothing to me about a visitor. It was only after lunch that day when he pulled me aside and told me his concerns. He said that someone knew about the letter he'd found and he was worried it could lead to trouble. He didn't say what kind of trouble but asked if I would hide it for him, keep it safe. I asked whom he wanted to keep it safe from, but he didn't say."

"The relic," Sean said.

The priest's eyes twitched open a little farther. "I'm sorry?"

"The letter you sent with Commander Bodmer, it spoke of a relic, something powerful that Napoléon needed. He said something about how not having it would result in his defeat at Waterloo."

"Good memory," Klopp said. "I believe you are correct. There was some mention of a relic."

"That would jibe with the story about the message Jarllson received, as well," Tommy added. "If the guy was looking for something...you said something that had been stolen from him?"

Klopp affirmed with a nod.

"The relic in the letter must be what this guy was talking about."

"Or gal," Adriana corrected.

"Right. Male or female. Whoever took it must have known the letter mentioned the relic."

"Which means," Sean continued, "that the letter you sent us was no ordinary correspondence. We initially thought it was some kind of undiscovered memoir from Napoléon on his deathbed. Now, I'm not so sure."

"You don't know what relic the letter is talking about, do you?" Tommy asked.

"Unfortunately, no," the priest said with a twist of the head. "I have no idea what relic it could be talking about, and I certainly don't know where it is."

"The killer," Sean said, making the short leap to the conclusion that whoever sent Jarllson the message was also the one who killed him, "said the relic was stolen. Thievery doesn't seem like it's the church's thing."

"Indeed," Klopp agreed. "I doubt any of our order would have done such a thing."

"Napoléon's letter suggests the thing was missing. He didn't say anything about it being stolen, but maybe it was taken from him," Tommy offered. "Could it be one of his heirs, a descendant of the Bonaparte line? I know there are still some of them around."

"Yes," Klopp said. "They hold a special mass for his descendants at his tomb every year in Paris."

That was something that none of the visitors knew.

Sean started connecting the dots. As he ran through the logical order of things, the timelines, the messages, the threat, the information contained in the letter, he began to form a new hypothesis.

"So," he said, "if Napoléon was missing this relic, that means it was either stolen or lost; or there is one other option."

The others looked at him with eager interest.

"He hid it."

Klopp pressed his lips together. His brow furrowed as he tried to understand what exactly Sean was saying. "Hid it?"

"Yes, but it's just a theory."

"The problem with that is," Tommy picked up the conversation, "is that we don't really have much of a clue."

"Clue?" Klopp asked.

"Yes, sir. We've seen this kind of thing before, more times than I can remember. Every single time we've stumbled on some kind of note or letter like that, it's contained a clue that leads to something else."

"Like a treasure map?" the cardinal managed.

"Yes, just like that. Sometimes, we even encounter real maps. Hiding precious items, valuable jewels or treasures, relics, artifacts, money, is ingrained into human nature. People don't want to lose what they've worked hard for."

"Or have those things stolen," Sean added.

"Right. During the American Civil War, soldiers from both sides would secure loot during various expeditions and missions. Sometimes, those men fought away from civilization for weeks or months at a time. There were no banks around, especially if they were in enemy territory. So they would bury their plunder and leave markings on trees, rocks, or even use existing landmarks to identify where the secret stash had been left."

"Jesus told a parable about a man who was given money and buried it in a hole to protect it," Sean said. "It's not a new thing to hide something valuable and leave clues that only the person who hid it, or a very clever hunter, could find."

Klopp suddenly felt overwhelmed. It was a lot to take in, and he struggled to wrap his mind around it all—despite the fact that he was a highly intelligent man.

"So, you think that the letter is a treasure map?" the cardinal asked after he felt like he'd grasped what they were saying.

"Maybe," Sean said. "But that's just it: We don't really see much on there that could give us a jumping-off point. I'm sorry, but I'm not sure how much help we can be beyond offering an idea of how the killer got into Cardinal Jarllson's apartment." Sean's tone was despondent. He regretted not being able to help more, but what else could he do?

He glanced at Tommy to see if his friend had any ideas. He could see the gears turning through the windows of Tommy's eyes. The answer wasn't clear, but Tommy wasn't giving up, and Sean recognized the look on his friend's face; the one that always seemed to get them into trouble.

As he gazed at Tommy, Sean started to wonder about himself. What was he thinking, giving up so easily on something like this? They'd flown to Europe to assist with a murder case, which he felt like they'd done, but that wasn't the real reason behind Klopp's invitation, or not the only reason. The cardinal must have had his own suspicions about the letter, but the man was keeping something from them. The question was, what?

Klopp looked defeated. He lowered his palms to the armrests and started to rise, but Sean stopped him.

"What else is there, Your Eminence?"

The old priest froze in place and cocked his head to the side. "What do you mean?"

"There was something else, something we needed to see. Bodmer alluded to it before."

The cardinal's cheeks swelled with pale red circles. He couldn't lie. Maybe he could try, but Sean was fairly certain there was a rule against that in the church doctrines. Sean was well aware of the commandment about bearing false witness.

Tommy and Adriana focused their intense stares at the man, as if their eyes alone could seize the information he had locked away in his mind.

"It...it's embarrassing."

"What is?" Tommy asked, a confused frown contorting his face.

"The letter I sent you; it bears a mark at the bottom."

"Right, two people staring at a rose."

Cardinal Klopp nodded. "Yes. Well, there was another fragment of that included with the letter. I...I'm ashamed to say, I disposed of it."

"Disposed of it?" Sean asked. He did his best not to sound upset, but this was a two-hundred-year-old piece of history, and this priest had just thrown it in the trash?

"The figures," Klopp explained, "they're pagan gods. We do not permit such things in the house of God."

"But the letter?" Adriana persisted.

"I returned it to the archives within our vaults."

"So, it's okay in the vaults, but not up above ground?"

"I know it sounds silly," Klopp admitted, "but I was torn between my devotion to preserving history and my devotion to the church."

Tommy let out a sigh of relief for the document not being damaged, not that he would ever get a chance to put his hands on the original letter. Getting down into the vaults of the Vatican was no small task, and he felt like he'd already pushed his limitations on a prior visit.

"I compromised," Klopp finished.

"So...that means the emblem was present in two places. The letter and on another document."

"There was nothing else on the other piece of paper. I believed, from my analysis of it, that it was the envelope at one time, or perhaps a kind of wrapper. I'm not certain. It didn't look like the traditional size of an envelope."

"But Jarllson gave both to you, which means they were together when he found them," Tommy stated.

"That is correct."

Sean stood and paced to the other side of the room.

Bodmer watched him, his ears pricked as he absorbed the conversation going on before him.

Sean stopped at the wall, spun on his heels, and took two more steps back toward the center of the room. He paused there again and tossed his arms over his chest. His white button-up shirt was rolled up at the sleeves, untucked at the waist so the tails and front could hang over his khaki shorts. He raised his right hand to his mouth, and the beads of his bracelets jingled momentarily.

He pressed his palm to his cheek and sighed. "So, we know that those symbols are important for some reason, but why?"

Tommy agreed with a nod and turned his focus back to the priest. "You said the images were pagan. I thought they looked familiar. Pagan deities, you said?"

"Yes," Klopp answered curtly.

"I knew it. At first, that's what I thought, but then I figured it could have been two heroes or kings or emperors."

"Which deities?" Adriana asked, inching forward in her chair, hands folded on top of her knees.

Klopp hesitated, as if contemplating whether or not he should answer the question. "Minerva and Apollo." The cardinal crossed himself for even saying the names within the walls of the church.

"Minerva and Apollo," Sean repeated. "Now why on earth would Napoléon have put two Greek gods on his letter and on the, whatever that other thing was, along with a rose in the middle?"

"Napoléon loved roses," Bodmer spoke for the first time in what seemed like a year.

Every other head in the room spun around and stared at him.

Sean swiveled his torso to fully face him. "What?" he asked.

"Napoléon Bonaparte, that's who you're talking about, yes?"

The others all nodded simultaneously.

"The general...he loved roses. I thought everyone knew that."

Sean arched one eyebrow. "Um, no." He turned to Tommy. "Did you know about that?"

"Actually, yeah, now that he mentions it, I recall reading about Napoléon's fondness for roses." It all started coming back to him at that point. "Something about his wife, Joséphine. She loved them, too."

Bodmer beamed proudly as if he'd just solved the entire mystery. In fact, it was the first time any of them had seen the hardened man smile since they had met him. "Yes, General Bonaparte's wife was passionate about roses. He built her a château with an immense rose garden that still stands to this day."

Tommy smiled, head bobbing excitedly. "That's right," he exclaimed. "It gets tons of visitors every year. I've never really thought much about going there before now."

"So...we're going to France then?" Sean asked, cutting through the bonding moment Tommy and Commander Bodmer seemed to be enjoying. "Is that what I'm hearing?"

"It would seem to make the most sense," Tommy said. "We could investigate the property and see what we could dig up." He noted the suddenly disturbed look on the cardinal's face. "Not literally dig up— I hope. I'll make a few calls and see if we can get private access to the place, though it would likely be in the evening when they close to the public."

"That could make our search efforts somewhat more difficult."

"True, although maybe we won't need to look long. Asking the head of the property for some assistance might cut down on the search time and focus our efforts."

"Sounds good," Sean said.

"There is one other thing to consider," Adriana said.

All eyes turned to her. She leaned back in her chair, raising her right arm to prop it up on the top of the chair's back. Her hand dangled behind it, making Adriana look like she was just hanging out at a friendly poker game.

"What's that?" Tommy asked.

"Napoléon had a nickname for his wife, Joséphine. He called her Rose."

10

THE VATICAN

T ommy's eyes lit up like they always do when he gets excited about a case.

Sean internally scoffed at the word *case*, thinking it a funny way to express what they were doing. Then again, it seemed to fit. They were embarking, once more, on what was undoubtedly a dangerous adventure filled with intrigue, murder, and tantalizing clues from history.

Cardinal Klopp allowed a thin smile to crease his lips, and he again steepled his fingers together over his lap. "It would appear I've called on the right people for this job," he said. He cast a glance over to Bodmer that was probably meant to gloat, but the priest wouldn't permit himself something so trivial. Saying I told you so wasn't really in his nature.

"Indeed, Your Eminence," Bodmer agreed. His cold, unfeeling demeanor returned, and he stood at the door with his arms crossed, wearing a statuesque expression.

"So," Sean said, "I don't mean to break up this lovefest and dampen the excitement, but we need to do a little research first. We also need to come up with a plan. Flying to Paris is one thing. Traipsing around the city and the property where Napoléon and his wife lived without some idea as to what we're looking for doesn't sound like the best use of our time."

"Agreed," Tommy said. He turned to Adriana. "You said Napoléon called his wife Rose?"

She nodded. "Yes, from time to time. Though I wonder what he called her after their divorce."

"Probably nothing sweet, I'd guess." He snorted a short laugh.

"Maybe we're not looking for something in the garden or at the estate," Sean offered.

All heads turned toward him as the rest of the group stared his way. It didn't bother him. He was accustomed to being put on the spot, sometimes stickier spots than this.

"What if we're looking for something related to Joséphine? It might be that the rose we're trying to find is actually her." Sean turned to the cardinal, who was listening with rapt attention. "Is there a place in here we can do a little research?"

"Certainly," Cardinal Klopp answered. "What do you need?"

"An internet connection," Tommy answered for his friend. "And I need to make a phone call."

"Of course. Cell service down here isn't the best, but you're welcome to use the landline. And our internet service is fast. You may use my computer if you like, although I suspect you may have brought your own."

"We did. But we don't want to intrude. It's a little cramped in here, too." Tommy tried not to sound ungrateful.

"No problem," the cardinal said. He wasn't offended in the least. "You're right. You need a place where you can spread out." He turned to Bodmer. "Commander, take them up to your headquarters and put them in the conference room—unless it's being used at the moment."

"It isn't, sir. I'd be happy to show them there," Bodmer spoke like a true military man, concise and to the point. "Is there anything else?"

"No," Klopp said with a shake of the head. "That's all for now. I appreciate you bringing them here, Commander. I know it was a strange ask and one that required no small measure of travel on your part."

"Not at all, Your Grace. I am at your service."

"I appreciate that, but you know me, I'm a simple priest, nothing more."

He could tell Bodmer was ready to argue that point, so he raised his hand and waved off the forthcoming rebuttal. "You may show them to the conference room now." He turned and looked at the other three. "If you need to speak to me again, you know where to find me." There was a mischievous twinkle in his eyes. "I'm not going anywhere."

The man made it sound like he was really under arrest, despite the fact that he was being detained for his own protection.

"Thank you for your time, sir," Sean said as he stood.

Tommy stood as well and bowed his head low. He wasn't sure if he should extend a hand to shake with the cardinal, or simply leave it at the bow and walk out.

Adriana stepped forward and offered her hand to the priest. "Thank you, Father. We'll see what we can do about bringing this killer to justice and figuring out what the contents of that letter could mean."

"You're welcome, my child. And thank you."

His hand was soft against hers, the skin of his fingers and palm felt like a baby's. This was a man who had never done a day of manual labor in his life, not that she was surprised by that or judged him for it. She'd always thought it interesting how you could glean insight into a person's past with a simple handshake. Sean had talked about that with her at one point, as he'd also found that subtle gesture to be a telling one, in his experience.

She let go of the cardinal's hand and Sean took over, shaking it twice as was his custom, before letting Tommy do the same.

"Commander, please keep me informed of any progress you make. I hope that you can find the person or persons responsible for this."

"I will, sir."

Bodmer gave a curt nod, turned, and led the way back to the exit.

No one said much on the elevator ride back up to the main floor.

They were too busy mulling over all the new information they'd just received and the theories that had been offered. It was also partially due, more than likely, to the occupants feeling like it was social convention to be silent on an elevator. Few people ever engaged in conversation on a lift, and when they did it often felt forced or awkward.

The moment the doors opened on the main floor, this notion was proved correct as Bodmer stepped out through the doors.

"So, the conference rooms are down the hall this way." He motioned past a series of desks to a wide hallway with stone arches bracing the ceiling, much like they'd seen in the bowels of the facility. "We have three primary conference rooms, but none of them are in use at the moment. We normally don't use them often."

"Why's that?" Tommy asked. He sounded like a kid touring a chocolate factory for the first time.

"We don't have any committees, and there are few reasons to have meetings other than to discuss security details for upcoming events."

"Such as the pope making appearances?"

"Correct."

"He makes lots of appearances, doesn't he?"

"He does," Bodmer confirmed as he continued striding down the corridor. He stopped at an open door that led into a sparsely deco-rated conference room. The table was long and rectangular, made from thick oak. The chairs around it were ordinary desk chairs, not like those fancy leather high-back things that would be found in a billion-dollar corporation's conference room. "We plan everything far in advance, that way we don't encounter any surprises."

Like one of your priests being murdered right under your nose? Sean thought. He didn't dare voice his inner snark.

One by one, the group filed into the room and took their seats at the table. They'd left most of their gear in the main office when they'd checked in, but Bodmer had allowed them to carry laptop bags and small backpacks in case this very scenario were to play out.

Tommy slid his computer out of his bag and flipped it open. The screen was black for a moment before it bloomed to life.

Sean and Adriana also retrieved computers from their bags and opened them on the table.

Bodmer gave them the Wi-Fi name and password so they could perform the necessary online searches while working on the case.

When he saw they were all situated and comfortable, he stepped toward the door. "Is there anything else I can get the three of you? I'm sorry, but I have a few things to attend to and I can't put them off any longer."

Tommy wanted to ask for a cup of coffee but thought better of it, not wanting to infringe on the commander's time.

"We're good," Sean said, seeing that caffeine lust in his friend's eyes. Truth was, he could have used a cup of joe himself, but he decided to pass and get down to work.

"Very well. I'll be out of the office for the next hour or so. If you need anything, talk to Vincenzo at the front desk. He'll be happy to assist you, and I'll instruct him to be accommodating."

"Thanks, Commander," Sean said.

The man disappeared around the corner. His footsteps clicked on the floor as he strode away, the sound fading until it finally evaporated.

Sean looked across the table as Tommy logged in to his computer, his fingers flying across the keys.

"Just another day in the life of the IAA, huh, Schultzie?" Sean said with a smile.

"Looks that way, although we did have a good amount of time off between jobs this time."

"Not long enough to enjoy our vacation."

"True." Tommy tilted his head to the side and raised his shoulders. "What are ya gonna do, though? This is who we are."

"I know."

Adriana was staring at her computer screen, lost in thought. "I wonder what the killer wanted from Jarllson," she said, ignoring the conversation the other two were having.

"I guess we have to figure that out," Tommy answered, entering a search query into the bar at the top of his screen. The monitor flickered for a moment, and then a new set of search results appeared on the page. He clicked on the top one and started scanning the images and content. "So, it looks like Joséphine Bonaparte was buried near the Château de Malmaison in a place called Rueil-Malmaison. She died there, apparently, and was interred at a nearby cathedral."

"The church of Saint Peter-Saint Paul," Sean said, still having done nothing with his laptop except for opening it.

"That's right!" Tommy said, surprised. "How did you know that?"

"Went by there once when I was in Paris on...assignment."

Tommy knew better than to ask for details of his friend's previous career. Many of them, no doubt, were grisly in nature, and while Tommy was no stranger to violence or trouble, he did his best to avoid that stuff whenever possible. It brought him down and caused him to lose focus. Neither was something he needed at the moment, so he got back to finding Joséphine.

"So that sounds easy enough," Tommy said. "They allow visitors there. Seems like a good enough place for the three of us to start our little investigation."

Little? Sean chuckled at the notion. There was nothing little about it. One of the highest-ranking officials in the Catholic Church had been murdered within the confines of the Vatican. They'd flown across the Atlantic Ocean to investigate the case, and now it appeared they were going to be leaving Italy soon to head to France.

No, Sean knew there was nothing little about any of this. And he also realized that they were heading into this investigation almost blind. For evidence, they had nothing but the ramblings of an old war general and a strange set of symbols at the bottom of the letter as their guiding light. Hardly the best set of circumstances.

He leaned closer to his computer and started typing. Google appeared on the screen and he entered a new query. Within seconds, a new page appeared with several results in blue highlighting the page. Adriana leaned close to see what he was doing. Sean playfully twisted his computer so she couldn't see the screen, as if he was a high school kid taking a test and didn't want the other kids cheating off his answers.

She let out a short laugh and then punched him in the arm. "What are you doing?" Her tone was playful and curious.

"Reading up on Napoléon," he said matter-of-factly. "I admit, I studied the guy in high school and a little in college, but there's a lot I don't remember, and I'd like to get some context if we're working on something that involves him."

"He always does this," Tommy said without looking up from his monitor.

"And you don't?" Sean joked.

"I'm doing it right now." The two shared a laugh.

"I know you are. Seriously, though, Napoléon was a fascinating study. While he wasn't a particularly religious man, he understood how to use the religious beliefs of a culture to his advantage, and he always did his best to show respect to those he would subdue."

"Which is a high contrast to the typical visage of him that history portrays."

Adriana nodded. "Yes, everything I learned about the man was that he was brash, ambitious, and egotistical. He wanted to control the entire world. Anyone with goals that big must have a gigantic ego."

"Indeed. And he could be a cruel leader at times, too," Tommy added.

Sean was busily reading the passages on the page. "He was really in love with Joséphine, though. She was a few years older than him. He built her that immense rose garden, the Château de Malmaison, and from the sound of it, even after their divorce he still thought of her. The argument could even be made that he spent the rest of his life trying to get over her."

Tommy's eyebrows knitted together as he thought about what Sean had said. "What was it in the letter, something about his greatest strength?"

"Yep. The great general was afraid he was going to lose the Battle of Waterloo because he didn't have the relic—we still don't know what that could be—and because he'd lost his greatest strength."

"Joséphine died in 1814, a number of years before him," Adriana said, looking at Sean's screen. "This says she passed soon after walking in the gardens with Czar Alexander the First of Russia."

"That's interesting. Makes you wonder what the two were talking about in her private garden."

Sean arched one eyebrow at his friend. "You think the czar had something to do with her demise?"

"Don't know," Tommy admitted. "And I'm not sure what that would have to do with this case, other than the fact we think the letter is pointing at Napoléon's ex-wife for the location of the relic."

"So that's where we'll go," Sean said. "To the tomb of Joséphine Bonaparte."

"Shouldn't be too difficult to locate," Adriana said.

"No," Sean agreed. "We can get there easily enough." He pushed the rest of his comments to the back of his mind, deciding to keep them to himself for the time being.

He was concerned that there was a killer on the loose, a killer looking for the same artifact or relic that they were searching for. That could mean trouble, which also meant Sean would have to stay on his toes. It had been months since his skills had been put to the test. He hoped it wouldn't take much to knock the rust off.

"Paris it is," Tommy said, leaning back in the chair. "That was easy enough. Maybe we didn't need this whole conference room after all." His statement was tongue and cheek. Tommy knew all too well that there was no way everything had been solved in just a few minutes with their computers. There were still a million questions looming around the case. Luckily, he had a few other resources he could depend on for assistance with difficult problems like this one.

"Sean, can you make the arrangments with the Vatican's pilot? We need that plane ready."

"Sure. When should he expect us?"

"Within the next two hours. Tell him we're going to Paris. He'll know what to do."

Sean didn't need his friend to walk him through the basics. He'd taken the IAA Gulfstream by himself on plenty of occasions. He picked up his phone and dialed the number.

"Adriana, see if you can book us a place to stay, preferably close to Rueil-Malmaison."

She nodded at the order, slightly impressed with Tommy taking charge of the situation. He'd done it before, but it still caught her off guard since he was usually the quieter of the two and certainly the less domineering.

"What are you going to do?" Sean asked as he pressed the phone to his ear.

"I'm going to call the kids and see what they can make of all this."

He pressed the phone to his ear. It only rang twice before a young man's voice came through the earpiece. "Hey, Tommy," Alex said. "Having fun in Rome?"

Tommy blew air through his lips in a short whistle. "Yeah, about that, it's more work than fun right now."

"Which is why you're calling us."

"Bingo."

Alex Simms and his wife, Tara, worked in the lab in the bowels of IAA headquarters in Atlanta. They were both highly intelligent, extremely curious about all things related to both science and history, and were gifted with the almost superhuman ability to seemingly never need sleep. Tommy knew they left the building to go to their home, but they were nearly always at the building before and after him. Tommy had even installed a couple of cots in one of the unused closets, but from the looks of the makeshift beds, they'd never been used.

While Tommy and Sean had significant investigative resources close by, the quantum computers back at the lab could search for information exponentially faster than almost any other computer on the planet—save for some of the higher-end tech developed by private industry and sparingly shared with only the most classified of government agencies.

"What can we do for you today?" Alex asked.

"We're here in the Vatican," Tommy started.

"Oh, cool. I've always wanted to go there."

"Really? I thought you guys didn't get out of the building. Wouldn't your roots wilt and die?"

"Hilarious," Alex said. The twenty-seven-year-old had a good sense of humor, and he knew how to throw it back just as well as he could take it. "Just let me know when you get back and I'll have the Sanka ready for you."

Tommy blurted out a laugh. "How do you even know what that is?"

"I'm not that young."

"And I'm not that old. I'm only like twelve years older than you."

"Try thirteen."

"Whatever. Can we please get back to the subject?"

"Sure, boss. What's up?"

"I need you to see what information you can dig up about Minerva and Apollo."

"The two gods from Ancient Greece and Rome?" Alex asked.

"Yeah. But I need you to dig a little deeper. I know the basics about them. My specialty isn't really in mythology, but I learned enough to understand enough to get by, as in the deity's specialty or what they were the god of."

"Right. Like gods of war or agriculture."

"Correct," Tommy said. "I need to know any other details about them. Maybe there's something I missed."

Tara's voice came on the line. "Hey, Tommy. You're on speaker-phone. Are you saying that you're at the Vatican, the home of the pope and the seat of the Catholic Church, and you're looking for information about pagan deities?"

"Yeah," Tommy sighed. He could already see where she was going with this.

"I'm guessing the pope doesn't know."

"I'm not sure, but we're leaving within the hour."

"Oh, where are you going?"

Tommy rubbed his forehead. "Paris. We're looking for a connection between those two pagan gods and a letter Napoléon wrote."

"As in *the* Napoléon?" Alex asked.

"Is there another one? Besides the one in that movie from a few years back?"

"Good one. No, I suppose there isn't."

"What's the connection between Napoléon and Minerva and Apollo?" Tara asked.

Sean eyes were locked on his friend, and he couldn't help laughing at the question.

"That's...that's what I'm getting at," Tommy said. "Seriously, guys. Are you messing with me?"

There was a pause on the line for a few seconds.

"Guys?" Tommy asked. He looked at his phone and saw the connection was still live. "You there?"

"Hello? Who is this?" Alex asked.

"It's...Alex, it's me."

Sean was dying of laughter at this point. Adriana didn't seem to understand what was going on, but she put two and two together when she glanced at Sean's lap and saw he was holding his phone under the table. He'd been texting the kids, and she guessed he was telling them to mess with Tommy.

She snorted and shook her head. "Would you stop."

"Sorry," Sean mouthed. "Couldn't resist."

"We got ya, boss," Tara said finally. "Dig up whatever we can about those two gods and Napoléon. We'll let you know as soon as we find something."

"Thank you," Tommy said, exasperated. "You can reach me anytime. Call as soon as you have something."

"What are you doing in Paris?" Alex asked.

"You mean other than trying to find a connection between those deities and Napoléon?"

"Obviously."

"We're going to the tomb of Joséphine Bonaparte. We think there might be a clue there that can help us figure out this whole murder mystery."

"Murder mystery? What are you, cops now?"

"How dare you! Secondly, no. The Vatican asked for our help, as you know, so we're doing what we can. But from the looks of it, there's something deeper going on here."

"As usual."

"No kidding. Anyway, we have to get moving. Call me if you find anything."

"You mean *when* we find something," Tara corrected.

"That's the attitude. I'll speak soon."

"Bye, boss," the two said cheerfully.

He ended the call and set the device on the table. His eyes lifted and met Sean's mischievous gaze. "What?" Tommy asked. Then he realized what Sean was trying to contain. "Oh, you put them up to pushing my buttons, didn't you?"

Sean shrugged and started laughing.

Adriana shook her head disapprovingly, though she had to fight to contain the smile that tried to escape. She stood up and closed her laptop. "Come on, boys. We need to get to Paris."

11

MALBORK

Berger pressed the phone to his right ear as he stared out of the window of his study. Rain lapped against the glass, spattering intermittently. Every few minutes, thunder boomed from somewhere a few miles away, seeming to never draw closer or push farther away.

"They're on the move, sir," Michael said. There was no urgency or panic in the younger knight's voice. Only information.

"Where?"

"They left the Vatican seventeen minutes ago and are on their way to the airport."

"Do you have any idea where they are flying next?"

Michael drew an audible breath through his nostrils. "Paris. They believe that there may be something to find at the tomb of Joséphine Bonaparte."

That was interesting information.

During his investigations, Berger had considered the possibility that Napoléon might have hidden the relic with his former wife. She died several years before him, and while they had divorced in typical fashion—messy—the great general had always held a place for Joséphine in his heart.

Berger couldn't imagine feeling something like that for another person. Perhaps it was his upbringing with the order. His entire life, he'd been surrounded by men and taught that chastity was important, though not required. They were not priests. There were no oaths requiring them to live in celibacy.

He'd been with women on occasion. None had ever impressed him the way it seemed Joséphine had done to Napoléon. Then again, maybe the great general, one of the most powerful men to ever live, was weak in that department. Everyone had their weakness, a chink in their armor. Berger had worked hard to make sure any weaknesses he possessed were minimized. Napoléon, it seemed, had made no effort.

After the split with Joséphine, he was never the same. From the outside, it looked as though she'd moved on, completely cutting off emotionally and physically.

"Rose," Berger said, almost a whisper.

"I'm sorry, sir?" Michael's voice only twitched slightly amid his confusion.

"Rose," the grand master repeated. "Napoléon called her Rose. That was her middle name, I believe." He knew he was correct. While the general used the name as a term of endearment, her middle name had, in fact, been Rose.

Still, why would Napoléon choose to hide the relic with his ex-wife?

In the final days leading up to the Battle of Waterloo, the general had been erratic, bordering on aloof in his behavior and actions. His mind had been all over the place. Some of his contemporaries had suggested that ever since his exile at Elba, he'd been different.

Berger knew why. The order had moved on him. They'd seen the man's sudden rise to power, the stratospheric level of his command, and known exactly how it had happened.

He'd taken something that didn't belong to him, something that had been placed within the confines of a Teutonic stronghold in the middle of the Mediterranean. The grand master of the time had sent out his best agents to retrieve the relic and bring it back to where it belonged. While they understood the relic's importance as a holy item, something to be kept sacred, it was Berger who understood its true power.

The knights tracked Napoléon, ever watchful of the man's every waking moment as they sought a way to exploit a weakness and retrieve what was rightfully theirs. The general was no easy mark, though, and was under constant and careful watch by his own guards, men who were highly trained warriors in their own right. Even so, the knights managed to infiltrate the abode of Napoléon— but found nothing. The relic was nowhere to be seen. If the man had it, he'd secreted it away in some hidden vault or safe, which he told no one about.

The knights who searched Napoléon's home considered killing the general while he slept, but they knew if they did that, they might never uncover the relic's location and it could be lost to history.

So they let the man live—for a time.

The assassins retired to the shadows and watched, but they didn't leave that fateful night without also reminding Napoléon of his transgression. They left a piece of cloth with their crest sewn into it, the mark of the Teutonic Knights. It was a simple design—a black cross on a white backdrop—but they knew that the general would get the message. He knew what he'd done, and the mere fact that the knights could infiltrate his own bedchamber meant that they held his life in the balance.

Somehow, though, Napoléon had managed to get the relic out of France, to where, no one knew. For hundreds of years, grand masters had sought to discover its location, but it was next to impossible. With no leads, no rumors, legends, or myths to go on, no clues anywhere, the relic had been lost forever.

Until Cardinal Jarllson discovered the letter.

If only Berger could have retrieved it.

Unfortunately, he'd had to make a quick escape. He'd gone to the Vatican himself to handle the situation, leaving specific instructions for Michael and the other knights on what to do if he didn't make it back.

He'd scaled the walls bordering the narrow alley with the strength and agility of a man fifteen years his junior. While his joints and muscles didn't work the way they had in his youth, Berger still found that his training and rigorous daily routines kept him in prime shape.

Jarllson hadn't had the letter, though, and once more it seemed the knights would be thrown into an endless wild goose chase, grasping at ghosts and shadows at every turn.

But fate, it seemed, was now smiling on them. These Americans were on to something, and if the order played things correctly, Berger and his knights would be led straight to their prize.

"We have a man in position at Charles de Gaulle in Paris, Grand Master," Michael said. "What would you have him do?"

He thought back on what he'd been told regarding the demise of Napoléon and the true cause behind the general's death. One of their own had followed him to Saint Helena, at the general's second exile. The knight had tortured Napoléon for weeks, slipping poisons and toxins into the man's food and drink—although nothing that would kill him quickly.

No one was the wiser. The doctors blamed it on stomach cancer, a common cause of death at the time due to poor diet. As Napoléon gradually slipped in and out of consciousness, and sanity, he began rambling about strange things. His friends believed he was losing his mind from the pain, but that was only part of it. He was also fighting the drugs he'd been given that would cause him to reveal the truth about the relic and its location.

Unfortunately, the general succumbed to his ailment before he could be coerced into giving away the details. It was a nightmare scenario for the knights, one that resigned them to their new lives as mercenaries, businessmen, and assassins. If they were going to rebuild their empire, it would be the hard way, and through many lifetimes of toil and anguish.

Berger's predecessors had stayed the course, knowing full well they would likely never hold the powerful relic Napoléon had stolen from them. It was just as well, Berger believed. They only thought the object to be something sacred, an item to be housed in a closet or museum so it could be revered. The truth, however, was that the relic possessed something greater, something more powerful than any of them ever understood.

Berger considered this as he pondered Michael's question—what to do with the Americans when they arrived in Paris.

"We know what they are after," the grand master said. "But do they?"

There was a pause. "I'm not certain, sir. I don't believe so."

"Ah, so these three are on what they think is just some treasure hunt."

"That's possible."

"Very well. Follow them to the tomb of Bonaparte's wife. Watch them closely. If they find the relic, kill them and bring it to me."

"And if they don't?"

Berger flashed a toothy grin as he stared at the birds eating just outside the window. "Take the letter and kill them anyway."

12

PARIS

S ean stepped onto the tarmac and looked around, taking in the sights and sounds of Charles de Gaulle.

It was loud as jets taxied to the runway a thousand yards away. Others were taking off and landing, one right after another.

Sean was used to seeing busy airports. Atlanta's Hartsfield-Jackson International Airport was usually the busiest in the world.

He watched planes stacked several layers high as they took off and landed in some sort of odd, perpetual motion. This airport was one Sean had visited several times in the past, most of those when he was on missions with Axis. There'd been a few for pleasure and another couple of visits with the IAA.

For tourists, the location of the airport was something of a nightmare. It was a long train or car ride back into the city, so anyone hoping to snap some quick pictures of the Eiffel Tower on a long layover would be pressed for time.

Fortunately, he wasn't pressed for time, not that he knew of, although solving the mystery behind the murder of Cardinal Jarllson would be better done in less time than more. Obviously.

"Yeah," Sean muttered to himself. "Best not to keep the Vatican waiting."

"What's that?" Tommy asked, sidling up next to his friend.

Sean tossed his head back and forth. "Nothing. Just thinking we need to solve this so we don't upset the Vatican."

"Yeah," Tommy agreed and looked over his shoulder toward the Vatican's jet.

Bodmer was still on board, collecting his things.

Adriana was already ahead of the two friends, stowing her rucksack and duffle bag into the trunk of a black luxury SUV waiting fifty feet away.

"The other thing I don't need is them trying to block me every time I apply for a permit."

"They would do that?" Sean turned his head and stared quizzically at his friend.

"I don't know," Tommy admitted with a shrug. "But I don't want to find out."

Commander Bodmer descended the stairs of the plane with his gear bag slung over his shoulder.

Sean started toward the SUV, and Tommy followed. They put their gear in the back, Sean deciding to keep his laptop bag with him instead. The driver was standing by the open front door of the vehicle and stepped out to extend a hand to the men.

"I'm Mattias," the man said. He had light brown hair, almost dirty blond, and was thin, probably 165 pounds and a hair under six feet tall. He wore a black suit and matching tie with a white button-up shirt underneath. His face was slender, like the rest of him, with a pointed chin and a short, squat nose that seemed out of place with the rest of the man's appearance. "I'm your liaison and driver."

The outfit made Sean wonder if he was going to drive them to the prom or to the tomb of Joséphine Bonaparte.

Tommy cut in front of Sean and shook the man's hand. "Mattias, good to see you again. I hope you've been well."

Mattias took Tommy's hand and shook it. The grip wasn't strong but not soft, either, like a person who was trying not to be too firm or too weak.

"A pleasure," Mattias said dryly. "What are you hoping to see at Joséphine's tomb? I heard that's where we are headed."

"To be honest, I'm not sure. It could be anything. All I know is that's where we think we're supposed to go."

"I don't suppose you'll tell me what you're searching for?" He turned as if he was about to get into the car.

"I would if I knew," Tommy said. "But we're as much in the dark about it as you."

Mattias seemed to accept the answer, twitched his nose, puckered his lips as if trying to work out an itch, and then nodded. "Well then, shall we?" He motioned to the car.

"Sounds good."

Tommy went around to the front passenger door and climbed in, leaving Sean and Adrianna in the second row while Bodmer crawled into the last row. The tall man looked scrunched, even though there was more than ample head and leg room in the vehicle.

"So," Mattias said as he shifted the vehicle into gear and started driving toward an exit, "you're visiting Paris and the tomb of Napoléon's ex-wife, but you don't know what you're looking for or why you're here?"

Tommy knew better than to divulge too much information, even with someone he knew and trusted. He'd worked with Mattias before on a few projects, though none were laced with danger and mystery like this. They were essentially part of a murder investigation. Not only that; they were part of an investigation that was centered directly in the Vatican. Something like that would require a great amount of care and discretion.

"We found something we think is a clue," Tommy said. He wasn't lying. He wasn't telling the whole truth, either. None of the passengers wanted anyone else, not even Mattias, to know the real reason they were in Paris. "What it leads to is anyone's guess."

"And so you and your friends have traveled all the way across the world to try to figure out what this is, and you don't have any idea what it could be or what it could lead to?" Mattias sounded skeptical yet uninterested at the same time. He was a fascinating study in that regard, how he was able to sound almost like he cared but remain a jerk all at once.

"Yep," Sean cut in. "You wouldn't believe how many times we've done this sort of thing and come up empty-handed."

"Sounds like an inefficient way to run things."

"Well, you win some, you lose some," Tommy chirped.

"Indeed."

The conversation fell off as Mattias steered the SUV out onto the street and turned away from the airport, merging onto the road that led to Paris. Once they were on the main highway, the vehicle's occupants engaged in some general banter, most of which was centered around catching up with Mattias and what he'd been doing since the last time Tommy saw him.

Mattias was a local historian specializing in French Revolutionary history and government affairs. He was a freelancer, which meant he was never tied down to an office or bosses that could dictate his schedule. He'd written several books, which helped fund his lifestyle, though from what Tommy knew of the man, he didn't have extremely expensive tastes. The SUV was a rental Mattias had picked up on Tommy's behalf. Mattias's car was more practical, and his apartment in the city was small: only two bedrooms, a living room, and a kitchen. One of the bedrooms was used as his office, though the sofa pulled out into a bed in case he ever had guests. Tommy got the impression that wasn't often. The man was one of intense focus and study, always with his nose in a book trying to learn as much as he could. And once he'd done that, his nose moved to his computer, where he wrote on the subjects he'd learned about. It wasn't an extremely lucrative job, but he seemed content and had no designs on trying to do better for himself. Mattias was a man of simple needs. Tommy appreciated that about him.

By the time they arrived at their destination, the sun had already begun to sink below the horizon, the sky growing ever darker in the east. The trip didn't take as long as Sean thought it might, only about forty minutes to reach Rueil-Malmaison.

It was a part of the city Sean had never seen, and from what he could tell, neither had Tommy.

Adriana, however, remained oddly quiet when they reached the wealthy suburb of Paris.

Sean wondered why for a brief moment but let it go. Perhaps she'd been through here on one of her quests for stolen art. Then again, it could have been anything. She was born in Madrid, educated in the UK, traveled the world, had United States citizenship, and had—as he'd recently learned—been trained by a secret order of ninjas, which still sounded ridiculous to think or say despite the fact he knew it was true.

"This is a nice area," Tommy said as he stared wide-eyed out the window.

Mattias guided the car through winding streets and straight corridors between lavish apartments and condos. There were immense châteaus and manors, all designed in that same palatial aesthetic that reflected a tony mix of Renaissance, neoclassical, and so-called French Empire styles.

"I can't believe I haven't been here before," Tommy added.

Mattias kept his eyes straight ahead. "Not much to find in the way of archaeology out here, my friend. So I suppose there was never really a reason for you to be here, *non*?"

Even speaking English, the driver ended his sentence with his familiar way of saying no. It was an endearing tick.

"Yeah, I guess that's true," Tommy said. "Except we're here now because of something related to history."

Mattias made a short humming sound to affirm what his friend said. He steered the vehicle past another row of townhomes and then a roundabout before cutting to the right and passing another massive mansion. This one was surrounded by huge shrubs, and flowers dangled off balconies that were lit by exterior floodlights pointing toward the building.

They kept going until they reached another collection of apartments, where Mattias turned left onto a side street. A parking area opened up on the right and he swept the vehicle in with a quick flick of his hands on the steering wheel. He expertly maneuvered the SUV between two compact cars, leaving plenty of room on both sides for all his occupants to get out without scratching one of the other vehicles. That was quite a feat considering most of the cars parked in the lot were dangerously close to each other.

Mattias shifted the transmission into park and everyone started climbing out as he killed the ignition.

The air was cool and humid, unsurprising for the late spring months in Paris.

Mattias led the group to a black gate in the rear of one of the buildings. It was preempted by a square yard separated from the others by brick walls. Beyond the gate, a lush green grass grew on both sides of a narrow stone walkway. Pink, red, purple, and yellow flowers hung in flower boxes from windows on either side of the red door leading into the house. There was a patio made from concrete pavers that jutted out ten feet from the house. A couple of teak chairs sat diagonally across from one another with a matching coffee table in between.

"This is a lovely little spot," Tommy commented.

Sean and Adriana nodded.

Bodmer remained quiet, as he'd done since they'd arrived in France.

Sean noted the man's odd silence but said nothing to him about it. Maybe the commander just didn't have anything to say.

Mattias opened the gate and led them to the back door of the townhome. He fished the key out of his pocket and unlocked the door, swung it open, and then held out the key to Tommy. "This one is yours. I have a duplicate. When your time here is done, feel free to leave it under the welcome mat. I'll come get it when I have a chance. Just be sure to lock the door."

Tommy's eyes squinted as he smiled. "Will do."

Mattias gave a curt nod and then stepped into the house. "This building is three hundred years old," he said, waving his left hand around in a swirl as if showing off the house, but also bored with the notion of doing so. "The original owner was one of the king's emissaries. Now, it belongs to a friend, a very wealthy, very never-home friend. Honestly, I don't know why he bought it other than as an investment or to tell women he has a place in one of the wealthier neighborhoods in Paris."

Sean chuckled.

"He also travels constantly and, since this is one of his many residences, he is almost never here."

"Where is he now?" Bodmer asked, suddenly curious enough to speak.

"Rwanda," Mattias said plainly.

"As in Africa?" Tommy asked.

"I know of no other place by that name. He's there establishing a supply chain for coffee. Apparently he thinks the market for coffee from that region is wide open and he's looking to take advantage of that gap."

Sean and Tommy were both impressed, their eyebrows climbing up their foreheads as they listened.

Mattias pointed at the kitchen to the left. It was bathed in white tile all the way to the ceiling. A huge steel vent hung over the gas stove. The cabinetry was cream, distressed maple with black hinges and hardware that also appeared to have been artificially distressed to match the general look and feel of the space.

"There's your kitchen. Over there is a small living room, as you can see." Mattias pointed his other index finger in the direction of a space to the right where a fireplace sat idle, surrounded by two leather chairs and a matching sofa. A painting of Paris in spring hung over the mantel, the bright and colorful flowers contrasting sharply with the black-and-white décor that surrounded it. Bookshelves hugged the fireplace on both sides, displaying dozens of tomes that looked like they'd never been touched, save to place them on the shelves. They were perfectly arranged alphabetically based on author name.

"I'll not give you the entire tour since I'm sure you want to get settled in, and I have some other matters to attend to." Mattias turned to Tommy, holding the key to the SUV. "There is a master bedroom downstairs, two more upstairs, as well as an office. Make yourselves comfortable, and feel free to stay as long as you need, though based on how you operate, Thomas, I doubt that will be more than a day or two." There was a joking glint in the man's eyes.

"You know me," Tommy said, throwing his hands out to the side with his confession. Then he took the key from his friend and arched an eyebrow. "How are you getting home?"

"I'll do a ride share," he said. "Or a cab. Whichever gets here first. I only live fifteen minutes from here. It's not a problem."

"We can take you home," Adriana insisted.

He raised a dismissive hand. "Don't be silly. It's no problem. I'm just glad I could help."

"Thank you, Mattias," Tommy said with a nod. "I appreciate your help. Especially on such short notice."

"You're most welcome. I know you would do the same for me. In fact, you've done more for me than most." The man's voice was unemotional, but there was an underlying current to it, one that made the others in the room wonder what Tommy could have done to help this young man in such a way that he would feel so indebted.

"You bet," Tommy agreed.

"I bid you adieu," Mattias said and turned to the door. He stepped out into the Parisian evening air and closed the door behind him before walking to the parking area and disappearing around the corner.

Inside the house, Sean and the others looked around, getting adjusted to their temporary accommodations. He only realized that he was hungry when his stomach grumbled. They hadn't eaten since breakfast, which was a fact he regretted since they'd been in Italy, surrounded by exceptional dining options. Luckily, now they were in Paris, and the options in that city would be just as good as in Rome.

"You guys up for a little dinner on the town?" Sean asked.

"Yeah, that sounds great," Tommy said. "I'm starving."

Adriana and Bodmer also added their approving sentiments.

"Great. Let's get situated, and we'll leave here in a few minutes."

"You two take the master down here," Tommy insisted. "Unless the commander wants to share it with me," he glanced jokingly toward the head of the Swiss Guard, but the man didn't seem to get the joke.

"Why would I want to share a room with you when there are two empty rooms upstairs?" There was nothing but dead seriousness in his eyes.

"Yeah, good point," Tommy said, suddenly made uncomfortable by his own sense of humor. "We'll take those rooms."

Sean snorted a laugh at his friend.

Adriana bit her lip and watched as the two men took their things and climbed the steps at the other end of the house, near the main entrance.

She and Sean took their belongings into the master bedroom and took in the surroundings again. The room was opulent, featuring a dark-stained armoire in the corner. It was made from sturdy oak and sat next to a large window with dark red drapes hanging down from the twelve-foot-high ceiling. The room smelled of lavender and lilac, and there were candles resting atop a dresser to the right of the window. In the corner to the right was another door that led into the master bathroom. The bed was covered in pristine white sheets and a navy-blue comforter. The oak sleigh bed matched the color and style of the armoire and dresser.

There were more paintings on the wall, but they were mostly of scenes from Paris and could have been mistaken for hotel room art as much as anything that would be displayed in the private residence of a wealthy patron.

"So," Adriana said, "your friend Mattias is an interesting fellow."

"He's not my friend. He's Tommy's. I just met the guy. But you're right. He *is* interesting." He eyed her suspiciously. "You think we can't trust him?"

"Oh, it's not that. He just seems emotionless. I've encountered people like that before. It's not always a bad thing or a good thing. They're just floating through life like non-player characters in a video game."

"Except he's written books and helps preserve history."

"True."

He smirked at her. "Come on. Let's change out of these clothes and go get something to eat."

She grinned back at him and pulled him close, planting a short kiss on his cheek. "Okay, dear."

13

PARIS

The food from the night before soothed Sean's slumber and still occupied his thoughts the next morning.

They'd ordered Roquefort and caramelized onion tarts, a spinach soufflé, at least three kinds of breads, a cheese plate, and the best crème brûlée Sean had ever tasted—and there were two places that did it pretty well back in Atlanta and Chattanooga. Those didn't come close. They'd also ordered a Napoléon dessert—a kind of fluffy cake dish with heavy whipping cream and powdered sugar.

Normally, Sean did his best to eat healthy, but not on this occasion.

The group had shared their entrées, passing them around as if it was a family meal or a holiday. They'd munched on crunchy bread with Boursin cheese, tomatoes, and a balsamic vinaigrette drizzle on top.

After the incredible dinner, the four retired to the house in Rueil-Malmaison and slept through the night. Even Sean, who was normally a light sleeper—both from training himself that way and from the fact he fought occasional bouts of insomnia—slept like a dead man. He only recalled waking one time during the course of the entire evening, and that was when a police car drove by with sirens blaring.

Sean lay in the bed for a minute as his eyes creaked open like ancient doors on rusted hinges. The room around him was foreign for a few fleeting seconds before he remembered where he was. Thoughts of last night's meal returned as he sniffed fresh coffee brewing in the kitchen and heard the sound of the brown liquid dripping into a pot. He turned to his left to discover that Adriana wasn't there.

He rose and stretched his arms and legs, then headed to the kitchen. Adriana was setting up fresh cream and a canister of sugar she'd found, probably in one of the pantries.

"You ever sleep in?" he asked as he scratched the back of his head.

She turned slightly, unsurprised by his mild intrusion. She'd known he was standing there. Adriana's acute sense of hearing was a skill honed through hard training and it had served her well, especially when behind enemy lines.

"You know I don't. And don't act like you do, either. Most of the time, you're up when I am." She raised an eyebrow and then turned back to the pot of steaming coffee. The dripping had ceased; the brew was ready. So was Sean.

He made his way into the kitchen and wrapped his arm around her waist for a moment, pulling her tight against him. He kissed her neck.

She smiled at the affection, putting off coffee for a few more seconds. "I do enjoy it when you do this to me first thing in the morning," she said.

"And I enjoy it when you make the coffee."

She slapped his shoulder at the half joke.

"But no French press? We're in France, after all."

She rolled her eyes and pulled away from him, shaking her head. Then she took the pot and poured the coffee into a white mug, set the pot back on the percolator, and turned to the sugar and cream.

"I guess I have to make my own."

"Mm-hmm," she hummed. "For the French press comment."

He chuckled and grabbed one of the three remaining mugs she'd set out for them. He poured the java into the container and then spun around, added a splash of cream and a sprinkle of sugar. He preferred not to overdo it.

"You sleep okay?" he asked as he sidled up next to her and took a sip of the hot liquid. His eyebrows lowered, and he grunted his approval. "This is good, by the way."

"Thank you," she said with an appreciative nod. "And yes, I did sleep well. I know you did."

He laughed again. "Yeah, I guess I didn't realize how tired I was."

"Or how all that rich food could knock you out."

"That, too."

"Well, we're going to eat healthy this morning."

"We are?" He wasn't sure he liked the sound of that. "Because, for the record, I regret nothing about last night's dinner. Nothing."

She snickered and shook her head. Her dark brown hair swished back and forth with the motion. "Fruit, bread, coffee this morning, Mr. Wyatt. We don't need any of that other stuff slowing us down."

"Just as well," Sean moped, "I doubt any of those places are open. Although—"

"No, no rich French breakfast foods, either. Besides, we need to get going soon. Your buddies upstairs awake yet?"

She was starting to sound like his mother, and Sean realized it had been a few days since he'd spoken to his parents. He kept his communication with them private in most instances, though in recent months since getting married, he'd found himself a little more domesticated and calling them more often, sometimes with Adriana in the room. He could text his mom later, maybe with a picture from the tomb of Joséphine, though he almost never did that kind of thing.

"Fine, healthy breakfast, but I make no promises about lunch or dinner. As to the other two, I walked straight in here. I'm not Schultzie's keeper."

"Who's my keeper?"

They turned and saw Tommy coming around the corner. His hair looked like a wet, tangled mop. He had on a Nirvana T-shirt and some faded blue jeans. Sean was surprised to see his friend dressed so casually. Normally, Tommy would have a button-up shirt of some kind, often tucked into his pants. Not today. Instead, he looked like he was going to a rock concert.

Sean was used to wearing stuff like that. He had on his gray Spider-Man T-shirt and some jeans instead of his usual khakis, but seeing Tommy dressed that way threw him off.

"Going to a show while we're here?" Sean asked.

Tommy looked down at himself, inspecting his clothes. "Nope. Just wanted to be comfortable. It's going to be warm today, and besides, I get tired of trying to look semiprofessional all the time."

"Wow," Sean gasped. "It's a whole new you!"

"Stop it," Tommy said, blushing slightly. "Anyway, I'm figuring we need to blend in, just look like normal American tourists."

"Because the locals will treat us better?" Sean asked with a sardonic tone.

"Fair enough. I guess you do have a point, but I'm not changing now. Besides, you're basically wearing the same thing." He walked over to the counter and poured a cup of coffee, then noted a white box to the left with a bakery's logo on the top. The words Au Bon Pain were embossed in gold lettering, with golden vines and leaves wrapping up and around them. "What's in the box?"

"Nothing as good as last night's dinner," Sean grumbled.

"It's breakfast," Adriana said. "Apparently, our friend here isn't hungry."

Tommy shrugged and opened the lid. Inside were croissants, an assortment of fruit, and three containers holding honey, jam, and marmalade.

"Looks good to me," Tommy said cheerfully.

"Did you sleep okay?" Adriana asked as she drew the cup of coffee to her lips and took a sip.

"Yeah, we slept great."

Sean nearly spit out his coffee and had to fight to choke it down without making a mess. "What?"

Tommy scrunched his eyebrows for a moment, looking puzzled.

Then he realized what he'd said and how it sounded. "No, I mean I slept great in my bed, and Commander Bodmer didn't say anything to me so I assume he slept fine, too." His face washed red, cheeks blazing from embarrassment. Tommy had the habit of walking into insults.

"Suuuurre," Sean said. "I won't tell June."

Tommy rolled his eyes, picked up a croissant and a few grapes, berries, and banana slices, and placed them on a white plate to the left of the box.

Footsteps on the stairs told them that Bodmer was on his way down, his boots clunking heavily on each step.

"Mornin'," Sean said in a deeper Southern accent than normal. "How'd you sleep?"

Dark rings hung under Bodmer's eyes and he wore a grumpy frown. "Not great," he said. "The bed was...softer than I'm used to."

"Oh, yeah, they were a bit on the soft side, weren't they."

"I didn't mind it," Tommy said. "It was like lying on a cloud all night."

Bodmer grunted, which could have meant any number of things. It was all he could do to slog over to the coffee pot and pour himself a cup. He slurped the hot liquid, unaffected by the searing heat against his lips. All he wanted at the moment was caffeine so he could shake off the effects of the poor night's sleep.

"There's some food over there, too," Adriana said. "Nothing fancy. Just a simple breakfast, sort of light."

Bodmer nodded absently. "Thanks."

"So," Tommy diverted the conversation, "I've made arrangements to have the tomb to ourselves for thirty minutes before it opens for the public. We'll need to get over there soon to check in and have a look around. I'd prefer not to have tourists looking over our shoulders while we're conducting an investigation."

Sean nodded in agreement. "Good idea. And thanks for calling ahead to make those arrangements. Should make things go smoother."

"I hope." There was a small measure of doubt in Tommy's mind, probably based on past experiences just like this one with his friend. No matter how thoroughly they planned, how careful they were, trouble seemed to find them like a heat-seeking missile. And it always ended up with a similar kind of explosion—sometimes metaphorical, sometimes literal.

They finished their coffee and breakfast in relative silence. Sean looked up the directions to the tomb on his phone and mapped out the path they would take to get there. It was only a five-minute walk from the house, and after a quick check on the weather app it appeared like the day was going to be a nice one for a little walk.

When the group stepped outside, that suspicion was confirmed. The sun was already rising into the sky; a few wispy clouds coasted through the light blue backdrop; the air felt warm against their skin, tickled by an occasional breeze that blew through the canyons of old apartments, condos, and townhomes; and flower petals fluttered in boxes hanging from windows and along the sidewalk, where they'd been planted around trees that lined the street.

Tommy admired the architecture of the corridor, stopping multiple times to appreciate the design of a doorway, an arch over an entrance, or the steep roof of a home.

Sean and Adriana were less interested in those things, though they enjoyed the scenery and could appreciate the style of the buildings surrounding them. They were more concerned with making sure no one got the drop on them. Both of them had been trained extensively to watch for tails whenever they were on a mission. Those skills had saved them more times than not, and while they hadn't encountered any trouble on this particular adventure, it was still a murder investigation at its core, which meant there were killers on the loose. If they got sloppy, they could end up the same way as Cardinal Jarllson had.

As the directions predicted, the walk took roughly five minutes before the group reached the building that housed the tomb of Joséphine.

The Church of Saint Peter-Saint Paul was just as Sean remembered it—unique. Most cathedrals he'd visited were enormous buildings with high-sweeping arches, huge domed ceilings, and immense sanctuaries. This particular church was smaller, though still quite large in its own right.

The beige stone building was set in the middle of a square, between pedestrian streets and normal automobile thoroughfares. A fountain in front spewed a circle of streams into its center. Across the street, and on all sides, the church was surrounded by shops, cafés, and restaurants.

Statues of the cathedral's patron saints, Peter and Paul, were carved of the same stone as the walls and set into shallow alcoves on either side of the blue doors of the main entrance. Above were two more statues. These were angelic creatures, their feathered wings folded down along their backs as the creatures stared perpetually at the saints at their feet.

Tommy led the way to the entrance where a young woman was standing to the right. There was no line of patrons waiting to gain entry to the building yet, but Tommy figured that would change shortly as Joséphine was a fairly significant historical figure and this place would certainly be at the top of many visitors' lists.

The young woman recognized Tommy and cracked a smile. She was of Asian descent, with long black hair that flowed down her back from a tightly tied ponytail. She wore a pretty blue business suit and skirt with white flower designs imprinted into the fabric.

"Bonjour," she said to Tommy as he approached.

"Bonjour," Tommy replied in kind.

"It is such a pleasure to meet you. My name is Monique. We spoke on the phone this morning."

The two shook hands as the other three caught up and halted behind Tommy.

"I'm Tommy. Yes, thank you so much for helping us out on such short notice," he said. His tone was as apologetic as he could make it. "I know it's a hassle."

She shook off his comments. "Not at all. We're more than happy to help you. You and your agency have done so much to preserve French history. It's the least we could do. Honestly, when I realized who was trying to contact me, I thought it was a joke."

Tommy's cheeks flushed, and he bowed his head. Fame never sat well with him, but it was something he'd had to deal with since the agency's first big find more than a decade ago.

"These are my friends," Tommy turned and motioned to the others.

They took turns introducing themselves and shaking hands. Once they were caught up with the introductions, Tommy continued. "So, we have about thirty minutes?"

"Yes, that's correct. I'm sorry we can't give you more time, but that's the best we could do."

"No, it's fine," he insisted. "Not a problem. We'll be in and out before you know it."

She grinned at his amicable demeanor and pulled back a loose strand of hair that had broken free from the bunch. She hooked it over her ear and then motioned for the four visitors to come inside the building.

They stepped through the blue doorway and into the atrium of the cathedral. The familiar scent of time filled their nostrils. It was a scent they'd grown to expect when entering an old building like this. The odor was a mixture of stone, ancient wood, and a musty feel that seemed to almost always permeate these structures.

A faint waft of incense floated through the space and tickled their olfactory senses as well, forcing a sort of sweet and pungent aroma to the mix.

"Right this way," Monique said as she motioned down one of the corridors.

The open doors across from the entrance gave the visitors a full view of the sanctuary, and rows of wooden chairs were set up for a mass. Once inside the building, it appeared far larger than it had when they were standing outside. The narrow sanctuary ran the length of the church. Unlike many of the more opulent cathedrals they'd seen before, this one appeared remarkably plain. There were no frescoes adorning the ceiling, no images of some long-dead master artist painted on the walls or columns. The floors were ordinary, made from stone and drab tiles. It was as if those who'd designed this place didn't want the distractions that other cathedrals had to offer. There were a few pieces here and there, a relief of a saint or an angel, but very little luxury that could be found elsewhere. Instead of a temple of worldly glory, this place looked like a church where parishioners could focus on the simple act of worship, undistracted by fancy trinkets and artistry.

Most of the color in the sanctuary came from behind the presbytery, where stained-glass windows displayed images of four men, two of whom were the saints for whom the church was named; another was Jesus; and the fourth was too difficult to make out as the group continued walking.

Sean noted alcoves along the side of the main sanctuary. Huge chandeliers hung from the ceilings in those recessed areas, casting bright light into the spaces, light that also spilled out onto the empty rows of wooden chairs.

Monique led them around a corner and down another passage where more light shone from above at the end of another domed room. The fixtures hanging from the ceiling and walls combined with light pouring in from windows fixed high up where the walls began to angle upward.

The beams of light seemed to point instinctively toward a single form in the center of the room, set against the back wall. As the group drew nearer, they made out the shape of a large stone box on the floor. Atop the container was the statue of a woman, kneeling in eternal prayer over an altar. She was dressed in the finest gowns of the period, and the tomb on which she knelt was adorned on all sides with wreaths and garland.

The detail of Joséphine's likeness was impeccably realistic, so much so that Sean and the others couldn't help but wonder if Napoléon himself had paid for the finest stone craftsmen and sculptors in all the world to come and create this final, lasting tribute to the woman he'd loved and subsequently detested.

"So," Sean said as he put his hands on his hips and stared up at the sculpture. "This is the tomb of Joséphine Bonaparte."

"Pretty spectacular," Tommy said.

"So regal," Adriana commented.

"Fitting for the former empress," Monique added. "Even though Napoléon and Joséphine were divorced, many people still considered her to be a queen-like figure. Despite some regrettable decisions in her life, she was still lauded as a popular public persona. Her rose garden is a popular attraction for tourists, and while she was alive she hosted several important dignitaries from around the world."

"The last of which was the Russian czar," Sean noted.

"Indeed. She died shortly thereafter."

Sean let his mind linger on that fact for a few moments longer. It was a strange occurrence that only days after hosting the czar, Joséphine died of a strange ailment. Of course, the doctors told everyone it was of natural causes, but Sean couldn't help but wonder if foul play was involved. At the moment, that didn't matter. They weren't there to figure out why or how Joséphine Bonaparte died. They were there to see if there was any kind of connection between her tomb and the note they'd been given by Cardinal Klopp.

14

PARIS

Sean looked over his shoulder, sensing movement at the other end of the corridor. The passage, however, was empty. He let his gaze linger for a moment. He'd learned long ago that if someone thought they'd been detected, they would take cover for a short time until their target had believed their senses were fooling them. Sean had used that very tactic on a mission in Tokyo. He'd been following his mark along a sidewalk in a city park when the man turned and looked back. Fortunately, Sean sensed the man's paranoia and ducked behind a tree a fraction of a second before he was spotted. There, behind a thick trunk, he waited until he was fairly certain the target had moved on before setting out to tail the man once more.

In this instance, Sean continued to look down the corridor while Monique spoke to the others about the history surrounding Joséphine Bonaparte and her late ex-husband, the former emperor.

There was no sign of movement, and no one appeared from behind the columns on the right or around either corner. Sean reluctantly turned his attention back to their liaison and listened as she finished her story.

He felt like he was on one of those guided tours in a museum or an art gallery, but didn't say anything for fear of offending their host, who'd been gracious enough to allow them private access to the cathedral.

Monique completed her five-minute spiel and excused herself, telling the visitors that they could take a look around and that if they needed anything she would be where they found her upon first arriving.

When Monique was out of sight and probably out of earshot, Tommy was the first to speak up. "So, we're here. What is it we're looking for?"

Sean stepped closer to the stone box. He stared up at the likeness of the dead empress and considered the riddle. His eyes drifted upward to analyze the ceiling, the supports that arched their way up to the top, and the stonework all around them. Then he dipped his head and scanned the floor.

The others did the same.

Adriana split off from the others and made her way to the side of the tomb, checking to see if there was anything hidden there that couldn't be seen from the front.

Bodmer worked his way over to the far wall and investigated the columns. He ran his fingers along the smooth surface, as if the act might reveal a secret doorway or hidden shelf.

Sean shifted a few steps to his right to stand next to Tommy. The two friends gazed at the shiny marble columns that supported a sort of portico-style arched roof over the kneeling Joséphine. Rows of carved flowers lined the inside of the portico's ceiling. Over the roof, light poured in from a skylight carved to look like a flower, similar to those over Joséphine's final resting place. Perhaps thinking they were flowers was a stretch. The petals, if that's what they were, looked as much like stretched out teardrops as flower petals. Still, it was compelling.

"What do you think?" Sean asked.

"I...I don't know," Tommy confessed. He crossed his arms and tilted his head to the right, still staring at the tomb. Then he moved to his right and inspected that end of the marble box.

Adriana joined her husband in front of the tomb and looked up into his icy-gray eyes. She still hadn't decided if they were blue or gray. At the moment, they appeared gray, but she swore they changed from time to time, despite not believing that sort of thing was normal.

"I don't see anything here," she whispered. Even though she lowered her voice, the sound echoed off the marble façade of the tomb and the stone walls.

"No," Sean said with a shake of the head. "I don't, either." He stepped closer to the marble monument that gave the name of the woman buried there. The words À *Joséphine Eugène Et Hortense* and the year *1825* were chiseled into the façade. That date was around ten years after the woman's death, based on what Sean had studied on the subject. "I wonder if the wreaths bear some significance to our plight," he theorized.

Three wreaths adorned the front and back, all aligned at the same height and evenly spaced. Similar wreaths were carved into either end of the tomb.

"Eight wreaths," Adriana murmured. "One for every nation he conquered?"

"How many *did* he conquer? I never bothered to look that up."

"I don't know, but I'd guess it's more than that. Napoléon waged war in many places."

"So, perhaps that's not the answer. The letter said that he would have to win at Waterloo without his strength and without the relic. What if his strength was something else, not his former wife?"

Sean's question brought them to a point they all should have considered before hopping on a plane and flying to Paris from Italy. Had they all acted too hastily? No, certainly not. They were going on limited information, even more so than usual. Paris was the best answer. And this tomb made the most sense based on what little intel they had. Then again, that didn't mean they were in the right place. He'd been around long enough to know that there was always another way to do things, always another method of coming up with an answer.

He thought back to high school and college math classes where he found alternative ways, easier ways, to come up with answers to complex math problems. The teachers, of course, hated when he did that, especially when his solutions proved correct.

The thought gave him pause. "What else could we be missing?" he wondered out loud.

Adriana didn't immediately respond.

Tommy ambled up to his friend and looked at him sideways. "What did you just say?"

"Sean isn't sure we're in the right place," Adriana answered.

"Where else would it be?" Tommy asked. "Napoléon called Joséphine, Rose. She's the rose. She has to be. Doesn't she?"

"Not necessarily," Sean said. He moved backward a few steps to take in the entire scene. He knew their time was running out for this private visit. Soon, tourists would pour into the building, and then finding anything meaningful would be nearly impossible.

But time, Sean realized, wasn't their issue. They could stay there in the Church of Saint Peter-Saint Paul for days and not find what they were looking for. There was a striking absence in the quiet hall, indeed around the entire church.

"It's not here," Sean said.

"What's not?" Commander Bodmer asked, stepping closer to find out what was going on.

"I don't know, but whatever it is, it's not in this place."

"What are you saying? I hope you haven't wasted our time coming here."

Sean took a step toward the entrance, but upon hearing Bodmer's insinuation a spark flared in his gut that attempted to ignite a fast-burning fire. He spun on his heels and faced the commander. "Waste our time?" Sean took a menacing step toward the man. "We are here at no cost to you or your church, Commander. We are helping you because that's what we do. If you think it's a waste of your time, then feel free to head back to the Vatican and we'll be on our way. It may seem like we always have the answers, are always on a quick and easy path, but that isn't the case. We strike out. A lot. That's what you do if you want to hit home runs now and then."

The commander looked confused by the baseball analogy, but he seemed to get the gist of what Sean was saying.

"There must be another place," Sean went on before the man could speak up again. "I am going to find out where that is."

He whirled around again and stormed toward the entrance.

Adriana followed quickly behind while Tommy lingered back, attempting to apologize. "He...well, he's actually right. So, you know, maybe let us do our thing. Okay? Pumpkin?" Tommy patted the man on the shoulder and scuffled ahead to catch up with his friends.

Bodmer stared at them as they strode down the corridor. He'd never been put in his place like that before, and it unsettled him. He also found a sense of respect for the man who was willing to stand up for himself. That was a commendable trait and one he admired. He shrugged off his irritation, swallowed his pride, and caught up to the others.

"I...apologize," Bodmer said as he fell in line behind Sean. "I didn't mean to insult you. You're right. I was out of line. The cardinal believes you are the best people for this. I should believe, too."

Sean looked over his shoulder at the commander, but he only slowed his pace, not stopping completely.

"It's okay," Sean said. "I'm as frustrated as you are. Even when we strike out, we don't have to like it." He winked at the man, and that seemed to disarm his concern.

"So, what are we going to do now?" Bodmer asked.

Tommy and Adriana were wondering the same thing, but it appeared their friend had an idea.

"Talk to the tour guide, of course."

They passed through the entrance and spotted the young woman in her blue-and-white dress standing exactly where she said she'd be. There was a short line of tourists waiting to get in. A few of them were wearing berets, others had shirts with the French flag on it. A few were clearly Americans, sporting their favorite college football team's logo on their shirts.

Monique greeted them with a polite smile and then glanced

down at her watch. "Is everything all right? You still have five more minutes. Or did you get enough time?"

"No, we had plenty of time," Sean said. "And thank you again for being so accommodating. Really, it's been extremely helpful."

"We were happy to do it." She narrowed her eyes at him with suspicion. "You look like you're about to ask me a question, though. Is there something else I can help you with?"

"Actually, there is," Sean said. The other three stood slightly behind him, Adriana to his right. "What do you know about the mythological gods, Apollo and Minerva?"

"Not much," she said after a brief moment of thought. "My area of expertise is more on French history, not Greek and Roman history."

Tommy jumped in, seeing where his friend was going with his line of questions. "We were hoping maybe you could tell us if there are any signs of those two deities in this area, specifically anything related to Napoléon."

Monique's jaw set firm and she pressed her lips together as she considered the request. At first, nothing came to mind. A full minute passed before she spoke up once more. "I'm sorry," she said. "I don't believe I know of anything like that around here, or that has to do with Napoleonic history or the revolution. However, if you're looking for something regarding Napoléon, might I suggest visiting the château? That is where you can find the rose garden and the personal library of Napoléon."

"Personal library?" Adriana asked.

"Yes. When he was still alive, the collection was quite impressive. Many of the volumes still remain as he left them. In fact, from what I understand, his study has not undergone any major refurbishment since he died."

"So the place will be almost exactly as he left it?" Sean clarified.

"Yes, I believe so."

Sean turned and looked at his friend, then his wife, and then Bodmer last. The Swiss Guard commander gave a curt nod. Even the pragmatic commander appeared to think that was a good bet.

"Great," Sean said. "Thank you so much for your help. We'll check it out."

Tommy stepped forward and shook the woman's hand. "Thank you. Truly, we appreciate all of this. You have been very accommodating. If there is anything I can ever do to help you, please do not hesitate to ask."

Monique smiled shyly. "Merci," she said. "And you are most welcome. Anytime."

"Merci," Adriana said.

Bodmer added his own thanks, and the group made their way across the plaza toward the Château de Malmaison. There was no reason to take the car since they could reach their destination on foot in a matter of minutes. Plus, it was a nice morning so far. The sky was crystal clear, and the air was cool, but not cold.

Tommy took a moment to enjoy the weather. He loved Paris when it was warm and the flowers were out in their planters, some hanging from windows of homes, others placed in city gardens and parks or along the sidewalks next to trees.

Sean tripped and nearly fell on his face. Luckily, the other two men didn't notice since they were walking in front, but Adriana did.

She braced him with a firm hand on his shoulder to keep him from falling over completely. As he regained his balance, he noticed what had caused the clumsy trip. The shoestring on his left shoe was undone.

"One sec," he said, and his wife stopped next to him.

"Guys," Adriana said. "Hold up."

Tommy and Commander Bodmer paused and looked back at Sean, who was down on one knee rapidly tying his shoelace. He made quick work of the loose strand and had started to rise when he saw something that made him freeze in place.

Tommy knew something was wrong the second Sean's expression changed.

"Nothing to worry about," Sean said, standing up fully and straightening his shirt.

There was no confusion, not to Tommy.

Sean's eyes flicked to the right.

Tommy wasn't stupid enough to look blatantly in the direction Sean had suggested. His friend's subtle motion was enough. There was trouble over there, and Sean had spotted it.

"You okay?" Tommy asked, taking a step toward his friend. "Get that shoelace tightened?"

"Yep, all good." Then in a hushed tone, Sean added, "Two of them. Watching us. Park bench near the fountain."

Tommy nodded and smiled, slapping his friend on the back. "You need to be more careful. I thought you knew how to tie good knots." As Tommy ushered his friend forward, he twisted and caught a glimpse of the two people Sean believed were following them, or at the very least, watching them.

"Man and a woman," Tommy said through clenched teeth. "And on bikes."

Sean had seen the motorcycles first, momentarily admiring them from a distance. They were twin Ducati Monsters, the newer 821 Stealth models with matte-black paint highlighted by red-and-silver trim. Then he'd seen the couple sitting near them. Tommy's assumption of the bikes belonging to the man and woman could have been a big one to leap to, except that the man had made the mistake of keeping his helmet on the ground at his side, whereas the woman's helmet hung from the right handlebar grip.

If Sean had looked their direction in another moment, he might have seen the two staring at birds or watching the clouds float by above. He had looked in that moment, however, and it was in that second he saw them watching. Even through their dark sunglasses, there was no mistaking what the two were doing. They were following Sean and his companions.

He'd instantly forgotten his admiration of the two motorcycles— the objects of his desire—and taken to retying his shoelace while having a quick scan of the area.

"You know," Sean said, "my ankle is acting up again." He winced in dramatic pain and reached down to the lower part of his leg, gripping it with fingers from both hands as if that would alleviate his ailment. "Old basketball injury. Would you guys mind if we take a cab? I know it's not far, but I just need to rest it for a few minutes and I'll be fine."

Bodmer was the only one in the group who didn't get the hint. "Ankle injury? Are you certain you can't make it? The château isn't far." He pointed in the general direction they were heading. The truth was, the palatial former residence of Napoléon was nearby, but they weren't within view of it yet.

"Sorry, man," Sean said, leaning on Tommy for support. "I'll pay the cab fare. Of course, you can go on ahead on foot if you like, but I thought it best we stick together."

Bodmer shrugged, seemingly unwilling to pick this battle. It wasn't a big deal, except that waiting for a cab might slow them down. That concern was immediately alleviated when a taxi whipped around the corner and pulled up in front of a shop not thirty feet from where they were standing.

"There's one," Adriana said. "I'll ask them to wait." She didn't pause for confirmation or permission. She simply jogged over to the cab and leaned toward the window, resting her elbows on the roof of the vehicle as she spoke to the driver. She nodded and then motioned the others over.

The cab was a minivan with black wheels and a navy-blue paint job. The driver looked like he was of Turkish descent, a common occurrence in this part of Europe. Turkish immigrants had been flowing over the borders of European nations for decades, and it seemed more were coming all the time. Shawarma carts were appearing on more and more street corners every month, as were hookah lounges; cafés featuring Turkish fare. These were some of the more notable changes to the culture that Sean also witnessed the last time he was in Germany.

Turkish people, in his experience, were friendly and accommodating toward Westerners. Turkey was one of his favorite places to visit, and he had been happy to see an attempted military coup thwarted a few years prior since it seemed the people favored keeping the leader in power. Sean found himself wondering how this cab driver might have arrived in Paris, if indeed his origin was the nation of Turkey.

The group piled into the minivan and the driver took off, flipping his rate flag down to begin the fare.

"You hurt your leg?" the driver asked Sean as he wheeled the vehicle to the left and stopped at a light.

"Yes, something like that," Sean said. "Although it's feeling better already."

"Oh, that's good. Doesn't make for good sightseeing if you can't move without pain."

Sean disregarded the man's less-than-astute observation and nodded, noting more about his Turkish accent than anything else. "Where are you from?" Sean asked, already knowing the answer. He only asked to divert the conversation away from himself. The less attention he conjured, the better.

"Paris," the cabbie said.

"That accent isn't Parisian," Sean countered.

"Ah, yes. I am originally from Turkey. Came here seventeen years ago with my family. We lived in Istanbul."

Sean nodded. "Wonderful city, Istanbul. Wouldn't you agree, honey?" He looked at Adriana.

"Definitely."

"Well, that is nice of you to say. I appreciate that. Unfortunately, I haven't been able to go back as much as I'd like. Money, you see."

"It can be elusive," Sean said.

The driver steered the minivan through traffic. A row of trees lined the streets on both sides, and a gray palace appeared up ahead. At least, Sean thought it was gray. As they neared the grand château, a few clouds overhead dispersed and the full power of the sun struck the enormous manor. The exterior walls seemed to change color from gray to a bright beige.

Tommy was busy on his phone, ignoring the others as he locked his gaze on the screen. He was looking at images of something, but being in the front with the cab driver made it impossible for the others to see what he was doing.

He'd been silent since entering the taxi. Sean realized his friend was doing something he deemed important. But what?

"You okay up there?" Sean asked.

Tommy nodded absently. "Yeah, I just...I think I figured it out."

"Figured what out?" Bodmer wondered.

"The solution to our problem."

15

PARIS

The group exited the cab and waited until the vehicle was out of sight before they hurried to the entrance of the Château de Malmaison. The scent of thousands of roses filled the air and washed over them in the gentle summer breeze.

"Smart move," Tommy said to his friend when the cab was gone. "I was wondering how we were going to get out of there."

"Those two on the bikes won't be far behind. Let's duck over there and wait for a minute." Sean pointed at a row of large, finely manicured shrubs to the right and started for them.

"What is going on?" Bodmer asked.

Sean didn't stop, instead looking over his shoulder as Tommy and Adriana followed. "We're being followed, Commander. I suggest you come with us to stay out of sight. As my friend suggested, they'll be here within seconds."

Bodmer reacted even though he still wasn't sure what they were talking about. He followed the other three into the shadows. They each crouched down, which wasn't entirely necessary, but it didn't hurt to be overly cautious.

It was less than ten seconds after they had secured their hiding spot that the sound of two motorcycles roared close by. Sean peeked through some of the thinner branches of the bush he'd chosen and noted the twin Ducatis rolling by slowly as their riders turned their heads in every direction in an attempt to locate their quarry. Their helmets' visors were darkly tinted, making it impossible to see the riders' faces. Sean had already seen them, though, and would easily make them out in a crowd, whether they were wearing their helmets, their sunglasses, or nothing over their faces.

The bikes slowed as they neared the entrance to the château and its grounds. For a moment, Sean and the others wondered if the two riders were going to stop and get out to search on foot.

That's not what Sean would have done. He guessed that these two would act in a similar manner, which would be to follow the cab at a safe distance. If they assumed the group had kept going, the bikes would take off in pursuit of the taxi. If they believed the visitors had gotten out of the cab to search this place, they would park their bikes. And then there would be trouble.

Sean felt the weight of his weapon tucked inside his pants. It was an interior-style holster, padded against his leg for comfort; though wearing it was hardly comfortable. It also only provided enough wiggle room for a single-stack magazine instead of the usual double-stack mags he preferred. He also didn't like the thin profile of the weapon when it was in his hands. It felt unnatural to be able to wrap his fingers so far around the grip and trigger, but the demands of necessity and practicality outweighed comfort. Paris was no city to be walking around with a gun fully visible to the public, even if he had the proper paperwork, and at this moment in time, he did not.

In the winter, this would be less of an issue since he could wear thicker clothes and outerwear that would conceal almost any sort of sidearm. The good weather of summer, it seemed, came with a price he hadn't considered—other than when he began preparations for this trip.

His right hand unconsciously reached for the pistol, and he felt the grip's corrugated surface against his thumb. If he needed to draw the weapon, he would do so with blinding and deadly speed. He had no cover, not from bullets anyway, and he knew that if it came down to a firefight, first blood would be paramount. Taking down one of the enemies would immediately make things harder for the remaining attacker and would force them to consider running. Sean had already chosen his first target if a fight ensued. At this distance, he could expect reasonable accuracy, but not impeccable.

He noted the weapons that were poorly concealed on the riders. The guns were strapped to their calves, sticking out of boot tops near the motors. Sean also didn't think those to be advantageous places to carry a firearm.

A wave of relief crashed into the four hiding behind the bushes when the riders apparently decided there was nothing for them to find there. The bikes revved hard and the throaty sounds of the motors faded as the two pursuers disappeared from view down the street.

"That was lucky," Tommy said as he emerged from the shrubs.

The others joined him on the street, all staring after the bikes despite the fact that they were already gone.

"What was all that about?" Bodmer demanded. It was the first time in a while the man had sounded like the commanding leader of the Swiss Guard.

"We have a couple of tails," Sean answered plainly. "Tommy and I noticed them as we were leaving the cathedral."

Bodmer turned his head back in the direction they'd come. The church was no longer within sight, but that didn't stop the man from staring that way. His head snapped back to Sean, then toward the church of Saint Peter-Saint Paul, and one last time to Sean, finally settling on the man. "You noticed them back there?"

"Yes. Sorry, I lied about my ankle, though only partially. I do have ankle issues from time to time, from my basketball days. Dad always pushed me to be a better rebounder, even though I was a shooting guard. Lots of ways to sprain an ankle in the low post. Know what I mean?"

Bodmer's confusion had shifted from the issue of the two people following them to Sean's recounting of his athletic days. The commander didn't follow basketball, and that fact was evidenced by the bewildered look on his face.

"Never mind," Sean said with a chuckle. "Look, just know that we spotted them in time, and now it seems we've lost them." He turned his focus to Tommy. "Now, what was it you found on your phone during the cab ride?"

Bodmer didn't appear fully satisfied with the results of his query, but it seemed—for the moment—there was no going back. In fact, the other three were already strolling toward the entrance to the château.

"Wait!" Bodmer exclaimed. "Where are you going?"

"The château, of course," Sean said, glancing back at the man as he caught up. "That's why we're here. And I don't think standing on the street is the best idea right now. If those two come back, it would be a good plan to either be gone or at least not be visible. If you want, you can go hide in those bushes again."

The commander bit his lip and fell in line behind the others. He knew Sean was right. Being in the open on a street corner was not a good position to be in, especially if the two bikers bore ill intent.

Tommy paid the small entry fee for the four adults to enter the palace grounds, and they immediately made their way to the nearest employee, who happened to be standing in the center of the path leading into the main building. The man was in the same uniform the ticket person wore. His hair retreated back toward the rear of his skull and left a shiny, pale bald spot over most of his head. The remnants of his brown strands clung around his ears. He wore a bright, welcoming smile, though Sean wondered how long that lasted as the man answered tourists' questions all day long.

"We need to find out where this is," Tommy said, showing his phone to his friend as he'd intended when they were entering the property.

The image on the screen was of a room. It looked antiquated, like a museum that was made out of someone's home. It was the same look Sean had seen in other places, like the White House, Monticello, or Mount Vernon. Those old homes featured rooms that had been preserved to look the same as they had in the days of old.

The two stopped short before they were too close to the attendant. Sean stared at the image. There were wooden chairs, bookshelves, a drab green ceiling, a desk, and other furnishings and everyday items that would have been used over two hundred years ago by someone of means.

"What's that?" Sean asked.

"That's Napoléon's library. And it's here, somewhere. We need to find it."

"Why?" Sean wondered. "What's the—" He didn't finish his sentence as Tommy expanded the image to zoom in on the ceiling.

"That's the point," Tommy answered his friend's unfinished question. "Minerva and Apollo. They're right there in the general's study."

Bodmer and Adriana each took a shoulder to look over as all four stared at the image.

"How did you find that?" Sean asked.

"Well, um...I Googled it." He sounded ashamed at the admission. In their line of work, performing ordinary internet searches was something amateurs did, and they almost always settled on the first result, which was often loaded with incorrect information.

Sean bellowed a laugh, then realized how loud he'd been and clamped his mouth shut. "Sorry. I mean, there's nothing wrong with that. I do it all the time."

"I know. I do, too. It's just, we're historians, archaeologists. You know?"

"Since when are you worried about image?" Adriana asked jovially.

"Yeah," Sean agreed. "And technically, you're the only real archaeologist here."

"You guys know what I mean."

"Is there anything I can do to help you?" A voice cut through their conversation like a saber. Sean and the others looked up and saw the attendant standing awkwardly close—too close for a private discussion, anyway.

"Oh, sorry. Hi," Sean said. "We were just...talking about how to get to Napoléon's library. Is it true that it hasn't been renovated since his death?"

"*Oui*, that is true," the man answered in mixed French and English. "Most of the grounds here have remained in the condition the emperor left them."

The way the guy said "the emperor" caused Sean to wonder if he actually wished Napoléon was still in charge of things.

Sean twisted his head and looked for Tommy's reaction.

His friend gave a casual nod, though Sean could tell Tommy was doing his best to suppress his excitement. It was rare to find places that were untainted by human hands. While the efforts to maintain historical sites and preserve them for generations to come was something to be lauded and appreciated, it was extremely rare to find anything authentic anymore, at least a place as important as this was. It was a gem, hidden in plain sight.

"Thank you," Sean said, cutting back in before Tommy started geeking out. "Would you mind showing us the way there?"

The man directed them with a few short directions that were emphasized by finger pointing and waving.

The group thanked the man, saying "*merci*" as they departed.

A massive terrace was in the back of the château, and wide steps led down into the gardens, passing tiers of roses and a variety of shrubs along each landing. At the bottom of the steps, rows of hedges were arranged neatly, wrapping around the feature attractions of the property: more roses.

Sean led the way around the palace until they came to the entrance the attendant had suggested. They walked into the palatial residence and then down a short corridor lined with golden sconces, paintings that depicted scenes from early nineteenth-century life, and a few choice furnishings such as upholstered chairs and cherry wood side tables.

A couple of tourists with cameras dangling from their necks passed them. Sean noted a German flag patched to one of their daypacks. He gave them an extra look to make sure they weren't also following him and the others. They were a little old for assets or hitters, but Sean had got sloppy before. He wasn't going to make the same mistake again.

Satisfied the German couple were no threat, he kept walking until they reached the entrance to the library. There, he slowed his pace and stepped across the threshold.

That old familiar museum smell filled the room, and Sean consciously slid one foot to the side to let his friend pass. He knew Tommy was in heaven and could sense his friend mere inches behind him despite Tommy not having made a sound.

Adriana peeled to the left, also detecting the same thing as her husband.

Tommy walked forward as though he were entering the most hallowed temple in all the world. How had he never been to this place? How had he not known that Napoléon's library was pretty much still in its original condition? He walked over to the chairs and dared himself to brush his fingers across the upholstered cushions or the wooden backs, though he stopped himself short.

Four columns, stained to match the reddish cherry wood finish of the furnishings, stood at both ends of the room, at the entrance under one archway, and on either side of the desk under a second archway. In the middle, a lavish rug rested on the floor. Its primary pale blue color contrasted with the pale cream color woven into the center, outlined by a burgundy wheel of sorts. Directly over the rug, a seven-sided domed ceiling arched upward, creating a false sense of roominess. A round, brass table with a shiny glass top stood in the center of the floor. It was a strange place for a coffee table, if that's what it could be called.

The volumes of books on the shelves still looked the way they did when Napoléon last visited this room. Tommy could see the general sitting in one of his chairs, slumping with his belly protruding out slightly over his pants as he pored over one of the tomes. Tommy wished he could pull one of the books from a shelf, but he imagined the volume might disintegrate if he were to do so.

Ironically, it was Bodmer who snapped Tommy back to their original reason for being there.

"Look," the commander said, pointing up at the ceiling in the center of the room.

There, in the middle of the nearest arched portion of the ceiling, about ten feet above, two faces stared toward each other. A narrow chandelier hung from the center, and it was the same on the other end near the desk. The two deities were painted in white and surrounded by olive-green wreaths that matched much of the ceiling's paint, and even the drapes at the window.

"Apollo and Minerva," Tommy whispered.

He stepped forward until he was directly under the first chandelier and gazed up at the two images.

"This is where you'll find it," Adriana said. She'd inspected the room within seconds of entering. The wooden floor planks were arranged in an intricate design that looked like the great general was going for some kind of geometric feng shui. It reminded her of an Escher painting.

An attendant was standing outside the room, watching the group as they looked around, taking in every detail.

Sean noted the man's casual watch over the area and lowered his voice. "So, I don't know about you, Schultzie, but if I had to guess I'd say that all signs are pointing to that spot." Sean motioned with a tip of his head toward the center of the room where the table was positioned.

"The table?" Tommy asked. It sounded like a dumb question when it came out of his mouth, but he couldn't stop it in time.

"I doubt it's that," Sean said, glancing over his shoulder at the man standing guard. The guy clearly didn't care much about his job, which was something that Sean planned to use to their advantage.

"So, under the table?" Tommy suggested, still dubious.

"Yep."

Tommy looked around again, panning the room for the same clue his friend must have found. Then it hit him. The four faces of the deities, the circle in the rug that seemed to be designed to flow into the center, the four chairs pointing toward the little table. Sean was right. Everything appeared to be directed toward the middle of the study.

"You think whatever we're looking for is under the rug?"

Sean nodded.

Tommy leaned close. "How are we going to move the table and rug while that guy is standing at the doorway?"

Sean was already thinking of that problem. "I have an idea," he said.

Tommy's brow furrowed with concern. "Why do I have a feeling I'm not going to like this?"

"Oh, not to worry, my worrisome compadre," Sean said, placing his hand on Tommy's shoulder and giving it a gentle squeeze. "I think it's time our friend the commander made himself useful."

Bodmer eyed the two suspiciously, only catching fragments of their conversation.

"What?" the man asked.

Sean simply offered a wry smile in reply.

16

PARIS

The cab pulled into a spot along the curb, and the driver put the transmission into park. He looked around, hoping the lady in the red dress walking in his direction would be his next fare. For a moment, he let his eyes linger a little longer on her well-defined legs as she strolled by. The scarlet skirt fluttered in the wind and he forced himself to have at least a little respect, refocusing his gaze on the street and sidewalk ahead.

He hung his elbow out of the open window and bit his thumbnail as he waited for another fare. It was a glorious day, one of the reasons he loved Paris in the summer. He wished he could cut out for the rest of the day and go play chess with his friend Pierre, but he knew that had to wait for another two hours. Chess would always be there. Money had to be made.

He heard a rumble from behind and glanced in his rearview mirror. Two black motorcycles approached, their engines grumbling loudly as the two riders pulled into a tight spot behind the cab. There was barely enough room for the two bikes, and the cab driver wondered if he was going to be able to get out of his spot. He'd been careful to leave a little extra space between his front bumper and the car ahead of him, but even with that he wasn't certain he could clear the other vehicle.

The two riders climbed off their bikes and stalked forward. The cab driver was glad. He fully intended to give them a piece of his mind or at the very least, ask them to park somewhere else or risk having their expensive motorcycles knocked over—not on purpose, of course.

He leaned out of his window a little farther and looked back as one of the riders approached. For a second, he wondered where the other was until he heard something to his right and turned to see that she'd come up on the other side of his car.

When he swiveled his head back around to the left, his eye came into contact with the end of a long, black cylinder with a hole in the end.

Terror coursed through the driver. Who were these people? What did they want? Why were they pointing a gun at him?

Back in his days in Turkey, he'd run a few drugs here and there to make some extra money, but he always promised himself that as soon as they had enough, he was going to move them out of Istanbul and start a new life, a legitimate one.

Things hadn't gone as planned, but he managed to make it work.

During those wild and dangerous times, he never once had a gun put to his head. No, he had to come to Paris and start driving a taxi for that to happen.

"What do you want?" he asked nervously.

"Where are they?" the gunman asked.

"Where are who? Who are you talking about?" The man could feel his bladder unclenching slightly and he had to force himself to hold it tight. Why hadn't he gone to the loo after that last fare?

"The group you just had in your car. Where are they? There were four of them."

The driver couldn't place the man's accent. He thought maybe it was German, but it was difficult to say, especially disguised by the helmet. Neither rider gave anything away. They were covered head to toe, so making out any physical details, other than the fact that one was a man and one was a woman, was nearly impossible.

"The..." Realization set in as he immediately understood what these two wanted. "The Americans?"

"Yes. Where are they?" The gunman pressed the pistol's suppressor barrel harder into the man's skull.

The driver managed to wiggle slightly, just enough so that the suppressor muzzle was no longer pressing into his eyeball. Still, it hurt with the hard metal digging into the bone of his eye socket.

"I...I dropped them off at the Château de Malmaison."

The tinted motorcycle helmet didn't move, as if the wearer didn't understand what the driver said or perhaps was processing the information.

"What were they doing there?"

The cabbie shook his head vigorously, causing the loose skin around his jaw and chin to shake back and forth. "They didn't say," he stammered. "I don't know. I swear. Please. Just let me go."

"What were they looking for?" The gunman asked, pressing the barrel deeper into the cabbie's skin.

"I just told you. I don't know. They just wanted a ride there. They didn't tell me anything. I swear it. Please. Don't kill me."

The gunman looked across the top of the minivan at the other rider, as though he was waiting for her command.

She gave it with a simple shake of the head.

The gunman nodded curtly and then leaned back. The woman glanced to her left then right then issued a single nod to the gunman.

For a moment, the cabbie was awash with relief. Another close call in a lifetime of near misses. He was lucky. That much was true.

Then the back quarter of his head exploded, accompanied by a quiet click from the pistol. The cab driver's body slumped over to the right and onto the center console. The killer quickly opened the door, rolled up the tinted windows, and switched off the light declaring he was open for business.

He closed the door, leaving the dead man inside his vehicle and, satisfied that no one would notice unless they really looked, walked back to his bike and joined the woman.

The two were gone within seconds, ghosts that people perhaps believed they'd seen but couldn't describe other than them having been on motorcycles.

The murder had been executed perfectly; in broad daylight, on a usually busy city street, and no one had seen a thing—at least nothing they would recall. The two riders whipped their bikes around the nearest corner and disappeared from the crime scene. There was no telling how long they had until someone discovered the cabbie's body. It could be one minute or thirty, it was impossible to know. It didn't matter, the two killers would hide the bikes and their clothing and when they entered the Château de Malmaison, they would look just like another couple of tourists.

They'd been delayed, but that would be remedied soon enough.

17

PARIS

B odmer doubled over and pretended to retch at the doorway of Napoléon's library. The man was hardly an actor, he'd never win an Academy Award, but the sound was realistic enough that the nonchalant attendant took notice with immediate concern.

"Monsieur?" he said, rushing to Bodmer's aid. "Is everything all right?"

Bodmer spoke fluent French, which was another reason he was the perfect candidate to be a decoy.

"I...don't feel well," he said, stuttering through the declaration. "Where is your bathroom?"

"Let me show you. Please, right this way."

Sean knew where the restrooms were. He'd noted their location on the way in. Just like so many other things in his life others might think unusual, for him it was an old habit.

When Bodmer and the attendant were gone, Sean scanned the room one more time to make sure there were no cameras. Just because he didn't see any didn't mean they weren't there.

He took the phone out of his pocket and opened the camera. Tommy and Adriana did the same as the three positioned themselves around the circular table in the center of the room with their backs to each other.

Each of them held out their phones as if about to take a picture.

"Ready?" Sean asked, checking the other two over his shoulder.

"Yep," Tommy said.

"Ready," Adriana added.

"Go."

The three pressed the buttons on their phones, and all three devices emitted a sequence of bright flashes, ending with a more pronounced and brighter flash.

"Okay, now," Sean said.

The three spun around. Tommy grabbed the table and pulled it back toward the desk while Sean and Adriana rolled back the carpet. Tommy stepped out of the way as the other two moved past him. He took the flashlight on his phone and held it up, shining the bright light around the room as he spun in a circle, once more sending a blinding beam into any potential camera lenses.

The initial flash should have incapacitated any recording devices for a few seconds, but they would need to keep hitting them if they were, indeed, there.

Sean and Adriana stopped rolling the rug and stared down at the floor. It was astounding to discover something that they assumed hadn't been seen in two hundred years.

Sean stepped away from the middle and looked at the image carved into the floor. His eyes were narrow as opposed to Tommy's wide-eyed reaction.

There, carved expertly and intricately into the floorboards, was a rose.

The flower was only a couple of feet in diameter; three at the most. At first glance, the rose appeared to be nothing more than a decoration, one last tribute to the general's love—his ex-wife. As Sean got down on one knee to have a closer look, however, he realized that there was more to this symbol than he first thought.

He stood quickly and strode around the room, looking for any other signs of a camera. It was the second time he'd swept the space and, convinced there weren't any electronic devices—aside from their phones—he told Tommy to stand down with the flashlight.

"I guess that whole exercise was one of futility."

"Shut up and help me lift this," Sean said, trying to work his fingernails into the nearly invisible seam between the rose's wooden disk and the rest of the floor.

"Can I get a please?" Tommy joked. Then he caught a flash of irritation in his friend's eyes and apologized. "Right. The attendant will be back any second. My bad."

Tommy got down on the floor and started working his fingernails in the same way Sean was doing, but both were futile. The narrow seam was too tight, nearly a perfect fit.

"We need a tool or something," Sean realized.

"Like this?" Adriana stepped closer and knelt down beside him. She held up one of the tools from her lock-picking kit that was almost always on her person. This particular tool was a thin metal shiv with a small hook on the end. It wasn't a tool Sean had seen before, though his experience with lock-picking utensils was sparse.

She stuck the thin object into the seam and then tilted it back like a lever. She pried hard and the other two thought that the metal tool was going to snap in half. It held firm, though, and gradually, the disc slid up.

When there was more than an inch to grab, Sean pressed his thumb to the edge and pulled up, keeping constant pressure on the side of the disk to make sure it didn't fall back down into place.

Tommy joined in when he had a surface area to work with, and within a minute the rose disk popped free of the floor.

All three of them stared into the cavity and marveled at the wooden box within.

The object was stained the same color as everything else in Napoléon's library: dark cherry. Just like on the surface of the disk, a rose was carved into the lid of the little box.

Sean stopped wasting time and bent down. He removed the box with the greatest of care, putting his hands under each end as he lifted it gently from the hole. It was lightweight and only about the length of his forearm, and maybe four or five inches wide.

Sean set the box down on the floor and looked back to the doorway. The attendant would return any second. Bodmer could only keep the man at bay for so long. Sean was surprised the commander had been able to delay the guy's return for this long.

He gave a quick once-over to the container, making sure it wasn't rigged to damage whatever was inside—or his fingers. Then he pulled up a golden latch and pried the lid open.

Inside was a piece of parchment rolled up into a scroll. The document was nearly the length of the box. Sean glanced at Tommy. "You don't happen to have any gloves, do you?"

Tommy arched one eyebrow suspiciously, then shook his head. "Yeah, they're right here in my back pocket."

"You don't have to be a jerk. Besides, I thought you would be irritated if I just picked up the paper."

The two caught movement in front of them and saw Adriana lift the document from the wooden box.

"Would you two shut up and stop screwing around," she hissed.

They watched with mouths agape and eyes wide as she unrolled the parchment and stared at the surface. The two men scooted toward her and looked over her shoulders at the faded ink on the page.

"That's..." Sean didn't know what to say.

"Strange?" Tommy finished.

"Yeah."

There was only one sentence on the parchment, written in dramatic cursive, as was common in Napoléon's time.

"May their victory stand eternal, heroes of the Empire." Adriana read the line out loud.

"Victory stand eternal?" Sean muttered. "Whose victory?"

Their eyes fell to the letters at the bottom of the page. They were nonsensical, jumbled, and without meaning.

DLOWONOG

"Any idea what that means?" Sean asked the other two.

"Nope," Tommy said. "Although, notice how the letter *O* is spaced evenly."

Sean had noticed that, but he'd blown it off as having no meaning. "Yeah, but there are two consonants before the first one and only one after the last."

"It's a puzzle," Adriana said. "Like in the newspaper."

The other two looked at her with disbelief.

"What?" Tommy sounded incredulous. It couldn't be that simple. Could it? He'd seen ciphers, puzzles, and riddles that could bend the minds of some of the best code breakers, archaeologists, and treasure hunters in the world. Perhaps, in this instance, all that experience from the past, all the complex clues he'd unraveled, were causing him to over think this. After all, there have been many instances where the simple solution was usually the right one. Occam's razor, it seemed, had been applied here.

"So, you think it might be a word scramble?" Sean asked.

She nodded. "We just have to think of what word would be related to Napoléon and contain these eight letters." Her smooth tone mixed with the Spanish accent was aural caramel in Sean's ears and he caught himself staring at her for moment with complete admiration.

"What?" she asked, catching him in mid-stare.

"Nothing," he shook off his daze quickly. "Just a nice view. That's all."

Tommy rolled his eyes. "Okay, can we please get back to solving this riddle? Pretty sure the guy who was guarding this place will be back—"

"Soon?" A new voice cut in from the doorway.

The trio raised their heads in unison and stared at the entrance. The attendant was standing there with his arms crossed and a bewildered expression on his face. Bodmer was behind him, looking disappointed and irritated all at once.

"What is the meaning of this?" the attendant asked.

The scene before him couldn't have been worse. Three tourists were huddled around the center of the floor in Napoléon's library.

They were on their knees next to a hole that had, he assumed, been cut into the antique wood. There was a little wooden box next to them.

The second the new voice entered the room, Adriana reacted with pure instinct, shoving the parchment into the back of her pants. She'd flipped her shirt down over her waist to conceal the page, though it was up in the air if she'd acted fast enough or not.

"We, um, well...." Tommy couldn't find the right words, none that he believed would satisfy the attendant.

"We're historians," Sean blurted. "Archaeologists. Tell him, Tommy. We're with the—"

"Sorry," Tommy interrupted.

Sean cast his friend a wary glance, wondering why he'd cut him off, but he let Tommy continue.

"We just noticed that there was something odd in the floor. I took the liberty of rolling back the rug and moving that table out of the way to see what it was. I'd hate for the foundation to be sinking or something. Could ruin this entire wing of the palace."

He waved his hand around as if displaying the library to a new visitor.

The man shook his head, and a stern look of disapproval washed over his face. Bodmer was lost, uncertain what he should do.

He put his hands out at his sides, as if seeking the answer from the other three, but there was nothing they could say or do. They'd been caught red-handed.

18

PARIS

"It was bound to happen sooner or later," Sean said in an almost cheerful voice. "I mean, think about how many times we've been in situations like this over the years and never got caught."

Tommy let out a pronounced "Pfft." He tried his best to feign offense. "You make it sound like we're criminals."

"Well, I mean, we did sort of vandalize a historic site that's gone untouched for the last few hundred years. Kind of a big deal when you think about it like that."

"You're not helping. You know that, right?"

Sean chuckled and stepped over to the white bars of their holding cell. He wondered why some jails painted their bars white. Best he could figure was that there was some kind of psychology behind it, but what that was he didn't know.

The corridor beyond was empty save for a guard standing at an electronically locked door to their right, about fifteen feet away.

Tommy sat on a bench with his face in his hands, fingers tickling the hair at the front of his head.

"Sorry," Sean said after a moment of thought. "I got sloppy back there. I should have been more careful."

"Yeah, well that goes for both of us."

"I know, but that's kind of my thing. I'm good at that stuff. At least, I used to be."

"You still are, man. I just hope this doesn't tarnish my reputation or hurt the agency. Hopefully, we can keep this out of the media."

"I can...pull a string to make sure that happens," Sean said.

Tommy looked up through the gaps between his fingers. "Emily?"

"Worth a shot." Sean shrugged. "Although, I think she's probably tired of bailing me out of spots like this. I mean, I've been arrested before, but not for vandalizing a historic site. Certainly not one that was the library of the former emperor of France."

Tommy snorted a forced laugh. "Yeah, no kidding."

"I already called Emily earlier. Had to leave a message. She'll get us out of this mess. I'm sure of it."

"I didn't call anyone," Tommy admitted. Truth was, he didn't know anyone else who could help them out of this situation. His parents might have been of some use, but they were in California playing golf. He doubted he could reach them, and even if he could they didn't have much pull with the French government. Most of Tommy's connections were through Sean. So there was no need to make the same call twice.

Sean spun around, suddenly struck with an idea.

"Word scramble," he blurted, bordering on incoherent.

"What?"

"The word scramble," Sean said. "I need something to write with."

"Pretty sure they're not going to give us a pen. That's a weapon in this place."

Sean already knew his friend was correct and had no intention of asking for a pen or pencil from the guard looming at the end of the corridor.

Sean's eyes darted around until they came to rest on a piece of ivory soap on the sink. He stalked over to the basin and picked it up. It was still dry. Then he turned to the grayish-blue wall and started writing on it with the edge of the soap.

Tommy's head lifted in curiosity as he watched his friend work.

It took only a few seconds before Sean was done.

"The letters from the parchment," Tommy realized.

"Yes. I memorized them."

"Okay...that's great, but it's not going to do us much good in here. Even if we figure it out, we're stuck in a French prison."

"Jail," Sean corrected. "A prison would be way worse than this. You might as well consider this place a Holiday Inn."

"Fine, whatever. We're stuck is the point."

"Indeed we are, my pessimistic friend."

"You don't have to sound so jovial about it."

Sean snickered. "Well, there is a silver lining."

"Oh? What's that?"

"To start, the people who were following us can't get to us in here."

"Unless, of course, they have connections with the guards or the cops. Which they probably do."

"Why you gotta be Johnny Rain Cloud?" Sean asked. "I doubt that whoever was following us has connections to the cops. Even if they do, what are they going to do, kill us while we're in custody?"

Tommy's eyebrows lifted slightly, and his lips slightly pursed. He chuckled.

"No," Sean quickly added. "They're not. And besides, just because we're in here doesn't mean our entire team is."

Tommy's face twisted into a frown. "Adriana is detained, too, you know. They just took her to a women's cell."

"I know that," Sean said, giving his friend the best *Thanks, Captain Obvious* face he could. "But the three of us aren't our entire team, are we?"

"The kids."

"That's right: The kids are back in Atlanta. If we can figure out what this code, or whatever it is, means"—he pointed at the scrambled soap letters on the wall—"we might be able to send them to the next spot and stay ahead of the bad guys."

"Whoever they are."

"Exactly." Sean beamed with pride as though he'd just solved the fabled unified field theory.

"You want Tara and Alex to go out in the field where they could get hurt or killed?" Tommy sounded skeptical. "I wouldn't feel good about that."

"Okay, first, it wouldn't be their first time in the field," Sean countered. "Second, they handled themselves well enough in Japan that one time."

"True."

"And I trained them myself. They're more than capable of taking care of themselves, and besides, if you're right about the people who are following us, the ones probably responsible for the death of Cardinal Jarllson, they're more than likely watching the doors of this jail as we speak. There's no way they would figure on a—"

"Hail Mary like this?" Tommy finished.

"I was going to say an audible, but yeah."

"It's a long shot. So, it's a Hail Mary."

"Fine, whatever. The point is, if we can figure out where they need to go next, you still have a call to make. You can tell them exactly where to go and what to look for."

"Yeah, but what if we get out of here in the next few hours?"

"Then there will be more of us to help out. Like one big happy family."

Tommy chuckled and shook his head. "Okay, fine. We'll call the kids. But first, we need to figure out just what in the world all those letters mean. I'm still surprised you remembered all of them."

"It's only eight letters, Schultzie," Sean said plainly.

Sean's memory bordered on eidetic, though certain things, like people's names, escaped him more often than he liked or cared to admit. It was a glaring and otherwise infuriating exception to his considerable talent. When it came to numbers and letters, however, he could memorize often complex or lengthy words or numerical values within seconds. He also possessed the ability to recall odd details, something that had proved useful when he was writing essays in college. His professors were always impressed that he knew things about certain events or people that no one else did.

"I guess," Tommy resigned. "So, what do you think it spells?"

Sean hadn't taken his eyes off the string of letters for the last couple of minutes. He'd been working through it in his mind while carrying on the discussion with his friend.

"The only vowel is the letter *O*," he commented. "That's odd."

"Must be a name."

Sean resisted a witty reply and simply nodded. "Yes. That's what I was thinking. A place, but where?"

In his mind, Sean saw the letters moving, rearranging themselves in different patterns. Sometimes they formed two words, but nothing ever made any sense. He continued shuffling the letters around his head, shaking off the nonsensical combinations, and frustrated by the few discernible words that had no bearing on the mystery.

"Wood," Tommy blurted suddenly.

"What?"

"Oh, that's it. Longwood," Tommy added. "Longwood."

"Okay...so it's a song by Green Day?" Sean made no effort to hide his skepticism this time.

"Yes. We found a clue to a Green Day song in Napoléon's library."

"All right, big guy. Settle down. So, let's say it's Longwood. What does that mean for us?"

Tommy stood up and paced the cell for a minute. He put his hands on his hips as he stalked back and forth, pausing momentarily to rest his chin on his thumb to think before picking up the movement once more.

When the answer hit him, he snapped his fingers. "That's it!" He made the proclamation slightly louder than he intended.

Sean tilted his head toward the bars and looked around the corner. The guard appeared to be unfazed by the abrupt noise as he stood there looking at his phone, something Sean was certain to be a breach of security protocol.

"What's *it*?" Sean asked in a hushed tone he meant to be a hint to his suddenly boisterous friend.

"Longwood," Tommy exclaimed again, more reservedly this time.

"Yes, we established that. What about it?"

"Napoléon's exile," Tommy said. The words weren't coming as fast as the thoughts, and his mouth couldn't keep up. "Napoléon was exiled on the island of Saint Helena. His residence there, after the first few months, was in a place called Longwood House."

Sean's eyebrows stitched together with doubt. "I thought Napoléon was exiled on the island of Elba."

Tommy nodded eagerly. "Yes, he was, but that was his first exile. After his defeat at Waterloo, the British sent him to Saint Helena, a small island in the middle of the South Atlantic. Its closest port with transport to the island is Cape Town."

"That's right. I forgot about the second one. I always think of Elba. I guess some people never learn."

"He learned the hard way," Tommy offered. "Some of the accounts suggest that his living quarters were pretty rough. There were rats, the rooms were cold, and I imagine the food couldn't have been great. Of course, there are other accounts that say he lived in a sort of luxury on the island until the day he died. I'd guess it was probably somewhere in the middle.

"Saint Helena is also the place where he was initially interred until his body was moved to Paris some years later; I can't recall the exact date. The grave site is still there, though it's empty. Some people take a long boat ride from Cape Town to visit Longwood and the vacant tomb."

"So, you call the kids and tell them they need to get to Saint Helena." Sean said it like it was a simple matter.

"And look for what?" Tommy asked. "That's the problem. We don't even know what we're looking for. Not to mention that the boat ride from Cape Town takes a really long time."

"Charter a floatplane," Sean said. "Fly them in and out. Should be something like that available in Cape Town."

Tommy bit his lower lip and nodded. "That's true. I never considered that as an option. But we still don't know what we're trying to find."

Sean thought for a moment. He rubbed the scruff on his chin with a thumb and forefinger. "The clue said let their victory stand eternal, heroes of the Empire. It must be a reference to men he considered heroes of France."

"Good one, but which heroes? That could be thousands of men who served under Napoléon." Tommy stopped to think for a second. "Although it was probably some of his officers. That would narrow it down to a few hundred. Still too many names to consider."

"If we find those names...that must be the secret," Sean realized. "We find the names of the heroes."

"There must be a clue, or clues, where these heroes are buried," Tommy added. "The list of these heroes might be on Saint Helena. So, if we send the kids there—"

"They'd need to search for a document with those names on it."

The two were finishing each other's thoughts in rapid succession.

Tommy nodded. "Exactly. Okay. It's still a long shot even if we're right, but it's worth a try. I'll call them and let them know. I just hope you're right about them being safe. I wouldn't forgive myself if something happened to those two."

"Schultzie," Sean said, putting his right hand on his friend's shoulder, "they're going to be fine. Like I said, I've trained them myself. They work hard on their skill sets every day. Honestly, I kinda feel bad for anyone who gets in their way."

Tommy considered what his friend was saying and then gave a reluctant nod. "I hope you're right."

19

MALBORK

Lucien strolled through the garden outside of his countryside manor. He took in the sweet smell of late spring flowers that wafted through the property. He'd been waiting patiently for an update from his people, but as the hours ticked by, Lucien realized he was going to have to take his mind off things for a while.

The garden was small, taking up a few thousand square feet of the backyard behind the manor, but it was a pleasant day out, and walking among the flowers and shrubs was something he'd done for the last few years to help relieve the stresses and concerns that could so easily fill his mind.

He stopped by one of the rosebushes and reached out to touch a petal. The flower was soft against his fingertips and he rubbed it for a moment, appreciating the delicate feel against his skin.

Lucien's moment of peace was interrupted by the vibrating of the phone in his pocket. He wasn't one given to being easily startled, and his reaction to the abrupt interruption was as calm as if he'd simply seen a cloud appear in the sky.

He pressed the device to his ear after glancing at the screen. Not that anyone else would be calling. Only the people on his team would be calling this number. Most of the other members of the order didn't have that direct line. Some of his higher-ranking knights did, but they had no reason to call him...yet.

"Yes?"

"Hello, Grand Master," the woman's voice came through the line. Throughout their history, women had not been part of the Teutonic Order. It was more tradition, now, than anything, but for this particular woman, Lucien Berger had made an exception. She was the only female member, though not the first. There had been a few others in the past, but none as skilled as this one.

She'd basically spent her entire life living in the care of the order. Berger did his best to train her, to make her into a ruthless killing machine. She was an assassin, a soldier, a warrior in the truest sense of the word.

Her name was Kallia, a name Berger had given her when she was a baby. It was the name of an ancient warrior princess he'd read about and he thought the name fitting for her.

Especially as she was his daughter.

Berger appreciated that she didn't call him dad or daddy or father on the phone. It was rare when she did that anyway, but all through her adult life she'd kept things professional. He'd cautioned her about it early on since he knew the rest of the knights would expect the same. They would not tolerate nepotism in any form, and they'd been careful to keep to that code.

Kallia had been an orphan, only three or four months old when fate brought her into Berger's life. It was sheer happenstance. He'd been in the city, walking through the open-air market. He had paused by a stand of produce and was eying some vegetables when he heard something in the alley behind the cart. The old woman running the stand apparently didn't hear the noise.

Berger hadn't been surprised. His ears were well trained, better than most. And he honed his skill constantly to be more lethal in the dark, and safer. When he ventured into the shadow-filled alley, he discovered the child in a wicker basket, wrapped in newspapers. Berger didn't spend much time trying to find the girl's parents. Even if they'd only left her there for two minutes, people like that didn't deserve to be in charge of a child's life.

He took it upon himself to raise the girl as his own, training her in the deadly arts as well as in religious and cultural values. She'd grown to become a fine young woman, relentless and cunning. He was proud, though he rarely allowed such feelings into his heart. To do so was against the rules, guidelines set forth by his predecessors to keep the knights humble and focused.

"What news have you, my child?" Berger asked.

"We've run into a bit of a problem, sir," she answered.

"Oh?" This surprised the man greatly as he'd grown accustomed to his daughter's keen ability to work through almost any problem and find a suitable solution, even when doing so required extreme measures.

"The targets...they...were arrested."

That caused lines to form on his forehead and he rubbed the side of his skull with his fingers. "Arrested? Where?"

"Paris, sir. They were detained at the Château de Malmaison."

"That's not a problem," he countered her original statement. "We have loyal vassals in the Parisian police."

"Yes, sir. I am aware. I spoke to our connections in the department. They said the men had nothing with them."

They'd found nothing? Surely, if they were on the right track they would have discovered something of interest. Then again, it was entirely possible they were *not* on the right track.

Berger pondered the issue for what felt like several minutes. In actuality, it was only twenty seconds. What were these two men up to? They were supposed to be good, but they went and got themselves arrested? Perhaps Berger had overestimated his opponent. It was always better to do so since underestimating someone could have grave consequences. It was part of his training to always assume one's enemy was highly skilled. In this case, that should have meant his opponents could evade the police.

Maybe they were just sloppy.

"What are they doing to get out of French custody?" he asked finally.

"They have made only two contacts since they were arrested," the woman answered. She knew what his next question would be and so addressed it. "The first was made to a building in Atlanta. We are unable to isolate the identity of that call's recipient."

"Unable?" That was strange. The knights, though nowhere near the might of their ancient predecessors, still had formidable technology on their side, and they'd accumulated a significant amount of money over the course of the last few decades as the previous grand masters, and now Berger, had continued to rebuild what had been lost so long ago.

"It's much like the results I get when I test out tracking calls to and from secret government agencies such as the CIA or NSA, but even those organizations are trackable and I can get some kind of identification. This one was completely locked down. I don't know who is there."

"That *is* strange." The man considered what he knew about Wyatt. There was a portion of the man's life that seemed unusually secretive, hidden from files that would normally be no problem for his people to access. He had a stable of hackers at his command and had used those cyber soldiers extensively to collect information on most of the important people in the world. Dignitaries, politicians, even kings were not immune to what his hackers could do. The venture of delving into peoples' secrets had been a lucrative one. Those with the most to lose always paid the most.

"The other call," the woman on the line went on, "was to their headquarters, also in Atlanta."

That part made sense, at least in some regard. The captives were likely trying to reach out to friends to see if they could muster the resources for bail or legal help. It was always a hairy situation when visitors in a foreign land were arrested. The amount of red tape that had to be navigated in those situations could be extensive and take far longer than it would for an ordinary citizen.

"Who is there that could help them?" Berger asked.

"That's just it, sir. Right now, most of their agents are out in the field working on dig sites or helping deliver artifacts. They run a small operation with only a handful of people who work there. From what I understand, they have a team on site that does much of their research and analysis in a laboratory within the confines of their headquarters."

Berger considered the problem. It was possible that Wyatt and Schultz called IAA to seek help in getting out of their sticky situation with the Parisian police, but that didn't add up in his mind. The two would need to call the embassy; someone connected who could help them navigate the legal complexities of being detained in a foreign country.

He doubted there was anyone on their payroll who could do that. It's not like they kept an ambassador on retainer.

So, why did they call the IAA building in Atlanta? If it wasn't to help them get out of jail, what possible reason could Wyatt and Schultz have, unless....

"Find out who is working there," Berger ordered. "I want to know whom they contacted and, if my hunch is correct, where those people are going next."

"You think they are going to Paris to get Wyatt out?"

"I doubt it. They wouldn't have the proper channels to navigate. It's possible that our captives might have found something after all."

"What?" she asked, more out of curiosity than doubt.

"I'm not sure," he said. "But it could lead us to what we're looking for. Find them and see what they're up to."

ST. HELENA

Tara and Alex stepped off the floatplane and onto the dock leading to shore. Each carried a rucksack with some clothes and a few other supplies for what was supposed to be just a two- or three-day excursion. Both gear bags contained a full-size pistol—the standard issue .40-caliber Springfield XD that Sean and Tommy preferred. Carrying weapons wasn't a requirement when on assignment for the IAA as much as it was a guideline.

The young couple was also armed with subcompact 9 mm sidearms that were hidden from view in holsters that fit inside their pants at the waist.

The holsters kept the weapons concealed but required pants that had a little more room for comfort.

Normally, the two wouldn't be armed in such a way on a trip such as this, but Tommy had suggested they be prepared and warned them they might encounter trouble.

The warning hadn't scared the couple. In fact, they found themselves growing restless in the lab. Most of their days and nights were spent there toiling over their computers or microscopes or some of the other equipment they used to analyze artifacts that were continuously flowing into the lab.

Thanks to their work, their laboratory had developed quite the reputation. Other treasure hunters, archaeologists, and historians were all too eager to use the skills and technology the IAA had to offer, and that had resulted in very little time off for Tara and Alex.

The sun beat down on them from high in the crystal-blue sky, warming their skin immediately. Gentle waves lapped against the dock's pilings and the pontoons on the bottom of the plane. The pilot stood there with his hands on his hips, wearing a pair of aviator sunglasses. He wore a white T-shirt that had more holes in it than the Robert Trent Jones Golf Trail. His khaki cargo shorts were frayed along the bottom and went well with his worn brown boots. The man looked more like a homeless traveler than a pilot, but he'd expertly guided the float plane and the flight from Cape Town was easy enough to endure, even though the aircraft's accommodations were minimal at best. The plane was old, essentially a flying tin cylinder, but it handled the flight with the graceful ease of an old war horse, which was to say it grunted its way through. It was a far cry from the luxury of the IAA jet Alex and Tara took from Atlanta to Cape Town.

"I'll be here when you two get done," the pilot said in a sharp South African accent, motioning to the dock. "If you run into trouble, you can radio me on channel two."

He held up a walkie-talkie, and Alex tapped the one on his belt. "Understood. Hopefully, this won't take long."

Alex thought about Sean and Tommy for a moment as he Tara walked down the docks toward the island. Tommy didn't explain why they were being detained, and he didn't need to. He'd asked them to do something for him, and they were going to do it even if it meant flying halfway around the world at a moment's notice.

Alex even wondered if Tommy and Sean were already out of jail. It wasn't a quick process to get to Cape Town even with the agency jet and by the time Alex and Tara arrived at the island, it was highly probable that their two superiors were already out and back on the street. At least that's what Alex hoped.

Now he and his wife were here on St. Helena and more than a little weary from the lack of sleep and the long journey. That didn't stop them from feeling excited about what they could find here on the island.

Tommy had given them the information contained in the riddle he had discovered in Napoléon's library. Now they were on the island where the general had spent his final days. There was a grave on the property, the original burial place of Napoléon. That tomb was empty now, and had been since the mid-nineteenth century. Still, it was a tourist destination for those willing to endure the long boat ride out to the isolated rock in the ocean.

The grave site wasn't their intended destination, however. The clue Tommy gave them specifically suggested that they should visit Longwood House, which is where Napoléon had lived during his final years.

They walked up the ramp toward a man in a white button-up short-sleeve shirt and khaki pants with flip-flops. He looked like he'd fully embraced his island position as a concierge for tourists. Tara and Alex, however, knew that the man was waiting specifically for them.

There were no boats there yet, but Tara and Alex did note one approaching from the northeast. It wouldn't arrive for another hour, but that still put their operation on a time frame, and as of yet, they had no idea how long this was going to take.

"Hello," the man said in a welcoming voice. His accent was mild but still clear enough to give away that he was from the southern French coast. His face and arms were tanned from constantly being in the sun. Most of his head was balding, but the hair that remained was cut extremely close to the scalp.

"Hello, Dr. Thuram," Tara said.

"Welcome to Saint Helena. You must be Tara and Alex." He stated the obvious while shaking their hands.

"Yes, sir. Thank you for arranging this on such short notice."

The man replied as if it were no big deal. "What? I'm more than happy to assist the world-renowned IAA with anything. Your boss has quite the good reputation."

They got the sense that maybe this man was hoping he would get his back scratched at some point in the future, but what that would look like they had no idea.

"Well, still," Alex said, "we know it was extremely short notice, but we were hoping we could get a look around the grounds before the rest of the tourists get here."

"Yes, of course. Right this way."

The man knew why they were there; at least he thought he did. The couple didn't elaborate on the exact reason they were on the island. They'd come in under the guise that they were interested in looking through some of the documents Napoléon left behind and that were now in the collection of his final documents.

That part was actually true. The two hoped to find something in the pages of Napoléon's last writings that could reveal the truth behind the riddle Tommy mentioned.

Tara kept the entire clue in her mind, repeating it from time to time so she wouldn't lose it. The riddle was easy enough to memorize, but it was vague, as were most of the things of this nature that they ran across.

Napoléon was a cunning leader, and if he'd left something of value behind for some future treasure hunter or historian to find, it wouldn't be easy.

Dr. Thuram led the two up a flight of wooden stairs and along a boardwalk until they reached the path leading to the main house. He'd been working the grounds for the last fifteen years, living on the British island among its four thousand citizens as the person responsible for preserving the historical landmark.

"So, what exactly are you looking for?" Thuram asked as they walked up the hill toward the house.

A perfectly manicured lawn ran fifty yards up the slope, bordered on both sides by small trees, shrubs, and flowers. The house was nothing fancy, certainly not suitable for the man who'd once been one of the most powerful leaders in Europe. Still, it was his final prison and, as such, could have been considered by many to be better than the man deserved.

"We're not sure," Tara admitted. "We believe it's a list of names that the general would have kept, perhaps of his officers."

"Ah," Thuram said. "That could be tricky. There were many documents left after Napoléon died. Some of those did contain names, although a simple list isn't something I recall having seen."

"Well, that's why we're here," Alex confessed.

"Do you know the names you're looking for?"

Alex's cheerful expression waned, and his face drew long. "No. That's the problem. We believe that the names we're trying to locate are probably men that served close to Napoléon, possibly some of his most trusted advisers and officers. According to what we know, there are three of them."

Thuram thought for a moment as they approached the main door. The porch had a pyramidal roof held up by seafoam-green posts. A picket fence of the same color ran around the building. Another smaller section of fence encompassed a flagpole proudly displaying the French tricolor in the wind.

The three walked up the steps, and Thuram opened the door for the two visitors. Alex allowed his wife to walk through first, and then he turned his head and looked out over the property. His eyes scanned the horizon first and then worked their way back quickly, pulling in every detail from the setting. It was something Sean had taught him to do when in the field: always be on alert, and always take account of your surroundings.

Alex knew that Tara had done the same, but he wanted to give one last look before dipping into the house. The recon effort took less than three seconds, and satisfied there was no immediate threat, he followed the others in.

Once they were in the building, the three were overwhelmed with the odors of history. The old curtains, upholstery, and wooden floors smelled like so many museums they'd visited. It reminded Alex of visiting his grandmother's house. Whenever he was in her closet, hiding as a child, he got that same distinct odor. It smelled like clothes that had been hanging around for too long without being worn or washed, possibly nibbled by moths.

Dr. Thuram gave them a quick tour of the building's interior. He took them to the sitting room, where the walls were covered in white curtains hanging from the edge of the ceiling. It was a strange décor, but the American couple kept their comments to themselves as they listened to Thuram give details about the life of Napoléon on Saint Helena.

The French caretaker led them to the general's bedroom and talked about the man's final moments on this earth as he was surrounded by supporters and friends, though many of those closest to him had already died long before.

They were shown the small study where Napoléon did most of his writing. With almost nothing else to do on the island except watch the waves roll in, Napoléon did a considerable amount of writing and contemplation during his years of imprisonment.

"The majority of the documents are in our vault," Thuram said, "though we have left a few out for visitors to see." He motioned to a glass display case next to the small wooden writing desk in the corner.

"What are those documents?" Tara asked, pointing at the case.

"Letters he wrote to some friends."

She nodded in acknowledgment. That didn't sound like the list they were looking for.

"If you'd like, we can make our way to the vault now. I believe the next boat will be arriving within the hour, and once that happens there won't be much peace and quiet—unless you want to remain locked in the vault."

"No, that's fine," Alex said. "We can take a more casual look around later." He understood that Tommy and Sean didn't have the luxury of time. Finding out what the riddle meant needed to be done quickly, and the fewer distractions they ran into, the better.

"Very well," Thuram said. "Right this way."

The curator took the couple down a narrow corridor and out a side door. They made their way down a pathway to a side building that looked more like a large shed than a vault for priceless documents.

Thuram stopped at the door and unlocked it with a key from his pocket and then pushed the door open and led the way inside. Once more, Alex took a look around before following the others in. He couldn't put his finger on it, but he kept getting the distinct feeling that someone was watching them. He'd not had that thought often, so the fact it was happening now either meant he was being paranoid or there might actually be a threat.

He didn't dare blow it off. That, Sean had said in one of their numerous training sessions, was how people got killed. By ignoring one's gut instinct that warned that danger was near, people often ended up dead, Sean had told him, especially in his previous line of work.

Alex heeded his instructor's warning and took to heart everything Sean taught them. He detected no movement in the courtyard or on the lawn to the left and right. The only motion came from trees swaying in the constant breeze or from the rustling bushes.

Satisfied there was no threat, Alex narrowed his eyes suspiciously and then stepped into the building.

The inside of the compound's archives was nothing fancy. It was a simple cottage with one bedroom, a small bathroom, and a kitchenette, all of which had been converted into a vault, of sorts.

It was difficult to believe that the only security measure Thuram employed was a deadbolt on the main door. There were no alarm systems in place, and from what Alex and Tara could tell, there were no cameras or sensors inside.

Thuram read their curious looks and answered the unspoken questions. "We don't rely on much security here because we're so isolated. No one who lives here knows about these archives, save for the few workers I have on hand a couple of months of the year. Most of the time, it's just me here, and I don't worry too much about someone flying in from the mainland to ransack a bunch of random documents."

The two accepted the answer and watched as Thuram pointed around the small room to the various cases, each containing parchments. "We also have a filing system over there." He pointed at a unique set of filing cabinets that appeared to be hooked up to a machine with a tube.

"Is that...a dehumidifier?" Alex asked.

"Yes," Thuram said with a passing wave of the hand. "We keep this entire building at a low humidity. I don't have to tell the two of you why."

"No, we're aware," Tara agreed.

"It is the one thing we've splurged on in regard to protecting the documents, as well as everything else here in this place. We must preserve these things as best we can for future generations to come and see. As you can imagine, keeping the humidity at an acceptable level is quite the trick. We have backups for the dehumidifiers as well as backup generators in case we lose power."

It was then that Tara and Alex could feel just how dry the room really was.

"Anyway," the Frenchman said with a nonchalant shrug, "have a look around. If you'd like to see anything in the files, please, don't hesitate to ask. Most of the important documents are out for anyone to see, but I am more than happy to assist you if you wish to see more."

"Thank you, Dr. Thuram," the two echoed.

"Of course. Now, I must go through my usual rounds. A group left a few hours ago, but we have the afternoon visitors on their way. I'll check back on you soon."

The two watched as their gracious host disappeared out the door. Then they turned to each other.

"Let's get started," Tara said with an excited smile.

Alex nodded but kept his excitement toned down. There was still something unsettling his gut and he didn't know what it was. He glanced out the nearest window and, having seen nothing unusual, set to work with his wife.

21

PARIS

Sean and Tommy had been imprisoned for nearly thirty-six hours, and the two were growing tired of it.

Sean worried about Adriana, wondered how she was faring in her cell. Then he reminded himself that it wasn't her he should be concerned about. It was anyone else in a cell with her. Heaven forbid she was in a big holding tank with several others. He doubted that was the case. The cell she occupied was probably much the same as his. But he'd hate to think what would happen if some other detainee tried to start something with her. Doing so would not go well for the other woman.

Tommy let out a frustrated groan and leaned his head back until the back of his skull pressed against the wall. He flapped his lips as he blew air through them.

"Don't ask," Sean said, irritated.

"What?"

"Why's this taking so long. Don't say it. You've already asked fifteen times."

"Well, we've been here for nearly two days and I haven't heard anything."

He did have a point. In the past, whenever they'd been in some sort of legal trouble such as this, their connections had always come through and usually with remarkable rapidity. This time, however, Sean might have gone too far.

His former partner and now director of Axis had warned him multiple times about getting into trouble. Most of the time, he blew off the warnings with bravado or bluster. Now, however, Sean was forced to rethink that. Maybe she really wasn't going to help him this time.

He shook off the thought. That couldn't be the case. Emily wouldn't just leave him there to rot—unless it was to teach them both a lesson. If that was it, she would eventually come to their rescue after she felt enough time had passed. Unfortunately, Sean didn't know if they had a lot of time.

Bodmer hadn't been arrested since he was with the attendant at the time and wasn't directly implicated in the vandalism, though the police had detained him for questioning.

If anyone had some pull with the police, it should have been the commander of the Swiss Guard.

Sean and Tommy had way too many connections to still be stuck there, which caused a small measure of concern to well up in Sean's belly. He felt the familiar tightness creeping up through his esophagus. It was driven by the thought that, perhaps, they had fallen right into a spider's web. Was someone else pulling some strings to keep him and Tommy detained while they searched for the lost artifact?

A commotion came from the end of the corridor. Heavy bolts clicked and slid through their housings as the barred entryway was unlocked in multiple gates. A couple of men spoke French to one another, and then there was a curt *"oui"* at the end of the conversation.

Footsteps followed, and within seconds two guards appeared. They didn't look happy. In fact, if Sean had to guess, they were there with nefarious intentions.

"Step back," one ordered with a sneer. He had his hand on the pistol at his side and appeared ready to use it if necessary.

They weren't going to shoot the two of them. Not there in the jail.

That would cause too many problems. There were witnesses, cameras, and then there would be the little matter of disposing of the bodies. It was unlikely these two guards could manage getting Sean's and Tommy's corpses out of the building without raising suspicion.

Then another figure appeared. It was Commander Bodmer.

The first guard shouted toward the other end of the hall, and a moment later the cell door unlocked with a short buzzing sound. It swung open, and the two occupants looked out warily.

The Frenchman didn't say anything like "you're free to go" or some other clichéd crack. Instead, he simply stepped back to his right to allow the men to pass by.

"Bodmer?" Tommy looked up, surprised that the commander was the one who'd managed to get them free.

"Sorry it took us so long. The...Holy See is not given to handling matters like this often, and when they do it is almost never a fast process." The commander's tone was sincere, and he looked both men in the eyes with sympathy. "I hope your stay here wasn't...uncomfortable."

"Well, it ain't the Ritz, that's for sure," Sean said. "But we've had worse." He stepped over to Bodmer and slapped the man on the shoulder. "Thanks for bailing us out."

"You can thank Cardinal Klopp when you see him again."

"He was the one who made the call?" Tommy's surprise heightened to match the rising tone of his voice.

"Let's just say he helped."

The guard to the right grunted, his way of telling them they needed to get moving.

"Yes, well," Sean chirped, "thank you boys for your company." He looked at the guard with chagrin. "You've been extremely hospitable, and please, give my compliments to the interior designer here. This place is lovely." He glanced back at the drab cell with feigned sincerity and then headed toward the exit.

The men collected their belongings after they were processed. Once they were back out on the sidewalk in front of the precinct, Sean took out his phone and inspected the device. The edges were smooth, and the seam was almost unnoticeable. It took someone who knew what they were doing to take apart a cell phone without damaging it in some way. If one or more of the cops was dirty, which was almost certainly the case, he would expect them to try to hack into his device. From what he could tell, there was no physical damage to the phone. That was only the first thing to check, however, and he set about scanning the screen when he unlocked it to make sure there were no new apps installed and that it was running correctly. The last thing he noted was the Bluetooth and Wi-Fi, inspecting those features to ensure no one was tracking him or connecting to his device from a remote location.

From what he could tell, it looked like no tampering had occurred. He saw Tommy going through the same process. It was something Sean had taught him to do the previous year, just in case they were ever captured or arrested—again.

"Thanks for getting us out of there," Sean said to Bodmer as they stepped away from the precinct entrance and walked down the sidewalk with the commander in the lead.

"I apologize for it taking so long," the man said.

Tommy scoffed with an audible pfft. "Please, none of our other connections seemed able to help us. And we're friends with a former president."

Bodmer arched an eyebrow but said nothing.

"Wait," Sean said, halting the procession. "Where's Adriana?"

"She's in the rental car I picked up. Just up the street."

Sean felt a wave of relief wash over him. For a moment, he had started to panic, and for no reason. Of course, Bodmer would take care of her first. It was the chivalrous thing to do.

Sean was about to say something, but his phone started ringing. He recognized the 404 area code and shook his head. "Of course she is."

"What?" Tommy asked, looking mildly concerned.

Sean raised one finger, indicating he needed a minute, then answered the phone. "Well, hello there, Emily. How are you?"

"Sean? Are you okay? Wait. How are you answering the phone? I thought you were in jail. Again."

"Just got out." He was tempted to add "no thanks to you," but he knew better. His friend and former partner had bailed him out of trouble like this more times than he cared to recount.

"Oh. How?"

Sean eyed their Swiss companion casually. "We had a little help from a higher power." He emphasized the last two words with a layer of mystery.

"Oh...kay," she said, dubiously. "Well, I'm sorry. I've been monitoring an undercover mission we're running, and I've been out of contact with the rest of the world for the last three days."

"Did it go okay?"

"Yes. Everyone got out safely. Well, everyone except the target, of course."

"Of course." Sean thought back on the times he'd been the trigger man for that target and how he'd handled things. It never bothered him, taking the life of someone who was going to hurt others. It wasn't until later, years after his time with the agency, that he realized why it didn't bother him. That part of him still felt foreign, like a person he'd just met and wasn't sure he liked or wanted around.

"Well, if you're okay, I'll leave you to whatever...thing you're doing over there."

"Keep your phone on next time. I might need your help again."

"That wouldn't surprise me."

"Thanks for checking in, Em. I'll talk with you later."

Sean ended the call and stuffed the phone back into his pocket. The three walked along the street and then cut over to the crosswalk, backtracking twenty feet until they reached a black luxury sedan.

Sean's eyebrows lifted as he noted the smooth ride the commander had procured. He made out a figure inside and recognized Adriana immediately.

The three climbed into the car with Bodmer taking the wheel.

Sean eased into the back with Adriana, letting Tommy ride shotgun.

"You okay?" Sean asked his wife, putting his arm around her and pecking her on the cheek with a gentle kiss.

"Need a shower," she said, "and some fresh clothes. Why did they keep us so long?"

"We vandalized a historical monument," Tommy said with more than a dash of regret in his voice.

"I have a room not far from here. Since I wasn't detained, I had to find accommodations. We can get something decent to eat near there at a little café I've been to before. They make excellent sandwiches and quiches, as well as some terrific desserts."

"That sounds amazing," Sean said. "Let's refuel, get cleaned up, and find out what's going on with the kids."

Tommy was holding his phone to his ear as Bodmer pulled out onto the road. "Way ahead of you."

22

ST. HELENA

Nearly forty minutes had passed, and Tara and Alex hadn't found anything of note in the "archives" of Longwood House.

Dr. Thuram returned about thirty minutes into their investigation and made himself comfortable at a little workstation in the corner, reading over forms and checking email on the computer.

The two visitors had looked through everything on display and come up with nothing. It was time, they figured, to have a look at the hidden files.

Thuram was more than happy to assist them and disappeared for a moment to retrieve some white gloves from a closet in the back of the cottage.

Once everyone was wearing the gloves, Thuram unlocked one of the file cabinets and pulled out the drawer. A new smell flooded their nostrils. It was the scent of old paper; parchment to be exact. Thuram rechecked the humidity of the room for a second time and then nodded to his guests.

"Feel free to look through any of these you like. Just...be careful. Not that I need to tell you two that."

Tara and Alex smiled appreciatively.

"We will," Tara reassured.

The man gave a nod and returned to his workstation, removing the gloves to continue pecking away at the keys on his computer.

Inside the file cabinet, rows of plastic sleeves hung from rods on either side. This kept the contents of each sleeve from settling or crumpling on the bottom of the drawer.

Tara removed the first sleeve and took it over to a wooden table. She laid the plastic onto the flat surface, while Alex retrieved a second document and repeated the process. They looked carefully over the parchment but found nothing of use. With each failed attempt to find anything meaningful, the couple replaced the documents and retrieved others.

There were random memoirs of long ago battles, people the general had known during his time in the military, friends he'd made along the way, and even some poetry. What they didn't see, however, was anything that related to the riddle Tommy discovered in Paris.

They pushed on, working their way through the first drawer, then the second, and then the third.

Another half hour passed as the two moved on to the second file cabinet. The ferry's horn groaned in the distance, and they realized that the boat would be arriving soon, which meant their time in the vault was probably drawing to a close.

They worked faster, though still careful enough not to concern their host and certainly not so much that they would damage anything.

While these documents were, apparently, less important than the ones on display, they were still precious, invaluable pieces of history that had been penned by one of the most domineering figures to have ever walked the earth.

They were into the second drawer of the second cabinet when Alex found a sheet he thought looked a bit odd. He furrowed his brow in confusion at the parchment, staring at the empty page. Empty—save for the image of a rose at the bottom and a few words.

"What is it?" Tara asked, noting his curiosity and abrupt silence.

"I don't know," he said with a shake of his head. "It's just a list of three words. They look like names."

"Set it aside, and move to the next one. We're running out of time."

"No need to rush," Thuram said. "I will go meet the new arrivals and then come back. It's not a problem."

She heard what he was saying, but Tara didn't want to be a burden, and the man had already gone above and beyond what was required of his station.

Despite what Tara told him to do, Alex continued to stare at the page as if searching for an invisible answer. "Why would this be in here if it didn't have anything on it but a couple of names?" he wondered out loud. "And what's with the rose?"

"I don't know. Maybe it was a mistake."

Thuram took notice of their conversation and turned around, twisting his body and resting his right forearm on the back of the wooden chair. "What is it?" he asked.

"This page," Alex said, holding it aloft so the man could see it. "It's just a list of three names and a picture of a rose on the bottom. Why would Napoléon create this?"

Thuram rolled his shoulders. "They say he wasn't in his right mind during his last days. He started calling out to people who were long dead—friends, usually—people he lost along the way. That's a common occurrence, from what I've been told."

Alex had heard the same, though he couldn't confirm it. He'd never been around death much growing up.

He frowned and took the sheet over to the table where he laid it flat on the surface.

"What are you doing?" Tara asked.

"I don't know," he uttered just above a whisper. "There's something odd about this. And look at the spacing between that last name and the one before it. Why is there a gap between them?"

"A gap?" Tara leaned over her side of the table and gazed at the parchment. "I mean, yeah, I guess it looks like there's more space there, but who cares? The guy wasn't using lined notebook paper.

Plus, you heard the caretaker. The general wasn't in his right mind during the final days."

"I guess," Alex said. He stared at the names, unwilling to let them go.

"Dumas, Masséna, Augereau. What do those names have in common?"

He took the phone out of his pocket and snapped a picture of the parchment, making sure he kept the rose in the shot as well. Then he tapped the screen and sent the image to Tommy and Sean. They could take a look at it when they got out of jail, if they weren't already.

He noticed that the images weren't going through and quickly surmised that the cell signal was too low to send any kind of pictures or video. He grimaced at the inconvenience and moved over toward the window, holding up the phone to find a place that might have just one more bar that would allow the message to go through.

"Trying to get a signal?" Tara teased.

"Yeah. I know you don't think that sheet is anything worth looking at, but think about the clue they gave us. Heroes. It mentioned heroes. Maybe these are the names of those heroes."

Thuram shrugged.

Alex was at the window now, holding the device as high as he could. The sun shone brightly in the sky. Its rays glistened off the sparkling water of the ocean. Alex was about to turn away from the window when he caught a glint of something from the tall grass of the slope that ran between the beach and Longwood House.

Fear ripped through him, and he instantly dove backward toward his wife.

"Get down!" he shouted.

His shoulder barged into Tara's back as she was leaning over the table, analyzing another letter from Napoléon. The force of his tackle drove her into the door with a thud. Pain surged through her shoulder, but it would pass.

A small pecking sound cracked through the room just as the two hit the floor. There was a second, then a third. The last two were followed by thumps on the far wall, and it didn't take a genius to realize what was happening.

The glint of light Alex had seen through the window was the reflection from a scope.

"You okay?" he asked, staring down at his wife as he covered her body like a human shield.

She nodded. "Yeah. Shoulder hurts. You should have played football."

He snorted at the insinuation. "Not big enough." He crawled off her and drew the pistol from his hidden holster. Their gear bags were on the other side of the room, which looked like a long way considering the circumstances.

Alex stared at the door, keeping his weapon trained on the entrance.

Tara drew her weapon and looked toward the workstation where Thuram had been working when the shooting began.

"Alex?" There was a coating of sadness in her tone. Her question pulled his attention from the door and he followed her gaze to the little computer desk.

Thuram was slumped over, his face pressed against the surface next to the keyboard. A clean bullet hole leaked blood from his forehead.

A surge of bile tried to rise in Alex's throat. Tara felt the same sudden reflex, but they both pushed it back down like Sean had taught them. It was easier said than done, but he'd warned them that this day would come if they got out into the field again.

It wasn't the first time they'd been close to death. They'd taken out bad guys in Japan once. This, however, was someone on their side, an innocent victim guilty of nothing but helping the two of them on their search for...what? They didn't know what Tommy and Sean were looking for, but one thing was now abundantly clear: whatever it was had to be extremely valuable, so valuable that someone was willing to kill to get it.

"How many are there?" Tara asked, diverting her attention to the problem. They could mourn or process Thuram's death later. Right now, they had to get out alive. Assessing the situation, Sean had told them, was the best way to refocus.

"Only one, I think. Best to assume two."

"Right."

Another thing Sean had taught them: Always assume that there are twice as many threats, especially if there is only one visible. Most assassins preferred to work alone, Sean had told them. That didn't mean it was overzealous to suspect there were more on any given hit.

"You saw their position, yeah?" Tara asked.

"Yep."

"You think we can circle around and flank them?"

"Probably," Alex said. "Unless they change their position."

"Which is likely. We need to find out." She looked over at the dead caretaker and a pang of regret washed over her, tightening her stomach once again. Tara swallowed hard and belly-crawled over to the window that the bullets had come through. She paused for a second and then reached up close to the keyboard, careful not to touch it or the dead man's face. She felt around for a moment and then pressed her fingers down, dragging a sheet of paper from the desk. Within seconds, she held the sheet. It was an invoice for landscaping at the property.

"When I raise this, be ready to go out there and flank them. Okay? I'll keep them busy while you circle around."

Alex didn't like the idea of leaving his wife there alone, but her plan was solid. It's what Sean would've done if he and Tommy were in the same situation.

He gave a nod and moved to the door, turning the knob quietly so that he could make a quicker exit.

He turned and looked over his shoulder at Tara. She gave a single nod and then raised the paper up into full view of the window.

More holes punctured the glass, cracking spiderwebs throughout the frame. Shards fell from the window and clattered on the desk next to the dead man's head. Three bullets tore through the paper in Tara's hand, and she shuddered with immediate fear as she let the sheet go.

She yanked her hand back down and waited for a moment. Then she looked to the door and saw it was open. Alex was already outside and stalking his prey.

Tara summoned every bit of courage she could muster. Her heart pounded in her chest and her breathing quickened. What was it Sean always said? Slow your breathing first by taking methodical, deep breaths and count to ten. That, he claimed, always did the trick. Sometimes, it took a few seconds. Other times, it could take minutes. But it always worked.

Tara focused on something calming. She envisioned being at her and Alex's home, working on cosplay costumes or props in the garage, playing video games, or watching baseball. All of those happy images ran through her mind as she steadied her breathing and shook off the fear. She knew what to do.

Keeping out of the line of fire, she shifted to a crouching position and raised her weapon. If the shooter was more than twenty feet away, she most likely wouldn't hit a potential target, but she could at least scare them into taking cover. Her job wasn't to hit anyone, but to buy Alex time.

She kept the pistol out of view until the last moment, then raised it just high enough that the muzzle would clear the glass. She knew it was going to be loud, but in the small cottage, the report was like an explosion. The hard floors and walls only made the sound worse, but she didn't stop. Tara fired her weapon once, twice, three times, and once more for luck, then she brought the smoking pistol back down from the window and waited for a reply from the other shooter.

———

ALEX STALKED through the tall grass like a lion on the hunt. He crouched and used the natural surroundings as cover. He snaked his way to a small tree standing in the meadow that overlooked the ocean and stopped for a moment, looking out at the position where the shooter had been just seconds before.

He heard the loud pop of Tara's pistol and took that as a cue to hurry up. While her weapon fired four steady shots, he maneuvered around the tree and farther around to the left. He didn't want to take a direct route to the shooter. That would put him in the line of fire. By curving his approach, it would take longer, but he could get behind the sniper and take him out.

Alex noticed the ferry approaching the docks but refocused immediately on the task at hand as he turned back toward the shooter's position. He was close now. The breeze over the meadow rustled the grass, giving some cover to his approach. Not that he needed it. Alex moved like a true predator, using the exact techniques Sean had taught him in their routines. He made certain never to step on a loose twig or leaf. The earth underfoot was soft, and the thick, unkempt grass helped cushion every minuscule noise he could have produced.

That didn't keep him from hearing things. He listened carefully and heard the shooter; he was still in the same position. The person was rifling through a bag from the sound of it, and they weren't doing a good job of being quiet. It sounded almost like a panicked search. Then Alex heard the gun firing again, near-silent pops muffled by a suppressor on the end of the barrel.

He ducked down and approached cautiously, using his hands to maintain balance but with the pistol extended toward the shooter's position. When he was fifteen feet away, Alex could make out the form of the gunman. The man was dressed in drab green pants and a matching shirt, much like the old military uniforms in the 1940s. The color blended well with the surrounding grass, making the shooter nearly invisible from a distance.

Alex raised his weapon and pointed it at the killer's back. He didn't want to shoot the man, but if the sniper didn't surrender he would have no choice. Alex noted another figure in the grass to the right of the shooter. He furrowed his brow as he realized it was a young woman, probably in her mid to late twenties. Blood oozed from a wound in her chest, and she lay motionless with her eyes staring lifelessly into the sky.

"Put the gun down!" Alex shouted at the shooter.

The man startled and spun around. Alex was so taken aback by the sudden, almost instant reaction that he couldn't make himself squeeze the trigger before the other man did.

Luckily, the killer was in motion and moving quickly, so when his silenced barrel popped, the bullets sailed over and around Alex.

It only took a second for Alex to react and he dove into the grass to his right, behind a scraggly shrub.

He rose to one knee and swept the scene with his pistol, trying to locate the sniper.

"Give it up!" he shouted. "We have you surrounded!"

He hated the way it sounded so stupid and insincere coming out of his mouth, but what else was he supposed to say? The truth was, Alex was overcome with fear. He couldn't see the sniper, but he had the sneaking suspicion that the sniper could, in fact, see him. Not the way he planned this little offensive.

Alex felt a wave of panic push into his chest and he swallowed hard to force it back down. He lowered himself deeper into the grass behind the shrub and pressed his torso into the earth. Now he couldn't see much at all. The tall blades of grass might as well have been trees from his position.

Still, he managed to catch a glimpse through a few gaps in the stalks and kept watching for any movement from the sniper. His patience was rewarded when the man suddenly popped up about fifty yards away. How in the world had the guy been able to get so far so quickly and without being seen? No way he could belly-crawl that fast, could he?"

Alex grunted in frustration as he jumped up from his position and chased after the gunman, who was now sixty yards away and sprinting toward the beach.

When Alex came over the crest of a small rise, he could see where the shooter was going. Nearby on the shore, a boat waited, decked out with a center-console dashboard, wheelhouse, and two big outboard motors.

Alex raised his weapon and fired three times, but missed badly. The sniper heard the shots and didn't even risk a look back as he increased his speed, making for the boat.

To their left, the ferry approached the docks, and Alex noted his plane still sitting there moored to the pilings.

The shooter was too far away to hit with his pistol, and Alex knew that the second the man reached the boat, he would easily escape.

Alex doubled his efforts and pumped his legs. He felt the slope of the earth under him, which made running more difficult albeit faster. The gunman was on the dock now. Alex knew he wasn't going to reach the man. The other guy was too fast and was nearly at his destination. Then the sniper spun around a few feet from the vessel. He raised his weapon and took aim. Alex felt a wave of terror crash into him, and he did the only thing he could think of.

He dove to his right and tried to disappear in the weeds. Bullets pounded into the ground where he'd been a moment before. They continued hitting the earth in small explosions as Alex crawled as fast as he could to get away from the hail of metal.

Then the barrage stopped. He lay there for a moment, covering his head with his hands as if that would somehow keep him safe from a high-caliber bullet.

He heard the sound of a boat motor revving to life and risked a peek over the top of the grass. Sure enough, the shooter was in the wheelhouse of the vessel and spinning the wheel as he turned away from the docks and back out to sea.

Alex let out a sigh as he stood and watched the boat leave. The guy was going to get away, but at least he didn't get what he was looking for. He rushed back up the hillside toward the spot where he'd first encountered the shooter and found the young woman's body still lying there.

He shouted toward the house and waved his hands round to signal to Tara that it was all clear. She joined him within a minute, trotting across the meadow with both gear bags slung over her shoulder. When she reached the body, she lowered the bags to the ground and looked closer at the woman.

"Who is she?" Tara asked.

"I don't know," Alex admitted. "I think one of your shots hit her."

The statement didn't bother Tara. This woman had come there to kill them. If Tara hadn't shot her, she might still be a threat. Tara could deal with the mental stuff later.

The two searched the woman's pockets and a small satchel next to her but found no identification. There were five hundred euros, some South African currency wrapped in a rubber band, and three spare magazines for a Glock 19, plus two sniper mags.

"Who is she?" Tara asked the same question again.

Alex shrugged. "We can figure that out later. For now, we need to go. The last thing we want is that ferry full of tourists thinking we killed her."

"We did kill her."

"Yeah, but they don't need to know that. And we certainly don't want them thinking we offed Dr. Thuram."

Tara nodded. Good point.

The two looked back at the cottage with a heavy sense of regret, then turned and started toward the airplane.

23

PARIS

Tommy didn't get an answer from Tara or Alex, and he had tried calling both. He looked down at his phone and shrugged. "I guess they don't have a good signal where they are."

"You mean out in the middle of the ocean on a tiny island that only has four thousand or so inhabitants? Yeah, that's crazy." Sean rolled his eyes.

"Touché."

"We did get their text messages from Cape Town, so we know they at least made it that far safely. Surely they're on the island now."

"I guess, but that leaves us in a sit-and-wait mode."

Sean's shoulders raised an inch and then dropped. He looked down at the almost empty plate in front of him. He pinched a crusty piece of bread between his finger and thumb and popped it into his mouth. The hard outer layer combined with soft middle and the buttery flavors in a divine dance on his palate. Sean reached for his café au lait and took a sip. It was still hot since the server had just come by and topped it off.

"There are a few perks to sitting and waiting in this place," Sean quipped, motioning to the spread as he set the coffee back on the table. He turned to Bodmer, who had been on edge since they had sat down to eat. "Honestly, I don't know how any of you stay in shape over here in Europe. We have good food in the United States, but over here is next level. Especially the bread." He finished chewing the last morsel of a piece of cheese and then leaned back.

"We move more here," Bodmer said simply. "Americans, from what I hear, are sedentary. We tend to be more active because of the layout of our cities. We walk more and drive less."

"That's something I've always appreciated," Sean confessed. "How active so many Europeans are."

He eased back in his seat, allowing himself to feel satisfied for a moment before realizing he was relaxing a little too much and then stiffening back up.

The café was like thousands of others he'd seen in the big French city, as well as some of the smaller towns. There were red-and-white umbrellas over folding metal and wood chairs and tables strewn across a section of sidewalk that reached nearly to the street, all cordoned off by a black metal fence.

People walked by in a mishmash of colors and styles. Some looked to be tourists, carrying cameras around their necks and day packs on their backs. Others were in business suits, probably taking a little time off for lunch. Then there were the casual citizens who roamed around as though they didn't have a care or responsibility in the world. Maybe it was their day off or they worked a later shift.

The smells of fresh-baked bread and baking cheeses wafted out of open doors and filled the nostrils of all who passed, luring them in.

The moment of peace ended abruptly.

Sean's phone suddenly buzzed on the table, causing his plate and fork to rattle. A second later, Tommy's phone started dancing, as well. The two picked up their devices and looked at the screens. Their eyes met for a moment.

"Text from Alex," Sean said. He could see from the home screen preview that it was an image.

Tommy nodded and tapped on his screen.

Sean did the same.

Bodmer leaned forward, looking intently at the two devices as the men examined the messages they'd just received. "What is it?" the commander asked impatiently.

"It's a parchment," Tommy answered first while the words hung on Sean's lips.

"Parchment?" Bodmer didn't seem satisfied with the answer.

"Yes. And there are three names on it, as well as a symbol of the rose like we saw before."

Tommy lifted his phone so the commander could see it.

Bodmer stared at the image for several seconds. He cocked his head to the side and narrowed his eyes in an effort to focus.

"The only name I recognize on that list is Dumas," Bodmer admitted and then leaned back in his chair again.

"Dumas," Sean said reverently.

Bodmer raised one eyebrow and looked at the man questioningly. "What? What about Dumas?"

"Great author," Sean said. "Wrote *The Count of Monte Cristo*. One of my favorite stories of all time."

"One of the original treasure hunter stories."

Sean snorted a laugh. "And a jailbreak story."

"All rolled into one."

"Shouldn't it be filed under education in the library?"

The two shared a laugh at the reference.

Bodmer didn't seem to get the inside joke, and so he crossed his arms, waiting for the two to be done with their fun.

"Sorry," Sean added quickly. "One of our favorite stories. Anyway, Alexandre Dumas wrote *The Count of Monte Cristo*. It's an adventure story filled with revenge, intrigue, murder, betrayal, treasure, and eventually justice. Really good book."

"I have heard of it," Bodmer confessed, which caused Sean to feel a little stupid. "So, what does this author have to do with the mystery surrounding Napoléon and the murder of Cardinal Jarllson?"

Sean turned to his friend, who merely offered a blank stare in response.

"You don't know?" Bodmer sounded irritated.

"To be fair, Commander, we don't have a whole lot of information to go on."

"And we just got the message," Tommy added. "Can we at least have a few minutes with it before we wave our magic wands and make the answers magically appear?"

The commander wasn't entirely sure what the lingo meant, but he had a feeling it was dripping with sarcasm.

Sean went back to staring at his screen and the three names on it. His eyes stayed locked on the one at the top, though, reading it over and over again in his mind. Dumas. What did Alexandre Dumas have to do with all of this? Was there a hidden treasure under an island off the coast of France, like in the story? Is that where the relic could be found?

He still didn't know what relic they were looking for. That fact had been niggling at him for the last few days.

He doubted the theory about a buried treasure underwater. That was fantasy, nothing more. And besides, it couldn't simply be some location related to the Dumas tale. There were two other names on that list. What did they have to do with it?

Sean turned his head in frustration and slid his phone over to Bodmer so the man could have a look for himself. While the commander was investigating the image, Sean looked out over the busy city street. He noted a young couple—blonde woman and brunette man—walking along the sidewalk, holding hands.

The sight made him think of his wife, and right on cue she appeared in the doorway of the café, holding a cup of coffee. She was drinking an espresso, which wasn't something the wait staff could refill as they made their rounds.

"What's going on?" she asked and slid into the empty seat next to Sean.

Tommy pushed his phone toward her and it stopped flush with the edge of the table.

She picked it up and looked at the image while sipping the hot coffee.

"Just got this message a few minutes ago from Alex. Seems he and

Tara might have found something down on Saint Helena. We're not sure what it is, though," Tommy said.

"Three names," she said absently. "Dumas?" She looked up from the phone with the question reflected in her eyes. "The writer?"

"We thought so at first," Sean said. "Now, I'm not so sure."

"No? Why not? He's definitely French."

"True," Tommy agreed, "but the other two names are ones I don't recognize. We're not sure what they have to do with any of this."

"Ah," Adriana said with a nod. She returned her focus to the screen and studied it while Sean let his eyes wander again.

He looked back to the street once more. The young couple were gone. On the other side of the road, another café, similar to this one except with pink umbrellas, looked to be just as busy as this place. He noted people drinking wine and beer and laughing. Occasionally, the smell of seafood wafted across the street, bypassing the vehicle exhaust and hitting Sean's senses. He didn't care for seafood, save for the occasional salmon or tuna sushi. That was about all he could handle. For whatever reason, he'd never acquired the taste for cooked fish, and he couldn't make himself eat shellfish.

Sometimes, people asked him if it was a religious thing. He always said that it wasn't, that instead it was simply a decision not to eat things on the lowest rung of the food chain.

Truth was, those creatures disgusted him, and he didn't fully trust what eating them would do to his body. He was like a four-year-old unwilling to eat when it came to sea fare.

His thoughts snapped away from the topic of food and locked in on a person he'd seen every single time he looked across the road.

The first time it didn't seem unusual. Sean had noted the man sitting there alone at a table. He was reading a newspaper while the majority of the patrons around him were busy on their phones or tablets. A few appeared to be working busily on their computers.

The man wasn't old, not by a long shot. He had a thick black beard with traces of gray in it, so he could have been anywhere from mid-thirties to mid-sixties as far as Sean could tell. He was too far away to get a clear picture from the few details he could muster. The man was also wearing sunglasses, which was not unusual given the bright sunshine pouring down on the city.

None of that would have been suspicious in the least except for a couple of factors: The first was that the café where the man was sitting appeared to be a place for a younger crowd. It was trendy, or at least looked that way, and might even be considered a kind of cyber-café. Sean made that assumption after seeing rows of laptops inside the building along the left-hand wall, all atop a counter that stretched into the back of the building.

If the man was in his sixties, he was the only one there of that age, though Sean figured him to probably be in his late forties. His skin was tight and tanned, and even though the guy was sitting down, Sean could see he was in good physical shape.

He wore a black button-up shirt with the sleeves rolled up and a pair of khaki cargo shorts. Sean had to admit he liked the man's style. Unfortunately, Sean was going to have to interrogate him.

To the casual observer, the man across the street was simply enjoying a cup of coffee while he read the daily news. Sean, however, knew better.

He'd spotted the man looking at them at least three times now, and each successive time the guy slowly averted his gaze, as if trying to look like he hadn't been caught.

It was a subtle move and one that would have fooled an ordinary person. It didn't fool Sean. He recognized the tactic, even applauded it internally.

"Sean?" Tommy interrupted his thoughts. "You okay?"

"Yeah," Sean said. "Just keeping an eye on a new friend over there."

Tommy followed his gaze but didn't spot who his friend was talking about.

Bodmer and Adriana also directed their eyes across the street.

"Man in the black button-up with the khaki shorts," Sean said. "Sunglasses. Thick black hair."

"Looks like something you'd wear," Tommy joked.

No one laughed, and he immediately felt a tad idiotic for the ill-placed comment.

"He's been watching us since we got here," Sean added.

"So?" Bodmer questioned. "There are lots of other people there, as well. And they've been there longer."

"My point," Sean said with a nod. "He got there at the same time we arrived at this place."

"How could you know that?"

Sean's head twisted to face the man. "How could you not?" He arched both eyebrows and went back to the problem. "I observed him sitting down at the exact same time we were sat at this table. He's at a table for four. Why? There are precisely three other two-seat tables on the patio. Two are in the sun, and one is in the shade, which means he could have had his choice of table when he arrived. There are six servers running the outside, though one of them is also waiting tables inside, along with one more who is strictly working the interior guests. That means they have enough staff and enough tables to put that man at one of the two-seaters, but they put him in one with four. Why?"

Bodmer stumbled for the answer to Sean's overly thorough analysis of the situation. "Well...maybe he likes the view better at that table."

"Or he could be one of those types that just likes more room," Tommy offered, but he knew better. Sean was onto something. Offering one more carrot for his friend to snatch would help drive home his point to the skeptical commander.

"True," Sean said, "but two of the other tables offer similar views, which rules that idea out. Plus, what would someone be hoping to get a better view of? The cars driving by? I don't think so. And then there's the issue of the newspaper."

"Newspaper?" Bodmer asked. His voice sounded like a forlorn child.

Adriana watched on with a slim smile on her face as her husband continued to conduct an investigation workshop.

"The newspaper hasn't changed pages. He's been staring at that same page for the last thirty minutes."

"How could you know that?"

"I wouldn't be able to," Sean admitted, "if he had the front page facing us. Luckily, he had it folded over, as if he's been working his way through the rest of the paper. If that was the case, I would have seen a new page by now. Perhaps he's the slowest reader in the world, but I doubt it. Based on the other facts, I'd say we picked up a tail."

Bodmer shifted uncomfortably. "What should we do? You think he's the killer?"

"No," Sean said with only a hint of doubt. "I don't think he's the killer. He may work for the killer, but I won't find out until I talk with him."

"Talk with him?"

Sean gave a nod as he stared intently at the man. The guy across the street had his face hidden behind the paper now.

Instead of answering, Sean stood up and walked out of the café and over to the crosswalk. He waited for a moment, and when the light changed took off at a trot to the other side of the street.

The other three watched with rapt attention as the man with the newspaper glanced around the corner of it and realized one of the people he'd been watching was gone. He looked around frantically and, when he spotted Sean, got up from the table and disappeared inside the building.

Sean reached the entrance to the other café a mere twenty seconds after their watcher went inside. After a few minutes of searching, though, Sean came back out to the sidewalk and threw up his hands.

He looked down the street in both directions, as if expecting the guy might reappear half a block away, but that wish never came to fruition.

Sean put his hands on his hips for a moment and then returned across the street. He plopped down in his chair with a frustrated sigh and fidgeted with his coffee cup.

"Lost him?" Tommy asked, already knowing the answer.

"For now," Sean said. "We'll see him again."

"How do you know that?" Bodmer asked.

"Because once a dog is on a scent, they don't stop sniffing until they get what they're chasing. That guy is working for someone. I doubt he stumbled on our search by accident. I don't know who he works for," he said, sensing the next question from the commander, "but that will reveal itself eventually."

Sean pulled his phone back across the table and looked at the names on the image Alex sent. "We have to figure out who these people are and why they would be on a piece of parchment in the house where Napoléon was exiled."

"Heroes," Adriana blurted suddenly.

The three men looked at her, confused.

"The clue we discovered at the library, the one in the château. It spoke of heroes."

"Heroes of the Empire," Sean added.

"Right," Adriana said. "Heroes of the Empire. It also said, let their victory stand eternal. If these names were the names of, say, officers under Napoléon's command, it's possible that we need to look up those names and find where they are buried."

"Eternal," Tommy said, his face suddenly brightening. "Eternal rest. That makes perfect sense. So, we just have to figure out who these guys were and where they are buried."

"It sounds like you're going to do some grave robbing," Bodmer said with disgust.

"Not if we can help it," Tommy countered. "I'd rather not have to go through the process of digging up all those permits, no pun intended."

Bodmer didn't get the joke.

Sean was already busily looking up the first name. "I'm checking on Dumas. You two check the other names. See what you can find. Adriana, take Masséna. Tommy, you look up Augereau." The other two nodded their assent and began working.

The commander watched as the others searched the internet for any information they could gather about the three mysterious names on the parchment. The group sat in silence as the Americans pored over information on their devices. It was a strange sight, or it would have been to someone trying to do the same research thirty years ago.

The world had changed in many ways, not all of them bad. With so much information available so quickly, quests such as this one could be conducted faster than ever before.

Adriana was the first to speak up. "I found out who Masséna is," she announced. "And where he is buried."

Sean looked up from what he was reading about Dumas.

Tommy chimed in immediately after her. "Pierre Augereau was an officer under Napoléon's command. He's buried at the famous Père Lachaise Cemetery here in Paris."

"Same for André Masséna," Adriana added. "He was an officer and is buried at Père Lachaise."

Sean had been to Paris many times, but of all the places he'd visited, that cemetery was one on his list he'd never had the chance to see. His reasons for wanting to go there were personal. He'd been a big fan of the American rock band The Doors since he was in high school and first saw the Oliver Stone movie. After that, he was obsessed with them for months. That obsession eventually turned into a casual love affair, but he never stopped appreciating the poetry and music that the band produced, especially from the mind of their singer, Jim Morrison.

Morrison's grave was also in Père Lachaise, and Sean wondered, even though he knew it was foolish, if he would have the chance to at least glimpse the legend's resting place.

"What about yours?" Tommy asked, cutting into his friend's thoughts. "What did you find on Dumas?"

Sean ticked his head to the side as if still working out the details. "Well, we weren't far off the mark. We're looking for Alexandre Dumas's father, Thomas-Alexandre Dumas. He was one of the highest-ranking officers of African descent ever in the French military. He died poor, which put his wife and children in a desperate situation. He was also a writer, though not to the level of fame his son, Alexandre, reached." Sean finished the sentence just above a whisper. He always felt a sense of reverence when reading about the history of someone who was no longer around. Even if it was a person who died long ago, Sean understood that the dash between the year of their birth and the year of their death contained a lifetime of memories from childhood all the way up through the final years of adulthood. That dash represented a life, full of trials and triumphs.

That's what the clue meant. The realization hit him. That dash was their triumph, their victory.

"He's buried in a cemetery elsewhere. It's not far, and there is a translation near it. We could be there in less than an hour, I think."

The others looked at each other for a moment and then back at Sean. They nodded.

"Let's go," Tommy said eagerly.

"Right," Sean said as he peered across the street where the mysterious man once sat. "The only question is, what's the plan?"

24

MALBORK

Lucien Berger stopped in his garden to admire a particularly robust rose. The flower was in full bloom and its vibrant red color was at peak perfection. He bent down toward it and took a sniff of its delightful perfume.

He allowed the scent to linger for a moment before he stood up straight again. Berger appreciated the simple things in this world, especially things from nature. He felt that his connection with God was heightened by the things that remained untainted by man. Plants like this rose were one such natural, simple thing. It grew almost in spite of man, with a will of its own. There was a kind of spirit to a plant, especially the rose. Perhaps, Berger thought, he wasn't the first one to consider that.

His phone vibrated on the table at the end of the courtyard and he turned, irritated. He narrowed his eyes and stalked over to the table, looking down at the electronic abomination that had just interrupted his meditative time.

He looked at the screen and pressed the answer button. "What's going on? It's been too long since your last check-in."

There was a pause on the line, only broken by gasping breaths.

"Hello?" Berger said, suddenly concerned.

"Grand Master," a weary voice said. "We...we encountered a problem."

Berger knew who it was. Only a few had this number, and Michael was one of them. His daughter was the other. Everyone else contacted him through other means.

"What is the problem? Did you handle it?"

"We...we went to Saint Helena, as you requested, sir. We tracked the...targets."

"Yes? Spit it out."

"We didn't anticipate that they would be so well armed and well trained."

Berger didn't like where this was going. His asset sounded like he had been running from someone. He was outside; that much the man knew because there was the subtle hint of wind in the microphone and he could hear birds singing in the background. It sounded like seagulls, which meant the asset was at a port somewhere, most likely Cape Town.

"It was an ambush, sir. There was nothing we could do." The man offered the explanation, doing the best he could to hide the hopefulness in his voice.

It was not lost on Berger. "Ambush?"

"The couple, sir. They led us to a building. We tracked them, like you told us to do. But then things got out of control."

"Why do you sound like that? You sound weak and pathetic. You are a Teutonic Knight, are you not? Get yourself together, or I will flog you myself when you return. Where is Kallia? Perhaps I should have her do it for me and save the time."

Another pause came through the line. This time, it wasn't accompanied by deep breathing. The young man had fallen silent.

Berger fought off the suspicion. "Did you not hear me, boy? Where is my daughter?" He found his voice booming louder than intended.

A swallow preempted the answer. "She...she's dead, Grand

Master. We were in a gunfight on the island. They counterattacked. We...we had them pinned down. It was...it was a lucky shot, sir. Whoever was firing at us from the house, they...they were shooting randomly. Kallia and I ducked for cover, but one of the bullets hit her in the chest. She...she's gone, Grand Master."

Berger sighed through his nose. He immediately took another deep breath and ran a hand through his thick hair, letting the fingers tug on the strands.

It wasn't real. This wasn't happening. It couldn't be. The asset was lying.

"Listen to me," Berger sneered through gnashed teeth. "I want to know where my daughter is. Do you understand?"

"Yes, Grand Master. She is...still on the island."

A renewed anger surged through the man and he slammed a fist down on the table. He struck it so hard that the glass top shuddered under the force, and a piece chipped off the end.

"My daughter is dead?"

"Yes, sir."

"And you left her there for the birds and beasts to consume?"

There was no answer, not at first. The man choked on his words. "I...it was all I could do to get away with my own life, Grand Master. I barely escaped."

Berger inclined his neck and scratched the stubble under his chin. His daughter was dead, and this moron had left her there on the island. The military man had, for a moment, been merely a father crippled by the sudden and unexpected news of his daughter's demise. The pain was still there, still burning in his chest, but the commanding knight, the Grand Master, returned and took over, pushing away grief until it could be handled at a later time.

"You escaped?" Berger asked.

"Yes."

"I assume, then, that you recovered whatever the targets were looking for? Surely, that is why the firefight broke out and why my daughter's body is on an island in the middle of the ocean."

There was another uncomfortable swallow on the other end, and Berger didn't need the idiot to speak to know the answer.

"Things got out of hand, sir. We...we were compromised. I had to abort the mission, sir."

Compromised? Berger knew what that meant. The man wouldn't dare suggest that Kallia was at fault or that he'd made a mistake. Instead, the young knight would try to offer a word that would lead the grand master down his own thought path, one that would make him think there was someone else to blame. Berger wasn't stupid. He knew the psychological strategy better than most.

"You failed me," Berger said. "I assume I don't have to remind you of the price of failing me, do I?"

"No...no, sir. You don't. Please, I will go back and recover your daughter's body."

"No," Berger snapped. "You have already failed at that task once. I will send another. Wait for him there, and then when he arrives you will return home."

That didn't sound so bad to the young knight, though he expected a berating when he got back to Malbork. He would not be well received, to say the least. "Yes, sir, Grand Master. Thank you."

"Do not thank me yet, boy. Stay there until otherwise ordered."

Berger didn't wait for a reply. He ended the call and set the phone on the table. He took a deep breath and let it out slowly, doing his best to push emotions out with the air in his lungs. His heart tightened at the thought of his daughter's death.

She was young, full of life, and was to take over the order someday as the first woman to become Grand Master. She would have been there for his glorious triumph in recovering the relic and reclaiming all they'd lost so long ago.

Now, she was dead, lying in the grass or on the beach on some faraway island. He didn't know for certain who had pulled the trigger, but whoever it was would pay. That much was certain.

Berger would find these brigands and bring them to justice, and he would have his revenge. He picked up the phone and dialed a number. The man on the other end sounded gruff, older than the young knight he'd just spoken to.

"Yes, Grand Master?"

"I need you to go to Cape Town, South Africa. There's something there I need you to take care of."

25

VILLERS-COTTERÊTS

S ean stepped off the train and onto the platform. He took a moment to survey the quaint town.

Villers-Cotterêts was small and looked like it hadn't changed much in the last century or so, perhaps longer. A massive church rose up from the center of the village, encompassing a vast footprint in the city proper. The cathedral was equal in size, if not greater than, the old castle that rested atop a rise in the middle of the town.

The village was surrounded by plains on all sides. Sean had noted the farms on the train ride in. That told Sean most of the towns-people were likely involved in some form of agriculture or another.

The others looked out on the scene as they stood on the train platform. New passengers scrambled into the cars, some of them apparently in a hurry to get on board.

Sean felt someone brush against his side, and he glanced back to see a small boy being dragged along by his mother. The woman was holding the child's hand as she hurried to get on the train. The kid looked back at Sean, who offered a smile and a wink.

The boy smiled back and then followed his mother up the stairs.

Sean rechecked his hip to make sure nothing had shifted. The pistol was still there, concealed under his belt.

He'd been impressed that Bodmer's pull was able to get their weapons back from French police. Carrying a weapon in Paris, or anywhere in France, was illegal without a hunting or sporting license. Those had to be renewed every year, along with an annual psychological evaluation. Some studies suggested that there were twice as many illegal guns in France as legal ones, a fact that merely reinforced Sean's opinion on the matter: Bad people were always going to get weapons one way or the other. It wasn't fair to keep them out of the hands of law-abiding citizens.

Whatever Bodmer had done had worked, though, and Sean was glad to have his gear back. He wondered how the cops in Paris felt about that.

Sean would have to ask the commander about how he pulled that trick, but that question would have to wait. They had more pressing matters.

The group made their way out of the train station and onto one of the main streets leading into the heart of the village. They strolled at a brisk pace but did their best to look casual, as if they were nothing but tourists taking in the sights.

They passed a bakery and a coffee shop, a pharmacy, a clothing store, and a collection of other retail shops.

Sean noted the windows of the two- and three-story buildings surrounding them, checking each one to make sure no one was watching them. Perhaps that was a tad overzealous on his part. No one knew the group was there, and if they'd been followed, whoever was on their tail would be behind them not in some building ahead, unless they'd called in advance. Doubtful. Still, doing a little recon was never a bad idea, and it kept his senses on alert.

The two left streets opened up into a square. A rectangular fountain pool occupied the center. Water sprayed up into short arcs and splashed down again. Overlooking the pool, a statue stood tall, staring out across the little city. It was the figure of a man in a heavy cloak that dated from the mid-1900s, unless Sean missed his guess.

His hair was thick and unkempt, as was also stylish at that period in history. He held a hand away from but across his chest. His fingers clutched a pen while the other hand rested on a stack of papers atop a pedestal.

The group drew near and realized that the figure was that of the great writer Alexandre Dumas.

Sean caught his breath for a moment.

Tommy swallowed with an audible gulp. It wasn't the burial place of the famous author, but it was the next best thing.

The two friends had been fans of Dumas most of their lives. His adventures were the model, the blueprint, of what they imagined archaeology and history could bring to their lives. They hadn't been wrong about that.

Sean reached out and touched the base of the monument. He grazed it reverently with his fingertips, as if the act itself might bring down the entire thing.

"So, is this where we will find the grave?" Bodmer asked, insensitively.

"No," Tommy said, clearing his throat. "The cemetery is that way." He pointed down the street leading away from the fountain and statue.

Adriana put her hand on Sean's shoulder. "Come on, tough guy. We need to find his father's grave. I'll bring you back here later if you want."

He smiled at her with a childlike look in his eyes. It was a look she'd seen before and one that she imagined few others had beheld. It softened him, a man who'd fought against evil, taken lives in battle, and who was constantly forced into the fire again and again. This hardened man still possessed the unflinching passion and curiosity of an innocent child. It was only one of the many reasons she loved him.

Sean nodded. "Yeah, you're right. Time for sightseeing later. We have a relic to find."

The group made their way out of the square and down the adjacent street. The foot traffic dissipated, and soon they found themselves very much alone save for an occasional pedestrian wandering lazily down the sidewalk or walking their dog.

Villers-Cotterêts was a stark contrast to the busy city of Paris. Here, it seemed life was much more laid back. No traffic. No throngs of people moving around on the concrete, scurrying to get to their jobs or to a meeting or to get a quick bite before returning whence they came.

Sean appreciated it. He enjoyed the slower life. It was one of the reasons he kept a residence in Chattanooga. While Atlanta was fun and had lots to offer as far as entertainment, it was busy and sprawling. Traffic always got in the way, and without a solid metro system it was only getting worse.

This place was the kind of town he wouldn't mind living in.

They walked around the corner and then made a left, following the directions on Tommy's phone. The blue line on the screen's map said it was only three more minutes until they arrived at their destination, the cemetery where Thomas-Alexandre Dumas was buried.

The next street was lined with thin trees, planted forty feet apart. The sidewalks were cracked and beaten from neglect. Old homes dotted the lane, much older than most houses in the United States. They were classic French designs, probably built by merchants several hundred years ago or possibly by local or regional dignitaries. Now, they were just average people's homes, no longer a statement of success or political prowess.

Still, the buildings were beautiful. Sean and Tommy appreciated them with quiet contemplation as they walked by.

Of course, Bodmer and Adriana didn't think much of it. Being from Europe, they were accustomed to such things. It was stuff they'd grown up with their entire lives.

The group made their way to the right at the next intersection, and the cemetery came into view. It was occupied by several large oak trees to provide shade to those in eternal slumber, and was surrounded by a black iron fence. The barrier was little more than decorative, and it had started to fall apart in some places where oxidation had taken its toll over the years. The grass and landscaping, however, were well maintained, and it looked as though the lawn had been mowed recently.

Tommy led the way in, and the group stopped once they were through the gate. It was a public cemetery and had no place for security or guards.

Sean panned the entire area before turning his attention to his friends. "We can cover more ground if we split up," he said. "I'll take that corner and work my way in. Tommy, you go over there," he pointed at the opposite corner. "Adriana, there, and Bodmer, there." He finished by jabbing a finger to the prescribed zones.

The others nodded and started toward their corners.

"Remember. We're looking for Thomas-Alexandre Dumas."

More nods came from his companions, and he started off toward his own corner.

Sean walked between the rows of simple headstones and gaudy monuments, his eyes scanning each surface for the name *Dumas*. He reached the end of one row and met Adriana as she was finishing her pass.

"Anything?" she asked, though she immediately regretted the question since, if Sean had found something, he would have alerted the others.

"Nope. Lots of graves to check, though."

She nodded and turned away, proceeding back the way she came on the next row.

Each of the four investigators kept moving, sweeping through one row and then the next. Sean's progress was slower than the others because he took on the task of also watching for trouble with every step. His method was simple enough. He checked a headstone, checked the fence. Checked a headstone. Checked the fence again in a different area. He didn't know why, but the strange man he'd seen at the café earlier that day made an impression on him, and that impression was of someone who wasn't going to stop just because he'd been caught once. Well, sort of caught. Sean regretted not being able to catch up to the guy. Maybe Sean had scared him, though he doubted it.

He turned at the end of another row and began the process all over again. Sean didn't have to go far before he found what he was looking for.

The grave was simple, not what he would have expected from one of the great heroes of Napoléon's legion of officers. It was no different than some of the other graves surrounding it. Then Sean recalled what he'd learned about the man, about how he had fallen into poverty after enduring several injuries with the army. His pension hadn't supported his family after his death, and this simple monument was likely all they had been able to afford.

Sean thought the tale a tragic one, righted only by the son who went on to become one of the most celebrated writers in history.

He read the name to himself and noted the birth year as well as the year of death. It matched up with what he'd seen regarding Dumas.

"Guys?" Sean shouted to the others, though he tried not to sound disrespectful in the cemetery. Graveyards had always been a reverent place to Sean. He'd grown up near one that his grandmother took care of. When he was old enough, about eleven or maybe even twelve, she started paying him to mow the grass. Even as a youngster, he felt a deep respect for those who had passed and did his best not to tread heavily on the ground within the confines of the cemetery's boundaries.

The other three joined him where he stood to the side of the headstone and gathered around.

"Good," Tommy said. "Now what?"

Sean knelt down, pressing his right knee into the grass next to the sunken earth where the man's coffin had been placed so many years ago. He stared at the writing carved into the stone, but there was nothing unusual, no clue as to what they should be trying to find there.

He heard a sound like a twig snapping and turned his head to the right but saw nothing. A few birds chirped in an oak tree on two low-hanging branches. Other than that, there were no signs of life save the sounds of the occasional car rolling down the road or intermittent hammering coming from a construction project nearby.

Sean's head twisted back and forth. There was nothing here. Surely they weren't really supposed to dig up this man's bones to find the next clue. That wouldn't fly with him or anyone in his group, much less the people of the little town. And they couldn't afford to go back to jail again. He doubted Bodmer would be able to pull the same strings twice.

"There's nothing here," the commander so aptly noted.

Tommy spun around on his heels, scanning their surroundings. A tree stood nearby with low-hanging branches and a thick trunk. It provided shade from the afternoon sun. Other than that, there wasn't much to distinguish this part of the cemetery from any other.

Adriana took a step away and stared out over the property, looking for clues in the terrain or perhaps the houses beyond the perimeter of the graveyard. Sean simply stared at the monument for a long minute, as if the simple act of observation would reveal some long-hidden secret of the stone.

He shook off his wandering mind and stood. There was nothing here, no sign, no clue pointing them to the next spot on the map. And there was certainly no X.

Sean pulled out his phone and took a picture of the headstone. Then he looked at Tommy. "Let's go."

"Go?" Tommy groused. "What do you mean? We just got here, and we haven't found anything yet."

"I know."

"So...why are we leaving?"

"Because there isn't anything to find, and we aren't going to dig up this grave to see if the man was buried with a clue."

"Well, obviously," Tommy managed. "Still, we can't just leave."

"I took a picture of the marker," Sean said. "The only thing I can figure is that the dates must line up with the dates on the other markers we're supposed to find. Or maybe those stones have a clue that goes with these dates."

"Coordinates?" Adriana ventured, putting her hands on her hips.

"Maybe," Sean said. "Maybe not. But we aren't going to find out until we visit the other two graves. Lucky for us, those two are in the same cemetery."

"Yes, but what if they're not?" Tommy asked. He felt his voice rising a little.

"Then we come back."

"Sounds like a lot of wasted time."

"Maybe," Sean agreed. "But there's nothing here. If you want to stay and have a look around, that's fine. I'm going back to Paris."

Sean started toward the gate.

Adriana lingered for a moment and then followed.

"Seriously?" Tommy asked, throwing up his hands in indignation. "We've been here less than five minutes, and you're going to just give up like that?"

"I'm not giving up," Sean said. "I'm going to the next grave to see what else I can find."

Sean trudged through the entrance to the cemetery and back out onto the sidewalk. Then he thought for a moment. He couldn't leave his friend behind like that.

He looked back at Tommy and shouted over his shoulder. "Hey, we're gonna wait for you in that restaurant we passed on the corner of the square. When you're done looking around, come find us."

"What's with you?" Tommy countered. "Why are you acting like this?"

"We'll save you a seat," Sean blathered.

"Fine. Whatever."

Bodmer's head swiveled back and forth as he watched the exchange.

When the two were done talking, Tommy said, "Come on, let's keep looking. There must be something here."

"That or you're going to have to get a permit to dig up the body."

Tommy sighed. "Yeah, let's hope not. That could take months. And we don't have that kind of time."

26

VILLERS-COTTERÊTS

S ean and Adriana sat at the patio table on the cobbled patch of street that ran into the café's outdoor seating. He watched people passing by, a few kids playing in and around the fountain, and the birds that were perched on a dangerously close gutter across the street.

"You're not mad about something, are you?"

Sean furrowed his brow. "Me? No."

"Because you sounded angry back there—or, at the very least, frustrated."

He cracked his neck to the right and then rolled his shoulders. "Nah. We don't have time to beat around the bush. There's a dead cardinal back in Rome, and we're supposed to find the killer or what the killer wanted. My problem with all of this is that Klopp doesn't seem to know what we're supposed to be looking for. No one does. We have the commander of the Swiss Guard with us, which is really weird by the way. I mean, who is running things for him back at base?"

"The Vatican."

"Yeah, exactly. My point is, yes, it's frustrating. We spent nearly two days in jail. Who knows where Tara and Alex are at this point, and we can't seem to get through to them. On top of all that, we come here and find nothing but a poor man's grave."

"Maybe Tommy will find something out there." She was trying to be helpful, but it didn't feel like it.

"Maybe," Sean said. "It just gets frustrating sometimes."

"These things are never easy," Adriana said. "If they were, anyone could do what we do. What you do." She cocked her head to the side and tilted her wine glass to the right. The red liquid shifted but didn't spill. She eyed it thoughtfully, considering what to say next. "Honestly, I'm glad stuff like this isn't easy. I enjoy the challenge, the roadblocks. It makes the triumph that much sweeter."

"Triumph," Sean muttered. Then he chuckled to himself. She had a point. Easy wins were rarely worth celebrating. He wasn't going to give up. That wasn't his point. He'd assessed the situation in this town and believed there was nothing to find. Did he make that call too quickly? Perhaps, but he stood by it. That didn't mean he was giving up.

He planned on going back to Paris, to Père Lachaise, where he could find the other two graves and compare them to what he was seeing here, in Villers-Cotterêts. The truth was, Sean was unsettled. Something else was going on here, and he couldn't figure out what it might be. That was the overarching frustration in his mind. Riddles, clues, mysteries, all of those had answers set in stone. That didn't change the feelings tugging at his chest cavity. There was something else. What was it?

"Lovely day for a stroll through the cemetery," a man's voice said from behind them.

Sean started to turn.

"Don't," the man said. "It won't help you to know who I am. Not yet, anyway."

"What? You gonna shoot me here in the middle of a café in broad daylight, in front of all these people?" Sean muttered so the other patrons couldn't hear. There weren't many since it was a slow time of day.

"Shoot you? Mr. Wyatt, I have no intention of shooting you. Make no mistake, though, there is a gun pointed at you right now. So, please, don't make a scene. I truly don't wish to kill you."

The man's limited facility with English was expected in Europe, but his accent was strange, unlike anything Sean had ever heard before. He tried to place it but couldn't. It could have been from one of the Mediterranean countries, but that was still a wide swath. Then again, the man sounded almost Middle Eastern. And was that a hint of...French in it? Sean couldn't tell, and it was fruitless to worry with it.

"Okay, let's say I believe you. I already got a good look at you before."

"Ah, very astute," the man groused.

Adriana was tempted to turn and look, but she kept her head still, paying close attention to everything around them. If there was one of them, there might be more surrounding the little café. After a quick-and-dirty assessment, however, she didn't notice anything unusual, save for a guy reading a newspaper. The culprit may well have been on his own.

"What do you want?" Sean asked. "Why were you following us in Paris? And why here?"

"Those are good questions, Sean. I'm glad you asked. Because you already know."

Sean's brow tightened. It was then he noticed the second gunman, a guy across the street, reading—of course—a newspaper. Whoever these people were, they weren't creative. "Never use the same gag twice," Sean muttered, only loud enough for Adriana to hear.

She'd already noticed the man with the paper the moment he sat down. How many more reinforcements were going to show up? She got her answer in seconds when another man pushing a baby stroller stopped at a lamppost and started chatting on his phone. The bundle in the stroller looked real enough, but Adriana knew it was a doll. The man was well dressed, with black pants and a slim-fitting white button-up shirt. Those facts helped give him away.

He turned in various directions, clearly trying to look casual. He even took a couple of steps away from the stroller as he pretended to be nonchalant and oblivious to the group at the café. Adriana knew no parent would do that, leave their kid sitting alone on a sidewalk. Of course, cultures varied. She was well aware of that, but this man was dressed like someone who took parenting seriously, like a responsible person. Not some deplorable from the gutter. This man, like the other, was watching them.

"I already know what?" Sean asked, continuing the conversation with the mystery man. He, too, noticed the second tail appear on the sidewalk about fifty feet down from the first.

"What it is I want. The same item you and your friends are searching for."

"And what item is that?" Sean asked sardonically. He sensed the man's hesitancy to speak again and so continued. "If you're talking about whatever we're looking for on this particular trip, we actually don't know."

Sean saw the two men across the street getting into position, casually checking the weapons they hid, one behind a newspaper and the other in—of all things—the baby stroller.

There was no panic in Sean's voice even as he watched the gunmen getting ready for—what, he wasn't sure, but he knew it wasn't going to be quiet. Were they going to wait until their leader was done with his chatter?

The little town would be thrown into chaos; people could get hurt, people who had nothing to do with any of this. That was Sean's concern, the people. And most importantly, his wife.

"What do you mean you don't know?" the stranger asked. His voice left no doubt as to his sincerity.

"We don't know what we're supposed to find." Sean said the words as though he didn't care. "We've been on this hunt for some relic, but we don't know what it is. You seem to know. Maybe you could tell us."

"You're...you're not serious." Up to that point, everything about the man screamed professional. He was stoic, emotionless, unable to be fazed. Sean's question and honest statement about their ignorance regarding the missing artifact had disarmed him.

"We are, Chief," Sean said. He flicked his fingers up as if discarding an irritating insect.

"How could you have made it so far and not know what you seek?"

"It's a funny business we're in. So, you gonna draw down on that smoke wagon or are you just gonna sit there and chirp? Because, quite frankly, I'm tired of the games."

"It is not my intention to shoot you, Sean."

"Oh," Sean said. "I'm sorry. I wasn't talking to you."

"What?"

"He was talking to me," Tommy said.

The stranger turned and looked up into the barrel of a pistol. Tommy was careful to make sure Bodmer shifted in front of him so any passersby wouldn't see the weapon and raise a stir. He shielded the other field of view with his own body and kept the gun out of sight from the people inside the café.

Sean twisted around and crossed one leg over his knee. "Well, it looks like we caught ourselves something."

The shock on the man's face was evident, and he clenched his jaw in frustration. He wondered how he could have been so careless.

"Yeah," Sean went on, "I didn't see you on the train. Even after we got off, you were doing a good job of staying out of sight. It wasn't until we were at the fountain that I first noticed you. By the way"— Sean glanced at the man's new lavender shirt—"that shirt was a nice touch." He bit his lip to keep from laughing.

"What? You..." The man couldn't form coherent words. All that came out was frustrated bluster. "You tricked me?"

"Yeah, pretty much. I could tell pretty quickly that there was nothing to find in that cemetery. I knew my friend would disagree at first. The only thing that made sense was that we needed some pieces of what's on the tombstone to combine with information from the others. As soon as we do that, we should be able to locate the artifact, or at the very least another clue. Seems like that's how it goes pretty often with these things."

"What do you want?" Tommy asked, tightening his grip on the weapon.

"We were just talking about that," Sean cut in. "Our friend here was going to inform us as to what it is we're trying to find."

"He knows?"

"Sounds like it."

Tommy's eyelids narrowed. "What is it?"

The man stared up at his captor, still in disbelief. "You truly do not know, do you?"

Tommy shook his head slowly back and forth.

"I can't believe it. You really don't know," he repeated his previous sentiment.

"We'll know when you tell us. Or I can take you out to one of the farms near here, and we can interrogate you." Tommy sounded tough. He made it appear as if he was willing to do whatever it took to get the information. It was all bravado, though, on his part. He wouldn't torture another human. Even if this guy was the one who had killed Jarllson.

The stranger searched Tommy's eyes for truth and found nothing but a cold, hollow stare. It was an expression he'd been working on for a while. Sean called it his poker face. It conveyed nothing but the absence of feelings, an emotionless vacuum that made it nearly impossible to tell if he was bluffing or telling the truth.

"I...I don't know what to say. This is all very awkward."

Tommy motioned with a slight incline of his head. "Put your gun down. Nice and slow." He couldn't see the weapon, but the man had on a windbreaker now, and one of his hands was shoved into the pocket.

The lightweight jacket was something the man wasn't wearing when they were in Paris. Had he been carrying the weapon there, as well? And if so, how did he conceal it? Those thoughts drifted in and out of Sean's mind quickly as he assessed the situation. He didn't give his full attention to Tommy and the gunman, instead choosing to only turn slightly. That way, he could still keep an eye on one of the gunmen across the street while Adriana watched the other. He noticed that the gunman with the newspaper looked momentarily confused by the sudden appearance of Tommy and Bodmer. Perhaps the two gunmen weren't expecting that move. Sean had never been good at chess, but in the game of life he was as good as they came.

"Look," Sean paused, suddenly realizing he didn't know what to call the man, "I'm sorry, what's your name?"

The stranger didn't appear angry. He was clearly frustrated that the Americans got the drop on him, but that seemed to be a mild irritation. He withdrew his hand from his pocket, careful to move deliberately so Tommy wouldn't put a bullet through his head right there in the café, if he was so brazen to do such a thing.

As the man's hand appeared from the pocket, Tommy saw the dry-erase marker clutched in his finger. It wasn't a gun at all.

The man shrugged as if to say "you got me" and then set the marker on the table. "I am...at the moment, unarmed."

Sean turned his full attention to the older man for a few seconds. He didn't dare take his eyes off the two across the street. "For the moment?" Sean asked.

The man put his hands up in surrender. "I am usually well armed, but I had no intention of hurting any of you."

Sean's eyes narrowed.

The stranger saw his doubt and set to allay it. "I am from a long line of priests," he said. "Though I am no ordinary priest."

"Yes, I can see that," Sean said dryly. "I don't know many priests who follow us around, or anyone for that matter."

"Like I said, I'm not ordinary. I'm part of a group of elite warriors. You probably have never heard of us."

Tommy kept his weapon on the man but had to pull it closer to his body as a couple of young kids—high-school age, most likely—walked by, chatting about what video game they were going to play when they got home.

"Try us," Tommy said.

The man tilted his head and looked up at Tommy with a quizzical expression on his face. "We are from an old order, long dead to civilization, at least on the surface. We're called *Deus Militibus*." He waited for a moment to let the information process.

"God's Warriors?" Adriana asked first.

"I had a feeling you all knew Latin," the man said. "Our original name was the International Order of Saint Hubertus. We were founded in 1695 by Count Franz Anton von Sporck. We no longer go by that name since it has been adopted by many others throughout the world since the Second World War."

"World War Two?" Tommy asked. He didn't admit it, but this particular secret organization was one he didn't know much about, if anything.

"Our order declined to permit Nazis into our ranks, and so Hitler dissolved the group—or so he thought. We simply ceased operations under that name and began working under the title of *Deus Militibus*."

The man looked at the others and assessed their demeanor. Seeing they were interested in what he was saying, he went on. "Most people believe that the order was put together simply as a sort of hunting club, if you will, a place for some of the best hunters of the nobility to enjoy their sport together. It was, however, much more than that. The reason we chose hunters is because they are the best at tracking, not only animals but signs, symbols, things that lead to answers. Certainly, many of the men who joined our ranks were expert trackers and hunters of all kinds of game. The purpose of our true hunt, however, had nothing to do with animals. It was for the same purpose you four now stand here in this place."

"The relic," Sean realized. "You were hunting the same relic?"

The stranger nodded. "I am Bertrand Wagner. I am the head of the order, the true order. It is our mission, and has been since the seventeenth century, to locate holy relics and bring them to the church. One relic, in particular, has held our...interest, since the early nineteenth century."

The dots connected.

"So, your...group," Tommy said the last word with chagrin, "has been looking for this thing for a couple of hundred years?"

"Yes," Wagner admitted. "We have seen clues but nothing

definitive. We've always kept in close contact with the Vatican, however, and when your friend the cardinal discovered that information in the archives, we knew about it within a few hours."

"How?" Bodmer asked. He was incredulous that some foreign entity, Catholic or not, could infiltrate his security systems, the detail, the countless measures that were in place to prevent just such an incursion.

"How did we get through the walls, the cameras, your Swiss Guard, Commander?" He added the last piece just to further display the order's capability. He knew who Bodmer was.

The commander twitched, momentarily unnerved by the comment.

"Those things are all of human design," Wagner said. "Because of that, they are flawed. Even your men, Commander. No one is perfect, and nothing designed by man is, either. We have our ways."

He left it at that, and Bodmer could see he wasn't going to get any more information, for now.

Sean looked nervously across the street and then back at the man. "So, you've told us who you are." He let his words hang a moment to show the stranger he still had doubts about his backstory. "What is it you...we are looking for? Why are you telling us this now?"

Wagner took a deep breath and sighed. "Sean, we have searched for hundreds of years for this particular relic. We have exhausted every lead, which were few and far between. We'd all but lost hope until that fateful day when the cardinal went into the vault and came out with the first lead we'd heard about in more than three decades. We believe you four are working for the same side we are. You are good people from what I understand. I know much about your exploits, Thomas," he motioned to Tommy with a nod of the head. "And yours as well," he nodded at Sean. "This woman, I know little of, but if she is with you two, I'm sure she is a good person, as well. And I know the commander serves the Lord."

Bodmer's face reddened, but he said nothing.

"And the relic?" Sean asked. He could see from the man's expression that he still didn't believe the group didn't know what they were looking for.

"One of the most prized and holy relics of all time. It was taken in the early 1800s by none other than General Napoléon Bonaparte himself." Wagner paused for effect. "You seek the ring of John the Baptist."

27

VILLERS-COTTERÊTS

S ean, Tommy, and Adriana had been through some pretty fantastical journeys together. They'd been all over the world, searched underground chambers, discovered priceless objects that had been long thought lost to history. They'd heard of most of those artifacts and relics. Some were more obscure than others. This, however, was one that none of them knew about.

"The ring of John the Baptist?" Sean asked with genuine curiosity.

"Yes," Wagner said, unmoving. "The ring was taken by Napoléon on his way to Alexandria. He and over thirty thousand of his men were sailing to the Egyptian port. It was a mission to take control of British trade interests in that region and effectively reduce Britain's strength there. Of course, there were other reasons for the campaign.

"Napoléon was a historian and a scientist. He desired to learn more about the ancient world from the ruins and cultural remnants of Egypt, Saudi Arabia, and Syria. It was on that campaign, I'm sure you know, that his people discovered the Rosetta Stone, effectively allowing us to decode ancient hieroglyphics."

Tommy and the others nodded.

They knew about the Alexandria campaign in that regard but didn't know anything about the ring of John the Baptist.

"On the way to Egypt," Wagner went on, "Napoléon made a stop on the island of Malta. While there, he sought to make a visit to the church in Valletta, Saint John's Co-Cathedral."

Tommy and Sean exchanged a curious glance. The church wasn't one they'd visited. In fact, neither man had been to Malta before. They were beginning to think that was a huge oversight on their part.

"He met resistance from the Knights of Malta, also known as the Knights Hospitaller. There was also a strong contingent of the Knights of the Teutonic Order on the island at the time since it was a period of strife and concern with the rising emperor in France. The knights knew the man was set on world conquest, and they feared he might stop there on his way to Alexandria to resupply.

"They called on every ally, every soldier they could muster, but the siege didn't last long, and in the end after a short stretch of fierce fighting, the knights were vanquished. Most died. A few managed to escape with nothing more than their lives. Their defense of the city was commendable, especially considering they were fighting over-whelming odds. The knights were outnumbered by tens of thousands, yet they still fought honorably."

Wagner sounded despondent for a moment, as if he'd been there for the battle.

"After the fighting ended, Napoléon made his way into the church. He threatened the priests, though it's doubtful he would've done anything to harm them. While Napoléon had a reputation for cruelty in certain circumstances, he wasn't always a monster. He respected the clergy—despite his doubts about their character from time to time. The general found the head priest of the church and demanded to be taken to the reliquary. There, Napoléon found what he was looking for. It was the golden glove that contained the skeletal hand of John the Baptist."

Sean and his companions listened intently as the man spun his yarn, while at the same time keeping a watchful eye on the two gunmen across the street. They appeared to be confused for some reason, and he couldn't pinpoint why. There was even a moment where he saw the two men glance questioningly at each other, as if they weren't sure if they should proceed as ordered.

Perhaps they were waiting for Wagner to give the command, but that would be foolish. Again, there were too many people around. Not hundreds but enough to make them keep their weapons at bay—for the time being.

Before Sean could ask what happened next, Wagner continued. "Napoléon went into the reliquary, removed the glove from its case, and then proceeded to take the bones out of their protective shell. It was then that he removed the holy ring from the hand of the Baptist. The priest protested, but Napoléon simply told him he could keep the hand of the Baptist, but that he would be taking the ring with him on his journey."

The man ended the story and leaned back for a moment, as if releasing a great burden from his shoulders.

"So, that's what all this is about?" Tommy asked. "Finding the ring of John the Baptist?"

"Yes. And we must find it so it can be returned to Valletta and Saint John's Co-Cathedral, the ring's rightful home."

Bodmer's face was stone, but a fire burned in his eyes as he listened to the story. It was obvious he didn't appreciate the implication that his security systems and team were unable to prevent events such as the one Wagner described. Still, there was something else that was bothering him, something that stoked the flames during the entire tale.

"So, you killed Cardinal Jarllson." He stated the words as if it was the obvious conclusion. To be fair, no one else in the group arrived at that same point.

"No," Wagner said, blowing off the insinuation. "Don't be ridiculous. We would never harm any of God's holy men unless absolutely necessary, and in this case it was not necessary. Unfortunately, we are not the only order that is looking for the ring."

Adriana arched one eyebrow even as she saw the gunmen across the street perk up. "Who else?" she asked.

Bodmer looked into her eyes, then Sean's, then Tommy's, making sure he connected with each for a moment.

"They are an old order, one that has been around since the First Crusade, even before then. Like us, many believe that they have transformed into a charitable operation, an organization dedicated to feeding the poor, helping the sick, and much more. Those groups are the ones ordinary people see. They put up their signs on the streets, host public events, assist with fund-raisers. Those men are not of the same order."

"What order is that?" Tommy pressed.

Wagner was about to answer when Sean caught a sudden movement out of the right side of his eye.

"Get down!" he shouted.

Adriana saw the movement as well and reacted a split second before her husband. She flipped the table over and ducked behind it as the two guns on the other side of the street began spitting bullets in their direction.

Sean ducked behind the metal table a second before the rounds plunked into the surface. The shield was big enough for the two of them to crouch behind, and because of the angle, the shooter across the street on their left didn't have a good viewpoint. The one to the right, however, was another story.

Thankfully, Bodmer reacted nearly as fast as Adriana, and he dove forward and tipped another table over, effectively giving them a temporary barricade.

Wagner crouched behind Sean while Tommy and the commander took refuge with the second table.

Sean drew his pistol, though he knew it wasn't going to be as effective as the weapons the men across the street were using. His usual .40-cal. Springfield would have been fine. It had decent range for a sidearm, and the targets on the other sidewalk would have been manageable. It was close by—stuffed in his rucksack on the ground next to his chair. Unfortunately, he didn't have time to grab it, so the subcompact on his hip would have to do. It was a weapon that was much more useful in closer quarters, say inside a building or for personal defense in a home invasion.

Even with his expertise, he doubted his ability to take out the gunmen, and he knew his companions were likely going to face the same issue.

The shooters were firing CZ Scorpion EVO 3s submachine guns. The weapons were compact enough to keep hidden with the right gear, and were more powerful with a greater range than the small arms Sean and the others carried. Apparently, the gunmen also had the automatic versions, which allowed them to spray the patio with bullets.

Screams filled the air from all around. A woman tried to take cover near Bodmer and was ducking behind the man as she sobbed hysterically. A young man with a goatee and a knitted cap was crouched behind Tommy. He, too, was crying and covering his head, saying something about not wanting to die.

Most of the civilians on the street took off the second the guns appeared in broad daylight. When the shooting started, their speed quickened, and within seconds the corridor was devoid of pedestrians. A few were still trying to escape past the fountain in the square, but other than that, it had taken less than a minute for the citizens of the small village to evacuate the area.

The fact that these gunmen were shooting in the middle of the day, surrounded by witnesses, told Sean that they were either desperate, gutsy, or stupid.

He hoped it was the latter, but doubted it.

This was a hit.

The other thing that bothered Sean was that they were trying to shoot at Wagner, too. If they were Wagner's men, why would they be trying to take him out—unless he was about to release information he wasn't supposed to? But if those men were with Wagner, he would have played that hand. He would have at the very least given them some kind of order by way of hand signals or a hidden radio. But Wagner hadn't done that.

Sean glanced over at the man and saw a tear in his windbreaker.

One of the bullets must have struck the guy in the shoulder. To his credit, Wagner wasn't complaining. It almost looked as if he hadn't noticed the injury yet.

Perhaps the man was well trained. Or maybe it was just shock.

There was a pause in the shooting, which told Sean the men were reloading. He popped out from behind the table and fired his pistol. One, two, three, four shots erupted from his muzzle before he ducked back down for cover.

His reply to the initial assault had been meager at best. He'd hit the baby stroller with one of his rounds, but that had only served to push the gunman back behind the park bench for cover as he reloaded. The man hadn't even jumped at the sudden counterattack.

Whoever these two were, they were trained killers and wouldn't be easily dispatched. They'd been so bold as to allow themselves to be seen for several minutes before opening fire. That brought a new question to Sean's mind: What had they been waiting for? They could have easily picked off every member of the group by simply opening fire right away. That meant they weren't there simply to take Sean and the others out. They were there to get information.

More bullets thumped into the metal table. Little dimples dotted the underside of it with every successive shot. The metal held true, though, and not one round managed to sneak through.

They needed to get out of there. The tables were holding up for the moment, but that wouldn't last. As soon as the gunmen changed positions, the group would be exposed again.

Running out into the street wasn't an option. They would get mowed down the second they popped up from behind the tables. It was doubtful Sean or any of the others would even get one foot onto the sidewalk.

No, that was an obvious no-go.

That left retreating back into the café as the only viable option. It was also a risky move, but so was staying put.

Sean turned to Adriana. "Take them and head out the back. I'll cover you."

She didn't like the idea of leaving Sean there, but she knew that he had a plan and that once it was set in motion, trying to stop it was futile. She preferred to stay there and take the fight to the gunmen.

But this was no time to argue. They had minutes, if that, before the cops showed up. Then there would be questions, and she had a bad feeling getting arrested twice on the same trip in the same country wouldn't end well, despite their high-up connections.

Adriana reached out and snagged the loop on top of her rucksack. She slung it over her shoulders and then shouted at the others, motioning for them to go to the café through the open door behind her.

The men looked at her skeptically, then Tommy nodded and waved his hand at Wagner and Bodmer.

"Go!" he yelled. "I'll be right behind you."

Tommy stood up from behind the table and fired five rounds, three at the shooter on the left and two at the man on the right. His volley sent them ducking for cover again and gave his charges the moment they needed to escape into the café. Tommy stood there with his weapon extended and flicked his hand at Adriana, a silent order for her to go next.

"Get to the train station," Tommy said sternly, directing the brunt of his order at Bodmer and Wagner. He didn't even know if the train would be there, but that didn't matter at the moment. It was their only way out of town, something he wished he'd thought of prior to embarking on this journey.

Adriana gave a nod and darted into the building, firing one shot at each gunman as she made her escape. One of the rounds came dangerously close to an exposed foot as she fired at the man on the right. The boot snapped back as the bullet hit the concrete next to it.

"Go," Sean ordered his friend.

"Not until they're clear," Tommy protested.

"I'm not waiting until they're clear," Sean said with a furrowed brow.

He popped up and squeezed the trigger again, twice in each direction. The shooters were forced to stay hidden for another couple of seconds, which was more than enough time for Sean to dash into the café.

Tommy was caught off guard for a moment, but he snapped back quickly and hurried to catch up. He thought maybe Sean would try to give the others more time to escape, but now he realized that wasn't the plan at all.

Sirens screamed in the distance. From the sound of it, they were still three or four minutes away.

Adriana led the other two men through the back of the café, past the counter at the coffee bar where, just minutes before, people were relaxing with a hot cup of their favorite caffeinated beverages, chatting about the usual things people talked about at a café. There'd been a couple of people working on their laptops, probably freelancers of some kind, or perhaps developers.

Now the café was empty. The baristas had taken refuge behind the counter, while most of the patrons were cowering on the floor or under tables.

Adriana sighed. She couldn't just leave all these people here.

"Quickly!" she yelled. "Everyone out the back of the building. Go! Go! Go!" She waved her hand like a windmill, ushering Wagner out first. Then she turned to Bodmer. "Help these people outside. You're armed. If you see trouble in the back, take them out."

Bodmer removed the pistol from his waist and nodded.

"Let's move!" he shouted in French. "Everyone through the rear exit."

Some of the patrons were quick to scramble to their feet. They clawed at the floor, all too happy to have a way out of the war zone that had suddenly exploded in their peaceful abode.

Others were less eager to move. Their fear was evident and for good reason. If they moved, they could accidentally get into the line of fire and catch a bullet. There was no time to explain to them that the same thing could happen if they stayed put or that their odds of being struck by a random bullet were actually higher by not moving.

Sean saw the issue and helped get the rest of the patrons out. He ordered them to stay on their hands and knees.

Adriana and Tommy assisted him, also keeping low and out of the gunmen's sights. More bullets punched through the windows, shattering one and sending cracks through another. The rounds plunked into the back wall, sailing over a few customers' heads before finding their end point in the drywall or in the framed pictures.

"Come on," Sean urged, seeing one older man struggling to keep up with the others.

Sean stayed low and returned to the door, pressing his back against the wall for cover until he heard the firing cease again.

Tommy rushed to aid the older man. He looped his arm around the guy's back and helped him crawl to the back hallway, past the bathrooms, and around the corner leading to the rear exit.

Sean heard the sirens drawing closer with every second. There would be cops everywhere in less than two minutes, if that. He spun around the corner and into the open door. He raised his weapon and squeezed the trigger. His sights lined up just left of the gunman with the stroller. The attacker had just reloaded his gun and was raising the weapon to fire again when Sean emerged from the café.

Sean missed with the first shot, but he stepped out and into the open, lining up the pistol's sights with the target's chest. He fired again and again, emptying the magazine at the gunman as he stepped forward like an immortal demigod.

One of the bullets caught his target in the clavicle. Another tore through the man's side. The remaining shots missed, but the damage was done. The gunman dropped to the ground on his knees and twisted around in a sudden snapping motion. He writhed on the concrete in agony while his partner resumed the attack.

Sean picked up his rucksack and dove back into the café in a single swift motion. He rolled onto his feet and stayed low as he maneuvered into the corridor and into the back of the building.

When he made it to the rear exit, he stuffed his weapon back into his holster. It was empty anyway, and his reserve mags were in the car. There were more than a dozen panicked people running down the sidewalk away from the center of town. Based on the sound of the sirens, it appeared the citizens were moving toward the oncoming police. They would be safe soon enough. Sean and his companions, however, needed to get out of there. The street was empty, though that didn't help Sean relax. He had no intention of lowering his guard now.

They split away from the main group and hurried across the street to the train station. A horn honked, signaling that the train was getting ready to leave.

His eyes shifted to Wagner. The man was running in the back of the group now, between Tommy and Commander Bodmer. The thin trickle of blood from his arm didn't seem to be bothering him much, which was a further tribute to the man's training. He must have been through some intense work to be able to ignore the sting of a gunshot wound. Nerves would be screaming to his brain at that moment, yet the man didn't wince, didn't moan or complain. He simply pressed one finger to the wound to stem the flow of blood.

"Who were those guys?" Sean asked pointedly. "Clearly, they're not with you."

"No, they aren't."

"Then who are they?" Sean demanded. "I thought they were with you. I had my eye on them the entire time we were talking. We believed they were your backup."

Wagner shook his head and sighed. "No. They are not with us. They are from another order. Those men are with the order that is responsible for the death of Cardinal Jarllson. They are the ones who murdered him."

Everyone was focused on the man who claimed to be from a secret organization of relic hunters.

"They are Teutonic Knights," Wagner said, "and they are here for the ring of the Baptist."

28

VILLERS-COTTERÊTS

G etting on the train had been easy enough. The group had purchased tickets that would allow for a couple of trips more than they needed, just in case. It was also the way the ticket pricing structure was set up. Sometimes, that worked in favor of travelers. Sometimes, it worked in favor of those running the railways. In this instance, it worked out for Sean and company. They had enough tickets for Wagner to join them, though they soon realized he also had a train pass. As it turned out, Wagner took the train to Villers-Cotterêts as well—the same train Sean and his companions were on. They simply never realized it.

Sean cursed himself for being so sloppy. He would have to be more attentive to his surroundings.

They filed into the train and found an empty car near the back. Based on what they'd witnessed on the way in, more people would be piling onto the train as they stopped at each subsequent station on the way into the city.

Adriana led them to a cluster of seats in the middle of the car and took a spot next to the aisle, motioning for Wagner to take the window seat beside her. It was a strategic suggestion, as was the selection of seats in the center of the car. With her positioned on the aisle and Sean across from her, the two could watch both ends of the train for suspicious activity. If anyone chose to get on this car, they would know it and have a strategic advantage.

Bodmer sat in an aisle seat by himself, across from the others, which made him feel a little like a fifth wheel at the moment.

Tommy took a seat across the row from Wagner. "Did you say Teutonic Knights?" he asked incredulously. "Seriously?"

"Yes. As I believe I mentioned before, the Teutonic Knights were also on Malta when Napoléon invaded the island and stripped it of its holiest and most precious possession. The Teutonic Knights fought alongside the Hospitallers in their resistance, but it was not enough. In the end, they lost everything. And not just on the island of Malta."

With slits for eyes, Sean looked across the row. "What do you mean, not just on the island of Malta?"

"Exactly what I said. The knights of both orders lost everything. The Hospitallers lost their foothold in the Mediterranean and were forced to withdraw deeper into Europe. The Teutonic Knights faced a similar plight. They'd lost Acre, the city in Israel where they were founded so long ago. They adapted, of course, and moved to Europe, initially to Venice. After some years there, they relocated to Marienburg, a small town in Poland—known as Malbork in the local language. Their headquarters and castle were there for over a century. It was there that they established their base of power. The Teutonic Knights were shrewd businessmen, cunning and respected. Over the years, they built up their wealth, their landholdings, and their influence. They controlled most of the region and found themselves in the precarious position of being primary rulers without the title of king or emperor. They, however, were not the only people to make that realization."

Wagner pinched the wound in his arm and then pressed his thumb back into the blood. It was starting to congeal, and soon it would be a dark scab. He was lucky in some ways. The injury could have been much worse. It could have been five inches to the right, too, which would have put it straight into his chest. They would need to keep that blood out of sight when the conductor came through, otherwise there would be more trouble with law enforcement.

"The rightful rulers of that area did not appreciate the growing amount of power and wealth the order was accumulating. They were becoming dangerous, indignant, and soon could take over everything if nothing was done to keep them in check. A plan was put together by the political leaders and the church. The knights were stripped of their lands, their titles, and most of their fortunes. False accusations were forced upon them. Some were executed. Many fled never to return. A precious few stayed, hidden in the shadows to watch and wait. Those knights hoped that they could be the ones to return their order to greatness, to undo the great wrong that had been visited upon them. Their wait, however, was in vain all those years. They never had even a glimpse of their former glory. As I said before, they lost everything."

Tommy listened to the man with fascination, never taking his eyes off Wagner as he relayed the information about the Teutonic Knights and their history. He'd known of the group, even read a little about them at some point in the past, but they and the Hospitallers always seemed to take a back seat to their brothers, the Templars, who were perpetually shrouded in secrecy and mystery.

"These guys, the Teutonic Knights, they don't sound like a group with many resources," Tommy commented. "And what do they want with that ring?"

Wagner took in a long breath and looked down at his wound again. Bodmer noticed the man's concern and stood up.

"I'm going to get him something to stem the bleeding," the commander said.

Sean nodded his assent, and Bodmer stalked toward the bathroom at the end of the car. He reappeared a moment later with a first aid kit and sat down in his seat again. After he removed a packet of gauze, he took out a can of disinfectant spray and hosed down the wound. He knew it stung, and for a guy who hadn't flinched at being shot, the spray seemed to finally hit the nerves Wagner had been ignoring since they left the café.

Bodmer gently packed the dressing over the wound and then taped it down with the adhesive strip from the kit. When he was done, the commander sat back and admired his work with a certain air of pride.

"Thank you," Wagner said. "I am in your debt."

Bodmer waved off the praise but allowed himself a slim smile.

"The Teutonic Knights," Wagner went on, answering Tommy's question, "take orders from the grand master. Like in many secret organizations, the grand master is the leader in all things. While he is not a king and doesn't wield total authority in most situations, it seems that with the Teutonic Order that is exactly what is happening."

"Who is this grand master?" Adriana asked. "Do you know him?" She looked at the man as she asked the question, then returned to watching the door and the aisle to make sure it was clear as she listened to his answer.

"A man named Lucien Berger," Wagner said. "He's been in control of their organization for several years now. He's fanatical, believes that the order should have all their previous landholdings returned to them, and the fortune that was taken."

"Land?" Sean asked, incredulous. "Land that has been in the possession of other people, families, for hundreds of years? There has to be some kind of statute of limitations on that, right?"

Wagner snapped his head. "No. Not in his mind. He believes that if they can find the ring, it will legitimize their place in the holy kingdom, that it will prove they are in God's favor and that all wrongs must be righted. I'm not certain, but if I had to guess, I would say they likely want the castle at Malbork returned to them, as well."

Sean glanced at Tommy, but his reply was a blank stare. Another place they hadn't heard of or visited. Malbork didn't ring a bell, although that wasn't a huge surprise. There were thousands of castles all over the world and twice as many ruins of ancient fortresses, palaces, and temples. They could spend five lifetimes and never see them all.

"So, once this guy has the ring and all his old stuff back, he's going to, what, just sit back and retire on his newly regained fortune?" Sean's question was riddled with doubt. Nothing was ever that easy, not that they were about to hand the ring over to that guy—a ring they didn't yet have, if ever.

"Lucien will not stop once he has the ring. He will use it to rally tens of thousands to his cause, perhaps hundreds of thousands or more. Once that happens, all of Europe will be set on fire."

That last part was a pretty big jump—for this audience, anyway.

"What do you mean, set on fire?"

"Lucien believes that the world is dying and that the cause is due to a lack of morals, an absence of religious guidance. This pope is weak, weaker than any who have come before him. He makes compromises with church doctrine, promotes tolerance in ways that the church never did before. Some call him a progressive. There are circles, however, who consider him a traitor, a treasonous snake who is working to undo the church from within."

"What do you believe?" Bodmer asked from across the aisle. He'd been silent for a few minutes, but now the topic of conversation was venturing into his backyard.

"I believe that the pope is a good man and is trying to do what is best for not only the church but for the world and all of Christianity. Perhaps he is misguided at times, but that is not for me to judge. Only one who has ever lived can judge that and it is not me or any other mortal."

Sean knew whom he meant. He'd lived his life according to the same belief, though he had often been the sword of what he hoped was the side of good and not evil. After what he'd seen in the government—the things that were covered up, the lies that were told to the American people and the rest of the world—he wanted no part of it. That was the biggest reason he'd left Axis, and it was a reason he could never really tell anyone about, even Emily. Especially Emily. She was still there, still grinding out work for the United States government as if everything was fine. Truth was, good people like her were needed in roles like the one she commanded. Emily Starks represented a light that could potentially guide others. Sean, however, knew he couldn't do it anymore. He'd left without a single regret about the decision, though there were still lingering doubts about the things he'd done before he joined Axis, and a few things he'd done after.

"The pope is the figurehead," Sean said. "The man could be firmly rooted in the doctrines and values of the church, and it wouldn't make any difference. He's the target of this...Berger's ambitions, his lust for revenge or justice or whatever he thinks it is."

"Correct," Wagner confirmed. "And he won't stop until he has what he wants: a unified front against the enemies of the church."

"And...who are these enemies? In his mind, I mean." Tommy asked.

"They're everywhere," Wagner answered. "He is obsessed with eliminating people of differing beliefs. Muslims. Atheists. Hindus. Buddhists. Anyone who isn't of the same faith will be an enemy to the grand master. Faith, however, is only a façade. It's the machine he will use to wreak havoc. The truth is, I believe all the man wants is to see the world in ashes. He hates it all." Wagner's words lingered in the air like smoke from incense.

"And he believes that the ring of John the Baptist will give him the authority to command a new Crusade against all of those who oppose what he thinks is right," Sean finished.

"Exactly."

The train slowed and pulled into the next station. There was a cluster of children standing on the platform with what looked like a chaperone, probably a schoolteacher. The kids were no older than eleven or twelve. Most had backpacks on their shoulders. Several were talking happily with each other. When the doors opened, the children got on the next car up, to Sean's relief. He didn't want to end the conversation just yet, and there was no faster way to end a serious conversation than loading up a bunch of schoolchildren into a confined space.

Even though the kids were in the next car, Sean could still hear their raucous laughter, their squealing, their chatter. He'd never wanted kids of his own. The world was messed up, a broken planet filled with evil people around every corner. Even those who seemed righteous or good often disappointed or ended up with some horrible secret. The pollution in the oceans, the political corruption scandals, and the outbreak of violent crime across most cities in the world—all of it was just too much for Sean to even consider having kids. While he thought he would enjoy playing baseball or soccer or basketball or football with a child of his own, all of the negatives far outweighed the positives, at least in his mind. Throw on top of all that the fact that he was never home, always traveling to some distant place, as well as finding trouble far more often than he'd prefer.

No, Sean and Adriana weren't ready to have kids just yet.

Right on cue, there was a scream from the other car, followed by a series of playful screams. Sean imagined a boy must have played a trick on one of the girls, perhaps with an insect he'd picked up outside.

He brought his attention back to the conversation as the train began to pull out of the station.

"How do you know about all this?" Sean asked pointedly. He'd been listening to Wagner talk about this Lucien Berger, the apparent grand master of the Teutonic Knights. The man seemed to know a great deal about the grand master, and Sean wanted to know how and why.

"An excellent question," Wagner said. "I would have been surprised if you hadn't asked that." He flashed a grin at Sean and went on. "Berger believed that all of us—the Hospitallers, my organization, and a few others—should band together. He wanted allies of a like mind. In his logic, he figured that we'd all been stripped of our rightful possessions, our status, everything. Truth be told, my order lost very little. We have never owned much in the way of property or material goods. Our existence is based on service to the church. We hunt down holy relics and return them to where they belong. The Hospitallers, on the other hand, lost much, as did the Templars. I don't think I have to remind you of what happened to them."

He didn't. Sean, Tommy, and Adriana were well aware of the Templar history, including some things that no one else knew outside of a tight collection of powerful people. The three knew about their centuries-long war with the Order of Assassins, how the Templars had been nearly exterminated in France so long ago when the pope and king conspired to take everything from them. It was a similar tale, according to what Wagner was saying, to the fate that befell the Teutonic Knights. Wagner hadn't mentioned anything about a mass execution, so that part was different, though the repossession of estates and money certainly mirrored what happened to the Templars.

"Lucien Berger recruited us, all of us," Wagner said. "He wanted all of the knights to unite against a common enemy and in an effort to find the ring of John the Baptist. He promised us great power and wealth if we agreed to help. We were to establish a new kingdom. He is even so delusional that he claimed his purpose was to bring about the New Jerusalem."

"From the Biblical prophecies?" Tommy asked.

"Indeed."

"I guess he read that part differently than I."

"Lucien is bent on revenge," Wagner said, reiterating the conclusion Sean had already reached. "He's bent on lashing out against a world that he believes wronged him, including the church. He thinks the church, too, has lost its way, and he is the shepherd to guide it back onto the righteous path. The truth is, the man's only desires are vengeance and power. I doubt there is any real spiritual reason behind anything he does or says. If there is, it's highly misguided."

"So," Adriana interrupted, "what should we do to stop him?"

Wagner turned to her. His eyes burned with the intensity of a gas fire. "You must find the ring, of course." He said it as though it was the simplest of tasks. "Lucien wants the ring, and if he gets it there is no question he will garner support from some of the other orders' leaders, if not all the orders entirely. My order will not rally to his cause because we know the truth about him. With the ring, however, he will claim that he is a new pope, the rightful ruler of the church. He will take back everything that was stolen from them centuries ago, and with an impassioned global following it will be like World War Two all over again."

"What do you mean?" Tommy asked. "Who will go to war?"

"Not the war," Sean answered for the man. "The Holocaust."

Wagner nodded solemnly. "Lucien is the kind of person who will begin systematically calling out those who are in opposition to what he believes are the true teachings of Christ and of the church. Personally, I don't believe any of it has to do with righteousness or bringing the gospel to the world. Christ never would have condoned anything that Lucien does, nor will do if he finds the ring. It is all about power for him. The more he has, the more he will try to bring the entire planet to its knees. In a way, he has similar goals to the very man who took the ring in the first place."

"Napoléon?" Adriana asked.

Wagner nodded. "Yes. Napoléon, too, believed the ring would give him great power, the ability and the right to claim all of Christendom as his own. With that kind of power, he believed, he could conquer the whole world. Allies from every Christian nation would rally to his cause. The only enemies he would have to vanquish would be the British and the Muslim nations. The campaign to Alexandria was one where he hoped he could accomplish both, weakening the trade and economies of those two enemies. He nearly succeeded, too, though the loss in the Battle of the Nile was a major setback and essentially ensured the French forces would never have full control of the area."

It was difficult to grasp the idea that someone, in modern times, would seek to control the entire planet. It was ridiculous to even think it. Or was it?

The grand scope would suggest the notion impossible. No single entity could rule the entire world and all its nations, continents, territories. Then again, it wasn't so long ago when a man from Braunau am Inn, Austria, rose to power in a nation ravaged by war and international sanctions. It didn't take much for Hitler to convince the German people that there was a single source for their misfortunes, for the injustices that were forced upon them.

He'd blamed the Jewish population, and as a result the nation rallied around him, forsaking logic and reason for rabid nationalism and racism. Six million Jews were executed during that time. Some were worked to death. Others were killed by any conceivable means possible. Either way, it was a mass execution, a genocide.

Sitting on the train, Sean realized that was less than a hundred years ago. The world was not that far removed from the Holocaust. There'd been others, too, in various countries since the fall of Nazi Germany. Cambodia came to mind. All it took was a fanatical leader who understood the pain of his people and could provide a salve for that pain, and a way to cut out the cause of it.

Sean's mind spun with the possibilities. He doubted anyone could ever claim every island, every corner of every jungle in the world, but wresting control of the civilized world was certainly possible if enough people joined the cause.

There were billions of Christians across the world. If unified under the banner of a madman, it was easy to see how their hearts and minds could be manipulated into thinking the problems of Earth were directly related to unbelievers.

"He wants a new Crusade," Sean realized out loud.

The others turned to him and stared.

"This Berger...he seeks to use a worldwide religious Crusade to regain power and to plant him at the top of it all. He would make himself the king or pope of everything."

"Or both," Bodmer chirped.

Wagner confirmed this suspicion with a nod. "Which means it is all the more important that you find the ring before he does."

"But...how can he find it if he doesn't have a clue where it is?" Tommy asked.

"Perhaps he does, and we are unaware. Either way, we must find the ring and return it to Malta. There, it will be safe and protected for all time."

Sean wasn't so sure about that. Napoléon had been able to steal it once. Why couldn't someone do that again? He decided to leave that question out of the discussion.

"Fine," Sean said. "We find the ring. Problem is we aren't sure what to do next."

"You found the three names, yes?"

The other four exchanged curious glances.

"How did you know about the three names?" Adriana pressed.

29

PARIS

L ucien walked over to the window of the hotel and looked out onto the street with cold, vapid eyes. The people walking down the sidewalks did not register to him, nor did the cars passing on the road. His mind was elsewhere.

He'd been carefully orchestrating things from his headquarters in Poland, but they had gone south quickly. His daughter was dead, her body found on the island of Saint Helena some hours ago. Her corpse was en route to Poland, where she would be prepared for burial by the knights.

They always took care of their dead. Part of that came from not fully trusting the funeral homes or morticians to respect the bodies. Knights were to be honored in life and in death. Lucien Berger's daughter would receive the highest respect he could bestow. For the time being, however, there was still the matter of the ring, and Lucien was not going to let emotions get in the way of the ultimate goal.

They lived by a strict set of rules, guidelines that had been in place for hundreds of years. Lucien didn't create the rules, but he certainly adhered to them, allowing them to illuminate his life's path every step of the way. One of the first rules he learned long ago was to never let emotions get in the way of the mission. There was another rule that warned against getting emotionally close to individuals or groups. Emotions had no place in war. They caused people to make poor decisions, rush into situations they could not survive or escape.

But even as Lucien reminded himself of that, he felt a tightening in his chest when the image of his daughter filtered into his vision. He winced and fought off the sudden wave of emotion.

Lucien redirected his thoughts to the task at hand. He had received word from two of his knights, and things were looking promising. They'd tracked down Sean Wyatt and his companions, cornering them in the little town of Villers-Cotterêts. The Americans visited a grave there, though Berger's men were unable to determine which grave, but that didn't matter now. Not after what had happened.

His men reported something troubling, something Berger should have anticipated. But how could he have? There were no signs that his old enemy was still alive, much less on the hunt for the ring.

He loathed the word. *Hunt.* Of the sacred orders, that one was, in Lucien's mind, the most unnecessary. That was putting his opinion mildly.

In their first years, perhaps they served some purpose. Back then, the church was scrambling to find whatever relics they could, and if the objects couldn't be located, substitutes were created as place-holders until the legitimate ones were discovered. Of course, Lucien knew that many of the placeholder relics were still being touted as the real thing to millions of unwary pilgrims.

Few knew that truth. His old nemesis, Bertrand Wagner, was one of the select. He had to be, though, considering his station. It was his job to find the authentic relics, if possible, and return them to where they belonged.

That last thought caused Berger to laugh out loud. Where they belonged. What that meant was where the church claimed they should be. Berger clenched his jaw in frustration. What authority did they have? They'd abandoned their ideals, their beliefs, the doctrines that had been preached to millions for thousands of years. They'd forsaken the very orders that had protected them.

The knights had given Christianity an empire, and what was their reward? Exile. Humiliation. Poverty. Death.

Hardly justice.

Berger knew what Bertrand Wagner was up to. The man's objective was simple enough to deduce: Wagner was looking for the ring so he could return it to Malta, to the church in Valletta from where Napoléon stole it over two hundred years prior.

Wonderful idea, Berger mused. *Take the ring back to the place where it was stolen.* He scoffed at the ridiculous notion.

The church and the people of faith who managed it had already proved themselves incapable of protecting such an important and powerful relic. Returning the ring to Valletta would be a colossal mistake.

There was, however, another reason Berger could not allow the ring to return to its island home in the Mediterranean.

Napoléon stole the artifact because he'd heard of the legend surrounding the ring of John the Baptist. While he wasn't one to be given to superstition, Napoléon was also a philosopher and an advocate of science. He understood that there were many things in the universe that man had been unable to explain through logic, reason, and experimentation. Those things, the general believed, were possibly supernatural. That open-minded approach caused Napoléon to occasionally dip his toes into the metaphysical, and even the superstitious.

It was by pure accident that Napoléon had learned about the power the ring possessed. Initially, he merely sought the relic because of its heritage and the prestige it would bring. The general also believed that if he had the ring of the Baptist, no one anywhere in the Christian world could dispute his authority as emperor. He would be unquestioned and could unite the Christian world against all others. Not because he was so devout to his religion. He was a game player, a master manipulator. It was one of the reasons he ordered his men to respect people of all beliefs when they ventured into foreign lands.

Lulling the enemy into a false sense of security was one of the more powerful tactics Napoléon had adopted during his reign. His military prowess grew. He was feared in every nation across Europe, from the grandest throne room to the humblest tavern. No one believed Napoléon could be defeated.

Unfortunately for him, the general soon realized that bearing the ring of John the Baptist didn't just bring great fortune.

He felt hollow, discontented. With every victory, he grew more bitter, almost to the point of anger. He felt his energy being sapped, his life essence being sucked out of his body.

His officers grew concerned and worried the general might die before they completed their conquest. This illness was not one that received a great deal of documentation, but Lucien knew about it. He possessed one of the few letters containing information about the general's malady and his subsequent remedy.

Napoléon took the ring from his finger and gave it to one of his men. He ordered him to hide it and gave specific instructions as to how and where it should be taken.

Later in his life, Napoléon would resurrect the relic, but when people around him started getting sick and dying, he decided the effects of the object were too dangerous. With a heavy heart, he put it in hiding once again, leaving it to be discovered someday by someone who would know what to do with it and how to control it.

The ring of the Baptist, it seemed, came with a blessing and a curse.

Berger didn't care about either. The only thing he wanted the ring to do was give him total power. He could declare himself the true pope and usurp the power of the church for himself.

He scoffed internally at the idea of the church. While he was a religious man, one who still believed in the tenets of Catholicism, he felt no true loyalty to the organization. It had conspired with secular rulers to bring about the downfall of the order. His order.

Berger found himself in a tricky situation in which he believed strongly in the doctrines and teachings of the church but held on to bitter...resentment. That was the only way he could describe it. He hated what had been done to his order, to the men who were so much like him hundreds of years before, merely performing a task that was set before them with honor and perseverance. They served their church and their kingdoms with fierce loyalty, and for what: To have everything they earned, everything they built, ripped away from them by greedy monarchs and a paranoid pontiff?

The church had turned its back on him and his order. Until he came along, there was no one who'd been able to find a way to right the wrongs. They'd been slowly building up their resources over the decades—centuries, even—always waiting and watching for the right moment to emerge from the shadows once again.

Now, they were closer than ever before to uncovering the one thing that would right all the wrongs. Berger had waited for this day, as had the grand masters before him. Each of his predecessors hoped they would be the one to lead the order back to its prior greatness. It seemed the burden was Berger's, though, and he felt honored to bear it.

With the ring of the Baptist, he could wage a new Crusade against the enemies of God.

Things weren't going according to plan, though Berger knew life rarely did.

Wyatt and company were on their way back to Paris. He knew where they were going based on the information he'd received from his man in Villers-Cotterêts. Berger was...disappointed that the targets were able to escape. That should never have happened, despite the circumstances.

The surviving knight would have to be dealt with, though Berger would be merciful. He'd always been understanding with those who served under him. It was one of the reasons they were so loyal. He walked the walk, which was why he was here, in Paris, to oversee the final leg of this centuries-long journey.

Wyatt was close to finding the ring. Berger could feel it. Perhaps Wyatt's survival thus far had been divinely orchestrated, a blessing from above as the Almighty pulled strings one way and the other. Berger convinced himself that was the case, that God himself was doing all of this for the benefit of his most fiercely loyal warriors.

Berger arrived in Paris earlier that morning, choosing a hotel close to the Champs-Élysées. It was a location he loved in the grand old city. He'd stayed there on many occasions in the past. While some may have looked down on his frivolous spending on the lavish hotel suite, he was the grand master and by rights should afford himself a few luxuries from time to time.

Besides, it was in a central location and within view of the Arc de Triomphe. Now, more than ever, he believed his choice of accommodations to be fitting. A monument to Napoléon and his victories, the Arc de Triomphe was now a perpetual reminder to Berger of what had to be done to right the wrong of the brash general. Napoléon had stolen the ring.

Now Lucien Berger was going to get it back.

Wyatt and his friends were on their way to Paris via train. Berger would make certain they received the welcome they were due.

30

VILLERS-COTTERÊTS

W agner's eyes narrowed and his lips creased in a grin, as if looking into the face of an innocent child.

"My dear," he said, "we have been searching for this ring for over a century. We've seen the names on the document on Saint Helena. Unfortunately, that is where our trail ends. I can point you to the graves in Père Lachaise. That will save you time—considering it is an immense cemetery."

"So, you've been to the graves. The one we just left, as well?" Tommy jerked a thumb to the back of the train.

"Yes, though we have been to many graves. You, however, were the first to discover the clue at the Château de Malmaison; not that it would have helped us much. We discovered the document on Saint Helena but could not figure out how it was related to the ring, or what the names meant. We looked them up, of course, but were unable to decode anything from the monuments. We tried everything we could think of—mathematical sequences from the dates on the headstones, mixing the letters from the names to form new words. None of it was helpful, and in the end we failed."

"You learn more from failure than success," Sean quipped.

"Indeed. And those are wise words to live by," Wagner said. "In this case, however, failure means a crazy person will begin a new world-wide Crusade that will tear apart all of civilization."

"When you put it that way," Sean snorted a laugh.

Tommy's face twisted into a frown. "And you think we are going to be able to make the connection, figure out the code that you and your...order could not? I honestly don't see how that's possible. You guys would be some of the best in the world—if everything you're saying is true."

"It is true. And we are some of the best code breakers and mystery solvers on the planet. This one, however, has vexed us."

Tommy slumped back in his seat and turned his head toward the window. He watched as they passed by a farmhouse. Fields of golden grain waved around the building. In the distance, up on a lush green hill, the ruins of a gray stone castle stood watching over the region, probably the former seat of a duchy or barony, perhaps a regional kingdom from long ago.

Wagner looked around at the other faces. He could see that his words produced a significant amount of doubt.

"There is no sense in worrying about it," he added. "Worry solves nothing."

Sean chuckled. "I used to tell people that all the time. Is worry helping or hurting, I would ask. It's never helpful."

"Precisely," Wagner agreed. "Now, we will be in Paris soon. Tell me what you found that led you to the names of Napoléon's three officers."

The others exchanged uncertain glances.

The looks were not lost on Wagner. "I don't purport to know anything other than you four would not have come to Villers-Cotterêts had you not discovered something at Napoléon's château."

Their expressions didn't change with his explanation.

And so, Wagner continued. "And yes, I have been following you since you arrived in Paris, which you know since Sean spotted me." At that, Wagner sounded a touch embarrassed.

Sean wondered how he'd figured they would go to Paris, but that question would lead to the same answers. Bertrand Wagner had considerable resources behind him, not to mention that it sounded like his order was the only one that managed to escape the wrath of a king or pope. They were still active, still working to find holy items for the church. Wagner's order was, in many ways, similar to the IAA. They were both dedicated to safely recovering and restoring priceless artifacts. From what Wagner said, he and his order also spent a good amount of time following clues and solving riddles.

Those things they had in common still didn't prove this man was who he said he was. In fact, Sean suddenly realized that bringing him along was a huge safety risk. They were all putting a tremendous amount of trust in a person they'd just met within the last hour, and who had pretended to be holding them at gunpoint.

That last piece actually did set Sean's mind at ease, at least a little. If the guy was a real threat, he would have produced a real weapon, and he could have killed Sean when he had the chance.

"We found a clue in Napoléon's library," Sean said, deciding to go with his gut. He would trust the man until he proved that trust unfounded. "That's why we were arrested."

"Yes. I knew about the arrest," Wagner said, stroking the stubble on his chin. "I wasn't able to figure out why you were arrested."

"Vandalism," Tommy added. "We...moved some things in Napoléon's library, things that, apparently, hadn't been moved in a few hundred years."

Wagner's right eyebrow rose. He stared at Tommy for what felt like half an hour. "You...you vandalized Napoléon's study?" There was a lull, and then the man broke out in a full belly laugh.

Tommy looked at the others in an attempt to figure out what was so funny, but everyone else appeared just as confused.

It was Sean who first realized what the man thought was so hysterical.

"Oh, no, we didn't paint graffiti or anything like that in the general's study," he explained. "We pulled back a rug and then pulled up a section of the floor. That's where we found the clue. It was in a wooden box."

Wagner slowed his laughter and met Sean's gaze. The older man's eyes were full of tears from laughing, but he managed to pull it together as he realized the situation wasn't what he'd imagined.

"You...you found something in the study?"

"We did," Sean confessed. "And in that box was the clue that led us to the cemetery in Villers-Cotterêts.

Wagner thought for a moment, glancing down at the floor to collect his thoughts. He had so many questions, but he narrowed them down to just one. "What did the clue say?" he hedged.

"It gave the names of the three men you already know of," Tommy answered. "It talked about their eternal sacrifice or victory or something." Tommy knew exactly what it said, but he wasn't going to give away all the details yet. This man, Wagner, was part of an old, secret organization. Someone with those kinds of secrets and that sort of pedigree could be trouble, and they'd only met the guy that day. Tommy could tell from the look in Sean's eyes that he didn't fully trust the man, either, but didn't distrust him enough to part ways. Not yet.

The kids squealed again in the next car. The noise disrupted the conversation for a moment. Off in the distance, the Eiffel Tower climbed into the sky. It was one of the first things that could be seen on the train ride back into the city and signaled the journey to Paris was nearly over.

"So, we are all on the same footing now," Wagner said.

"Unless you are keeping something from us," Adriana said with suspicion in her voice.

"No," Wagner said offhandedly. "If I had more information, I would have probably already located the ring and delivered it safely to Malta."

It was a fair point but one that also showed the man was still on the hunt. His desire was to return the ring to the cathedral in Valletta. If that was the proper place for the object to go, Tommy and Sean wouldn't have a problem with it. They would need to fact-check everything first to make sure Wagner's story was true, but if the ring came from Valletta, then that was where it needed to be.

Sean pulled out his phone and sent a quick text message to Alex. The message was meant to be a request for information about the missing ring of Valletta, but what he got instead was an immediate return phone call.

"Hello?" Sean said, putting the phone to his ear. Then it hit him. Alex and Tara had been out of communication with them for...what was it, a day or two? Sean was losing track of time and what day it was. He rubbed his temples, one with a finger and the other with a thumb.

"Sean, thank goodness. We were out of cell range. Did you get the picture I sent?"

"We did," Sean said. "It helped. We're still investigating those names."

"Okay, good." Alex sounded relieved. "Our signal was really bad on Saint Helena."

"Are you two okay?"

"Yes. We...we had a run-in with a couple of assassins."

Sean's heart skipped a beat and he stood up, took two long steps away from the group, and lowered his voice. "What do you mean assassins?"

"We don't know that," Tara said in the background.

"They were trying to kill us," Alex said, now arguing with his young wife.

"That doesn't mean they were assassins."

"Guys," Sean interrupted. He looked back at the group. Every pair of eyes was staring at him, so he took another step away, lowering his voice again. "Guys, seriously. Someone tried to kill you?"

"Oh, sorry. Yes. A man and a woman were shooting at us, but your training came through, Sean. We took them down. Well, one of them, anyway. The female. The other one, he escaped. We left the island before the police showed up or before anyone could find the body."

"You...just left it there?"

"Um...yes?" Alex answered with uncertainty.

"No one saw what happened?" Sean pressed.

"No. We don't think so. We went back to Cape Town and tried to find the other gunman, but we couldn't locate him or his boat. We had...plane trouble."

Sean wasn't sure what that meant, but he figured it had something to do with the old plane they were no doubt chartering. Most of the readily available pilots in Cape Town were flying airplanes that should have been retired long ago. It was all they could afford, though, and many of these pilots found that a little duct tape here and some grease there could save them a good amount of money on a new rig.

"Do you know who they were?" Sean asked. "Who they were working for?" He had a feeling he already knew, but asking for some confirmation wasn't a bad idea.

"No clue," Alex said. "We got out of there pretty fast."

"You're safe now, though?"

"Yeah, we think so. We're actually in Portugal right now. Once we got back to Cape Town and couldn't find the other shooter, we decided it would be safer to leave than stick around in a town we didn't know."

"Okay, that's good thinking," Sean said. He admitted it: Their strategy was sound. If he'd been in the same situation, he wouldn't have ruled out the possibility of retreating to another country where he could reset the game and figure out his next move. He'd done that before when he knew a fight was one he couldn't win. "You two lie low for now."

Sean's voice grew quieter as he took the volume down to just above a whisper. "I need you to find out all you can about a ring from a church in Malta. Look at the text I sent you. I need this pretty fast if you can manage it."

"Sure thing, Sean. We're at a nice place. Their internet isn't as fast as ours, but its fine for ordinary people."

Sean chuckled. "Okay, cool. Figure out what you can and text me." He took another wayward glance at Wagner to make sure the man couldn't hear what he was about to say. "The main thing I need is to know if the story is legit or not. Anything else is a bonus."

"Sure thing, Sean." It was an unusual request for more than one reason, but Alex knew he and Tara could figure it out.

"Thanks. Speak soon."

Sean ended the call and slid the phone back in his pocket as he stepped back over to his seat.

"That was Alex," he said. "They got off Saint Helena safely but said their cell service wasn't great out there."

"I can imagine. That's probably why we couldn't get ahold of them before," Tommy said with a nod. "That island is way out in the middle of the ocean. It's extremely isolated. I imagine getting supplies must be expensive for the people who live there."

"Indeed."

"So, why are my two assistants calling you instead of me?" Tommy asked. There was a hint of joking in his voice but also genuine curiosity.

"Maybe they like me better than you," Sean jabbed.

Tommy snorted, and a big grin swept over his face. "Probably."

"I'm sorry to interrupt this little moment," Bodmer said, "but we are still in danger." He looked around, taking in the surroundings before continuing. "We're trapped here on this train. You realize that, yes?"

"I know," Sean managed. "And there's also the problem that they probably know where we're heading."

"Of course they know," Bodmer blurted. The man hadn't been talkative until that moment. It caught everyone in the group off guard except for Sean. He remained unflinching. "This train goes straight to Paris."

"There are other stops along the way," Sean pointed out.

"Sure, but the men who tried to kill us aren't going to simply sit around and wait. We left one of them alive back there."

"There was no getting around that."

"I know, but my point is he will call someone. The second we get off this train in Paris, there will be more just like him waiting to grab us."

"No doubt about it," Sean said casually.

"You don't seem concerned." Bodmer's tone softened as his curiosity spiked.

"Because we're not going to get off the train in Paris."

"We aren't?"

Sean's head turned one time. "No. We're getting off two stops away from the main train station. From there, we can take other transportation to Père Lachaise and lose the tails that way."

Bodmer inclined his head as he considered what Sean was saying. "So we're going to let them think we're taking the train all the way into Paris."

"Exactly. They'll have the cavalry waiting for us on the platform, or maybe by the exits, ready to nab us. But we'll be gone, and they won't be the wiser."

Bodmer's head began to bob as he grasped the plan. "Yes. That is a good idea. While they're wasting time looking for us, we can investigate the other two graves."

"There you go." Sean leaned back in his seat and crossed his arms as if in triumph.

"That might work," Bodmer admitted.

"I hope it does," Wagner chimed. "Everything is riding on this."

"Everything?" Adriana asked.

"If Berger is able to get to the ring before us, it could have catastrophic consequences. That relic, in the eyes of billions of believers, could signify that he is the rightful leader of the church. He will command legions of followers who will rally to his cause."

"And what cause is that?" Tommy asked.

"Getting back what was taken from the order is only one part of Berger's deranged plan."

"The other?"

Wagner sighed. "He wants to begin a new Crusade, a new campaign to bring the entire religious world under one banner. His banner."

"It won't work," Tommy countered. "There's no way he could garner that much support."

"You underestimate the power of religious fervor. You don't have to look far to see the atrocities that have been carried out in the name of religion, even today in our so-called modern era. People get swept up in things. Their emotions are played. Once Berger shows the ring to the world, much of Christianity will believe it to be a sign that he is a messenger from God, if not the rightful ruler of a new Heavenly Kingdom on Earth."

The older man may have been playing things up just a tad, but Sean knew he was right. If the relic they were looking for really was the ring of John the Baptist, and it could be verified in any way, this Lucien Berger would wield unimaginable power. Billions would believe every word that dripped from his lips.

Another thought occurred to Sean. It was in reference to something Wagner mentioned before. If the ring held some kind of mystical power, it would not only be a symbolic relic but one far more dangerous.

"Wagner," Sean said, his attention abruptly going back to the man. "You're keeping something from us."

The rest of the group looked surprised. Was there something Sean knew that the others didn't? Their eyes shifted to Sean, but his gaze was locked on Wagner. He was holding the man in his seat, as if Sean's stare possessed the power to turn a person into stone.

Tommy worried Sean had just offended the man, a man whose help they could probably use in solving the murder of Cardinal Jarllson, plus the mystery of the missing ring.

"Am I?" Wagner spoke softly. His lips barely twitched, and the words came out like a poison.

Sean didn't allow the man to play coy for long. A threatening glare set Wagner straight.

"You've been playing a good game," Sean commented, letting his guard sag for a moment. He visibly relaxed, his shoulders slumping and cheeks drawing out ever so slightly. "I believe everything you've said, by the way. Just putting it out there."

Wagner didn't move.

"But," Sean raised a finger that went only slightly higher than the pitch of his voice, "there is something you're hiding. I want to know what it is. What is it about this ring that is so important? It's not just a relic or some holy object. It's more than just a symbol. Isn't it?"

Wagner chewed on his response for what seemed like minutes. He knew there would be no lying to Wyatt. The man was cunning, clever, and far too observant to miss even the slightest misdirection.

None of the others had bothered to ask the question. They likely believed everything he'd told them. There was no reason to think otherwise.

Wyatt, though, was a different animal.

Wagner had been holding back the second piece of truth regarding the ring because stopping a madman should have been reason enough for anyone to pitch in and help out. Now, however, he could see he'd have to spill the rest.

"Legends suggest that the ring possesses certain...supernatural powers."

Adriana's was the first eyebrow to rise. "Supernatural?"

Wagner drew in a deep breath through his nostrils. "Yes. Some legends say that whoever wears the ring shall obtain immortality. Others posit that the bearer of the ring will be granted tremendous strength and military might. There are even a few who believed whoever wears the ring will be able to resurrect the dead."

Sean's brow furrowed, but it was Bodmer who spoke first.

"Immortality? Superhuman strength? Resurrection of the dead? John the Baptist died. He was not a warrior. He never resurrected the dead, not that we know of." There was disdain in Bodmer's voice. "It sounds like a bard's tale."

Wagner shrugged. "Like I said, they're legends. Perhaps they're not true. Or maybe they are. Either way, we cannot let Berger get to the ring. If he does, even if the ring possesses no mystical powers, what it represents to the people will be enough to throw the planet into chaos. Lucien Berger must not get his hands on the ring of John the Baptist."

The train began to slow again as it proceeded into the next station. Off in the distance, the Eiffel Tower loomed larger with every passing second. And so did danger.

"I guess we'll have to work faster," Tommy said. "When we get to Père Lachaise, we should split up."

31

PÈRE LACHAISE CEMETERY - PARIS

After a cab ride that took longer than it should have, the group stood just outside the gates of the main entrance to Père Lachaise. Sean noted the reliefs carved into the exterior of the gate. Each side of the opening was adorned with a sort of column, both rising to the height of the stone wall that encircled the cemetery. Stone torches occupied each corner of the columns. The most fascinating (and depressing), Sean thought, were the hourglasses engraved into the curved tops of the columns. The hourglasses were higher than the wall and a stark reminder that every person only has a finite amount of time in life. That was how Sean interpreted it. Right or wrong, it impressed him in a sad way.

He'd always known that someday he would die. He'd been close more times than he cared to recount. He noted the wings that were set in the background of the hourglasses as he and the others passed through the gate and into the cemetery.

Once inside, they stepped out of the main thoroughfare and surveyed their surroundings.

Sean didn't like the idea of splitting up as Tommy had suggested on the train, though he also realized his friend's assessment was probably the right course of action. "Sounds an awful lot like a bunch of movies and cartoon series I've seen," he offered. "Doesn't usually end up well for most people when they split up in a situation like this."

"I agree," Bodmer said. "Dividing forces in favor of speed may not be the best decision."

"Then we stay together and waste valuable time," Wagner countered. "Either way, there is risk."

Sean nodded and took charge. "We'll split up. But keep your phones unlocked and be ready to answer if you get a call." He cast a wayward glance at Wagner. It was a look that told the man Sean was giving him the benefit of the doubt. "Adriana, come with me. Tommy, you mind going with those two?"

Tommy's lips curled as they often did when he was trying to express that something was okay. "Not at all. Someone's got to take care of them." He slapped Bodmer on the back, but the commander didn't seem to care for the joke. Or maybe he missed it completely. Either way, he offered no laughter, not even the slightest crease of his lips.

The man, for the most part, had been a bore to bring along on the trip. Tommy figured it was merely his nature. Years of training and tremendous responsibility at the Vatican certainly would have taken a toll on anyone. Perhaps he was simply hardened from that and only sought to complete his duty. *All business*, Tommy figured.

"You three take Masséna," Sean said. "We will go to the Augereau grave."

The others nodded.

Sean held a map he had procured from the information desk on the way in. The glossy paper flapped in the gentle summer breeze. The smell of flowers filled the air and washed over the visitors in an array of scents that ranged from the extremely sweet to the nearly pungent and bitter. It was an odd contrast: so much life flourishing amid so much death.

"Looks like we go this way," Sean said after only a few seconds of analyzing the map. "You guys go that direction. Call me when you're there, and let me know if you find anything."

"If?" Tommy asked, sounding a little cocky. "It's here. The rest of the clue has to be in this cemetery. Be sure to take pictures of the headstone when you find it. That way, we can compare everything when we find a place to sit down and work."

Sean inclined his head for a second. Then he gave a word of warning, not that his friend needed it. Sean would be remiss if he didn't.

"Keep your head on a swivel, Schultzie. There is still the guy from before, and I'm certain he or whoever is behind this won't take long to figure out what happened, if they haven't figured it out already."

"Yes," Bodmer added, checking the pistol tucked into his hip holster. "We must stay vigilant. Clearly, these people will stop at nothing to get to the relic before us."

The man's comments were one of the first outward displays of leadership that Sean had seen since meeting the man. There was a fuel behind his words, a slow-burning diesel that flickered in his eyes. Sean wondered what his true motivation could be. He knew Bodmer held on to a firm sense of duty and honor. That much was clear, but Sean pondered how much of the man's intense desire to track down Jarllson's killer was for revenge and how much was for justice. It was still unclear if the two had been friends before Jarllson's untimely demise. Maybe it didn't matter—as long as the man was helping them.

Tommy led the other two down a path that branched off from the main one, while Sean and Adriana took another going in the opposite direction.

Père Lachaise's massive footprint occupied 110 acres and sprawled out in what—to the untrained eye—might have appeared to be a chaotic layout. Huge headstones and monuments, tombs, crypts, and stone caskets covered the landscape, some lined up in neat rows while others pointed at odd angles opposite to their neighbors. A dense row of trees laid out the boundary of the property along with the massive stone wall that lined the perimeter. More trees dotted the walkways, some between graves and others planted along the paths. A denser patch of forest occupied the center of the cemetery, providing a natural and relaxing feel to the somber resting place of so many. Sean found it hard to believe that in 1804 this place only had thirteen tenants. Now, it was bursting to the point of overflowing. Celebrities from all over the world wanted to be buried in the famous confines of the cemetery, though from what Sean had heard it was easier to get a cheap apartment in Manhattan.

Even as he constantly scanned their surroundings, Sean couldn't help but think of the one grave he wanted to see. He'd been a fan of The Doors in high school and knew that Jim Morrison's final resting place was somewhere nearby—so close he could almost hear it calling to him. In the back of his mind, he kept the exact location of the singer's marker dangling like a carrot over a mule: division 6, row 2, grave number 5.

Sean sloughed off the thought and refocused on the mission. So close yet so far. Maybe after they were done, he and Adriana could return to this place.

He sighed and kept walking, passing the lane he knew would lead to Jim Morrison's tomb.

Adriana's eyes darted in every direction and she constantly turned to look over her shoulder, wary that someone could be following them. With so many visitors to the famous cemetery, it was going to be a task to try to single out suspicious characters. People were everywhere, not that Adriana blamed them. She'd toured the cemetery before and considered it to be one of serene beauty, a source of calm in the storm that was cosmopolitan Paris. The world spun chaotically all around, but in Père Lachaise there was peace, a stillness that filled the soul of every person who walked the cobbled lanes.

Sean and Adriana walked at a steady pace, not wanting to look like they were in a hurry but also well aware that time was potentially against them. No one else in the cemetery appeared to be in a hurry to get anywhere. It wasn't that kind of place. Time was forgotten there; for the tenants it had ceased to exist.

The couple made their way around a curve that was lined with tall monuments and crypts. Some of the headstones were bizarre.

They saw one that featured a man's likeness lying on his back, hands raised slightly over his torso and holding another man's face.

Père Lachaise was known for such oddities and drew a strong contingent of its millions of annual visitors who simply came for the bizarre.

Sean recalled their destination in his mind. He'd memorized the names of the little pathways and boulevards they would need to take to reach the grave of Pierre Augereau. He knew exactly where to go, as far as an overhead map view was concerned, but being there in person was different. He likened it to watching an American football game from the nosebleed seats versus being down on the sidelines. It was a different world, especially when surrounded by thousands of monuments. He'd read that the cemetery contained the remains of around one million people. The number was mind-numbing, but as he and Adriana continued down a path that branched off to the right, he could believe it. He'd never in his life seen a place like this. Most cemeteries in the United States were spread out, giving at least a little space between occupants. Then again, the older cemeteries, such as in Boston or Charleston, were much more like this one, smaller but with graves closer to one another.

He snapped his head to the left at the sight of a sudden movement. His right hand instinctively reached to his hip. Sean's thumb rested on the back of the weapon's grip as he watched. He unconsciously slowed his pace, too, and fixed his gaze on the rows of gravestones and crypts that climbed up a short rise—like a staircase of sadness.

A squirrel's head appeared over one of the monuments as it climbed up and perched itself next to the cross that adorned its top. The creature looked around suspiciously and then began gnawing on an acorn.

Sean's hand dropped back down to his side as he exhaled. Adriana had detected his sudden concern and focused her attention on whatever had caught Sean's. She also watched their backs, making sure no one was flanking them.

"Squirrel," Sean muttered.

Adriana narrowed her eyes, sweeping the area one more time before continuing down the path.

Getting to the grave of Pierre Augereau took less than two minutes after the squirrel incident.

The tomb stood out among those surrounding it. The structure was tall and thin with a steeply angled roof. The narrow doorway was blocked with an iron gate. An ornately carved crest loomed over the opening. A cluster of hardwood trees stood behind the division of graves, framing the space with a touch of peace the likes of which only nature could provide.

Sean looked around and then shuffled between two graves so he could reach the row where Augereau was laid to rest. Adriana followed behind, still checking their surroundings as she moved. She made no sound, though the breeze and the rustling of the trees around them would have prevented anyone from hearing much.

Sean stepped close to the crypt's entrance and peered inside. He glanced over his right shoulder, then his left, to ensure no one was watching, then took his phone in his left hand and turned on the flashlight. He pointed it into the darkness beyond the tomb's door and peered through the iron gate. Sean noted the stone vault that contained the man's remains and then scanned the walls for anything of note.

Pierre Augereau had risen to the rank of marshal under Napoléon Bonaparte and was one of the general's most trusted officers. Augereau died when he was fifty-eight years old, several years before Napoléon's passing. Despite the man's rank and his good standing with Napoléon, the tomb appeared relatively ordinary aside from the fact it was a small building compared to the in-ground graves surrounding it. There was nothing ostentatious about it, no wreaths or crowns or visages to glory that would be expected of an honored warrior.

There was none of that, only the man's name and the dates of his birth and death. Sean furrowed his brow and scratched the back of his head. He'd had a bad feeling prior to coming to the cemetery. That concern proved itself right before his eyes with a glaring lack of evidence that any kind of clue was going to present itself at this man's grave.

Adriana moved close, like a wraith hovering nearby. "Do you see anything?"

He knew what she meant. Was there an object, a word, anything that could be construed as useful in their search for the lost relic?

"No," Sean said. "Have a look."

He passed his phone to her and stepped back so she could peer into the darkness of the crypt. She turned the light one way, then the other, pointed it at the ceiling and then at the floor. Adriana came to the same conclusion.

"What do you think?" she asked, handing the device back to him.

"I think it's just what I was worried about. There's nothing here."

"So you weren't merely doing that for effect back in Villers-Cotterêts?"

Sean shook his head dejectedly. "Only partially," he admitted. "But I felt like we were missing something. I can't put my finger on it."

Adriana looked at him with pity in her eyes. He was too hard on himself sometimes—most times, if she was honest. Sean bore the weight of being the one with the answers, the one who could solve problems with his mind or his fists. He was, in her eyes, the ultimate hero, and she loved him for it. She wondered, even though he'd never said anything about it, if that pressure was taking its toll.

His phone vibrated in his palm and took away any opportunity to say something about what he was thinking or feeling.

Sean expected to see Tommy's number appear on the screen, but it was Tara.

"Hey, Tara," Sean said, keeping his voice low so as not to attract attention from other visitors. There were only a few walking by in that part of the cemetery, but he wasn't only lowering his tone for their benefit. They were, after all, in a cemetery.

"Hello, Sean. You guys back in Paris?"

"Yes. We're at Père Lachaise as we speak."

"Find anything interesting there?"

"I've never been here before, so it's all interesting."

"I always wanted to visit that place but haven't had the chance yet. Maybe I can take a little time off soon and get Alex off his rear to fly over there with me."

Sean smirked. "Sounds like you have a plan."

"I do," Tara said cheerfully. "I also have some information for you on the...artifact you asked about."

Sean appreciated that she was savvy enough to keep things vague on the phone, especially a mobile phone.

"Hit me."

"It's an interesting story, actually. According to what we found, Napoléon did visit Valletta on the island of Malta during his Alexandria Campaign. He took something like thirty thousand troops, ten thousand sailors, and sailed from the South of France to Malta, laid siege to the city there, and then proceeded to invade the place. There was some fighting there between Napoléon's forces and the Knights of Malta, also known as the Hospitallers."

Sean already knew all of this, but he let her continue. It was, after all, what he'd asked Alex and Tara to do.

She continued. "It was difficult to find any evidence about the story with Napoléon stealing the ring, though." Sean felt his heart sink for a second. "But we did find a couple of citations about it."

Sean's hope returned as quickly as it had left, his breath catching in his chest. "What?"

"There were some old texts, books that were probably scanned in the old-fashioned way a long time ago, like when they used to do that microfiche stuff for libraries back in the day."

"It wasn't that long ago," Sean countered.

Tara chuckled. "Easy there, old timer. You don't have to get defensive. I'm not judging, but yes, it was a long time ago. Like a couple of decades, at least."

Sean rolled his eyes, but she wasn't wrong. It had been a couple of decades since he'd been in the library at the University of Tennessee. That was one of the last times he'd seen microfiche.

He swallowed his pride and got back on track. "So, you were saying you found something about the ring story?"

"Oh yes. There were a couple of references to it in some historical texts. But here's the thing." She paused for effect. "Those texts are not available anywhere."

"What do you mean they're not available anywhere?"

"Just what I said. You can't find those books in any library. The site where I saw them was an underground history website that posts stuff like that. It took quite a bit of searching, but we were able to use the quantum computers back in the lab to speed things up."

"I thought you were in Portugal."

"We are. Haven't you heard of doing things remotely?" Her voice hit a sarcastic pitch at the end of the sentence.

"Ha ha," Sean blathered. "So, these books—where are they?"

"No one knows. They were scanned and uploaded to the archive of this website and one other that operates similarly. Both sites are kind of dumping grounds for all kinds of historical information. Most of it is useless, but there are some nuggets in there that are priceless, and in this case exactly what we needed."

So, that was their secret. Alex and Tara used some kind of secret conspiracy theory forum to extract information. He had to admit: It was better than just doing a simple Google search. The way she spoke about this mystery website made him wonder if there was more to it than she let on, as in maybe she and Alex were the site's creators.

He decided not to dive into that rabbit hole for the time being. It wasn't pertinent, and he had a mystery to solve.

"So, these records," Sean said, "they're legit?"

"Looks like it. I'd say that what we saw corroborates the story that Napoléon visited Valletta and stole a ring from what is believed to be the hand of John the Baptist. Does that help you at all?"

"Definitely," Sean said. "It's a big help. Now we know we're not out here on some wild goose chase."

"Yeah, the story seems to be legitimate. Good luck the rest of the way. You guys aren't getting into too much trouble, are you?"

It was Sean's turn to chuckle. "Nothing we can't handle."

"That's what I'm worried about."

Sean was about to end the call when a thought occurred to him. "Hey, Tara?"

"Yes?"

"There wasn't anything unusual about the list of names you sent us from Saint Helena, was there? I mean, we saw the pictures, but sometimes little details don't come through on digital images. Know what I'm saying?"

"Yeah, I get what you're saying. It can be frustrating, especially so with old documents."

"Right. So, did you happen to notice anything odd about the document with the names?"

A brief pause of silence slid into the conversation like an evening fog slithering through a forest.

"No, not really."

Sean bit back the disappointment.

"Other than the fact that it was just a list of three random...people?"

"Yes, they were officers in Napoléon's army."

"Oh, okay. Well no, then. I don't suppose there was anything odd about it. There was the image of a rose at the bottom."

Sean knew that didn't mean much. They'd already been to the famous rose garden château and come up with the clue that led them to this moment. Visiting the tomb of Joséphine yielded nothing. As far as Sean could figure, the rose was simply a symbol that tied things together but had no bearing on the next step in the mystery.

He sighed in frustration. "Nah, I don't think the flower has anything to do with all this. I don't know what I was getting at by asking. I guess maybe there could have been some faded writing, invisible ink—cliché, I know—or like a combination of words or letters that seemed off." He snorted. "Then again, we could have seen that on the photo."

Sean was about to tell her goodbye again when Tara's voice cut him off. "Well, there was one thing I thought was strange, but I figured it was nothing. We both did, actually."

32

PÈRE LACHAISE

A familiar feeling crept into Sean's mind. He'd always been one to get his hopes up, in regard to pretty much everything. Usually, that ended in disappointment.

"The spacing on the list," Tara went on, "there was something off about it. We both figured it was nothing because it wasn't like they were using lined notebook paper or legal pads, but I guess if there was anything off about the document, that would be it."

"Margins," Sean muttered. That was all he had to go on? An incorrectly margined piece of parchment? Then he stiffened. "Wait. You said the spacing was off? Tell me again. What was wrong with it?"

"You can see it for yourself if you still have the images. "There's a little more space between two of the names. I can't remember which two, but I could look it up for you if you give me a second."

"No, that's not necessary," Sean said. "I have the images. I can probably see the difference."

"Well, we thought it was strange. Based on the spacing between the other names, it looks like maybe a name was missing?" She spoke as if she was uncertain, a question more than a statement of fact. "Yeah, now that I think about it, that's it. You could have fit another name in there."

"But there was none?"

"No," Tara said. "We sent you the image. There was no other document like that."

Sean looked up at Adriana, who'd drawn near. She stared him in the eyes. It was easy to tell the gears were churning through the two windows into his mind. Sean was on to something, and her ears tuned out nearly every other ambient sound to focus on his end of the conversation.

"Which means a fourth name was left out."

"Possibly, although we may never know what name. I honestly don't know how I would go about trying to find the fourth one."

A fourth name. That was the answer all along, not some coded message on the tombstones or some mathematical sequence to be extrapolated from the dates of birth and death regarding the three men in question. It was simply a missing name. Whose name, however, presented an even more perplexing issue. By comparison, taking the information from the three monuments to combine into some coded answer would have been easier than pulling a name out of thin air. On the other hand, the fact that there was a name missing from this list meant they must be close. Didn't it?

Sean wasn't sure, but one thing was certain: They weren't going to find what they were looking for in Père Lachaise. The answer, it seemed, was already on the piece of parchment the kids found on Saint Helena.

"See what you can figure out," Sean said after a long and thoughtful pause. "We'll do the same here."

"Oh...kay."

"Don't wear yourselves out. I know you two have been through a lot."

"You can say that again."

"I know you two have been through a lot." Sean cracked a smile he felt sure she could sense through the phones.

Adriana's face scrunched, not understanding why he had repeated himself.

"That was bad," Tara chided.

"I know." Sean snorted. "Just wanted to lighten the mood a little. Seriously, it's fine. If you can figure out who is missing from that list, shoot me a text. Apparently, we're spinning our wheels here at this cemetery. If we find anything, I'll let you know. I need to call Tommy and get out of here."

"You're not afraid of ghosts, are you?"

"No," Sean said. "But I am afraid of the living."

He ended the call and tapped the screen, returning to the home screen briefly before he tapped on the recent calls list.

Adriana continued to stare at him, waiting for him to fill her in.

Sean didn't disappoint. "This isn't where we're supposed to be," Sean said as he pressed the device to his ear. "There was a name missing from that document. I can't be sure, but I feel like if we find that name we can locate the ring."

"What name?" Adriana asked.

"That's what we have to find out."

———

TOMMY STOOD next to the grave of André Masséna, gazing at the monument with rapt admiration and appreciation. The man in the tomb was a French war hero, a leader, and a confidant of Napoléon Bonaparte. Regardless of what some said or thought about General Bonaparte, the men surrounding him were usually intelligent and highly skilled in the art of war. Masséna was no different, though the similarities between him and the other officers stopped there.

André Masséna had been born a commoner. Most of the nobles and the members of the upper classes were promoted up through the ranks of the military as a result of their standing in society. Masséna had no such privilege. The son of a shopkeeper, he worked hard at everything he did, whether it was in day-to-day tasks or in the military commanding thousands of men.

After his father died and his mother remarried, Masséna went to work on a merchant vessel as a young man of only thirteen. He was a cabin boy and toiled as hard as any of the men. He learned a great deal about the sea during his time aboard the vessel, often listening in on the crew's conversations or paying close attention when the captain issued commands. Dealing with pirates was the most fascinating part of Masséna's nautical education. He learned tactics and strategies that, while not offensive strategies, were still militaristic in many ways. He always believed he would join the military someday and thought learning some of the finer points of naval strategy might not be a bad idea.

When he did join the army, André quickly rose through the ranks, reaching the level of warrant officer, which was the highest a non-noble could go at the time. He left the army for a short stint as a smuggler and made good use of the strategies he'd learned from the merchants, both aboard the ship from his youth and from traders he'd encountered along the way.

He made some money, and had some adventures, but the army was where his true talent resided. Masséna was an exemplary commander, and within a short time of rejoining the military he had risen to the rank of colonel.

Napoléon often bragged about him, regaling Masséna as "the greatest name of my military empire." The emperor general also gave Masséna the nickname Dear Child of Victory.

Tommy recalled all that information within seconds. He'd spent some time on his phone, looking up as much as he could about the man. The train ride wasn't terribly long, and so Tommy did his best to make maximum use of it, focusing on some of the highlights of the officer Napoléon hailed as such a valuable resource.

The monument of André Masséna was a four-sided granite plinth. The sides of the column angled in slightly, giving it the look of an obelisk that had been cut in half, leaving only the bottom in place.

A four-sided cross that looked ominously similar to the Templar Cross was carved into the front façade of the monument. The sight caused Tommy to arch one eyebrow in suspicion. He'd had his fill of the Templars.

Below the cross, a short list of names occupied the remaining surface until, at the bottom, the dates of Masséna's birth and death were cut into the granite. An image of Masséna adorned the base of the pillar, cradled by a wreath underneath it.

Tommy's eyes returned to the names above the base. They weren't names of people. They were places. He wondered if that somehow figured into the answer of the riddle. Perhaps those names were to be put together in some kind of coded message. Or maybe Tommy needed a map. What if the names on this grave were supposed to be pieces of some grid that pointed to the location of the relic? His mind spun with the possibility, imaginary lines being drawn from one place to another on the incorrect map in his vision.

His heart quickened at the possibility. He loved this kind of stuff, figuring out riddles and ancient mysteries that had lurked in front of ordinary people for hundreds, sometimes thousands of years. Right under their noses.

Tommy took a step back, partly in disbelief and partly to get a better look at the monument. From his new perspective, he could see the pillar wasn't cut off at all but was merely shallow angled at the top, making a complete obelisk.

He tapped on the Google app on his phone and entered the names from the stone. It didn't take long for a list of results to appear. He selected the first one and scanned through the information.

They *were* places, as he already knew, but now the connection was clear. Every name was a location where Masséna had led the army to victory in key battles. They were an acknowledgment of his incredible leadership and valor. It was a worthy tribute, but the locations of those battlefields were far away from where Tommy stood. They were in foreign lands where Napoléon had sought to vanquish enemies and expand his empire. Finding those sites wouldn't be a problem. If that was the answer, perhaps there was a grid to be created from the famous victories of all three officers. Tommy was certain if they sat down with a map and outlined the battlefield locations, they would find answers, perhaps a single answer.

"What are you doing?" Bodmer asked. He sounded grumpy, which was normal for him. The man almost never smiled, his focus seemingly a permanent fixture that sealed his face in stone.

Tommy turned his phone around so his companions could see. For a moment, he'd forgotten they were even there.

"My apologies," he said, doing his best to sound formal. He wasn't sure why, but he felt that Wagner especially deserved his respect. "I was looking up the names on the obelisk to see what they had in common."

"Military victories of Colonel Masséna," Wagner said, as if it was obvious.

"You knew that?"

"Of course." Wagner's shoulders lifted and drooped. "We have searched for many years, across continents, and performed rigorous research into the men who surrounded Napoléon. We know much about the men upon whose shoulders the emperor stood."

"Oh," Tommy said, realizing he found himself in the unusual position of being behind. "Okay, then."

"You believe these places have something to do with the location of the relic?" Bodmer asked.

"Possibly," Tommy said. "It's possible that we need to find a map, a real map, like in a library. I wouldn't know where to find a world map here in Paris."

The other two cast a wary glance at each other, a confession of their ignorance.

Tommy went on when the two said nothing. "We could be looking at something where we need to chart out all the locations on a map in hopes of zeroing in on either the location of the relic or perhaps another clue. It's hard to know without sitting down and plotting everything out."

"You believe that whoever hid this might have created a map based on the victories of the three officers?" Bodmer made his doubts evident. "That would mean Napoléon planned out the campaign ahead of time with the sole purpose of hiding the ring in a specific location."

Tommy could see why the man thought that, though the logic was flawed. "I see your point, Commander, but it's possible that the locations on the map will not form a traditionally defined grid, as you're suggesting. I assume you've seen something like that before."

Bodmer confirmed with a nod.

"Washington is much the same as what you're saying. Its design was very specific. They've featured it on many television shows because people believe there is some kind of Masonic conspiracy behind its layout. Some have even suggested that when you connect certain streets on a map, it produces the symbol of the Freemasons. Perhaps that was on purpose, and maybe it wasn't. I haven't seen many instances where something that elaborate was done, though. This could be one of the bigger ones if that's the case. Still, it would have been done after the fact. Not before. Napoléon could have easily used the battlefield sites as markers to draw us to some other place. If we can find a map, one that will have all the places Napoléon visited during his campaigns, we should be able to tell pretty quickly whether this theory is workable."

Tommy's phone vibrated in his palm. The abrupt gyrations caught him off guard and he fumbled with the device, nearly dropping it to the hard stone path at his feet. The phone bounced off the fingers of his right hand and then toppled into the left. He was lucky to snatch it out of the air and breathed a sigh of relief. He hated buying new phones, and he had a strict policy about waiting two years before replacing his current one. It wasn't that he couldn't afford the latest or best models. He simply didn't like wasting money on something that was still functioning properly.

He looked at the screen and saw it was Sean. "Hey, what's up?"

Tommy listened as his friend described what he learned just a few moments before. A perplexed expression crossed his face, and deep wrinkles carved into his forehead. He rubbed his left temple with a thumb as Sean finished what he was saying by telling Tommy to get the other two and meet them back at the entrance to the cemetery.

"Okay, buddy. See you there in a minute."

Tommy ended the call and stuffed the phone in his pocket. He wore the look of dejection.

"What is it?" Wagner asked, sensing something was amiss. "Is there a problem?"

Tommy snickered, his eyes still staring blankly down at the pavement. He snapped out of it a second later. "No. No problem. But the map thing...yeah, it was a dead end."

"It was...is?" Bodmer corrected himself.

"Yeah, it seems Sean figured something out regarding the list with the three officers' names on it."

"What does that mean?" Wagner asked, his eyes showing concern.

"It means the map idea *was* a dead end."

"But Sean knows where the relic is?" Bodmer pressed.

"I don't think so. He made it sound like he has everything he needs to locate it, though. Something about a gap on the list of names. I don't really understand it. I saw that list and didn't notice a big difference between the lines."

"Perhaps he's wrong," Wagner said.

"We should go find out," Bodmer stated. "We have wasted enough time."

Tommy nodded, sensing the man's urgency. Bodmer was right. The gunman from Villers-Cotterêts could show up at any moment, and probably with reinforcements. If there was a gunfight in the cemetery, Tommy had no doubts that he and his companions would be outnumbered.

"Okay," he said finally. "Let's get to work."

33

PÈRE LACHAISE

Sean could see the main gate just around the bend. An elderly couple walked hand in hand along the path. Neither said anything as they passed Sean and Adriana. The two were looking around at the memorial stones on either side, entranced by the bizarre and classical alike.

For a moment, Sean lowered his guard and glanced at his wife. She was striking. Her features were a combination of elegant and powerful. Strange and dangerous circumstances had brought them together, but they'd developed a strong bond through the years, and he knew that bond would never be broken. He trusted and loved her with every ounce of his soul. Someday, he thought, the two of them would be that older couple walking down the lane of some distant park or cemetery or city.

Not now, though.

They strode purposefully toward the gate. There was no sign of Tommy, but that was to be expected. Sean and Adriana had a few minutes' head start on the others. It came as no surprise that Sean made it there first.

The two stepped off to the side where they'd split from the others earlier. Adriana's eye caught something to her right. Her head twisted

and she noticed the refreshment cart just outside the wall. She forgot
to bring a bottle of water with her and hadn't had time to pick one up.
Sean, too, was without anything to drink, and she realized that the
only hydration she'd received that day was from the café back in
Villers-Cotterêts.

"I'm going to step out there and get a bottle of water," she said.
"You thirsty?"

"Yes. Thank you. I didn't even realize how thirsty I was until you
said it. Here, take my card." He reached into his front pocket to pull
out his money clip, but she was already five steps away and shaking
her head.

Sean's chest rose as he chuckled, watching her walk away. She
was wearing black boots, jeans, and a white T-shirt. Nothing fancy,
but she made everything she put on look amazing.

She stopped in the back of the line of people waiting for refreshments, and Sean turned away to watch for Tommy. He didn't have to
wait long before he saw his friend appear from around a row of
monuments. Bodmer and Wagner were on either side, and all three
men stalked toward the gate, clearly in a hurry to get to their
rendezvous. Sean was partly disappointed. For the briefest of
seconds, he considered running over to the tomb of Jim Morrison to
take a quick picture of it, but he knew there wasn't time.

Sean started to raise his hand to wave to Tommy when he felt
something jab him in the kidneys. He laughed instinctively and
turned around expecting to see Adriana sticking a water bottle into
his back.

Instead, he found a face he didn't recognize. The young man had
onyx hair spiked up in a mess that looked as if he'd climbed out of
bed mere minutes before. He was wearing a gray windbreaker, which
was probably overkill in the warm sun, but Sean knew why he wore
it. It was much easier to conceal a weapon with a jacket or coat than
with nothing but a T-shirt on, though Sean was doing that very thing
with no outerwear.

Sean couldn't see the gunman's eyes behind his aviator

sunglasses, but he could see enough of the slits to tell he would not hesitate to pull the trigger.

"Stay where you are, and don't move," the gunman said in a heavy accent Sean couldn't place.

Sean watched as Tommy approached, and noted that Bodmer was slipping back a step or two behind Tommy. It was subtle, and most observers wouldn't have thought anything of it. But Sean did. He knew right then who was behind everything: the murder, the gunmen tracking them down, probably the shootout at Villers-Cotterêts. No, definitely the shootout. The only problem with that was they put their own man at risk.

Sean thought back to the gunfight. The memory flashed before his eyes. Bodmer was there. He'd fired shots, hadn't he? Sean had trouble recalling, but he thought for sure Bodmer had discharged his weapon. The man definitely took cover during the assault from the two shooters, but had he been the first to dive clear of the hail of bullets? Again, everything happened so fast, it was difficult to recall clearly.

None of that mattered. Sean saw the commander of the Swiss Guard retrieving the weapon at his hip. The movement was subtle, just like the slowing of the man's pace to get behind Tommy and Wagner. Sean saw the commander's eyes flick toward Wagner, the more dangerous of the perceived threats. He obviously didn't know as much about Tommy's background as he professed, or thought he knew.

There wasn't a second to lose. Sean had to act, despite the warning from the gunman behind him.

Sean shook his head, locking eyes with Tommy. Then he spoke to the gunman at his back. "How'd you manage to get that in here, into France I mean. They have pretty strict gun laws here, and you don't strike me as the law-abiding type."

"Stop talking," the gunman snapped.

"I'm just saying, it's weird that you have a gun." Sean let his voice grow louder with every word. "Here in France. You know? Did you get your gun illegally?"

People started looking at him as they passed by, like he was crazy. It was an easy act to pull off since many Americans joked about how Parisians looked at them with disdain when on vacation there.

"I heard that more than half the guns here were purchased illegally." Sean's voice climbed to a shout so that everyone walking by could not help but hear his seemingly random rant.

"I told you to stop talking," the gunman snapped, jamming the muzzle deep into Sean's back.

Sean grimaced at the discomfort, but his intent was already accomplished.

Tommy stopped walking, suddenly concerned at his friend's erratic behavior. He realized the danger immediately as he traced Sean's gaze over his shoulder. Tommy bolted to the left, his right hand instantly digging into his pants to retrieve the small pistol hidden there.

The abrupt maneuver by Tommy threw off the Swiss Guard commander. His intention had been to take out Wagner, or at least hold the man at gunpoint, then deal with Tommy.

Bodmer saw Tommy sprint to the left and dive behind a cluster of headstones and tombs before he could turn his weapon around and fire a shot.

Then everything broke loose. Women started screaming. Men yelled. Children weren't sure what to do, but there were only a few within sight. People everywhere panicked at the sight of the weapon. Those who'd been close enough to hear Sean's mad ravings realized —incorrectly—that the American was talking about Bodmer, who was now sweeping the path with his pistol.

Amid the chaos, Wagner vanished like a wraith, melting into the crowd and then out of view. Even Sean lost track of the man, which was no easy task.

Bodmer spun around to find the older man but couldn't locate him. Then his attention went back to finding Tommy. It was futile. Anarchy had taken hold, and now more people than Sean realized were in the cemetery, started pouring out through the gate, all running from the perceived threat.

Bodmer's face flamed. He stormed through the melee and stopped short, mere feet in front of Sean. For his part, Sean was happy he'd managed to save his friend and Wagner from whatever Bodmer had planned. His next thought was for Adriana, but she would be fine. The second people started rushing out of the cemetery, she would have probably tried to come help him, but then she would have also seen Bodmer and the guy sticking the gun in Sean's back. With Tommy and Wagner safe, Sean smiled like a child who'd just taken the last cookie out of the jar without anyone noticing.

"You did this on purpose," Bodmer sneered, slightly flicking his head to the chaos around them.

"Who, me?" Sean feigned innocence.

"Get him out of here," Bodmer ordered.

"Is there any chance you could take me by the tomb of Jim Morrison? I'm a big fan of The Doors, and this is the closest I've ever been to seeing his grave. It's sort of a bucket list item for me."

"Shut up. Get him to the car, and stuff something in his mouth so he can't speak."

"But then you'll miss all my witty banter," Sean whined.

Another man appeared out of the crowd and grabbed Sean's left arm, twisted it behind his back, and pressed it high in a way that seemed to strain every possible ligament in his shoulder. He winced at the uncomfortable position and felt a familiar tightness where he'd had surgery twenty years before on his rotator cuff. A burst of pain like hot needles swelled from the shoulder, and he feared that it might pop out of the joint for the first time in a few decades.

Then there was another pain. He knew what it was, and he knew what would follow, or he assumed he did. The tiny prick in his shoulder wasn't bad. It was barely noticeable, much less significant than the torqueing ligaments and cartilage in the joint. The result, however, was going to be far worse.

To his surprise, he didn't feel the drug being injected into his blood. Most of those that he'd endured sent either a cold or hot sensation through the skin and the blood vessels. He could definitely sense the drug entering his body, but it felt like nothing more than a sort of ooze creeping its way through the appendage.

The sensation reached his neck, and Sean knew he didn't have much time. He frantically scanned the area, looking for one face in the crowd. He couldn't see her. Was she safe? Of course she was safe. She was Adriana. She could take care of herself. Sean felt himself swaying as the effects of the drug wrapped their fingers around his mind and sent it spinning inside his skull. Everything tilted, and he would have lost his balance were he not being supported by...was it the gunman or Bodmer? Or was there someone else?

He heard the voices of the panicked cemetery visitors, but it was like thousands of people screaming into a giant blender. His arms and legs felt like Jell-O, and he was unable to make the muscles tighten enough to stand.

The gunman at his back swooped around and hooked his arm under Sean's armpit while the second man took the other arm. The two put a hat over Sean's head and a pair of sunglasses on his face. Sean was already out of it by the time they dragged him into the crowd. To most of the panicked visitors, he would look like some homeless vagabond, drunk on cheap wine.

Bodmer kept a keen eye on the gate and its surroundings as he and the other two passed through. He was specifically watching for Adriana, but didn't immediately notice her in the area. He thought he'd seen her leave the premises through the gate, though he wasn't sure.

Then he caught a glimpse of her only fifteen feet away as the flood of people surged through the exit and out onto the sidewalk beyond. She was swimming upstream, trying desperately to get through the hysterical mob.

Bodmer ducked his head as hers twisted slightly to the side. He wasn't sure if she saw him or not. He decided to slow his pace so the two men carrying Wyatt could get away.

"Get him to the car. You know what to do. I'll meet you at the rendezvous."

The younger man in the aviators nodded curtly and continued forward, vanishing a few seconds later into the crowd.

Sirens screamed in the distance. Bodmer knew he had no time to stand around, wading through throngs of people, to find Adriana. As long as she hadn't seen them leave, the plan would still work. She would have no idea where they went or what they were planning. She also wouldn't know who was involved, save for him, which would be of no concern soon enough.

He turned away from the gate after seeing her continue to plunge ahead into the now-thinning crowd. Adriana was focused on getting back into the cemetery and finding Sean. She didn't realize that he'd been dragged right past her, only a few dozen feet away.

Bodmer stuffed his weapon back into the holster and pulled his shirt down over his waist so no one could see the peculiar bulge on his hip. He glanced around, taking one last precautionary look to make sure no one had seen that *he* was the one everyone was freaking out about.

No one seemed to notice.

Calmly, Commander Bodmer strode away from the cemetery and disappeared into the mayhem.

Soon, the order would be restored, and he would be regaled as a hero.

34

PÈRE LACHAISE

Adriana plunged ahead, swimming through the writhing mass of people until she managed to break through at the gate. There, the crowd thinned and she was able to walk normally—albeit with a few bumps from rushing citizens.

She cut to the left where she'd last seen Sean and noticed that he was no longer standing there. Her head twisted back to the gate. There was no sign of him. A deep frown crossed her face. Something was wrong.

She'd overheard people talking as they tried to escape the cemetery. Most of them sounded like they'd never seen a gun before, which was probably the case considering the laws there, but the fact that someone was waving a gun around in the cemetery on the exact day and time Adriana and the others were there...that was a little crazy. She'd learned long ago to let go of the notion of coincidences. In her mind, there was no such thing.

Adriana spun in a full circle before she noticed something move between a cluster of tombs in the center of the graveyard—between the paths as they forked in several directions.

She reached down to her hip, but the sound of sirens on the street reminded her that she wasn't exactly supposed to be carrying a firearm, much less brandishing it in a public place in Paris. A famous public place at that.

Thinking better of it, she took one last glance through the gate and then jogged ahead, careful to run on her tiptoes so as not to give away her approach to the target, whoever or whatever they were.

She reached the peninsula that jutted into the thoroughfare. There, she paused for a moment, watching and listening to the spot where she first saw the movement.

Adriana cautiously stepped up onto the stone ledge that lined the path and turned her body sideways to fit through the narrow gaps between the graves. She slithered through the narrow gap, bracing herself on a wrought iron fence at her back. Even when she was safely out of sight of the gate and the approaching police, she kept her weapon holstered. There could be danger lurking around any one of the tombs, but if the cops came through the gate and saw her holding a gun, there would be no escaping the trouble it would cause.

If there were any enemies still in the cemetery, she was going to have to take them down the old-fashioned way. The Old Testament way.

She heard a leaf crunch barely ten feet away and immediately knew that her quarry was close.

Adriana's training kicked in automatically.

She moved deftly, without sound, maneuvering to her left and crouching low to keep from being seen. She stepped into the narrow path between a row of monuments and lunged forward as she caught sight of the figure.

Even as she attacked, she realized that the person she was pursuing wasn't an enemy. Or were they?

Her quick movement hadn't caught the man's attention as he hid between the tombs, apparently hoping to evade the cops. She slipped her hand around his mouth and cupped it tight, pulling him into her chest with the other arm and holding him tight.

"Don't speak," she whispered into the man's ear and lowered him back down to the ground.

Wagner nodded, though the panic in his eyes betrayed his uncertainty, and his fears.

"Where is Tommy?" she asked hissed.

Wagner raised a finger, pointing toward a row of tombs.

Adriana wasn't sure, but she assumed he meant the other side of the boulevard.

"I'm going to loosen my grip on your mouth. If you cry out for help or try anything stupid, I will rip your vocal cords out of your neck. Do you understand?"

He nodded without hesitation. It wasn't a fear-filled gesture. It was one of a man who had nothing to hide, who was innocent of any wrongdoing.

Adriana loosened her grip, and he whispered, "Other side of the boulevard." He motioned again with the same finger.

Wagner waited for a moment as she surveyed the area. Then he spoke again. "I think Tommy saw something suspicious. I don't know how he saw it, but as we were heading toward the gate, he took off running away from us, toward that section of the cemetery. At first, I didn't know what he was doing." Wagner's eyes darted around almost frantically.

Adriana understood why. The sirens were closing in. Some squad cars were probably already lining up outside the gate. Getting out through one of the other exits wouldn't be a bad idea. She recalled one such exit on the other side of the cemetery. It was right next to a metro station. If they could get there, it was possible they could evade trouble with the cops.

"What about Sean?" she asked. "Where is he?" She assumed he was hiding among the tombs, same as them, or perhaps he'd escaped with the throng of crazed people and she simply hadn't seen him.

"I don't know," Wagner confessed. "There was a man behind him. He was standing very close. I can't be sure, but it appeared the man was holding him there, maybe with a gun in his back. I couldn't tell, and I don't want to speculate on such things without having proof."

Adriana's heart skipped a beat. Sean was caught?

"How did that happen? Where's Bodmer?"

"That's just it," Wagner said, twisting his head around slightly so he could look the woman in the face. "Bodmer was the gunman everyone was running from."

The words processed quickly, and almost immediately their truth hit her: Bodmer was a mole. He was the one feeding information to the people chasing them, the Teutonic Order. It was Bodmer who'd orchestrated the murder of Cardinal Jarllson. He may have even been the one to carry out the deed.

It all made perfect sense. Getting away with the murder would have required intimate knowledge of the Vatican's campus, the apartment complex, the palace, the alleys and courtyards. No one would have more knowledge about the inner workings of every security feature, every square inch of the property like the commander of the Swiss Guard.

In hindsight, Adriana realized it was obvious and should have been all along. This wasn't some grand plot twist. Then again, maybe it was. Bodmer worked for the Holy See. While she wasn't Catholic, Adriana had always respected the religion and its adherents. Usually, no one was more loyal to the pope than the man directly responsible for his safety and the safety of all the cardinals on site. As she considered it, Adriana forgave herself for missing that piece of the puzzle.

She did not forgive herself, however, for losing Sean.

The rush from realization to the pangs of guilt took less than five seconds.

"Bodmer took Sean?" She nearly ran out of breath as she asked the question, so grave was her distress over her husband.

"Yes. I believe he did."

She gave a curt nod and then pulled the man up by the collar. "Come on. We have to find Tommy and get out of here."

"He could be anywhere," Wagner protested. "We need to leave. I was going to sneak into the center of the park and then cut across to the exit leading to the subway."

"We're finding Tommy. Then we go."

He saw the intensity in her gaze and realized there would be no convincing her otherwise. Not that he needed convincing. Wagner was a man of honor. He didn't want to leave Tommy behind, but he also knew the situation.

"Come," he said. "I saw him go in over there."

He wound through the tombs and headstones with Adriana tucked behind him so close that she was almost physically on his heels.

They climbed through the last narrow sections and crouched behind a stone crypt that stood around ten feet tall.

"Over there," Wagner said, pointing through an opening between graves across the way.

There was no sign of Tommy, but Adriana had to trust the man's claim.

She glanced over at the gate and heard the commotion as police swarmed the area. Some were yelling orders in French through a megaphone, mostly telling the citizenry to get clear of the cemetery in an orderly fashion, while some scurried about to get into position in order to prevent an escape of what they believed to be a lone gunman.

"Now," she said and leaped from her place.

Adriana sprinted across the path and dove between two tombs. There was barely room on either side of her as she rolled to a stop and onto her feet behind a bizarre monument featuring what could only be described as a zombie trying to escape from the headstone. It was one of the strangest monuments she'd seen in her life, and she wondered if the person buried there was a fan of horror stories or just deranged.

Perhaps it was both.

She shook off the distracting thoughts and watched as Wagner darted toward her, bounding across the path in four long strides. The man was more agile than he appeared, but she could tell from his build that he still trained and worked out frequently. This man may have been a decade or so older than her, but he didn't move like it.

Wagner dove out of sight a mere two seconds before cops took up positions at each side of the gate, awaiting further orders.

Adriana peeked around the corner of the nearest tomb and saw the armed police officers scurrying around just beyond the exit. They were getting people clear of danger and securing the perimeter in case the gunman was still inside the cemetery.

Adriana knew that the other exit would be smothered in cops within minutes. They had to move. But they also needed to find Tommy.

"Where is he?" Wagner hissed.

"You're the one who said he came in over here," Adriana countered. She didn't hide her irritation.

"I'm right here," Tommy whispered.

The other two turned around and saw him poking his head around a skinny obelisk. Tommy motioned them over, and they hurried to his position, keeping low as they maneuvered through the headstones to where Tommy crouched.

The three ducked behind an aboveground tomb and then exchanged concerned glances.

"Where's Sean?" Adriana asked. There was a hint of anger in her voice, but Tommy knew there was much more than she let on. She was holding back the winds of strife, knowing lashing out at Tommy would be counterproductive.

Tommy sighed. "There was a man. I think he had a gun. The guy had to be in his late twenties, maybe younger. Sean caught my eye. He didn't have to say anything." There was dejection in Tommy's voice. It wasn't the first time his best friend had been abducted, but Tommy wondered how many times they could push their luck.

"He warned me," Tommy said, his voice growing distant. "It was Bodmer. I didn't realize he'd slipped behind me and Wagner. By the time I realized what Sean was trying to tell me, Bodmer had already produced his weapon and was about to shoot Wagner here." He motioned to the older man.

"We can discuss all that later," Adriana interrupted. "Where is he now?"

Dogs barking at the gate cut off her question.

"He's gone. They took him. We have to get him back." Tommy didn't like his response, but it was the only one he could offer at the moment and under these conditions. Adriana knew that to be true, as well. There was no way they were getting past the cops. The metro exit was their only chance to get out.

"Come," Adriana snapped under her breath. "We must move quickly."

Wagner said nothing, simply nodding his agreement.

"No," Tommy argued. "We can't just leave him here. He's your husband for crying out loud, and my friend. We're not abandoning him."

Adriana sighed and felt a tightening in her chest. All of her life, she'd been able to suppress emotions during times of crisis or danger. Compartmentalizing feelings was a large part of her training. It was one of the rules she'd learned while under the tutelage of the ninja. The training had been brutal, and she'd been forced to do things that still disturbed her in the darkest hours of the night. She pushed the thoughts away and looked dead into Tommy's eyes.

"I love Sean as much as you. I haven't known him as long, but he is my husband. I love him with all my heart. There is nothing I wouldn't do to keep him safe. Do not think that our running is due to a lack of courage. A strategic retreat, Schultzie. We must retreat so we can attack again. I will find Sean. *We*," she said the word emphatically, "will find him. But we must leave."

That was it. She turned and started toward the other side of the park, snaking her way between monuments, careful to stay low as she navigated the maze.

Tommy followed behind them, checking over his shoulder periodically.

Adriana led the way through the rows of monuments and tombs. She knew there were more than a million people interred at Père Lachaise, but the scope of that number was truly unfathomable until you actually went there and saw the place—or tried to escape its maze under pressure.

The graves seemed to stretch on forever, only broken up by a few hills and outcroppings of trees where ancient forests would have stretched for miles prior to the establishment of the cemetery.

It wasn't a short trip to get to the metro exit, and their journey took longer because they were forced to stay off the cobbled paths, instead ducking and weaving through the array of tombs and graves. The clock in Adriana's head was screaming that they weren't going to make it.

She veered to the right and skirted the perimeter wall. Tommy and Wagner followed close behind. They passed a series of tombs that stretched nearly to the height of the wall. One was only a few inches below the wall's top edge. Two others nearby were shorter in a descending order, almost like a staircase.

Adriana pressed ahead and down a gentle slope. The slight incline allowed them to move faster as they continued through the vast cemetery. She scanned the area in front of them. There were no signs of trouble. That would change soon. She listened intently. Sirens whined on the other side of the wall. Adriana felt a flood of dread fill her stomach and chest. They weren't going to make it to the exit in time. They were trapped.

35

PÈRE LACHAISE

"There's no way we're going to beat them to the exit,"
Wagner said. Hearing the sirens, he'd arrived at the same
conclusion as Adriana. The cops were ahead of them now
and they would be swarming the metro gate, leaving them with no
way out.

Adriana spun on her heels, nearly bumping into the two men
who were following perhaps a little too close behind her. She darted
between them, leaving Tommy and Wagner staring at each other in
confusion.

"Where are you going?" Tommy asked, beleaguered.

"Back up here," she said. "Just up this rise." She motioned toward
the wall and a row of tombs they'd passed before.

He didn't know what plan she was concocting, but she must have
seen something they could use. Adriana was adept at such skills.
While Tommy was spending hours deep in research, working on his
field of expertise, he'd missed out on the kinds of training Sean and
Adriana had received in their younger days. He knew what skills they
possessed, especially Sean, though Tommy still didn't have a full
grasp on how Adriana had become what she was.

She'd disclosed the fact that she'd been taken at a young age by her father to a secret monastery where she spent years training under what was believed to be the last remaining sect of ninjas on the planet. Tommy couldn't imagine the rigors the young girl must have endured, what she'd been forced to do. He wasn't sure he wanted to know, either. Some stones, he decided, were best left unturned.

He shrugged and took off after her without so much as a single word of explanation to Wagner about what they were doing.

For his part, Wagner trusted what the other two were up to, though he was wary that the police were right on their heels. At the moment, they were running headfirst, back into the jaws of the enemy.

Adriana stayed low as she worked her way back up the slope. She used her hands to brace herself against the headstones and tombs. The technique made her movements more fluid, as though she herself was a ghost slipping through her domain, swinging through narrow gaps and paths.

The three were near the crest of the rise when Tommy realized Adriana's plan. Against the wall were the three tombs he'd noticed on their initial passing. Apparently Adriana had seen them as well, though she'd come up with a backup plan, or perhaps recalled the conveniently stacked tombs and crypt the moment they went by.

"You're going to use those as stairs to get over the wall. Aren't you?" Tommy asked suspiciously. He didn't hate the idea, but he wondered what was on the other side of the wall. There could be cops parked there, waiting for them to vault over, right into their trap. There was simply no way to know without taking a look or going over the lip.

"It's our only chance." She tipped her head toward the main boulevard that ran through the cemetery, "That, or we try to pry that manhole cover from the stones and get out through the sewers."

Tommy followed her line of sight down to the path and then shook off the idea. "No, the wall is probably a better option."

He knew that while the sewers were probably a better possibility in that the cops would have difficulty finding them, getting the lid off the manhole might prove impossible without the right tools. Then there was the little fact about what was in the sewers—something he'd rather not think about.

No, the wall was the best option, regardless of what awaited on the other side. They'd have a better chance that way than the other.

Adriana climbed irreverently onto the aboveground vault of the lowest tomb and stepped across it to the next in line. She pressed her palms into the top of the second tomb and pushed her weight up, letting her feet dangle momentarily until she was high enough to raise them over the edge and swing them onto the roof.

"Go," Wagner ordered Tommy.

Tommy wasn't planning on leaving the man behind, but he got the impression Wagner wasn't the type who was accustomed to having his orders questioned. Tommy gave a nod and vaulted onto the first tomb. By the time he reached the opposite edge, Adriana was already on the roof of the third, the largest of the crypts.

Its roof was slanted, not at a sharp angle but steep enough to cause trouble if they weren't careful. The real issue was the slick slate tiles that covered the top of the crypt. If it had been raining or even foggy, Tommy imagined the surface would have been too slippery to navigate.

Adriana, however, was having no trouble.

She deftly skirted up the back edge of the roof, using the wall as a brace until she reached the ledge. Then she swung her right leg over while balancing her weight with her left hand on the flat surface of the wall's top. She disappeared over the edge, and Tommy was left wondering what had happened to her.

He'd find out soon enough.

Pushing off the sudden sense of concern filling his abdomen, he climbed on top of the next tomb and quickly shuffled over to the third. He was only about six feet off the ground, but it felt much higher. He was exposed, an easy target standing out in the open. If any cops were within range, they would see him. Then Adriana's escape plan would be over as quickly as it began.

Tommy didn't see any, though, and he reminded himself that the park was massive, too vast for even a considerable force of cops to cover in a short amount of time. Still, that didn't mean he should linger about pondering the issue.

He pulled himself onto the third roof and copied the technique Adriana used to get to the wall's upper lip.

Wagner was right behind him now and waiting patiently as Tommy navigated the tenuous climb. A fall wouldn't kill him, not unless he landed on his head, but it would certainly hurt. A broken limb wasn't out of the realm of possibility, though the bigger issue was time. Falling now would slow them down, perhaps enough for the cops to catch up.

He was nearly to the top and had reached up to grab the ledge when one of the tiles under his right foot broke free. His shoe slipped. Gravity pulled him into the roof with a smack, and he felt himself sliding slowly down the side of the slate tiles.

His fingers dragged on the smooth surface, nails digging in as hard as they could. He kicked his toes into the roof and found purchase, stopping his descent. Tommy scrambled back to his feet and managed a couple of quick steps before he leaped toward the edge of the wall, even more eager now to get off the roof and over the wall.

He gripped the edge and used his feet to walk up the rest of the way until he swung one leg over the wall and found himself straddling the top.

Adriana was already on the sidewalk below and watching for trouble. Her head turned left and right, and then she looked up at Tommy.

The drop was around twelve feet, but for some reason it felt higher than that.

"Did you jump?" He hissed over the sounds of cars passing and distant sirens.

"Use your hands. Lower yourself down. Hang. Then drop." Her answer was curt out of necessity. She kept twisting her head back and forth to make sure no one was paying any attention to them, especially people wearing uniforms and badges.

Tommy hesitated. That hesitation was interrupted by Wagner as the man dragged himself over the edge, gripped the exterior side with his hands, and lowered himself down. In half the time it had taken Tommy to get up to that position on the wall, the older man was already dropping himself down to the ground.

Wagner hit the concrete below with a thud and then looked up expectantly. "Come on, son. This is no time to dilly about."

Tommy shook his head in disbelief, then spun himself around so his back was facing the street. He moved a little too quickly as he tried to position his hands and fingers on the edge, and when he lowered his weight, his fingers slipped, scraping against the hard surface of the stone wall.

He dropped awkwardly to the ground, but instead of hitting the solid pavement in what he was certain would be a painful landing, he felt a pair of strong hands cushion the fall and guide him down onto his feet. When Tommy gathered his senses enough to look around, he realized it was Wagner who'd steadied his fall. He peered into the man's eyes with questions that couldn't be answered at that moment.

Whoever this man was, he was far more than he let on. Or maybe the training he received as a knight of a secret order kept him young and vigorous. Tommy wondered how old the man really was.

He'd read an article once in a men's health magazine about a tribe of Mexican natives who lived in Copper Canyon, Mexico. The people had unnaturally long life spans, averaging around one hundred years per person. Researchers also learned that there were zero instances of cancer, heart disease, or Alzheimer's. Apparently, the Tarahumara, as they were called, had figured out the secret to longevity and extraordinary health.

It had fascinated Tommy to read about a chief, who was one hundred years old, outrunning the thirty-something journalist covering the tribe.

Tommy wondered if Wagner was trained in such a way, in such a lifestyle.

He shrugged off the thoughts. Maybe Wagner simply wasn't that old and just had a few gray hairs. The man's eyes, though, spoke of years, more years than Tommy for certain. He'd get his answers soon enough, though he wasn't sure how forthcoming the man would be with that information.

"You okay?" Wagner asked in a gruff tone.

"Yeah, I'm good. Come on. This way." Tommy motioned across the street toward the metro station. It was still a few blocks away, and by going in that direction now they would be running straight into the police. They could stay on the streets, taking sidewalks and alleys to get away from the cemetery. Had they been spotted? Was there any way to identify them?

All of those questions brought him back to one big question: Should they get on the train?

The three crossed the street at the next crosswalk and then proceeded toward the entrance to the metro. People were streaming out of the exit to Père Lachaise, though not at the level of the other entrance. Hundreds of people stood behind the police barricade that surrounded the entrance to the cemetery in a semicircle, effectively cutting off an exit for anyone the cops deemed a threat.

Gaps between the patrol cars allowed people through and into the plaza beyond. Tommy thought that strategy strange. The police weren't even checking to see if any of the people they were letting through were the gunman.

The dark green entryway descended into the bowels of the city. The railing, the façade, even the font of the lettering declaring the purpose of the entrance, harkened to a time many decades ago. They were all designed to affect an air of nostalgia and a smattering of history from Industrial Era France.

Tommy's eyes wandered to a surveillance camera perched atop a nearby light post. A terrible realization hit him: They were operating under the assumption that the cops didn't know what the mad gunman looked like. He knew from his time with Sean that making such assumptions could come back to bite him. It wouldn't take much for Bodmer to make a call to the Paris police and give them Tommy's description.

He fought to suppress the panic as they moved closer to the train. Getting on the metro would get them away faster, but it would also corner them. One thing he didn't want to be was stuck on a subway with no possible escape.

Adriana was about to descend the steps to the metro when Tommy halted her.

"Wait," Tommy said. "I have another idea."

"I thought we were taking the metro," she protested. "We need to get as far away from here as possible for the next few hours."

"Yeah, I know." Tommy looked back over his shoulder at the cops beginning to funnel into the cemetery. "But if we get on the train, we'll be stuck in there like sardines."

Wagner jumped in. "Agreed. If someone fingers one of us as the gunman, we'll be trapped. Best to stick to the streets and lie low for a bit until we can find a place to hide out until this boils over."

Adriana looked at Tommy, then at Wagner. "Okay. Let's move. Stay calm, but not too calm. Everyone else is freaking out. So, do your best to blend in."

Tommy nodded and started trotting away from the cemetery, keeping the pace of everyone around him. He glanced back now and then since that seemed to be what the rest of the population was doing. Adriana and Wagner were on either side of him. Adriana could have won an Academy Award with her portrayal of the terrified woman. Only he knew that she was anything but. The agonized worry on her face, though, would have fooled almost anyone.

The three moved quickly, though not too quickly, through the chaotic plaza until they reached the street on the other side where a strange convergence of curious onlookers and frightened escapees collided. Tommy considered the irony as they trotted over a crosswalk, watching more and more people hurrying in the other direction to see what was going on. He likened it to the way people would slow down to see horrific accidents on the highway. Humans were—apparently—fascinated with tragedy.

They slowed down once they were through most of the foot traffic. Adriana suggested they stop in a café or a bar to come up with a plan. The two men agreed, and when they were another block down, the three stepped into a darkly lit wine bar.

The hostess showed them to a small table in the back and handed them menus. No one had any intention of drinking or eating anything, but they couldn't just sit there. When the server appeared, Adriana ordered a few appetizers and three glasses of red wine. The young woman appeared to be less than thrilled to be working. Her brown ponytail sagged behind her as she tromped back to her station, where she began putting in the order.

The second the girl was out of sight, Adriana turned to Wagner. "Where did they take him?"

Wagner's head tossed from side to side. "I swear. I don't know. They could be anywhere in the city now." There was despondence in his voice, as if he'd given up hope. "With the resources the Teutonic Order possesses, they surely have dozens of safe houses here in Paris."

The girl returned with three glasses of wine and set them down in front of the guests. She spun and immediately disappeared again without so much as a smile.

Wagner reached forward and grabbed his glass. He took a long, slow sip and then let out a relieved "ah."

Adriana took a glance at the wine, then decided it was best to keep her wits about her.

Wagner clearly didn't have that concern.

"You don't know where any of those safe houses are located, do you?" Adriana's gaze met his.

"No," he said, setting the half-empty glass down and sliding it forward. Apparently, he wanted to keep most of his wits as well. "But I can see where you're going with that idea. If we could find one, we could draw out Bodmer and his puppet master."

"The grand master?"

"Yes. But we don't know where any of their holdings are." Wagner slumped back into the chair.

Tommy had been listening silently, but his mind was a raging torrent of thoughts. It wasn't the first time something like this had happened. Sean could handle himself. He kept telling himself that. In the past, Tommy had wasted time and energy worrying about his friend. Worry, he had learned, was counterproductive.

"They'll have his phone," Tommy realized out loud.

The other two looked up at him.

"We can call his phone," he continued. "One of the men who took Sean will answer it."

"Then they can track us down. That's *if* they answer," Wagner countered.

"They'll answer."

"And why do you think that?"

"Because," Tommy said with a distant hope in his voice, "we'll have something they want."

36

PARIS

T he late afternoon sun shone brightly through the open windows of the café. It was hour number two of the group's search for answers, and each one of them was beginning to grow impatient.

They'd scoured the internet for answers, trying to figure out the solution to the mystery of the missing name.

There was plenty of information to go around regarding the three men's names that *were* on the list, but that wasn't what they needed. Another phone call to the kids had resulted in nothing new, but they were doing the best they could with the resources available.

Adriana stared at her phone's screen, reading through more information about the three officers whose graves they'd already visited. She felt like she was reading the same text she'd read five or six times already.

Tommy was faring no better. He gazed at the laptop screen on the table in front of him with wide eyes, scanning through the text of site after site. He'd found a tech store close by and purchased the small computer, as well as a tablet for Wagner to use. Adriana insisted she was fine with the phone.

They could have all used phones, but Tommy was more than just a tad insistent about getting some larger screens to work with. He claimed he could go much faster on a computer or tablet. She understood his reasoning. Adriana also preferred to use a bigger screen. More information being displayed at one time made getting through it faster, plus it just felt better to be able to jump from tab to tab, window to window, to compare notes or examine one bit of information in conjunction with another.

Still, she insisted on using her phone, thinking it wasteful to buy expensive tools when the one she had on hand would work well enough.

Wagner flipped through more pages on the tablet, but his efforts produced the same results as the other two: nothing.

Tommy stood up abruptly and ran his fingers through his hair. He combed through the thick locks three times before he stopped, lacing his fingers behind his head and, keeping his arms up, stretched from side to side.

"What are we missing?" he said out loud.

"A name," Adriana answered dryly.

He snorted and cracked a smile. "Fair enough. We should have discovered something by now, though. Maybe Sean was wrong about there being a gap in the list of names. It was probably just a screwup on Napoléon's part when he created the list."

Adriana knew he was probably right, but she didn't want to consider that. Sean had been confident about his conclusion. There was simply a piece of the puzzle they were missing. Her head spun. The names of the three officers danced around in her brain like pieces of a baby's mobile dangling over a crib. *Masséna. Dumas. Augereau.* What did they have in common? Other than the fact they were all long dead and served in Napoléon's army?

Adriana entered a new search in her web browser, and a collection of blue links appeared on the screen. She tapped the first one, read through the information, and then tapped the back button to examine the next link, though she figured it would be like all the others.

Her finger hovered over the phone screen as she debated tapping on the next link in line. She peered at the options at the top of the search window. She hadn't considered looking at images or video. It was doubtful anything helpful would be posted under the news tab, though she could be wrong. Still, her focus remained on the word *images* in the row of tabs. She extended her finger and tapped the screen. Her fingernail made a clicking sound on the tempered glass, and a moment later several rows of images appeared on the display.

There were several pictures of the men she'd included in the search query. Most of the images were portraits the famous military leaders had commissioned when they were still alive and in their prime. There were a few monuments, as well, including some from the more prominent of the men's military victories, accomplishments, and achievements.

Adriana scrolled down the page until she found something interesting. It stood out from all the other images—probably because it was one she easily recognized. The Arc de Triomphe appeared in several places on the page, and she couldn't help but wonder why.

One row displayed several pictures of the famous monument's pillars and walls where names had been engraved upon its completion. She narrowed her eyes and tapped on one of the images.

Tommy eased back into his seat and resumed his searching, while Wagner continued to stare at his tablet screen with rapt attention. The man hadn't said much in the last hour, and barely anything before that. Clearly, he believed the situation with Berger was a dire one, and he didn't feel that discussing the danger Sean was in would be helpful. So, he kept his thoughts to himself and concentrated on the search.

Adriana tilted her head to the side as she scanned through the names on the first column of the Arc de Triomphe. She didn't see any she recognized so tapped the back button to go to the next column. Was this where she could find the list of names from Napoléon's parchment? Her hopes tickled the back of her mind, but she didn't dare let them run free. She had to stay focused.

The second column produced the same results as the first, and she hit the back button again to return to the main page of images.

She considered giving up but knew she needed to be thorough. She looked up and drew Tommy's attention.

"Do a quick search regarding the names listed on the Arc de Triomphe here in Paris," she said. The words came out a little more demanding than she'd intended, but Tommy didn't need niceties or social conventions at a time like this. He didn't need her to say pretty please.

"Sure," he said. "You got something?"

She rolled her shoulders. "Maybe."

Wagner looked up from his reading and his eyes drifted to Tommy's screen. He watched as Tommy rapidly typed in the search term. The monitor flickered, and then the two men scanned the results.

"From this summary," Tommy said, "looks like the names on the columns are soldiers who were loyal to Napoléon."

"Officers," Wagner corrected. "Most of them were officers and close friends of the general."

Adriana's pace quickened. She scanned the next column, the fourth, the fifth, and so on until she'd seen every one. Her shoulders slumped, and she let out a disappointed sigh. There was no sign of the three names from the list.

Unless...

She started working her way back through the pictures of the columns, eyeing each one carefully and forcing herself to work through every single name in the order they appeared, from top to bottom. She used her finger to make sure she didn't skip any, which is what Adriana feared may have happened on the first pass. She wasn't the careless type, quite the contrary, her diligence and focus were nearly unmatched, but that didn't mean she was infallible. She made mistakes, though she tried to make sure those errors weren't catastrophic.

She was halfway through the list when her breath caught in her throat. She didn't swallow, didn't breathe, didn't say a word for a moment. Then it all came rushing back.

Adriana took a deep breath and nodded. "Gentlemen, I think we have something."

Tommy's eyes darted from his screen and landed on hers in an instant. Wagner, too, was now fully distracted from his search.

"What is it?" Tommy asked.

"Come see for yourself."

The two men started to get up to move around the table, but Adriana held out the cell phone for Tommy to take, indicating he didn't have to move all the way over. He shifted in his chair and took the device from her, holding it off center from his torso so Wagner could see what she had found.

Tommy blinked rapidly, trying to make sure he wasn't imagining things. The words chiseled into the stone didn't change, though, and he felt overcome with a wave of excitement and, more importantly, hope.

"That's it," Tommy said. "The three names, plus the one that was missing. That has to be it."

Wagner nodded and began pecking away at the digital keys on the tablet's screen.

Tommy handed the phone back to Adriana and immediately started typing in a new search term. His fingers flew over the keyboard. When he entered the search, he waited for a couple of seconds as the café's Wi-Fi connected him to the internet again and wrangled a new set of results for his query.

Tommy clicked on the first one and started reading. He stopped momentarily and motioned Adriana to join him and Wagner on the other side of the table so she could see what he found.

The missing name from the Saint Helena list was Berthier.

Tommy's search had brought back some tremendous resources on the subject of the man whose name was wedged in the middle of three others whom Napoléon trusted and relied on during his attempts at global conquest.

The man was born on November 20, 1753, and died on June 1, 1815. According to the first search results, which was one of the more popular internet encyclopedia sites in the world, Louis Alexandre

Berthier was the First Prince of Wagram, a sovereign prince of Neuchâtel, a French marshal, and the vice constable of the empire. He also served as Napoléon's chief of staff.

Tommy left the site and went to the next one, digging deeper into the history between this mysterious officer and the French emperor. The resources suggested that Berthier was one of the most influential leaders in Napoléon's regime and that his abilities as a commander on the battlefield and as a strategist were held in extremely high regard by Napoléon.

Like so many others in Bonaparte's company, Berthier died before his general.

"This is the part the riddle was talking about," Adriana said.

"Which part?" Tommy asked. "There are more than one."

"What we've learned is that Napoléon was concerned about the Battle of Waterloo. Remember? He suggested that he was going to lose because he didn't have his most powerful asset. That asset would be Berthier. According to this information," she tapped on the screen, "Napoléon fretted over not having the man there to help him plan the battle. It seems the general relied heavily on Berthier, and without him he believed the battle was already lost."

"There was something about the victory standing forever, too," Tommy said. "That validates the Arc de Triomphe as the location for the four names, especially in regard to Berthier."

"That's right," Adriana confirmed. "Napoléon built that monument to stand as an eternal tribute to the men who served him loyally during his conquests."

Tommy beamed proudly at the connection he'd made.

"Don't get cocky," Adriana chided. "That still doesn't mean we know where the ring is. I doubt it's hidden in the arch."

"It's possible," Wagner spoke up for the first time in a while. "There are many ways Bonaparte could have hidden the relic in the monument. We'll need to consider every possible angle before we try to break something or dig a hole in the ground."

Tommy shook his head. "I'm with Adriana. I don't think it's there."

"No?"

"It would be too easy. Nothing about this entire mission has been easy. It never is. If there's one thing I've learned over the years, it's that if something is too easy, it's either not right, or there is something else waiting just beyond it."

"Okay," Wagner acquiesced. "Where is it, then?"

Tommy's lips were pressed together, but the right corner creased slightly as a mischievous grin crept across his face, causing his right eye to narrow to match the expression.

"I think I know, but I'm going to have to make a couple of phone calls first."

37

PARIS

Sean's eyelids scraped his eyeballs as he tried to see through the haze. Something smelled vile. It wasn't a scent of decay such as refuse or rotting meat. It was on the other end of the spectrum, pungent and acrid. It burned his nostrils and reminded him of bleach or ammonia, only stronger, like some kind of unholy sterile solution. Was that a hint of iodine mixed in?

He blinked hard against the dryness of his eyelashes, and the wetness slowly returned, washing away the irritating pain. He had a mild headache reverberating from the back of his skull, but nothing he couldn't handle. Sean had been in situations before where had woken in a strange place after being drugged or knocked unconscious. He had to admit that this was one of the less intrusive wake-ups.

As his vision returned, he looked around the room, gathering as much intel as he could, which was as common a practice as breathing for him. Sean noted he was in what looked like an old conference room. The windows to his right ran the length of the room from floor to ceiling.

He craned his neck to try to peek through the slivers between the blinds, but it was no use, although he could hear the bustle of a busy street just outside. From the sound of it, he was several stories up, maybe six or seven, but it could have been nine or ten for all he knew.

For the moment, that didn't matter. He had to figure out where he was and why he'd been taken. The second question wasn't as difficult to answer as the first. Bodmer was the mole; he was responsible for the murder of Cardinal Jarllson, and basically this entire fiasco. But Bodmer wasn't the one calling the shots. He was a pawn—powerful and clever, but a pawn nonetheless.

He'd played them all like a maestro, and now Sean was a captive. There was no telling what the knights of the order were going to do to him, but he had a bad feeling it wasn't going to be pleasant. The least he could do was offer them the same unpleasantries, if not physically, then verbally.

It seemed like hours had passed before he heard the sound of someone coming down the hallway just outside the conference room door.

The place was devoid of furniture save for the office chair cushioning his backside, though the generous amount of duct tape that strapped him to the seat removed any semblance of comfort the chair's cushion could offer.

The room had two doors. Sean could see through one of the doors, the one at the opposite end of the room. There were empty cubicles and desks stacked along a wall near a window in what appeared to be a much larger space.

It must be an abandoned office building, but why was he here? And why were the Teutonic Knights using it? He calculated their strategy in seconds.

Taking him out of the city would, no doubt, be in their cards, but they'd kept him here, in Paris. The sounds coming from the street below were from a city with a large population. Paris was the easiest to figure. If he'd been flown somewhere else, though, he wouldn't have known.

For now, imagining that possibility was not helpful in formulating a plan to escape.

Sean reeled in the straying thoughts and wiggled his arms and wrists. He knew it would be futile, but he had to try. As he suspected, he was secured tightly to the chair. Not only that, but his wrists were also bound together with duct tape that dug into his skin and cut off the circulation. His ankles were secured with what was probably too much of the thick tape. That only served to tell him that Bodmer knew who he was dealing with. Sean was a dangerous man, maybe the most dangerous that the commander of the Swiss Guard would ever meet. He wouldn't be stupid enough to leave Sean with any sliver of hope, no minuscule chance of getting away.

Sean had to hand it to him: Bodmer was smart in that regard. That didn't change the fact that Sean was going to kill the man if he ever got out of this chair.

He'd been working through his issues around killing. He only took lives when he had to and there was no other option, but with Bodmer it was already decided. The man had signed his own death warrant when he betrayed Sean and the others, when he killed an innocent man. It was one thing to stick a knife in Sean's back or the backs of his companions—that didn't sit well—but this guy killed a cardinal, a man Bodmer was charged with protecting, keeping safe.

It sickened Sean to think about it, and those kinds of things rarely got to him. He possessed an innate ability to compartmentalize that stuff. It was how he had survived this long, how he'd managed to get through so many missions a lesser agent would have questioned and likely failed at.

He would have treated the act the same if it had been an innocent child or a random stranger, but the fact that the cardinal was a person of importance, a person revered by many? That made it all the more pertinent for Sean to exact justice, his brand of justice that came without mercy.

Unfortunately, justice would have to wait until he could find a way out of this jam.

He snorted, frustrated, and managed to wiggle his toes enough to roll an inch or two toward the window. It was the only part of his body that could move, save for a full-on jerking motion with his torso, which he also started using in conjunction with his toes to move toward the window faster. When he reached the blinds, his knee bumped into one of them and the entire contraption moved in a slow wave, back and forth.

Sean peeked through the gap as the blinds rippled forward for a moment. He'd been right. He was still in Paris.

The blinds clapped against the window and ruffled again, this time for less than two seconds. Sean used the brief moment to take another look. This time, his focus was on a clock on a building across the street.

He had to assume it was the same day he'd been abducted. Based on the clock, he'd only been out of it for around three hours. It could have been much worse, though his situation was still less than optimal. In fact, it was dire.

This was no amateur he was dealing with; none of them were. He'd met challenges before from professionals, mercenaries, secret sects of warriors trained in ancient methods and martial arts. He'd faced madmen, too, though they were usually easier to handle than their underlings. He doubted that would be the case here.

Bodmer was an elite soldier and security officer, and the fact he was a knight of the Teutonic Order meant he probably had a higher level of training than most soldiers in the world. He couldn't be sure, and conjecture wasn't always helpful, but he had the feeling that Bodmer, along with his puppet master, likely spent most of their days working on techniques in a vast array of combat forms.

"Enjoying the view?"

The familiar voice echoed in the empty room as it bounced off the shiny black marble floors and the sterile ceilings.

"Not much to look at here, Commander," Sean said flatly. "If you're going to duct tape people to chairs in abandoned office buildings, could you at least pick one near the Eiffel Tower? Maybe one that overlooks a park or something?"

"Your jesting has made you sloppy," Bodmer said.

"Oh, sorry. You thought I was joking. Have you looked out this window? There's not much to look at."

"You were right about him, Brother." This new voice was deeper and had a baritone growl to it.

Sean turned his head and saw Bodmer standing just to the side of the doorway. Another figure appeared a moment later. He was older than Bodmer, probably by ten or fifteen years. Gray strands of hair streaked his locks and beard. Like Bodmer, the man was fit. His broad shoulders and taut muscles looked as though they might rip through the suit jacket covering his torso. He was decked out in black from head to toe: slacks, shoes, and shirt, all of it. It was a fact Sean refused to let slide.

"And who's your friend here?" Sean asked. "He certainly likes the color black."

"You know who I am," Berger said coolly.

"Do I? Because I don't think we've ever met. Pretty sure I'd remember. Have you considered incorporating some other colors into your wardrobe, or is this, like, a thing for you?"

The other two men turned their heads slowly toward each other, exchanging an annoyed glance.

"And did they only have youth medium? Looks like that suit is about three sizes too small."

"You know why we are here," Berger drawled. "I would appreciate it if you give us what we want, what is rightfully ours."

"Rightfully yours? I thought it belonged to the Hospitallers—you know, the Knights of Malta?"

"We were allies. The Hospitallers and the Templars worked with us, not against us. Their orders, as they once were, are no more. They're shells of their former selves, nothing more than symbols drifting in a sea of apathy. We, however, remained strong."

Sean chuckled to himself. "Shows how much you know."

Berger's face cracked with curiosity, but he didn't pursue Sean's teasing comment. He didn't care to hear anything from Sean save for one piece of information.

"Where is the ring, Sean? Tell us where it is, and we will give you the honor of a swift death."

Sean snorted another laugh and turned his head to face forward.

"Sorry, guys. Can't keep looking at you that way. My neck is starting to get a little stiff." He started struggling in the chair, wobbling it back and forth until it began inching its way around to the left. "If I can just...get...it...to turn." He let out a relieved gasp as if the exercise had required intense effort. "There," he said, facing the two men, "that's much better. I'm sorry; you were saying?"

"The ring, Sean. Where is it?" Berger's voice carried a deep rumble, reflecting the irritation that was surely swelling with every passing second.

"I'm sorry, I didn't realize we were on a first-name basis. And I'm sorry I'm not sorry, but I don't know where the bloody ring is. Your boy, Commander Bodmer there, stuck me with something before I could find it. I guess that means you two are out of luck, huh? Unless, of course, I take you to it."

Berger's right eyebrow rose with suspicion. "We both know you wouldn't do that."

Sean chuckled dramatically. He was stalling, hoping to find a way to break free from the bonds, though doing so at the moment would have been a bad idea. These two would cut him down before he took a step; of that he was absolutely certain. If he found a weak spot in the tape, he'd have to wait to exploit it, but with every passing second he realized that was fantasy. Without some kind of tool or a knife, there was no way he was getting out of the chair unless one of these two let him out.

"True," Sean said. "And you also know that torturing me won't do you any good. There's nothing you could do that would make me tell you a thing."

"Yes, I'm sure you're right, though we may hurt you merely on principle."

Sean nodded slowly. He was afraid of that. For all his bravado and the display of emotionless courage, he knew these two were likely experts in extracting every ounce of pain from the human body. He'd been through different kinds of torture before, the worst of which was waterboarding. He shuddered at the thought and hoped Berger didn't have that in mind. It wouldn't make Sean talk, but it would definitely make his life a living hell for however long they decided to do it.

"What if I do what you don't expect?" Sean asked. "What if I'm willing to tell you where the ring is if you promise to leave my friends alone?"

It was Bodmer's turn to laugh, but he quickly silenced himself. The man hadn't said anything since Berger appeared. It was a fact that didn't escape Sean's observation.

"You've been awfully quiet over there, Commander. Does Daddy not let you talk when he's around?"

Bodmer did his best not to let Sean's jab get to him, but Sean could see it struck a nerve. Bodmer's eyelids narrowed ever so slightly, but he kept his lips pressed tightly together.

"Don't try to instigate something with my associate, Sean. To your question: You know we can't offer that. You friends are going to die one way or the other."

"You won't find them."

Berger smirked at the insinuation. "You don't realize it, do you? The power we wield? The connections we forged long ago and have sustained all these centuries? We can find anyone, anywhere. Your friends will be found, and when they are, they will die long, slow deaths, just like you. And we will make you watch."

So, that was what they were keeping him around for. Sean knew they wanted the information he had in his head, but they were misguided. He didn't know where the ring was. The only new bit of intel he had on this hunt was the gap in the names on the list from Saint Helena. That list wasn't in his possession, and without it he couldn't determine how exactly it figured into the ring's location. He'd easily memorized the names, though he still kept that minor detail to himself.

A thought occurred to him. He might not be able to get out of this alive, but he could buy his friends time, draw these men away from them until they found the ring or, at the very least, got out of the country.

A deception bubbled in his head. It was nothing elaborate. He had to pick a place, any place where there was some kind of historical marker. The Eiffel Tower? No, that would be too obvious. Then he had another idea. He had to be careful. It was a dangerous game he was playing.

"If I tell you where the ring is, you may be able to beat my friends to it. If you do, I want you to swear you will let them live."

Berger stepped deeper into the room and strode casually over to the window. He twisted the long rod connected to the blinds, and the shutters turned, opening the view to the street below and the buildings surrounding them. The man stared thoughtfully through the window.

"No," he said.

"No?"

"I can't trust you, Sean. You're too bent on protecting your friends. You would happily mislead me to protect them." He kept speaking, cutting off any intrusion Sean may have offered to the conversation. "While I do appreciate your...sentiments around taking such an oath, I will do no such thing. And even if I did, how could you trust me?"

He slipped his hands behind his back and laced the fingers together. He turned his head slightly and glanced at Sean out of the corner of his eye, adding a short humming sound to reiterate the question.

"I don't, but you are a man of God, are you not? You hold oaths in high regard. They're sacred. Like the ones your order took to protect the church so long ago."

"Hmm." Berger's head turned back around to face the window, and for a moment he seemed pensive. "Do you think you can manipulate me?" His voice remained calm, eerily so. "I am aware of your abilities, how you use mind games to get what you want. Psychology was your first degree, no?"

Sean said nothing at first.

"Your attempts to dupe me won't work."

"I'd rather use my fists."

Berger allowed a short cough of a laugh. "I'm sure you would,

Sean. That's how you handle most of your problems—with guns and fists."

"It's not a matter of preference. I rarely get the chance, though with you I'd probably choose to shoot you dead."

Berger faced him again and eyed him dubiously. "Perhaps. Perhaps you would not."

The statement confused Sean, but before he could retort, Berger stepped away from the window and wandered over to the far end of the room. He stood there for a moment, staring at the blank wall where an old television mount was still bolted to the wall.

"Where is the ring, Sean? Surely by now, you can see that no matter what scenario you choose for this little game, you cannot win. The only way to save your friends is to tell me where it is. Do that, and they may not cross my path. Don't, and I hunt them down, picking them off one by one. I'll start with Wagner. Then I'll kill your friend Tommy. I'll make it hurt, too. But I will save the best for last."

Sean snickered. "Here's the part where you threaten to hurt my wife, and that's somehow supposed to get a rise out of me, make me lose my cool, inevitably coughing up the location."

Sean lowered his head in dejection. Berger was right. He'd used up all his moves, and now the only one he had left would land him in checkmate.

"Well?"

The first thought that popped into Sean's mind was that Adriana would be a handful for this guy no matter how extensive his training had been. He thought better of it. If Sean was going to help his friends, he'd have to delay Berger and Bodmer. He'd only get one chance. The second the two men realized they'd been lied to, they'd kill Sean without hesitation.

He had to take them somewhere. An idea emerged through the fog of thoughts hanging in his head.

It was perfect—unless of course the ring really was there. That could be problematic, but he'd have to risk it. It was the best option he could conjure that Berger would likely believe.

"The ring is in the cathedral at Notre-Dame," Sean said. He spoke with an even tone, emotionless and cool.

Berger arched an eyebrow and inclined his head as he assessed whether or not Sean was telling the truth.

"Is it, now?" The grand master didn't sound convinced.

Sean felt like the man could see through his soul, picking out every tiny inconsistency or falsehood.

Sean nodded. "We won't know for sure until we go look."

A vibrating sound cut off Sean's explanation. His head snapped back to Bodmer, who was still standing at the door with lips sealed. He reached into his black jacket pocket and fished out a phone. Sean's phone.

Berger turned to see what the source of interruption was. "Ah," the man said, "it would appear your friends are trying to reach you. Is that right, Commander?"

Bodmer nodded. "It's Tommy."

Sean bit his tongue. The immediate urge was to go on the defensive, to tell the men not to answer the phone, but it was no use and he knew it.

"Answer it," Berger ordered. "I'm interested to see if your friends came to the same conclusion you did regarding the cathedral."

Bodmer tapped on the green button and the call connected within a second. He pressed the device to his ear. "The prodigal son returns," Bodmer said.

Tommy snorted through the earpiece. "Seriously? That's the best you could do? Some worn out cliché? Come on, Bodmer. I expected better from you. Sounds like you've been watching too many spy movies. You should get out more."

"What do you want, Tommy?" Bodmer actively chose to ignore the barbs coming from the man on the other end of the line. "You know we have Sean, which is why you called his phone. That must mean you have something we want, or you want to make some kind of deal to get your friend back."

Sean's expression didn't change. He didn't widen his eyes at the hope of being saved from whatever fate these men had planned for him. He knew better. He knew that he was being constantly watched for any sign of weakness, and Sean Wyatt was not going to give them an inch.

"Yes, I'm aware," Tommy said. "Very astute of you to connect those dots." His tone was lathered in venom so thick it could have paralyzed a horse, or at the very least a weaker-minded person.

"It's simple, Tommy. We want the ring of the Baptist. Deliver that to us, and we can talk about letting Sean go home with most of his appendages." He let the threat linger for a moment, knowing that Tommy would wonder which fingers or limbs had been removed from his friend's body since they last saw each other.

When Tommy replied, it was in a deep grumble. "Let me tell you something, Commander. Your life is over. You realize that? I'm not just talking about your career with the Swiss Guard. I figure you were going to leave that behind anyway once you went down this path. So, let me put this in words you can understand. If you hurt Sean in any way, I destroy the ring. I find out you're lying about anything, I destroy the ring. If you piss me off, I destroy the ring. And then after I do that, I will destroy you. Do you understand me? I will end you." Tommy's sneering voice trailed off.

———

THE DARKNESS behind his words caught even Adriana off guard. It was a side she hadn't seen often from her friend, though he captured her exact feelings and everything she would have said with his little tirade.

There was a long pause on the line before Bodmer spoke again. "Where do you want to meet?"

Tommy glanced at Adriana and Wagner before answering, as if they could hear the question. He thought fast. "The Arc de Triomphe," Tommy said. "I'd demand no weapons, but you would demand the same. So, come as you are."

"I will. Oh, and Tommy? When this is all over, you're going to die."

Bodmer ended the call before Tommy's temper kicked in and he could say anything else. His chest heaved up and down as he tried to calm himself with breathing exercises. He was furious, but anger would do him no good. Still, he needed to reel it in before they went to the rendezvous point.

"Where are we meeting them?" Adriana asked.

"Meeting them?" Wagner sounded concerned. "We don't have the ring, and you just told them we do. If we show up without it, they're going to kill us."

"They're going to kill Sean if we don't."

"He's probably already dead."

Tommy's nostrils flared, and Wagner could see the big man's rage was beginning to switch targets. "Sorry," Wagner added quickly.

"He's alive. I know that. Our only option is to go meet them and find out where they're keeping Sean."

"You don't think they'll bring him to the meet-up?"

"No," Tommy said. "They'll have him somewhere out of sight. So, we'll work the same angle with what they want."

38

PARIS

Adriana, Tommy, and Wagner stepped out of the cab and waited as the vehicle pulled away. Each one of them was armed, though not as heavily as they would have preferred. With one pistol each, they weren't a formidable force, though the weapons they carried could land them in a French prison. Again.

The dark sky overhead was muddled from the humid air and muted by the light pollution from the city. Patches of clouds drifted lazily across the face of the moon. It was the perfect night for monsters to roam the old city. The three knew the monsters they were about to meet weren't like the fantastical beasts of old fairy tales. There were no vampires, no werewolves, no dragons. In some ways, those creatures would have been preferable. Human beings could be far worse.

The Arc de Triomphe was a few hundred feet away. The colors of the French flag rotated through a timed sequence of lights illuminating the monument. A huge French flag hung directly under the arch. It was well beyond prime time for tourists, but there were still a few dozen loitering around, taking pictures, laughing, posing like a bunch of...well, tourists.

"This is good," Tommy said. "Still plenty of people around. I doubt

Berger would be so bold as to try starting a gunfight in the middle of a crowd."

Wagner's gaze fell on Tommy. The older man didn't say anything. He didn't have to. The look he gave Tommy said enough. Berger *was* bold enough to do that. And cruel enough to not care about collateral damage.

"There he is," Adriana said. She didn't point, choosing to be subtle.

The other two followed the direction in which she nodded and saw the leader of the Teutonic Order leaning against one of the columns.

He was shrouded in shadow. The lights of passing cars, the flashes of phones and their cameras, even the beams that illuminated the surface of the arched monument seemed to avoid him, drawing close but only daring to cast wayward glows onto his face.

He was big, well over six feet tall, and his arms were crossed as he appeared to be casually watching people come and go.

"I guess we should go talk," Tommy said.

Adriana nodded, and Tommy stepped away from the car.

They made their way along the sidewalk toward the arch, walking deliberately and scanning their surroundings. Adriana noted a couple kissing behind a thin tree trunk off to the left. In the bushes nearby was another person, a silhouette if it could be called that. He was nearly invisible, but she'd spotted him. He wasn't paying attention to the kissing couple. He was watching Adriana and her companions. She flicked her eyes to the right and spotted another watcher, this one standing nonchalantly near a park bench. By the time they reached the base of the monument, Adriana counted nineteen men watching their every move. That wasn't to say she assumed they were the only ones. There could have easily been a dozen more hiding on the other side of the road or farther away, perhaps in sniper nests, ready to take them out when the order was given.

She didn't like being exposed like this, out in the open, easy targets. Adriana knew there was one thing keeping them alive at this very moment: restraint.

Berger knew that if he killed her and the two men with her, he wouldn't get what he wanted. The ring would be lost, although that was making the assumption they didn't have it in their possession. The grand master of the Teutonic Order was at least giving them that much credit—that they wouldn't be foolish enough to show up with the priceless relic. Then again, that also meant Sean would be nowhere nearby.

The grand master was still leaning one shoulder against the stone column as Adriana and the others approached. She slowed her pace, letting Tommy take the lead as they had discussed before arriving at the arch.

Tommy stopped several feet short of where Berger stood. The older man's eyes sized him up in less than a second. Tommy was certainly shorter than Berger, but what he lacked in height Tommy made up for in brute strength. Over the years, he'd continued his workouts, his training, and had honed his body into a stout structure that could both take and deal out punishment.

"I assume you're armed," Berger commented nonchalantly.

"We have a saying back home about what happens when you assume," Tommy said with a coy smirk. "Doesn't usually work out for the one doing the assuming."

"Ah. Well, I'm certain you know I'm armed." Berger pulled back the thin peacoat to reveal a .45-caliber pistol on his hip. It was brazen to wear a firearm in such an easily seen place, at least in this country. Doing so showed that this man didn't fear the cops. He probably owned many of them, which gave Tommy pause to wonder how they'd gotten out of jail alive.

"We knew you would be," Tommy said. "Just like we knew you'd bring reinforcements."

He let his eyes flit to the left as if signaling Berger to give a look to his men.

"You saw my men." He made the statement as if Tommy had merely noted the color of grass was green. "I did not position them in a way that they would be invisible to you. I wanted you to know what you're dealing with so you don't get any stupid ideas."

Tommy forced a chuckle, though he was not in the mood to laugh. They were in a tight spot, even though there were still dozens of innocent civilians standing around, doing what tourist's do best— take pictures.

"I don't expect a shootout here," Tommy confessed. He could feel Adriana and Wagner close behind him even though he didn't turn to check their positions.

"Why would you?" Berger asked, extending his hands out wide as if showing off the area. "So many innocent people. We wouldn't want any stray bullets hitting them."

Tommy inclined his head, uncertain if the man meant what he was saying. It didn't sound like he cared. In truth, Tommy knew he didn't. This guy cared only about one thing: getting the ring of John the Baptist. After that, who knew what he was going to try next? It was anyone's guess.

It was a dangerous game of poker that Tommy was playing with this man, and he knew he couldn't overplay his hand. His eyes narrowed as he considered what to say next, and he wondered what the other man was thinking.

Before he could say anything, Berger spoke again. "I see you brought some dead weight with you." He nodded, indicating Wagner. "Found an old knight of your own, did you? I'm sure he told you that he intends to take the ring back to Malta, to Valletta where it can be put back in the reliquary. No doubt, he's convinced you that his island is where it belongs."

"It is where it belongs. Don't for one moment try to pretend this is about anything more than your greed and a false sense of truth you've managed to twist and bend to justify your actions."

Berger's head rocked back for a second as he snorted a forced laugh at Wagner's comment. "Please. That useless rock of land you call home is undeserving of such a powerful relic. You already lost it once. If it ended up back there, you would simply lose it again. No, it will be safer with me, with someone who understands its true power."

Tommy wanted to keep the man talking, to stall as long as he could. He glanced around, as if hoping something might miraculously happen, but he knew no miracle was coming. Berger had been strategic about where he placed his men. If anything went south, the rest of his team would converge on the Arc de Triomphe with swift and deadly speed. Not only that; they might never locate Sean.

"I guess," Tommy said, keeping the conversation going, "this is where I ask you where Sean is. You ask me where the ring is, then I tell you it's not here."

Berger's eyebrows lifted slightly, but he kept his demeanor calm.

Tommy went on. "We go around and around a few times before we come to some kind of an arrangement where you show me a picture or video of Sean that convinces me he's safe, and I tell you where to find the ring."

"Direct. Blunt. To the point. I like that."

"Time is the one resource you can't get more of in this life. Why waste it with pleasantries and banter? You want the ring. We want my friend back. Tell us where he is. Show me proof. And I will tell you where you can find the ring."

Berger appeared to consider the offer for a moment. A sedan drove by with the windows down, playing a song by a popular electronic dance music DJ.

"Proof? Where will my proof be?" Berger asked. "You want me to tell you where your friend is, but you will likely take the information and try to leave without giving me details about the whereabouts of the ring. I don't think so."

"So, we're at an impasse," Tommy said. "You're going to have to trust me a little on this one."

"Do I have to trust you?" Berger shook his head. "No, I don't think I do. You see, I believe I'm going to take you three and force you to tell me where the ring is."

"That would cause a scene," Tommy said. "I don't think you want to cause a scene. Besides, if you do anything to hurt the three of us, any of us, you'll lose your chance at finding it. Maybe the new grand master will have better luck...in four hundred years."

"Oh, I know what's at stake here, but you have one problem with your plan."

"And that is?"

"You underestimate my willingness to torture everyone you care about in order to get the information we want. So, you can do this one of two ways, Thomas. You can tell me what I want to know right now and trust that I will give you the true location where I'm keeping your friend. Or you can put up a fight right now where there is the potential for accidents—you know, those innocent people you mentioned—all of which will end the same way. You three will be surrounded, captured, and taken somewhere I control. Once that happens, there will be nothing you can say or do to save yourselves. Even when I have the ring in my possession, I will continue to torture your friends right before your eyes until they succumb. And I promise, that breaking point will not come quickly. I swear it."

The man's words hung in the thick, humid spring air.

"You're quite the negotiator," Wagner said after hearing enough.

"I wondered when you might open your mouth, Bertrand."

Adriana's eyes darted around, a question in her head needing answers: Where was Bodmer?

"Your greed and quest for revenge are over, Lucien," Wagner hissed. "You think that ring will get you riches and glory. That's not what the ring is for."

"Oh, I know what it's for, old friend."

Tommy wondered how well the two knew each other, but now wasn't the time to question their backstory.

Wagner was too quick to continue anyway. "You think that if you trundle into Rome with it, you'll be able to command the Holy See. You believe it gives you the authority to take over the Vatican and, with it, the entire Christian world."

"It will. Of course, you will be able to witness it for yourself unless you do something foolish and I have to kill you."

"Kill me?" Wagner chuffed. "You can't kill me, old friend. You've tried before and failed."

More backstory. What happened between these two?

"That? I promise, if I was trying, you'd already be dead. No, your presence here was expected, and when you die it must have meaning, purpose."

"So you can root out all the wickedness in the world, starting with your own brethren."

"Your order forgot the oaths long ago, Bertrand. You betrayed us along with the now-extinct Templars. They got what they deserved. Now it's your turn, along with any others of your kind that managed to survive through the years."

Tommy watched the exchange with vested interest.

Adriana did, as well, though she spent more time watching the perimeter, making sure no one was trying to sneak up behind them.

"We are not like you or the Templars or the Hospitallers. We work for the church. We serve without greed or motive. The only fuel that drives us is seeking truth. Not some misguided selfish dream. Your order died long ago, Lucien. It's time you accept that."

Berger almost seemed to consider the statement for a moment. He tilted his head back and then lowered it again, maintaining eye contact with his rival. "No, I don't think so. The pope has lost his way. The church, too, has lost its way. They accept anything, anyone. They've become too tolerant. We lose members around the world every day. Why? Because people are tired of the soft stance the church has taken on too many issues."

"You mean like its founder?"

"You forget, old friend, the Kingdom of Heaven must be forged through the blood of the wicked. You know as well as I do that to provide peace, true and lasting peace, there must be war first."

Wagner shook his head dejectedly. "Then you are truly lost. You are beyond redemption."

"Funny," Berger countered. "I was just thinking the same thing about you."

"Then I guess we are at an impasse."

"I suppose so."

Berger turned his attention back to Tommy. "I don't wish to kill your friend—not yet, anyway." He reached into his jacket pocket and pulled out a cell phone. He tapped on the screen, and then an image appeared. It only rang twice before the recipient answered. It was Bodmer, who then turned the phone's camera so that it showed a man tied to a chair with layer upon layer of duct tape. His mouth was likewise sealed shut with the silvery tape. His head hung low, chin almost touching his chest. He appeared to be tired, maybe even sleeping. It was hard to tell, but Tommy could see that Sean's chest was rising and falling in a slow rhythm. He was still alive.

Where he was, however, was more difficult to discern. From the looks of it, he was in some kind of construction zone, surrounded by scaffolds, tools, paints, and huge drop cloths. Most of the area beyond the immediate field of view was dark, the only illumination coming from a couple of candles placed in the middle of the floor.

"You see?" Berger asked. "He's alive and well. You tell us where the ring is, and I give you Sean's location."

"I suppose you're just going to let us waltz in there and pick him up without a fight." Tommy sounded skeptical.

"Of course not. I will have my men positioned there. You will have to fight your way through to get to him, which I don't think you'll be able to do, not with just the three of you. Still, he is there, and you are free to try. Now, the ring. Where is it?"

"Where is Sean?"

Berger's lips creased. "Still forcing the stalemate? I've given you the proof you seek. You've given me nothing. Perhaps you don't know where the ring is. If that's the case, I see no reason to keep your friend Sean alive any longer." He had started to raise the phone to his face to give the order to execute Sean when Wagner stopped him. "I will go with you to where the ring is hidden."

The unexpected volunteering caught Tommy, Adriana, and Berger off guard.

"You would be my hostage?" Berger asked.

"Yes. If it means saving Sean and any other innocents from your madness."

Berger ignored the last barb. "Very well, Bertrand. You will be my prisoner. If Thomas is lying about the location, he knows what I will do to you." He turned back to Tommy. "Tell me where the ring is, and

I will give you Sean's location. You have five seconds, or I kill him. I've lived my entire life without the ring. I will find another lead. I doubt you will find another Sean."

Tommy knew he was right. It was the checkmate play that Berger had in his back pocket. He'd kept it there, waiting for Tommy to go through the entire scenario before showing his hand.

Tommy had hoped it wouldn't come to that. He knew there was nothing as powerful when it came to bargaining chips. He was going to have to trust that this madman wasn't lying, that Berger was going to give him Sean's true location.

"As a man of God, I hope you wouldn't lie to me," Tommy groused.

"As a man of God, you shouldn't stand against me."

"Perhaps. Perhaps not. Sometimes, even the men who profess to serve the Almighty still make bad decisions, do the wrong things for the right reasons."

"I'm sorry," Berger said abruptly, cutting off Tommy's thoughts. "We were in the middle of counting down your friend's execution. I believe I said five seconds. That was at least a minute ago. Commander, if you will?"

Bodmer set down the phone so Tommy and Adriana could see what was about to happen.

"No, don't do this," Tommy insisted.

Adriana said nothing, though she was clearly suppressing a million emotions. She'd seen Sean in predicaments before, always able to get himself out. Now, however, was different. He didn't appear to have a way to get free.

Bodmer appeared on the screen, standing directly behind Sean with a shiny dagger. The metal glinted in the flickering candlelight as the killer held the weapon with the point nearly touching the back of Sean's skull. Bodmer's intention was clear. He was going to shove the tip of the blade through the base of Sean's neck, and up into the back of the skull where it would kill him instantly.

He'd wanted to make Sean suffer, for his death to take a long time, but an execution like this would get his friends' attention, and it wasn't like time was on Berger's side.

Tommy sensed the man was growing apprehensive, as if afraid of something. Was it being exposed, out in the open in such a public space? Or was it something else?

"Stop!" Tommy shouted. "Tell him to stop."

"Three." Berger said, skipping five and four.

"Stop, I said."

"Two."

"It's here! Okay? The name we were missing from the list. There was a gap. It's Berthier. The ring is hidden in the tomb of Berthier."

"One."

"He just told you where it is!" Adriana insisted, stepping forward with her pistol showing just under her waistband. "You kill him. You die. Understand?"

Berger's lips cracked on the left side of his face. "You would die, as well," he said, motioning to the men who were now emerging from their hiding spots.

"If you kill Sean, I have nothing left to live for," Adriana said. "That happens, and killing you will be the only thing I care about. I'll die satisfied."

He searched her eyes for truth. "You carry a defiance unlike any I've seen in a woman. Or a man, for that matter. I wonder...who trained you?"

"My father. He taught me about people like you, cowards who stand behind hostages. I will end you, Lucien."

His smile broadened.

"He is in Notre-Dame Cathedral, though I don't know if you will be able to make it there in time."

"What?" Tommy suddenly seemed worried.

"Commander Bodmer," Berger spoke into the phone. The man reappeared on the screen a moment later. "Burn it."

A sudden flick of the man's wrist caught Adriana's attention.

Wagner and Tommy also saw it but didn't realize what had happened until it was too late.

The searing white light pierced their vision and caused the three to grab at their eyes. The painful flash only lasted a couple of seconds, but the damage it rendered took minutes to overcome as their eyes struggled to adjust to the dark city night.

Adriana was the first to recover her vision and looked around, careful not to brandish her weapon. The flash-bang device had already drawn the attention of far too many people. Some were pointing in her direction, and she knew that some form of authority would be making their way over soon, if for nothing more than to ask questions. It was an unaffordable delay.

Tommy stood at about the same time as Wagner. He rubbed at his eyes, trying to locate Berger, but the man was nowhere to be seen.

"Where did he go?" Tommy asked with deep concern in his voice.

"To get the ring would be my guess," Adriana said. She turned to Wagner. "Go to the tomb of Louis Alexandre Berthier. Do what you can. When we find Sean, we will head that way."

Wagner nodded, apparently having the same idea.

He took off and ran down the street before blending into the crowd. Adriana watched him disappear and then scanned their surroundings for any more of Berger's men. There was no sign of them anywhere.

"Come on," Adriana said. "We have to get to the cathedral."

39

NOTRE DAME CATHEDRAL - PARIS

S ean had been sitting motionless in the chair. He was surrounded by construction materials—plastic tarps, tools, and scaffolds. He was glad Berger's men hadn't knocked him out again before bringing him to Notre-Dame.

Bodmer had been the one in charge of securing the location amid the renovations that had been going on for the last several months. The place was in disarray, and with so many construction workers moving in and out of the building, it was easy enough to slip in and up to one of the higher levels. Bodmer and three other knights set Sean down in a wooden chair, though this time they didn't use as much adhesive to bind him to the seat. The tape was still wrapped tightly around his body, and he found that any movement at all took an exhausting effort, but it was also necessary as he was losing circulation in his wrists and ankles. His shoulders, too, were tightening from the lack of movement.

Then there was the other issue.

He really needed to relieve himself, but he knew there was no way Bodmer was going to allow that to happen in a civilized manner.

The man had been watching him like a very annoying hawk for

the last hour, barely taking his eyes away to even blink. Sean knew that something was going down, and soon.

Berger had gone, Sean assumed to meet Tommy and Adriana. He didn't like the idea, and concern for his friend and his wife overwhelmed any worries he might have harbored for his own well-being.

Luckily, he hoped, he had a plan. It was just a question of time.

The men who'd abducted him had taken everything from him. They removed his money clip, his phone, and his weapons—everything except one small item.

The wedding band on his left ring finger was still there. The thick groom's band was made from silver and had a harder upper edge that wrapped around the entire loop. It was engraved with Celtic knots, a symbol of his Irish heritage, along with a single Templar cross engraved in the center of the knots. That one was for personal reasons, reasons he'd never shared with anyone but his wife and Tommy. Even the kids didn't know the reason behind it.

Part of it was spiritual, a reminder to him of his Christian upbringing and the values he'd learned as a young person. The other purpose of the cross was to grant him access to a secret archive in Washington, a place few knew existed.

Now, however, none of that mattered. The ring had a different purpose, and Sean needed that purpose to work faster.

One of the few body parts he'd been able to move during his captivity was his ring finger. He'd managed to bend his left thumb over to where he could wiggle the object back and forth in a wobbling motion. Sean started the process while still in the abandoned office building and continued during the ride to the cathedral in the back of Bodmer's SUV. He'd been manipulating the ring for over an hour and wasn't sure how much progress he'd made since his hands were behind his back. Though at one point he was pretty sure he felt something give way. The tiniest sliver opened in the duct tape, and he felt the ring poke through it.

Bodmer was still watching him but couldn't see the subtle movement within the silvery mummy wrapping.

Sean doubled his efforts, doing his best not to move his body. If he rocked back and forth, Bodmer would realize something was up. Sean was only going to get one shot at this. The only reason he was still alive was because Berger needed information from Tommy and the others. He hoped that his friend hadn't given up the secret—if they had in fact figured it out. Knowing Tommy and Adriana, they likely had already reached a solution and retrieved the ring.

Maybe that was just being naïvely hopeful.

Sean felt his finger punch through the tape as the slit he'd created widened. He jammed another finger through and felt the adhesive give with a barely audible tear. Sean froze for a moment, glancing across the room at Bodmer with disinterest, doing his best to look calm.

Bodmer had finally taken his eyes off Sean and was busily preparing something with rags and...then he realized what the man was doing. He was dousing rags with paint thinner. They were going to burn down the cathedral with him in it.

He worked his fingers in the slit and continued tearing it until he felt the tape break free on the top. His wrists broke away and his fingers immediately began to tingle as blood began to flow unrestricted once again.

Sean checked his warden again. Then he stole a glance at the two guards standing by the door, knowing the third was just beyond on the other side. He thought it odd to place one man outside and two inside with Bodmer. Perhaps they were still concerned Sean might find a way to escape.

He didn't want to disappoint.

His fingers gripped the bottom edge of the tape that was wrapped around his back and began ripping it. He moved carefully, deliberately, stopping when Bodmer appeared to check on him, then began again.

The tape tore easily enough considering the awkward way he was forced to work. Sean knew he wouldn't be able to get it all the way to the top, but that was something he could handle. Once the tear in the adhesive was high enough, he could pull it off like a shirt, a task made far easier now that his hands were free. Facing Bodmer, Sean knew the commander wouldn't be able to see what he'd done unless he walked around behind the chair.

Sean got a little too aggressive and ripped the tape louder than intended. Bodmer's head snapped around to find Sean staring down at his lap, a despondent look on his face.

Bodmer grinned devilishly. "Why so glum, Sean? You'll be dead soon, and you're going to burn in one of the most famous cathedrals in the world."

"I figured you were going to set the place on fire," Sean said. He wasn't lying. The second he'd seen what Bodmer was up to, he knew. "I just gotta ask..."

"Why? Why are we burning down this icon to Christianity? You know why, Sean. This entire journey has been why."

"Oh, I see. You can't get to the Vatican, so you're going to tear down another symbol of the church. Got it."

"We can get to the Vatican," Bodmer said. "Who do you think killed Jarllson? How do you think that happened? I *am* the Vatican." His teeth flashed like a wolf's as he spoke. "It will belong to us the moment Lucien puts on the ring of the Baptist."

"Gotcha," Sean said with a nod that covered up his shoulder movements as he continued working the tear in the tape up toward the middle of his back. "So, what does that mean for you? Do you get to be like a second-in-command, or is there an assistant job you're gunning for? Honestly, I didn't know the pope had that kind of position. Or is what you're looking for...a little more intimate?" Sean let the insult hang for a moment.

Bodmer snarled and began to stalk toward Sean when the phone on a small worktable started vibrating. Bodmer's eyes flashed a warning blaze, and then he turned back, strode over to the phone, and picked it up. He pressed the green button and held the phone away from his face.

Sean listened to the conversation while he moved his hands faster. He halted when Bodmer turned his attention to him and pointed the camera his way. Sean knew he was being put on display for his friends' benefit. They likely wanted to know if he was still alive. It was smart on their part since Sean knew they were probably involved in some kind of negotiation with Berger.

It was obvious to Sean how everything was playing out. The grand master would demand the location of the ring, which Sean figured his friends were able to determine on their own. Why else would they have a meeting with Berger? Unless they were trying to trick him and give him a false location.

Bodmer turned the phone away and walked back to the table, finishing his conversation with Berger. Sean felt the tape break free at his back just as he heard the grand master give the order to burn it.

Sean knew what that meant. This wasn't just some small arson job. They were going to take down a symbol of the church; the church that Berger was convinced had wronged him and his order so long ago. It wasn't just an international icon, a place that was visited by millions of tourists every year. Notre-Dame was a display of culture and architecture from a time long ago. As important a site as it was, it belonged to the entire world, not just to a group of religious fanatics. These guys were going to burn it down. *The arrogance*, Sean thought.

He did his best to keep the tape from sagging as Bodmer strode back to where he sat and started drenching the floor around the chair with turpentine.

"I don't want to tell you how to do your job," Sean said, "but you should be careful with that, you know. With all the candles burning in here, only a matter of time until those fumes catch fire."

"That's the plan," Bodmer said. "And you're going to go up in flames with this beacon of betrayal."

Sean snorted a genuine laugh. "Beacon of betrayal? How long have you been sitting on that one? Seriously, that's what you came up with?"

"We'll see how funny you think it is when your skin is melting off your body."

"Eek," Sean said. "That's a grisly thing to think about."

Bodmer said nothing. Instead, he walked over to the worktable and picked up the knife and pistol he'd left there. He shoved the knife back in a sheath and holstered the pistol before turning to a collection of four candles on the table's surface. He picked up one of the candle holders before pivoting around to face Sean.

"You see, Sean, nothing can get in our way. We are going to destroy this temple of lies, as well as the one in Rome. We will rebuild the church as it was meant to be, and we will root out dissent and apostasy to put the rightful rulers in place."

"You being the rightful rulers—the Knights of the Teutonic Order."

"Exactly. Soon, the world will see what the church and the governments of the world did to us, and to them. They will see the pope for what he really is, and when we are done all will kneel before the true leader of the church and the ring he bears on his finger."

"So, a sort of kiss-the-ring kind of deal. Sounds like you guys are Mafia or something." Sean smirked at his own humor.

"Funny," Bodmer growled.

"I thought so."

"You won't be laughing as you burn along with this church."

Bodmer held the candle aloft, letting it waiver over a trail of paint thinner he'd sprayed on the floor, a trail that led to where Sean was sitting. "You know," he said, "when they get to the tomb of Berthier and recover the ring, none of this would have mattered. All of your efforts could have been avoided, and you wouldn't have had to die. Not yet, anyway," he said with a disturbing clown-like smirk.

Sean didn't take the bait, but he did make a note: Berthier. That was it, the missing name from the list. Sean rapidly processed the information. He seemed to recall reading something about an officer named Berthier who had served Napoléon. That had to be it. The ring was at this Berthier's tomb. He tried not to focus on that. It was, after all, the assumption of a man desperate to save his life. "Careful with that, Commander. With all this turpentine you accidentally spilled, you could start a fire with that thing."

"I know." Bodmer dropped the candle dramatically to the floor, but by the time the candlestick hit the wooden boards, the flame had been extinguished by the wind.

Sean couldn't stop himself from laughing despite the dire circumstances. Even though he was now free from the waist up, he still had to get the tape off his legs before he could move.

"I'm sorry," Sean said amid the laughter, "I just...one second. He wished he could pretend to wipe tears from his eyes for more effect. "That's just too funny. I mean, you were trying to be all dramatic and do a kind of mic drop with the candle and...it blew out!" Another round of laughter ensued.

Bodmer hurriedly picked up another candelabra and spilled glops of wax on his hand. He angrily shouted something in French and then lowered the flame carefully to the floor. "I'm going to make you pay for laughing."

"You sure you don't want to try the big mic drop again?" Sean joked.

The flickering yellow flame touched the paint thinner and the trail immediately caught fire. It was a slow burn at first but rapidly picked up speed. Bodmer watched it for a moment as the flames shot out in different directions, all following the different paths of fuel he'd poured to make sure the entire room would be engulfed within moments of his leaving.

He turned and motioned for the guards to open the door. The two men did so and stepped through, leaving Bodmer to watch as the fire neared Sean. The American struggled against the duct tape, fighting to get free, but the effort was futile.

Bodmer briefly contemplated saying something else to the prisoner, but he decided against it. Soon, this entire place would go up in smoke, and he needed to be as far away from it as possible.

40

NOTRE DAME

The second the door closed behind Bodmer, Sean ripped his arms out of the tape and started trying to free his legs. The flames danced wildly around him, lapping at the chair as the wooden floor beneath caught fire.

More flame trails crawled up the walls, surrounding him like liquid rivers of fire flowing upward until they reached the ceiling and joined in the center.

Sean knew he had less than a minute before the entire place was consumed in flames.

He tried to pull the duct tape down over his shoes, but it was wrapped too tightly. "Where is the end?" he asked out loud as the sound of the fire grew louder. Thick black smoke filled the very top of the building and loomed over him like a cloud of death waiting to descend on its prey.

He felt the back of the smooth adhesive, searching for the seam that would indicate the end of the tape, but he couldn't find it. He kept searching even as the flames licked at his hands and feet. The searing heat swelled, and he could feel it pressing in on his clothes and skin from every angle. Sean was about to give up on freeing himself and try to hop over to the door when he felt the edge of something graze his fingers.

The end of the tape.

He jammed a fingernail under it and pulled. At first, only a tiny patch pulled free from the rest of the bonds. Sean stayed persistent, though, and soon he had the entire end unwrapping from the bundle. He worked fast, working his hands over and under his legs even as the flames continued to build.

The heat in the room was nearly unbearable, even for someone like Sean, who been in a few infernos, nearly dying in one.

Sean forced himself to concentrate, knowing that if he tried to do things too quickly he could lose his focus and mess up, tangling the tape. The flames drew ever closer, encroaching on his personal space. He winced against the scalding heat and gave one last tug on the duct tape.

The adhesive ripped away from his pants and he jumped out of the chair to sprint to the door, but something was holding him back. He looked down at his ankles and realized that two strips were still attached to his legs, wrapping individually around the ankle and the chair supports.

"Oh, come on!" he shouted.

Sean bent down and ripped the tape on his right ankle, then the left. Now, however, a wall of fire stood between him and the door. Smoke was already trying to force its way into his lungs, and he knew he didn't have much longer before he succumbed to either the smoke or the irrepressible heat.

With only seconds to spare, Sean found a spot on the floor that seemed to be resisting the flames. It was one where Bodmer hadn't spread any flammable liquids. He dove to that area to buy some time and found himself standing next to a small wooden table. This one was similar to a bistro table, not as large as the worktable on the other side of the room but bigger than a common nightstand.

Sean could only think of one way to use the table to his advantage. It was pretty much the only thing left in the room that wasn't on fire, save for him, and that could change at any moment.

He flipped the table onto its top and started pushing it toward the door. His legs churned, the muscles tightening and releasing with every step. The table's surface squelched the fire in Sean's path, suffocating the flames of their precious oxygen so that Sean had a charred, but not burning, trail to follow to the door. He was nearly to the exit when the front end of the table caught on a jagged piece of floorboard. The end Sean was pushing lurched up, and the fire he'd tried to avoid flamed violently in his face. He jumped back and dropped the table, effectively putting out the surge of flame. He felt sure his eyelashes and eyebrows were singed, but he didn't care. He had to get out.

Sean tilted the front of the table just enough to get over the piece jutting from the floor and pushed hard the last few steps. His leg muscles burned, but they could have been burning in a much worse way as he felt the end of the table run into the wall next to the door. Luckily, there was still a small patch of floor that wasn't on fire. Sean stepped over to it and then tapped on the latch to make sure it wasn't hot. He knew metal knobs and handles heated quickly, a harbinger of a potential inferno on the other side. Thankfully, it was still cool and Sean pulled down on the latch. The door opened and he stepped out into the corridor, quietly shutting the door behind him to contain as much of the fire and smoke as he could.

Bodmer and his men were nowhere to be seen.

The short corridor ended just beyond the room where he'd been. There was a stone staircase at the other end, and he recalled being dragged up it, an exercise that had exhausted Bodmer and his men.

Sean hurried over to the stairs and began his descent. He did his best to do it quietly, but the sound of rafters collapsing and glass shattering covered up any noise his feet could have made on the hard stone steps.

He looked down into the narrow shaft between the winding staircase. He spotted a hand rounding a corner several floors down. The men he was after were already nearing the bottom. Once they were outside, it would be impossible to catch them.

A sudden explosion in the upper room rocked the building. One of the highly flammable cans must have caught fire. Where he stood remained stable, but as the fire spread things would rapidly deteriorate.

Sean plunged down the stairs, two, sometimes three steps at a time. He flew around the corners, vaulting himself down nearly an entire flight to make up time he'd lost above. He had no weapon, but it wasn't the first time he'd been in that predicament. He had to slow down Bodmer and his crew. That was the least he could do to help his friends.

Besides, Sean learned a long time ago that guns, knives, explosives, none of those things were weapons. They were tools.

He was the weapon.

His feet hit the final landing as a door slammed shut in the next corridor. The men he was after still didn't know he'd escaped. He jumped down the last couple of steps and wrested an iron sconce from the wall. The object was hanging loose and broke free with little effort. Sean removed an iron chain from a loop beneath it and then rushed to the door.

He flung open the heavy wooden door and stepped through into the next corridor. He saw Bodmer and his men near the end of the hall. They were almost to the exit. Sean wouldn't be able to catch them, and even if he could they would hear him approaching. He had to figure out a way to cut them off.

Think, Sean.

He remembered the men bringing him there. They'd brought him in a burlap sack, which had been its own kind of uncomfortable. The rough fabric scraped against his skin and reeked of turpentine, or whatever it was that caused burlap to smell the way it did. Still, he'd been able to see out of the top and noted where Bodmer's driver had parked. He also recalled the path they'd taken to get into one of the maintenance entrances to the church.

That was all just before they entered the musty stone corridors of the cathedral. Sean knew most of the other hallways would be occupied with people there to appreciate the historic site. What they didn't know was that they were all in great danger.

That fact smacked Sean squarely in the jaw.

Bodmer and his men opened the door at the other end of the corridor. A dim, orange-yellow light radiated into the dark passage. He couldn't see much beyond the exit, but he knew where they were going. Sean had to take a different path out, and on the way he had to warn everyone of the danger.

His mind made up, Sean took off in the other direction, and when he reached another door he tossed the chain and sconce onto the floor with a clank.

Bodmer and his three henchmen were already gone, which meant they wouldn't hear the noise.

Sean found himself standing next to an alcove where a priest was kneeling before dozens of candles and a sculpture of Christ on the cross. Sean didn't want to interrupt the man's meditations, but there was no time.

"Father," Sean said, tapping the man on the shoulder.

The old priest looked up at him with confusion in his eyes.

"You need to get everyone out of here."

The priest frowned at the insinuation. It wasn't an angry expression, merely one of bewilderment.

Sean clarified with his best French. "The building is on fire, Father. You must get everyone out."

The man's eyes widened just as a fire alarm pierced the air with its sharp beeping.

"Go," Sean ordered.

The old man nodded and stood quickly before hurrying out into the sanctuary, where Sean assumed he would help usher people out of the building.

Taking off in the other direction, Sean headed down another side corridor that ran perpendicular to the sanctuary, behind the presbytery, and out to the other side of the building. He reached a door set in the wall and tried to pull it open—but it was locked. He scowled, wishing he'd asked the priest for a key. The locked door also explained why Bodmer and his men had taken the long way around. For a moment, Sean was paralyzed by the distracting thought about how the four men were able to sneak a corpse-size burlap sack into the church, but that question would have to wait.

Sean sighed, looked to the ceiling, and said, "I'm sorry." Then he kicked the door with the heel of his boot. The hinges creaked, and the housing broke free as the bolt splintered the wood on the other side.

He sprinted through without a second thought. He also gave no thought to stealth or covert movement. Only his target occupied his thoughts.

41

NOTRE DAME

Sean burst through the door and found himself under
twinkling stars set amid a crystal clear sky. He blinked rapidly
for a moment, letting his eyes adjust, and then scanned the
area.

People were already gathering at a perimeter around the church.
They likely believed they were at a safe distance, though Sean would
have preferred them another hundred yards back.

He darted out of the doorway and headed toward the parking
area that he recalled seeing through the little hole at the top of the
burlap sack. It was entirely possible that he was going the wrong way,
but he couldn't hesitate to worry about that. If he was wrong, he'd
deal with it.

Sean filtered his way through the swelling crowd, almost having
to swim through some of the denser portions of onlookers. Notre-
Dame was one of the most famous landmarks in one of the most
historic cities in the world. It was no surprise that when smoke began
to billow from the rooftop, throngs would rush to the scene.

There was no time to look back and survey the damage Bodmer
and his henchmen had caused. He'd have to hope the fire depart-
ments and emergency personnel could save as much as possible. It

was lucky, in some ways, that the landmark was being renovated. There would be fewer evacuees, and most of the relics and important works of art had already been removed. Still, so much history would be lost if the building was totally destroyed.

He caught a glimpse of a jacket he recognized moving in the opposite direction to the flocking masses. He pulled his way past a smaller man who looked at him with a rude expression but immediately set his eyes back to the spectacle as Sean continued in the opposite direction.

Bodmer and his men were moving quickly, but not running. They were clearly doing their best not to look conspicuous.

The commander of the Swiss Guard was in the lead with the others trailing behind him in single file.

Sean searched the ground at his feet for anything he could use as a weapon but found nothing but the occasional empty cup and trash from fast food restaurants. He let out an exasperated sigh and scooped up a McDonald's cup as he kept moving, closing the gap between him and the four retreating knights.

Twisting his way through the sea of people, Sean reached the first of the Teutonic guards. He pulled the plastic straw out of the paper cup and bent it in half to form a sharp V. Then he stepped on the guard's heel, causing the man to stumble. Sean lurched forward, as if to assist the tripping man, and grabbed the back of his neck. To an untrained eye, he might have appeared to be helping. What the onlookers didn't see was how Sean shoved the end of the straw through the man's eye.

The knight's yelp was cut off as Sean "accidentally" fell forward and bashed the man's forehead into the pavement, rendering him unconscious, or possibly dead. Sean didn't stop to check. He had another target right in front of him.

He moved fast, catching the second guard in the same way, though this one required a more deliberate foot to the ankle to send him stumbling forward. The second guard managed to twist around as he fell to the ground, a move that made Sean's task much easier.

The knight's eyes widened as he saw the ghost of Sean Wyatt

surging toward him. Sean grabbed him by the throat and used all of his momentum to drive the back of the man's skull into the sidewalk.

Instantly, the knight's eyes widened and then closed as he lost consciousness.

Sean immediately found the man's pistol at his side and was happy to see there was a small suppressor attached to the end of the barrel. It was more of a flash can than anything else, but with the rising tide of shouts amid blaring sirens, no one would notice a muffled pop.

He tucked the weapon under his shirt until he reached the third guard. They were almost to the SUV in the parking lot when Sean caught up with the man. He planted the pistol in the guard's kidneys, wrapped his hand around the man's mouth, and pulled the trigger. Sean was careful to make sure he felt the hard spine under the man's skin before he squeezed. The bullet of the 9mm would hit bone and continue on another few inches before it stopped.

His plan went exactly as he knew it would. The bullet stopped in the man's abdomen, allowing for no exit wound and no stray bullet streaking into the crowd. It was a tactic he'd used before, but never in a crowd this dense.

The man grunted and collapsed onto knees that would never feel anything again. His face hit the pavement with a smack, but no one seemed to notice as the crowd pushed to get a closer view of the tragedy taking place before their eyes.

Sean hid the pistol under his shirt again as he hurried to catch up with Bodmer.

The commander reached out to grasp the handle on the SUV and turned to make sure the rest of his unit was with him, but instead was met by the deadly gaze of a man he knew to be one of the most lethal in the world.

Bodmer tried to retrieve his weapon, but Sean's was already drawn and shielded from view by his body. Not that the crowd would notice—their attention was focused entirely on the flames erupting from the roof of Notre-Dame Cathedral. A massive hole in the tiles dumped clouds of roiling black smoke into the otherwise clear blue sky.

Sean squeezed off a shot as Bodmer tried to slap the gun away. It was a quicker move than Sean expected and the round missed the target, instead tearing through the commander's right shoulder. It was only a scratch, though, and Bodmer immediately recovered, as would be expected from a highly trained elite member of the Vatican's security force.

Sean didn't lose his grip on the weapon, but Bodmer wasn't done. He jabbed his right hand at Sean's face. Sean whipped his free arm up and partially deflected the blow, though Bodmer's fist still grazed Sean's jaw and sent a sting through his skin.

Bodmer followed with a knee that Sean avoided with a subtle twist. Though the force of the strike was intended for Sean's groin, it landed on his hip with a thud that sent a deadening pain through his leg and lower back.

Sean felt his left leg give, and it took all of his focus to shift weight to the right leg for the brief moment it required to recover.

He twisted his gun hand back around to deliver another round, this time into the target's chest, but Bodmer sensed the move and quickly turned sideways, snatched Sean's wrist, and jerked him toward the car.

It was a move Sean had used a million times, or so it seemed, and unfortunately it was just as effective when wielded by the Swiss Guard commander. Sean felt his weight leave the ground, and for a brief moment he was flying.

The flight was short and ended with a rough, abrupt landing as his middle back struck the side of the open SUV with a crunch.

Sean felt the weapon in his hand slip as the pain surged through his body.

Bodmer went for the killing blow. He wrenched the pistol from Sean's hand, twisting it in a way that would have broken multiple fingers had Sean's grip not already been loosened.

Bodmer then switched the weapon around to aim the barrel at Sean, who'd fallen to the ground next to the vehicle. Just as the man pointed the gun at Sean's head, he ducked to the left and swung his elbow hard into the backside of Bodmer's hand. The muzzle popped and sent a bullet burrowing into the driver's seat. Then Sean grabbed the barrel and yanked it hard to one side, then twisted back and up.

Bodmer's grip wasn't loose like Sean's had been, and a series of small cracks sounded amid the chaos as the man's trigger and middle fingers were broken in multiple places.

He growled angrily, and fire filled the man's eyes as his battle energy and agonizing pain coursed through his veins.

People continued to flood past the two fighters, oblivious to the conflict as the massive cathedral was engulfed in flames that stretched up into the sky.

Bodmer tried to drive a knockout roundhouse punch to Sean's nose, but Sean ducked to the right and drove the silencer into his opponent's gut. Bodmer hovered over him for a moment as Sean sat on the ground with his back against the lower part of the open door. The commander's eyes narrowed slightly, a second before the muted puff sent a concussion into his stomach. It was followed by a hollow pain, then a sharp one as the man's body began to react to the bullet lodged against his spinal column.

Sean felt warm liquid oozing onto his fingers and he quickly withdrew the weapon and wiped it on Bodmer's jacket as the man collapsed in a heap to the ground.

The commander lay in a fetal position, clutching his gut with both hands as his life spilled out onto the pavement.

Sean glanced around and saw that no one was paying any attention to him. Every single eye was fixed on the burning church. Sean bent down and grabbed the keys that lay next to Bodmer's head and whispered into the dying man's ear. "Your death for Jarllson's."

Bodmer's face quivered in agony. He'd heard that a bullet wound to the stomach was one of the most painful ways to go, though he'd never administered such a death before. Now he was experiencing it for himself.

"That's...not very Christian of you," Bodmer said.

Sean's expression never changed. "I'm old school." He kicked

Bodmer in the face, smashing the man's nose, rendering him nearly unconscious. Then Sean climbed into the SUV. He was about to start the engine when he heard someone calling his name.

He frowned and clutched the pistol in his hand, ready for an ambush, when he noticed a familiar face wading through the throng of people.

Adriana was making her way toward him. Tommy was right behind him, to her left, and was also coming his way.

"Sean!" she shouted.

He got out of the car, gave another glance at the writhing Bodmer, and then stepped over him, securing the weapon in his waistband to keep it out of sight.

He stepped toward her and wrapped his arms around her. She looped hers around his neck and kissed him, hard, before turning her attention to the dying commander of the Swiss Guard.

"Bodmer?" she asked.

"He'll be dead soon. What are you doing here? How did you find me?"

Tommy skidded to a stop next to them and then saw the body on the ground next to the SUV. "Oh jeez. I...oh wow. Okay. So, maybe we shouldn't stay right here in this spot."

"Good idea. I'll tell you once we're in the clear."

Sean led the other two away from what was now a crime scene and toward the sidewalk across the street.

They turned at a coffee shop and headed deeper into the city and away from the tragic spectacle at Notre-Dame.

Sean risked one glance back, partially because he was making sure they weren't being followed and in part because he, too, was curious about the damage to the historic church.

What he saw was nothing short of devastating. He felt a wave of emotions pound into his chest with the force of five mules.

The cathedral's entire roof was ablaze. A thick black cloud streamed from the top of the flames and streaked through the previously clear sky.

Sean gasped. He actually gasped in horror.

Tommy and Adriana shared a shocked glance and then grabbed Sean by the shoulders.

"Come on, man. We have to get farther away."

Sean nodded and spun around, jogging behind them. "You mean we have to get to Berthier's tomb," he corrected. "I figured it out. Bodmer, he was chattering while I was tied up, and he mentioned the name of the tomb. I guessed that was where the ring must be. I didn't get a chance to tell you, but—"

Tommy veered right at the next street and kept moving as he interrupted. "Yes, we know." Then he slowed to a casual walk and stopped at a white sedan. He put his elbow on the roof of the car and grinned proudly.

Even Adriana seemed confused. "What are you doing?"

"Remember I said I needed to make a couple of calls?"

Adriana frowned and shook her head. "Yeah, I guess."

Sean wasn't getting any clearer on the subject. "Dude, let's go."

"I made two calls," Tommy said, putting one hand out wide.

"So?"

Tommy sighed and hung his head dejectedly. "Really, guys? What does my wife do? Hello?"

"So, you called June?" Sean asked.

"Yes."

"About a French tomb?"

"Yes. No. I mean, sort of. Yes." Tommy fumbled through the words and put his elbow back on the roof of the car. "Look, I called in the cavalry."

Sean inclined his head and then nodded. "Oh, you..." He pointed a bouncing finger at his friend. "Nice. Well played, sir." He stuck out his fist and Tommy pounded it with his own.

"Thank you."

"So, where is this tomb? Is it close?"

Tommy looked less proud than the second before. "Actually, no. It's in Bavaria."

"Bavaria?"

"Southern Bavaria, close to the Austrian border. It's out there."

"The town's name is Tegernsee," Adriana said. "It's south of Munich. Berthier's body was moved there in 1881. We have to assume that any relics interred with him at his original burial place would have been transferred to Tegernsee."

"That's a big assumption," Sean said. "If someone found the ring..."

"It's our only lead. Our best lead," she reinforced.

Sean thought about it for several seconds then nodded. "Okay, lead the way. I've never been to this Tegernsee place before. Sounds interesting. Hopefully, June and her crew can handle Berger."

"Oh, she'll be fine. She knows what to do." He nodded with a smug expression on his face.

"Hey!" a new voice yelled. A blonde woman in a red dress was walking toward them with a scowl. "Get off my car!" she screamed in French.

Tommy jolted away from the sedan and then motioned to the others with his head to start moving.

"Wait, is that your car?" Sean asked amid the woman's incensed yelling.

Tommy flashed a cheeky grin. "Um, no."

42

TEGERNSEE, BAVARIA

The little town of Tegernsee nestles close to Germany's southern border with Austria. Founded in the sixth century, this village had long nestled its eponymous lake in a valley teeming with ancient forests of spruce and pine, surrounded by ski slopes that wound their way down from the stratospheric peaks of the Alps.

At first glance, it seemed the twenty-first century—along with most everyone else—had forgotten this quiet, conservative corner of Bavaria. The only hints of modernity were the cars, the power lines, and some renovations here and there that reflected more current architectural tastes. Most of Tegernsee, however, looked much as it had more than a hundred years ago, its history pristinely preserved.

In the winter, visitors flocked to the tiny village to enjoy the sweeping views, skiing and snowboarding, and cross-country skiing. In the summer, snow gave way to flowers, green trees and grass, and sparkling water that glistened in brilliant sunshine. Summer visitors could also find world-class hiking and climbing, or kayaking and canoeing on the lake, and the townsfolk were known throughout Central Europe for the cultural festivals they hosted in the warmer months.

Still, despite its popularity with tourists, life remained much the same as it has always been for the fewer than four thousand locals.

Berger looked up through the windshield at a minuscule church called the Wallbergkircherl that sat at the top of one of the mountains high above the town. People who visited the little chapel were treated to a 360-degree view of the surrounding Alps and the picturesque valley below.

Lucien Berger stepped out of the black sedan and looked around, taking inventory of the plaza surrounding the abbey.

The twin steeples of the Sankt Quirinus Kirche monastery rose into the sky. The beige stone walls reflected bright sunlight and made the building difficult to stare at for more than a couple of seconds.

Berger slipped on his sunglasses, and his vision cleared.

The Sankt Quirinus Kirche had originally been a monastery, but the abbey eventually fell under the ownership of the Bavarian dukes of Wittelsbach, a Bavarian royal family that had at one time produced two Holy Roman emperors and a king of Sweden.

Berger was somewhat surprised, though not shocked, to learn that the building now housed both a brewery and a high school, a strange combination even for the Germans, whose drinking prowess was renowned throughout the world. He sloughed off the thought and walked across the street to the entrance.

A café abutted the abbey. Yellow awnings stretched out over the width of the sidewalk, stopping at a small black fence that encompassed the patio dining area. People were happily eating a breakfast of deli meats, breads, crackers, and fruit while they sipped cups of coffee or cappuccino.

Berger's men parked their cars in various places along the street and fanned out behind him, making sure they set up a perimeter to protect their leader, and to ensure every angle was covered.

He didn't have to watch to know the men were doing their job. They were trained for this. And today was the day they'd all been preparing and waiting for, for so long.

Berger stepped onto the sidewalk in front of the church and stopped at the entrance. He hadn't heard from Bodmer yet, which was unlike his second-in-command. The man was always prompt with his check-ins, and the fact that he hadn't bothered to call was disconcerting.

It was no matter. That's what Berger told himself. He'd seen the reports regarding the Notre-Dame fire, watching the headlines scroll across his newsfeed with great satisfaction. They had struck a blow to the church, one that would ring down through generations.

In truth, Bodmer and his men had done better than expected. The plan was to burn the place, but Berger wasn't entirely convinced it would go up in flames the way it had. It really couldn't have gone more according to his vision. It was a strong blow that would echo across the entire planet.

Once the ring was in his possession, Berger would claim that the fire at Notre-Dame was an act of God, a symbolic and catastrophic gesture that change was coming to the true church and that the things of old would be swept away, just as it was foretold in the scriptures.

He took in a deep breath of the cool mountain air, relishing how fresh it felt and smelled as it passed through his nostrils. He reached out to open the door, but it suddenly opened on its own.

He squinted as he tried to adjust his eyes to the darkness within. A musty scent wafted over him from inside the building, and he cocked his head to the side as he took a single wary step forward.

"That's far enough," a female voice said from the shadows.

"What?" Berger asked, incensed. "Who are you?"

A blonde woman with pale blue eyes and a striking creamy complexion stepped into the sunlight. She wore a black coat that ran all the way down to her ankles. Her matching boots climbed up to the top of her calves where her tight pants disappeared into the cuffs.

"Lucien Berger. So, this is what a knight looks like. I thought you'd be...shinier, you know, with armor and all that."

"Get out of my way, woman," he demanded.

She pressed her lips together in a tight sarcastic smile and shook her head. "No. You're going away for the murder of Cardinal Jarllson."

"What?"

The man twisted his head around and saw that all nineteen of his men were being rounded up and detained by men and women in black uniforms. Some of the Kevlar vests they wore were branded Polizei. Some identified themselves as Interpol. Then there were a handful of others that had no branding whatsoever, just as the woman before him.

Berger's blood boiled and his face burned pink before settling into a deep red. He watched as his knights were pressed against streetlamps, park benches, and unmarked police cars. They were then cuffed and loaded into vans and other vehicles. Lucien Berger watched as everything he'd built over decades evaporated instantly, right before his eyes.

His head snapped back to the woman in front of him. "Who are you? You will pay for this."

June's face curled into a faux pleasant grin. "I don't think so. And before you ask me how all of this was possible, you don't have to look far for the answer."

Berger narrowed his eyes and then followed her gaze over his shoulder. There, across the street, were Sean Wyatt, his wife, and Tommy Schultz. Berger couldn't believe it. He shook his head in denial.

"That's impossible. I saw him burn in the fire."

"Apparently, you saw wrong. Or maybe Sean Wyatt can't die. Honestly, I'm not sure which it is."

Sean stood on the opposite sidewalk with arms crossed and a proud smile beaming across his face. It was a condescending look, a gloating expression that only served to further anger Berger.

He spun around to face June and lunged for her. "I will have my revenge, for the order!"

He produced a pistol from within the folds of his jacket, whipping it around in hopes of catching the woman off guard.

Berger had no idea who he was dealing with.

June moved like a wraith, swift and deadly. She stepped forward and to the left so quickly that Berger barely saw more than a blur. Before he knew it, her hand was locked on to his. A sudden and horrible pain shot through his arm, radiating from his wrist as it twisted into an unnatural position. He felt the bone within straining under the force, and he knew that it would break within seconds.

He tried to counter with his other hand, swinging a fist wildly at her, but she caught it, jerked it around behind him, kicked the back of his knees as she turned his body, and then forced him to the ground.

Berger yelped in pain as June pushed the hand higher up his back, while at the same time wrenching the pistol from his fingers.

"You will pay for—"

"Okay, we're done here," she cut him off as she pressed her knee into the middle of his back and shoved him hard into the ground.

His cheek and temple hit the concrete with a smack.

June made quick work of the man's wrists, binding them with zip ties.

Sean, Adriana, and Tommy watched the display from across the street with something approaching glee. Wagner stood next to them with a more reserved expression, though in his eyes there was a hint of satisfaction.

"You sure you didn't mind putting her in that position, Schultzie?" Sean asked as they made their way across the road to the church entrance.

Tommy guffawed. "Seriously? Did you see what she just did to him? No contest. Besides, she's got plenty of backup."

Adriana cast him a sidelong glance. "I'm pretty sure June could take you down too, big guy."

Tommy's face flushed. "Yeah, sure. Okay, guys. Hilarious. Let's talk about how Tommy's wife can beat him up." His tone was goofy and deep.

"No need to talk about it," Sean quipped. "That's like talking about how all trees are wood. No reason to overstate the obvious."

"What? Wait."

It was too late. They'd already reached the other side of the street, where Sean addressed Tommy's wife.

"Hey, June! Nice work."

June looked up from where she straddled Berger's back. She

grinned and stood, extending a hand to Sean. "Thanks. I appreciate it."

Sean shook her hand.

Tommy threw his hands up in the air and let them slap against his hips. "Come on, guys. It was my idea to call her in the first place. How about a little credit?"

"I loved the way you spun him around and dropped him to his knees," Adriana continued. "Good technique. You learn that with Axis or your previous job?"

"Previous."

"Hello?" Tommy interrupted like a five-year-old.

"So," Sean said, crouching next to Berger's head, "it looks like you're going away for a long time, Lucien. I do hope you'll write."

The man grunted something, but June casually placed her heel on the back of his head and pressed his face into the pavement.

Sean chuckled and then stood up as four men in suits approached. They collected Berger and dragged him away toward one of the unmarked black cars parked along the sidewalk on the other side of the road. He didn't struggle, didn't try to get away. He didn't even shout insults. He merely hung his head dejectedly, staring at the ground, probably wondering how or when he'd screwed up and where it had all gone wrong. He was going to have quite a long time to ponder that.

"I appreciate your help with this," Wagner offered. "My brothers and I are truly grateful." He turned so that each person met his gaze. "All of you." He offered no gloating to Berger, no last words that would give Wagner superficial satisfaction. He was above that.

When Berger was safely inside the government sedan and the door was closed, Sean turned to Tommy, who was staring at him with bewildered eyes.

"What?" Sean asked.

Tommy pursed his lips and shook his head. "Oh, nothing. It's just that...well, usually, these things don't end this way."

"What do you mean?" Sean chuckled.

"Typically, there's a big gunfight, a fistfight, some kind of dramatic battle to the death. You know."

Sean frowned, his brow furrowing. "I was tied up in the top of Notre-Dame and almost burned alive. And did you see what I did to Bodmer?"

"Oh, right. I guess there were those things."

"Honestly, how much drama do you need, Schultzie? We got the bad guys." He slapped his friend on the shoulder. "Now let's go get that ring."

The four stepped into the shadows of the church and out of the morning sun.

43

MALTA

S ean, Tommy, and Adriana stood at the center of the sanctuary on a red carpet that stretched from the back of the church to the front.

The Co-Cathedral of John the Baptist was overflowing with parishioners. The crowd had come from all around Valletta and from across the Mediterranean to see the priceless relic restored to its former resting place.

The pope presided over the service and stood solemnly at the center of the room, at the base of the altar. Wagner stood curiously close to the pope, several feet to the left. He almost looked like a guard, which would make sense based on what the man had told Sean and the others about his order.

Sean and Tommy both felt uncomfortable with the proceedings, but they did their best to be reverent. They, along with Adriana, were receiving the highest honor the pope could bestow on a layperson.

As the older man in white vestments continued to speak the Latin words of the rites, he gave subtle nods to each of the three heroes, crossing his hands before them as he did so. The three took the cue and bent down to one knee for the last part of the ceremony.

They weren't Catholic, which was one of the primary sources of inner turmoil for the two men. Adriana, however, seemed more than comfortable with it.

When the pope finished the rites, he changed to English in case there were those in attendance who couldn't understand Latin.

"I knight thee, Sean Wyatt, Thomas Schultz, and Adriana...Wyatt, into the Order of Saint Gregory the Great." He paused when he said Adriana's last name. She had made the request to keep her last name a secret during the ceremony.

"The Holy Church of Rome owes you a great debt. You have returned one of our holiest relics to its home, and we will always honor you for that. Rise, Knights of Saint Gregory the Great, and be recognized."

The three stood and turned to face the crowd. Everyone bowed their heads in unison.

Adriana and Tommy looked comfortable with the attention, while Sean couldn't get out of the room fast enough. There was something disconcerting about hundreds of eyes focused on them. Maybe it was his training. With so many in the sanctuary, all looking at him, it was more difficult to detect a threat.

Security was tight, though, and he knew that the pope's unit, along with local security forces, would make sure everything had been locked down.

Sean let out a long breath and forced a smile onto his face.

When the proceedings were over, the pope personally thanked them and then made his way out of the building, touching people on the head and blessing them as he passed.

A familiar face emerged from the crowd as most of the people began heading toward the exits.

Cardinal Klopp approached them with a humble smile on his face. His fingers were laced together in front of his waist. The red cassock draped over him flapped in the wind, but it didn't seem to bother the cardinal.

"Cardinal Klopp," Sean said with a nod. "Glad you could make it."

"I wouldn't miss it," he said, squinting against the bright rays of the sun. "You three are my heroes. I will always be indebted to you."

"No debts," Tommy said. "We're not a credit agency."

The cardinal looked at him as if Tommy had a bus growing out of his head. "I'm sorry, I don't understand."

Sean arched one eyebrow. "Neither do we, sir." He turned to Tommy. "Was that even a joke?"

Tommy's laughter at himself ceased, and he bit his bottom lip in embarrassment.

"Anyway, I just wanted to say thank you for all you've done." Klopp shook Sean's hand, then Adriana's, then he stopped at Tommy. He held Tommy's hand for a long couple of seconds. "I have been granted authority to give you unlimited access to our archives, whenever you need them. This is a great honor and one that I'm certain you can appreciate."

Tommy's eyes widened. "What? Are you serious?"

Sean chuckled over the priest's shoulder. "He's a priest, Tommy. I doubt he's messing with you."

"The thought did cross my mind," Klopp said with a wink. "But no. I am being serious."

Tommy lost his composure in his excitement and let go of the cardinal's hand and wrapped his arms around the man, hugging him tightly. "Thank you! Thank you so much!"

He suddenly realized he was hugging a high-ranking cardinal and immediately let go, making sure he flattened out the man's robes before taking a step back.

Klopp simply laughed. "You're welcome, my son."

"History nerd," Sean said, barely masking it with a cough.

"You are, too," Tommy defended.

Sean snorted a laugh. "That I am, my friend. That I am. Speaking of, did you see that article the other day about the thing in the...oh, sorry, sir." He nodded at Klopp.

The cardinal smiled kindly at him and then waved a hand. "I will see you again. God bless you."

"And you," the three said together.

The priest turned and walked away, heading down the stone path toward a cluster of people. Two security team members were standing on pillars with rifles slung over their shoulders. Their eyes darted left and right behind dark aviator sunglasses.

"Well, I guess we're knights now," Sean said.

"I was expecting to get a sword or something," Tommy said dejectedly.

Adriana chuckled. "Maybe they'll send it to you in the mail." She nudged his shoulder with a balled fist.

"Anyway, we should probably get moving," Sean said as he turned and looked back into the sanctuary where the ring of John the Baptist was on display. It was a simple piece of jewelry made of solid gold. The surface was flat, not rounded like a groom's wedding band, with a thin white line that cut through the middle of it going all the way around.

Tommy had offered his lab to analyze the ring, but the church had declined, though they did say perhaps at some point he could bring some equipment to their laboratories.

The three turned to walk back toward their ride and looked out over the city of Valletta.

"Napoléon must have felt like the king of the world when he was standing here," Tommy said.

"You know what, buddy? So do I."

"Me, too," Tommy agreed. "Now, tell me about that article you were talking about a minute ago."

Sean's eyes gleamed, matching his broad grin. "You're not going to believe what these scientists found in South America."

THANK YOU

Thank you for taking the time to read this story. We can always make more money, but time is a finite resource for all of us, so the fact you took the time to read my work means the world to me and I truly appreciate it. I hope you enjoyed it as much as I enjoyed sharing it, and I look forward to bringing you more fun adventures in the future.

Ernest

OTHER BOOKS BY ERNEST DEMPSEY

Sean Wyatt Adventures:

The Secret of the Stones

The Cleric's Vault

The Last Chamber

The Grecian Manifesto

The Norse Directive

Game of Shadows

The Jerusalem Creed

The Samurai Cipher

The Cairo Vendetta

The Uluru Code

The Excalibur Key

The Denali Deception

The Sahara Legacy

The Fourth Prophecy

The Templar Curse

The Forbidden Temple

The Omega Project

Adriana Villa Adventures:

War of Thieves Box Set

When Shadows Call

Shadows Rising

FACT VS. FICTION

Hello again. You probably have some questions regarding this story as to what I made up and what is real. You obviously know all the characters and events are fictional (mostly), but what were some of the things I utilized or conceived to make the story go? Well, you've come to the right place. So, let's get started.

The Teutonic Knights- Everything I portrayed about the Teutonic Order was as accurate as I could make it. I took few liberties, if any, in regards to their history. The island of Malta is more well-known for its occupation by the Knights Hospitaller, a brethren group of the Teutonic Order, but a number of Teutonic Knights did live on Malta during the invasion by Napoleon.

The invasion of Malta was a real event in history. Napoleon took 30,000 soldiers and 10,000 sailors from the south of France and landed shortly after on the coast of Malta en route to their ultimate destination in Alexandria.

The story about Napoleon's visit to St. John's Co-Cathedral is accurate and actually happened. One of my primary sources for this portion of the story comes from a fan, David Nixon, who relayed the legend from a visit he made there in 1998. It took an incredible amount of digging and more hours than I can recall to find evidence to corroborate this story, but I found multiple sources and was delighted to be able to include this key moment in history.

Malbork Castle - This castle is quite the sight to behold and was the final headquarters of the Teutonic Order as it existed during its glory days. Does it still house some of the Order to this day in some secret chamber or perhaps a hidden headquarters beneath the surface? Who knows?

Rosemary Beach - This little beach town in West Florida has become one of my favorite places to visit. You can find me there on my birthday every year. If you do, feel free to say hi or visit the local book store in the town square. You'll also find the most beautiful beaches and water in the continental United States.

The Vatican - Everything I relayed about the layout of the Vatican and the apartments was as accurate as I could make it. I also did a great deal of research concerning the Swiss Guard and their procedures for various circumstances. Commander Bodmer might have seemed aloof during the first two thirds of the story, but that was by design. A man of his standing would be clever and alert. Making him appear to be less than aware in some cases was merely a hint to his true intentions behind the plot.

Paris- Napoleon's Chateau, the Tomb of Josephine, and the Library are all popular tourists spots in Paris. While the secret compartment may be fictional (or possibly real), everything about the layout and the history of the library is real, as is the content regarding the other locations.

I do find it extremely interesting that the library has remained almost untouched since Napoleon's last visit there. And the images of the deities combined with the room's architecture are certainly fascinating and worth the raise of an eyebrow.

St. Helena- This place is one of the more interesting spots in the historical landscape of our world. One of the world's greatest military leaders was exiled there and eventually died there, was buried there, and then exhumed and moved to Paris. I have so many questions about this place, about what happened there, who was involved, and what ultimately killed Napoleon—the common theory notwithstanding.

All of the details I included about this location are as accurate as could be. The only fictional item I added was the letter itself and the names on the sheet of paper in the museum section of the property. That sheet was a device of my own imagining.

Villers-Cotterêts - This quaint village was one of my favorite scenes to write in the story. The statue I describe and all the other details are as accurate as possible, right down to the shops, cafes, and their positions near the town square. It's a quiet place, and one I highly recommend you visit if you get the chance as it can be a welcome relief from the hustle and bustle of big Paris.

Arc de Triumph - The names mentioned in the fiction list from before actually do appear on the famed arch in Paris. And the order I included is also accurate. You can visit the arch and scan through them, just be sure you take my book along so you know which column to search for (wink wink). One little side note is that, as a huge fan of Alexandre Dumas, I found it extraordinarily fascinating that his father's name is on this monument, and that he was one of the most brilliant commanders in Napoleon's military. It's sad that Alexandre's father died destitute, but my admiration of him being one of the earliest civil rights pioneers cannot be overstated.

Père Lachaise - Perhaps the most famous cemetery in the world, this location is home to millions of visitors every year who come to Paris. It's a place shrouded in mystery, history, and the bizarre. You can find many of the headstones and monuments I mentioned in the story, though for the sake of flow, I did alter a couple of locations, so don't use my book as a guide for this area (I'm laughing as I write this). However, most of the facts I included about the cemetery are real and I highly encourage you to visit if you get the chance.

Notre Dame Cathedral - In 2019, a catastrophic tragedy to one of the most recognizable historical sites in the world took much of this beautiful cathedral from the world. While the rebuild effort is under way at the time of writing this, it is a terrible shame that so much destruction happened to the old structure. I fear the walls and ceilings won't feel the same as they did before, oozing with history as it did before. While my characters were obviously not responsible for the fire that consumed the cathedral, there are certainly more than a few conspiracy theories as to what happened that fateful day. Perhaps that is for another time.

Tegernsee, Bavaria - This is one of the most picturesque locations I've ever written. Just get online and search for it. The pictures are worth the effort. I did my best to convey the history of the town and its famous buildings, and took very few liberties here—none of which are worth even mentioning. This part of the world is one of my favorites. If circumstances fell in line, I would be completely happy living here.

One last fun fact. Alexandre Berthier fought alongside the American Colonists in the American Revolution, which for me is a huge deal. I've always loved the history of the American Revolution. It's one of my favorite subjects, and the fact that this man served to help give me the freedom I enjoy means a great deal. I'm truly honored to have been able to share a little piece about his life, and to bring him to the forefront of history if only for a few moments. I believe Berthier to have been an honorable man and a great warrior who fought for liberty for all, both in America and later in France.

I hope you enjoyed this little hike down the true or false trail. Be sure to come by next time for more fun facts. Or fiction....

BONUS MATERIALS

I love immersing readers into a story, and what could be more immersive than food?

Food is something that brings people, cultures, and worlds together. Cooking it is a journey. Eating it is a journey. The destination is connecting. Connecting with others, and with yourself. The journey begins anew every time we get together for a meal. To me, food is the greatest peacemaker of all.

I love cooking and I truly enjoy trying new things. No, I didn't eat escargot while writing this book because of my dietary restrictions, but I did try more recipes than I have for any other story.

I started including recipes and bonus materials like this with book 17 in the Sean Wyatt Series, The Forbidden Temple. Those were some terrific Indian dishes that I had a blast creating and still make every month in my home.

You can find that book here:

And if you want to see one of the cooking videos, go here:

Now, it's time for what you've been waiting for.

I try to eat vegan about 70 percent of my meals because it's good for the body and the environment, but I'm not fully vegan or vegetarian. So, for all my veggie friends, I'm doing some vegan style recipes along with some of the more traditional stuff. And most of the recipes I include have a vegan and even some gluten free ways of being prepared, though I don't necessarily get into that with all of them in the videos where I cook them.

You can start watching my Cooks With Books series on YouTube here: https://www.youtube.com/playlist?list=PLIRCasoDCUHoFJqFibKfVdmFH62xW5jnK

And here are the links to the recipes I highlight in the videos, plus a few more I included that I may cook later on down the road:

This site has a few dozen recipes for you to try and I used a couple of them for the story and for videos. Definitely worth a look — https://www.purewow.com/food/easy-French-recipes

Want to whip up some delicious Beignets like I did in the video series? Here's an easy recipe to throw together — https://www.foodnetwork.com/recipes/paula-deen/french-quarter-beignets-recipe-2014039

Crepes. I love these things and I immediately regretted learning how to make them, because I'm going to gain a ton of weight. Perhaps literally. Anyway, here's a good recipe to try for your own crepes — https://www.iheartnaptime.net/perfect-crepe-recipe/

Cheesy French Onion Bread—or something like it— was featured in this story, and I would be remiss if I didn't give you a recipe for it — https://www.delish.com/cooking/recipe-ideas/recipes/a58499/cheesy-french-onion-bread-recipe/

Chicken Marengo is the poultry version of one of Napoleon's favorite dishes. Check out this simple recipe here — https://www.foodnetwork.com/recipes/melissa-darabian/4-step-chicken-marengo-recipe-1949194

French Onion Soup has to be in here, right? Here's an easy recipe for it— https://www.simplyrecipes.com/recipes/french_onion_soup/

Bon appétit!

For two of my favorite teachers, Gary Pennell and Michael Peel. Thank you for helping foster my interest in history and other cultures. I'll never be able to express my appreciation enough. But I'll sure try.

ACKNOWLEDGMENTS

As always, I would like to thank my terrific editors for their hard work. What they do makes my stories so much better for readers all over the world. Anne Storer and Jason Whited are the best editorial team a writer could hope for and I appreciate everything they do.

I also want to thank Elena at Li Graphics for her tremendous work on my book covers and for always overdelivering. Elena is amazing.

Last but not least, I need to thank all my wonderful fans and especially the advance reader team. Their feedback and reviews are always so helpful and I can't say enough good things about all of them.

One of those fans is David Nixon, who relayed the story about Napoleon and the ring of John the Baptist to me. I'd been working on something for the Teutonic Order and when I heard that tale, I thought it was the perfect fit. So, thank you for the information, David. I appreciate it and I hope I did it justice.

I'd also like to thank my good friend Billy Massingale for his expertise as my military consultant. As someone who didn't serve, it is crucial to have knowledgeable military personnel I can go to with questions whenever I'm in need. I appreciate the assistance from Billy, and all the others I've spoken to in the past.

Special thanks for the Knights Templar Seal by Cristian Chirita

See you next time,

Ernest

Made in the USA
San Bernardino, CA
11 May 2020